Restless Warrior

About the author

British born Richard Mann has lived and worked in or been connected with Asia for more than two decades. His wife, Jenny, is from Sumatra, Indonesia.

Mann began his career in the Far East as a Senior Information Officer in the Hong Kong Government. Later he was in charge of the Government Secretariat Press Office. Quitting the colonial civil service, he became an Asian business consultant and, from the mid-1980s, began writing and publishing business books about Asia. To date, he has published thirty five titles, some of which have been printed in multiple editions - majority about Indonesia. His first volume of short stories, set in Indonesia, was published in 1995.

Mann received a Bachelor of Arts degree in Social Science from the University of York, United Kingdom, in 1967. Trained as a full service journalist his career as a reporter, editor and broadcaster in Britain, Hong Kong, Canada and the Far East has included newspapers, magazines, books, television and radio.

In 1996, his son, Ian, aged 19, is studying law at Southampton University, United Kingdom and his daughter, Sarina, aged 17, is in her final year at Takapuna Grammar School, Auckland, New Zealand. In 1997 she, too, plans to study at a British university.

$\mathcal{R}$ESTLESS

$\mathcal{W}$ARRIOR

Raffles' tragic
love affair with
the Indies

By
Richard Mann

© Copyright 1996

Published by:

Gateway Books

All rights reserved. No part of this publication maybe reproduced, stored in a retrieval system or transmitted by any form or by any means, graphic, electronic or mechanical and including photocopying, recording, taping or otherwise.

ISBN 0-921333-45-5

Cover paintings by
Drs. Mansyur Mas'ud

Dedication

The generous and far sighted sacrifices of my wife, Jenny, made it possible for me to write this book in the serene, quiet beauty of New Zealand.

Note about spelling

To assist the reader, Dutch spelling of place names in the Indies has been retained while the spelling of Indonesian place names follows current usage.

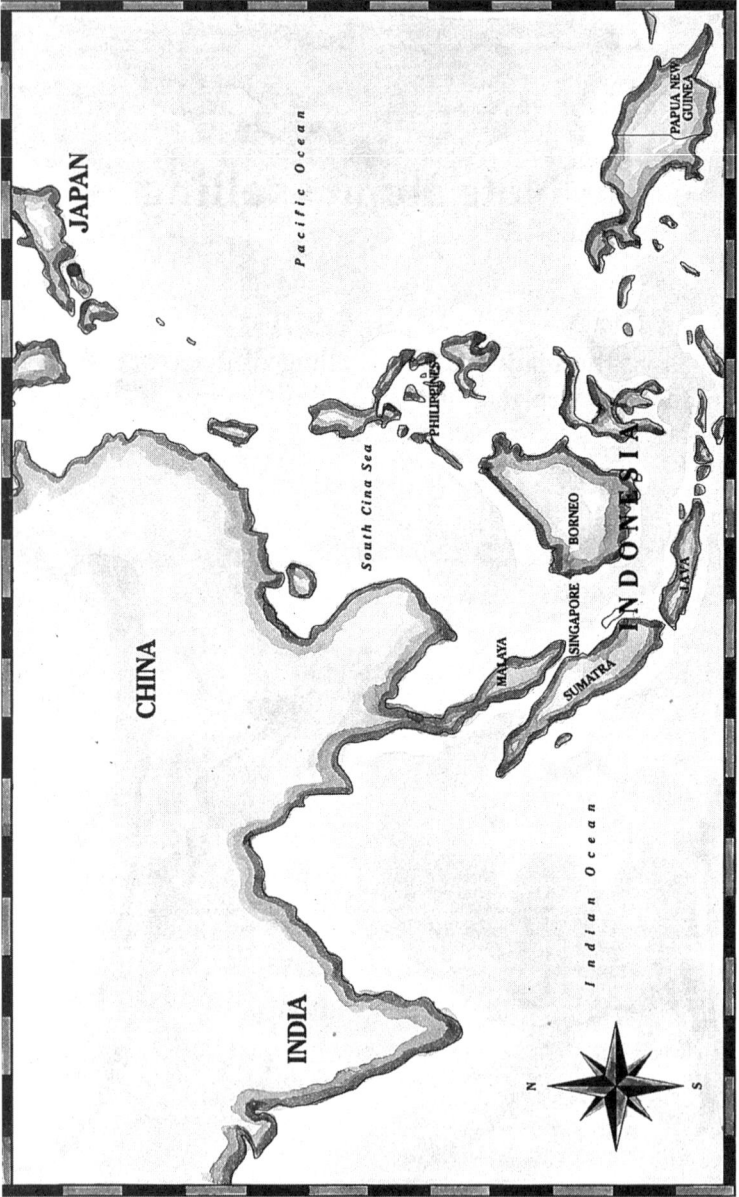

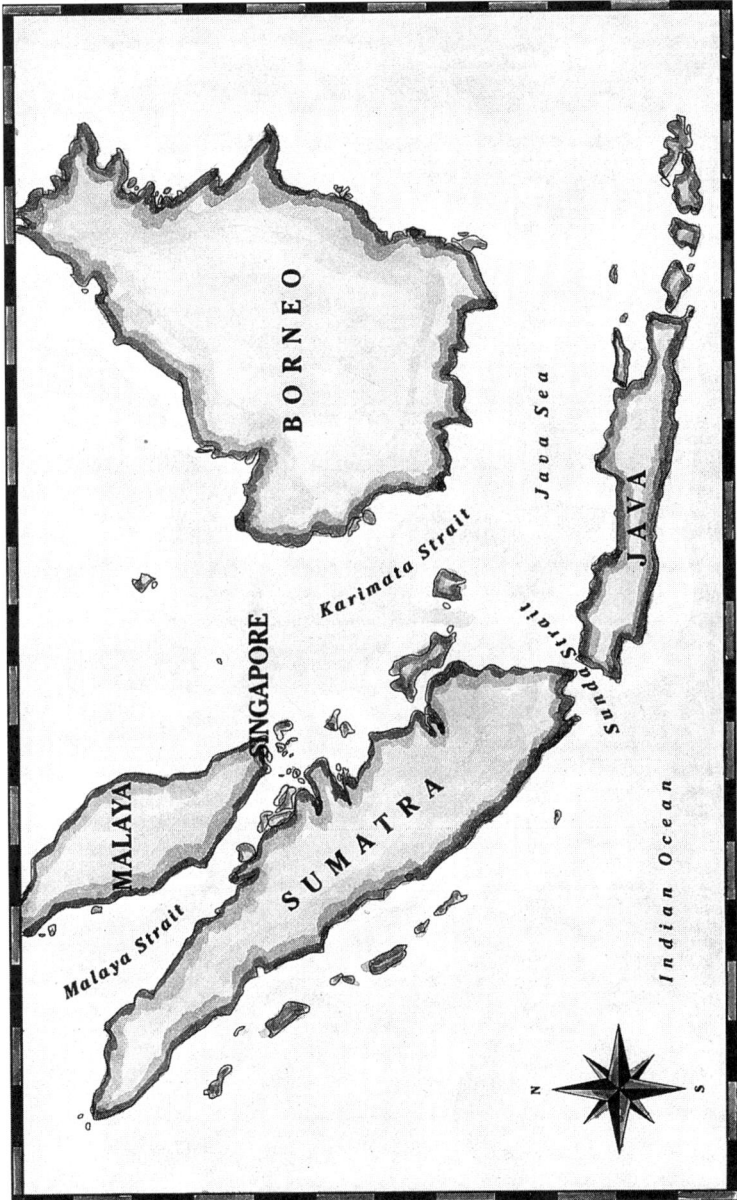

CHAPTER ONE

Although a diligent pupil, nevertheless there were long, hot, summer afternoons when even Thomas Raffles stole a glance out of the open school room window, while the teacher's voice droned on in the background.

In 1793, the London suburb of Hammersmith, in England, was still countrified but close enough to the great metropolis and emporium of London for Raffles to be fascinated by the lumbering wagons which creaked and clattered incessantly to and fro along the dusty road, their drivers constantly clucking their tongues or cracking their whips to keep up the pace of the horses pulling them. Other horses, bearing more bulky freights, passed by in long covoys. Stage coaches bounced by on their leather springs in a storm of dust and noisy hooves accompanied by the warning blast of the postillion's trumpet. Scarlet coated mail riders dashed passed so quickly that it was hard to focus on them. The liveried carriages of the rich swayed along on their way to or from important business 'in Town', or perhaps just on a shopping trip for the mistress of the house. Very occasionally a troop of cavalry clattered by, their resplendent riders ramrod in their saddles. Every day, at some time or other, the road became filled with the herds of cows, pigs, sheep, turkeys and geese needed by London to satisfy its ever growing appetite. And every day, the youths of a hundred villages trudged along on their way to hoped-for fortunes in London with their bundles of belongings slung, like Dick Wittington, over their shoulders.

Where were all these people coming from ? Raffles wondered. Where were they going ? Where had they come from ? What goods had they aboard their wagons and in their packs? What were the great houses like in which they lived ? Were there urgent dispatches in the mails telling of peace or war ? A boy of Raffles imaginative disposition couldn't have been more fascinated at his school room window than if he had already embarked on a perilous adventure to the unknown far places of the earth, across the seas, the mountains and deserts where he had read strange peoples lived.

Not that Raffles was a dreamer. Far from it. He was the kind of boy who is so fascinated by the knowledge gained from books that he would have read even without necessity. In fact, his school work often seemed to him but a complement to the reading he undertook himself, after hours, in the library. His reading was never uselessly diffuse. He delved into religion and philosophy, and into the sciences which explained how the world worked but, as he progressed, most of all he studied history, politics and trade.

Today, one day at the beginning of summer but the last day of term, his questions and fantasies were abruptly halted by the class master calling his name. Instinctively he thought it was a reprimand for inattention. While he gazed entranced at the busy crossroads before his window, a boy older than himself, and a prefect, had entered the room with a message for him to report immediately to the Head Master's study!

Raffles felt his heart palpitate! He had never been sent to the Head before. He knew of boys who had, but they had usually been bullies or transgressors. Small of stature, Raffles bullied nobody and transgressions were behaviour far removed from his academic pursuits and obsessions.

"Look sharp! Get a move on" You're for it now", the prefect taunted Raffles as they hurried together along the long, echoing, corridor at the end of which was the Head Master's room.

"What have I done?" asked the harassed Raffles as the older, bigger boy pushed him along by gripping one arm in a terrifying vice.

"You'll soon find out", he leered threateningly.

At the Mansion House Boarding School, Hammersmith, Raffles was not part of a particular group. He was simply there. And because he did well teachers respected him and liked him. Often, when other pupils failed to answer a difficult question a master would turn in desperation to Thomas Raffles.

"Raffles. You tell them. I am sure you know the answer".

Equally often Raffles <u>did</u> know the answer but knowing not only did not endear him to those thus humiliated but additionally earned him their undying hatred.

"Always think you know it all, eh," sneered the prefect. "Well, now you're for it and you haven't got a clue why! Have you?"

Raffles found himself propelled and prodded to the Head's heavy, oak door, on which the prefect rapped loudly. The Head, Dr Anderton, was a huge man who towered above little Raffles as he stood before him. But like many large people he was a kindly man and spoke softly. Like his staff, he respected Raffles and knew how hard he worked and with what a passion to learn. Raffles sat on the edge of a high backed wooden chair in front of the Head's desk and Anderton spoke sadly for a few minutes.

"What it all boils down to Raffles is that your sponsor, Mr Bingley, is bankrupt. There's no more money so I'm afraid that you'll have to leave the school."

Raffles' thin face turned white. His large, expressive eyes grew even larger. He clasped his long, bony fingers together in a death-like grip. Instantly, he saw himself looking for a job but not a job such as he had always dreamed; just a job, any job. Without the best education, impeccable antecedents or powerful friends, he feared that he could now be doomed to forever live not at the bottom of the social scale but definitely at the bottom of its higher levels. Raffles' mind was momentarily numb!

"Do you understand Raffles?" the Head asked, puzzled by his continuous silence. "You're a fine pupil but business is business. If our pupils don't pay us it won't be long before we are bankrupt too!."

Raffles was in shock but far from tearful. He was made of sterner stuff than that.

"Yes, sir. I understand, sir", was all that he said and the Head at once rose, walked round his desk, and, with a kindly arm round poor Raffles' shoulders, escorted him to the door.

"You're a talented young man, Raffles, and I am certain that you will be able to put your resources to good use."

"I hope so, Sir."

"Goodbye Raffles. And good luck."

How all powerful was money! One moment, with money, he had been a valued and respected member of the school's student body; the next moment, without money, he had been thrown out instantly onto the street!

Hearing no sounds of a ticking-off from behind the closed Headmaster's door, Raffles' escort had gone and, because it was empty, the long corridor seemed longer and quieter than ever. As he walked, with his arms hanging loosely by his sides, Raffles glanced into each of the class rooms lining the corridor, seeing with vacant and hopeless eyes the lessons he would never again attend.

He was a boarder and he wondered if his parents knew! Wondered, if they knew, why they hadn't told him! Once he walked out of the doors of Hammersmith School what was to become of him? What job could he get? And if he worked how could he study? And if he didn't study how would he ever be qualified to rise up in society?

Fourteen is a self-conscious age and Raffles walked back to his class with leaden shoes, fearful of the joyful sneers and derision from his peers if they learnt he had been thrown out of school. As he walked, his heart aflame with humiliation and shame, he decided that they should not be told and that he would quit the school as unobtrusively and quickly as he could. He said nothing when he returned to his desk and, stony faced, at the end of the session he gathered his few things together for the last time.

Mr Haswell, his Classics Master, was a kindly man, who, like so many of the teachers, liked Raffles and admired his determination to learn. It was lunch time and the classroom emptied quickly until Raffles was the last there. Haswell peered at Raffles above his oval spectacles.

"We are all so very sorry Raffles", he said. "Do you know what you are going to do now?"

"Thank you, sir. No, sir," replied Raffles with a heavy heart, knowing the chronic impecunity of his large family.

"Whatever you do I am quite sure you will do well", said Haswell encouragingly. "Never give up your reading because knowledge, you know, is power and with power you can do anything".

Raffles left the school building for the dorm where an old and battered sea chest of his father's stood ready packed at the foot of his bed, today being, in any case, the last day of term. The other boys would not be leaving until late afternoon but Raffles decided to slip away at once. Two years was only a short time to have been at the school and while he had made friends he still felt himself an outsider and, because of his aptitude and willingness, the object of countless jealousies by his fellow pupils. If they knew he was leaving they would only take the opportunity to pour ridicule on him for being too poor to afford the fees. At the school lodge there were no messages from his parents and having a few coins remaining from his term allowance he decided to take a stage directly to the family home on the opposite side of the city, close to the bustling inner London docks.

The nature of the journey home was a deception because there was nothing out of the ordinary about it. He would have been leaving school for the end-of-year holidays today anyway. And the joyous greeting of his four younger sisters was only to be expected after nearly two months away. But the sad countenance and demeanour of his mother reinforced his deep down realization that today was indeed a very different day and that he was in fact living through the greatest tragedy of his life to date.

"I tried to keep it from you," said Anne Raffles, burying her tearful face in his shoulder, as she hugged him to her. "Your father's still at sea and I've been wracking my brains for ways to raise money. It was all so sudden."

"What am I going to do?" Raffles asked his mother despairingly.

Anne Raffles was by no means a weak or timid woman. She was the wife of a sea captain and had spent many of her days aboard ship with all its roughness and privations. Raffles himself had been born in Jamaican waters in his father's cramped cabin on the trading ship he captained. Her attitude to the current disaster was that, while it was a set back, it was God's will. Now, they must find another way for Raffles to become successful in life.

While Anne Raffles would not have been human if she had not shared her son's disappointment at having to leave school, in her practical mind he was already aged 14 and capable of earning money the family needed so badly. Trade with the West Indies was depressed and Captain Raffles was barely managing to subsist. Extra money from any source would be like a gift from God. Now that the die was cast and Raffles had been forced to quit school, Mrs Raffles busied herself more than ever making enquiries about what work her son might do. Raffles, meanwhile, seized the opportunity to read everything his busy school curriculum had precluded - especially about science, trade and current affairs. The family was so poor that even knowing his interests, nevertheless, his mother one night reprimanded him for 'wasting' a candle by which he was reading. Unlearned herself, Mrs Raffles was by no means convinced about how much income was to be gained as a result of reading and preferred the certain benefits of the practice of a trade or profession.

Ever resourceful, she wrote letter after letter to family and friends asking for any help they could give in finding Raffles a job. One of her brothers in law, Elton Hamond, was in the tea trade and therefore very familiar with the opportunities to be had in the Far East and the enterprises engaged in exploiting them. He came to visit one day and told Anne Raffles about a vacancy for a clerk at the head office of the British East India Company.

"What do you think, Thomas? Would you like

to be in trade? he asked.

Raffles eyes shone with delight. If not the manufacture of the new industrial products, which no one could undertake without capital, participating in Britain's burgeoning trade was the goal of many-a-man who dreamed of riches for himself and his family. Only the previous year, that great apostle of free trade and one of Raffles' heroes, William Pitt, had been re-elected Prime Minister. The nation's manufacturers and merchants were in the mood to search for new markets and for trade reform. Captain Raffles was in the declining West Indies trade but Uncle Elton was in the glamorous Far East trade with all its fabled prospects.

Raffles had read or heard of many a man who made his career in India and returned to England with enough of a fortune to built a country house and live in riches. India and China danced before Raffles eyes. Far off places, ships heavy laden with treasure, personal fortunes to be made and fame more than a possibility. Out there, beyond the furthest seas, the fact that he was a nobody would matter to none. What would matter would be what he could do and, based on his reading and experience, Raffles had few doubts that there was much that a boy like him could do. Many times, as he lay in bed in the dark, thinking about his books, his heroes and his life he had the inexplicable feeling that he was destined for greatness, that no matter how bad were the things that happened to him, such as being poor or having to leave school, fate had something great in store for him. The very name of the East India Company seemed like an incredible beginning. The Company was a power in the City, in the Government and in the land. A clerkship was as good as a ticket to India, to untold riches, to a return to England and a big country estate and, maybe, even a seat in Parliament!

"I'll do it", he told his mother and uncle. I'll join the East India Company."

Nervous, yes, but how proud he was that first day to be entering the deceptively modest three storey offices of the East India Company in Leadenhall Street, in the City of London, stretching far back from its stone-faced frontage and spacious enough to provide not only facilities for an army of clerks but even apartments for its directors. He could almost walk there from home, along the narrow, cobbled streets, feeling a new sense of importance as he shared the pavements with businessmen, office messengers and fashionable ladies and gentlemen. The winding streets were busy with cabs and carriages of every description, their iron rimmed wheels grating and grinding on the uneven surface. On the brass plates at every door he read the names of trading houses and banks whose activities were making London the largest and most powerful business centre in the world. In the space of only one generation Britain's population had doubled, Britons had shown themselves uncannily able at finding new ways to make and transport the objects of trade and the nation's ports throbbed with the loading and unloading of sailing ships from around the globe.

After the payment of his first wages at the East India Company, the debacle of leaving school was totally forgotten. He had work, he had money, he was launched upon a career that might make him a baronet or a duke! "The Duke of Puddledock" his mother used to laugh with good natured cynicism when he told her his dreams, referring to an unsavory area of London, near the inner docks. Whether going to work in the morning or returning home at night, during those first introductory days, he felt as if he was walking on air. A strong individualist of independent mind, Raffles determined from the outset to work hard, to be noticed and to try to work his way to the top. If there was a God in heaven surely what he lacked in birth or social connections would be more than compensated for once his abilities and merits were known!

The euphoria of the first days eventually evaporated and Raffles found himself settled into a job that many times he fancied he might still be doing when they carried him to his grave. From early morning until late at night he sat on a high wooden stool in the company of about sixty other clerks, some young and others grey with the lack of fresh air and bent with years of sedentary employment. As each summer followed the other, many a hot afternoon he looked up involuntarily every few minutes at the great, dark clock that dominated the room, fancying that each time he looked hours must have passed! Despite his unpromising predicament, his inner voice told him, that <u>he</u> would never end up grey and bent.

However late he toiled, he went home and read the materials which interested him, which gave him an understanding of the world. His new maturity quickly led him to the realization that he did not want to be a mere spectator or even a passive participant but a man who applies his knowledge and as a result brings about change and progress. Everywhere about him was the fury of debate, the inrush or new ideas and new ways of doing things. Science was being turned upside down, industry and manufacture were being turned upside down. Politics was being turned upside down - not least across the Channel in France. Even the very ways in which people lived were being turned upside down. While no-one in his right mind could call Raffles' early work electrifying the times in which he lived <u>were</u> electrifying. Men were doing things unheard of a generation before. There were opportunities unheard of. Most important of all Raffles felt that there were beginning to be opportunities for any man - not just the rich and the favoured, though he was not so naive as to believe that these things didn't still matter. Indeed, he made it almost a crusade to do everything possible to please his chief at the Secretariat, William Ramsay, calculating that one day his exemplary service might be rewarded handsomely.

Pursuing this strategy, as at school, Raffles worked hard to attract the attention of his chiefs. Whatever needed to be done and whenever, Raffles was forever willing - a willing horse. Despite frustrated hours of clock watching, he was genuinely bright eyed about his prospects and above all, wanted to get on. During his first months with the Company he was little more than a mail clerk, learning the ropes, but as the years passed, and he became more experienced, his natural abilities led to him being chosen for ever more high level work in the course of which he met and learned to relate to ever more high ranking and powerful people. The British East India Company was a substantial banking and trading enterprise and in its trading division its clerks not only kept records about its extensive and voluminous commerce but also about the ships, settlements and servants for which it was responsible throughout its world. As he progressed in the Company, Raffles was just as likely to handle figures relating to goods purchased and sold as to postings, pay, pensions, transport and accommodation. The secretary's office, where he clerked, was the largest unit in the company and to Raffles extraordinary good fortune, through here, flowed not only the details of daily transactions but also the copious correspondence and minutes of meetings at home and abroad relating to policy, not only the company's trading policy but its policy to outsiders, including foreign governments.

Recurrent exposure over nearly a decade to the thinking of his seniors and their officers in the field coupled with his voracious reading and his visionary personality, put Raffles in a position to form his own views about what might be done and achieved in the Far East and, especially about what opportunities might exist for a man such as himself.

Clearly, he would never make his fortune as a clerk in Leadenhall Street. But out in the distant lands of the Far East anything was possible! Though quiet by nature, Raffles nursed in his breast a towering, burning ambition. It never occurred to him that it might not be proper for him to have views, that the highest expectation of his bosses was that he would do the job he was paid to do. Of course, he knew he had to do the job he was paid to do but he dreamed also of making a contribution, of making an intervention in the Company's affairs, of charting the Company's course in a direction of his personal making. To his bosses he was a clerk. To himself he was a boss in the making!

Just as at school, his zealousness eventually won him enemies among the other clerks, especially those of about his own age. But, just as at school, he was not only liked and admired by his bosses but even invited to their homes. Over time, he became a close friend to Bill Ramsey, the son of Company Secretary, William Ramsay, and many times while at the Ramsay's imposing home he was able to quietly observe some of the cream of Britain's business community discussing the issues of the day - the very issues that Raffles had read about and which interested him. The new and revolutionary ideas in economics and politics provoked fear in some, who saw the old order crumbling around them, and hope in others who saw more opportunities than had ever before been imagined. At such soirees were discussed the lessons of American Independence both for colonial policy and individual rights as well as the thinking of such men as Tom Pain, author of 'The Rights of Man'. Then, there was the French Revolution which in 1799 had so dramatically and gruesomely swept away the 'ancien regime' in France.

On the economic side, British entrepreneurs and would-be entrepreneurs were obsessed with the theories of Adam Smith and the extent to which they opened the way to make previously unheard of profits. Merchants were pressing for an end to regulation and the dawn of the age of free trade.

Raffles followed up ideas gleaned at the Ramsay's with midnight reading at home of such new-age thinkers as Paine, John Stuart Mill, Smith and Jeremy Bentham, reading by the light of a candle for which he was now able to pay himself. Not that he was stingy. Far from it. He spent hardly a penny of his pay on himself, preferring instead to sacrifice his wages to ease the life and worries of his mother and his sisters.

As the new century opened, so bright with prospects for the British, France cast a long shadow over British trade and industry. America had already been lost thanks to French intervention and Napoleon Bonaparte was not only gobbling up Europe but was turning his attention to Egypt, India and the Far East, threatening Britain's growing and lucrative sea borne trade. Despite these inflictions on Britain, Raffles found himself full of admiration for a man he could see was sweeping at storm force though France's ramshackle legal, fiscal and banking systems, introducing reforms and modernizations which were making France strong.

Despite his heavy work-load and personal reading programme, he nevertheless succeeded in learning French so as to keep fully abreast of everything the French were doing. Battle after battle were fought with the French on land and at sea and just when it looked as if peace had been clinched or one or other had been beaten new threats and hostilities appeared somewhere else. This seesawing of events even affected humble individuals like Raffles who could see their personal prospects held ransom to French power.

Ten years of hard work and exhaustive study took their toll on his health, and family and friends began to worry that he was suffering from tuberculosis because he looked so pale and thin. It was a popular belief that too much hard work and too little recreation could send someone into 'decline' by which was generally meant tuberculosis, a wasting disease for which there was then no cure. The twenty four-year-old Raffles listened to the old wives advice and decided that he would like to see the forests and mountains of Wales.

Shunning the stage coach, he walked there and back averaging an astonishing thirty miles-a-day. And why not? Frail though his health was he was, after all, an Englishman! And at the dawn of the a century, which seemed also to be a new age, many citizens of the world's first industrial power felt themselves to be invincible!

In Wales, the beauty of the green hills and valleys moved Raffles to tears and to poetry. Nothing gave him more delight than to scramble to the top of a mighty hill and look down on the world far below which now seemed small and himself almost god-like. He loved the wind tugging at his hair, loved the clouds tacking across the blue sky, loved to sit dreaming over a lunch of bread and cheese followed by a pint of ale at a local inn.

Raffles had become knowledgeable, sophisticated and worldly and his recent escape to Wales from the chains he now felt bound him to clerking put him actively on the lookout for some opportunity for advancement. Pacing up and down the family's tiny living room, usually with only his mother as audience, Raffles dreamed aloud his dreams, dreams which often seemed to become all the more viable for the role his mother frequently played as devil's advocate - not because she feared their impracticality but because she feared the loss from home of her only son.

Many-a-night he would lament that he could not spend the rest of his life chained to a desk.

"Just be grateful that you've got such a good job", came the invariable acid reply.

But, imperceptibly, as the months and years rolled past, Raffles developed the idea, not only that it would be nice to go to the country with which his daily work dealt but that it was only there that he could make the fortune his family so sorely needed. Wave after wave of British merchants and adventurers were going to India every year with exactly this motive in mind. And year after year those parts of India influenced or ruled by the company expanded, often at the expense of competitors, particularly the French. A plan to try to work in India formed solidly in Raffles' mind. His father had died two years after he joined the company and he knew well that his remuneration was key to the survival of his mother and sisters in some degree of comfort. While he realized that his mother would, of course, miss the only man in her family, he drew comfort from the fact that his younger sisters were still unmarried and living at home. On the other hand, should any marry, Mrs Raffles would still have <u>some</u> company but without the full burden of maintenance which, in any case, ended up with her son. Unobtrusively he scrutinized the pay scales of overseas officers compared with London clerks and was impressed at the advantage.

While thoughts of India were in his mind, toward the end of his tenth year with the Company, Raffles found himself handling the application for a pension of a Company wife from India whom he was amazed to see had married at twenty two but was widowed at twenty nine! Being himself only twenty three, he could easily understand what might be the feelings of one whose life and prospects had abruptly ended hardly after they had begun. More interesting still, Olivia Mariamne Fancourt wrote informing him that should her pension be granted she preferred it to be paid in England where she planned to arrive momentarily, lodging with an aunt at a house in London, close to the City. The day came when Mrs Fancourt duly arrived at the Company's offices in Leadenhall Street and Raffles was deputed to explain the details of her affairs to her in a private reception room.

He fell in love with Olivia from their first meeting, not least because she could tell him absolutely everything he wanted to know about life in the great and exotic sub-continent of India. Raffles work place was a world of men and he had not met or made time for girl friends. The ladies he occasionally met were more often than not quiet and demur, following their husband's leads and looking for all the world as if they had never had a single opinion about anything. Of course, he lived in a family of women, but his mother was extremely conservative and sisters were, after all, only sisters.

Olivia was proper but she was not quiet or conservative. She was not even English. Or Scottish, Welsh or Irish. Her mother was a Circassian Muslim from the Caucassus and, ten years before Raffles gave his first cry, she had been born in India to an Irish father. She had married Jacob Fancourt, an assistant surgeon at Madras, remaining at Fort St. George alone for four years after his death and before applying for a company pension.

Raffles slight figure disguised his wild heart

and in Olivia he found a corresponding wildness born from her ancestry, the influence of her Irish husband and her long years beyond the confines of 'civilized society' as defined by the luminaries and traditions of British life. Clever and accomplished, the spirit of adventure animated her smiling, dark eyes and she was as irrepressible in her questions about the England she had never seen as Raffles was about the India he had never seen.

They met with increasing frequency at either her aunt's or Raffles' mother's house. As Spring, 1805 approached, and buoyed by Olivia's descriptions of the prosperous life he could probably lead as one of the Company's officer's in India, Raffles determined that he would end his drudgery at Leadenhall Street by applying for the next most suitable post, particularly its rank and remuneration as well as its prospects. There were many discussions with William Ramsay as Raffles expressed interest in one vacancy after another posted on the Secretariat's internal bulletin board.

British interests in India were a rapidly moving frontier but Ramsay convinced him to temporarily turn his back on the sub-continent and instead accept an assistant secretaryship, not on the sub-continent but at Penang Island, close to the Malay mainland.

"You probably prefer India because you have heard so much about it and nothing much about the little island of penang," Ramsay smiled when he made the offer. "But Penang is a very important post for the Company. Our trade with China is growing fast but between India proper and China there is not an inch of ground, beside Penang, where British merchant ships can stop, refit or resupply. As you know, we are temporarily in charge at Malacca but when the war with France ends and we have to hand it back to the Dutch, Penang will be our only base between India and China. There's not much there at the moment but we want to build it up. A capable and energetic young man such as yourself could go far there."

Raffles was quick to realize that in India proper he might have been 'just another clerk but at Penang he was miraculously being offered an assistant secretaryship, a post only one removed from governorship. Raffles jumped at the opportunity not least because his salary would leap from a mere £70 to an unbelievable £1,500 a-year.

"The Directors are offering you this post on my recommendation Raffles," explained Ramsay. "I could have sent my own son and there were many here before you but you are one of the ablest of my staff and I think you will do well in Penang.

Raffles smiled and murmured his thanks, his heart pounding at the thought of his new assistant secretaryship.

"As you know," continued Ramsay in thoughtful tones, "the Company has many factories and posts in India but only three regional administrative centres or Presidencies at Bombay, Calcutta and Madras. Such is the potential we foresee for Penang that it has forthwith been upgraded to a fourth Presidency. For you to go to Penang as Assistant Secretary of a Presidency is honour and opportunity indeed."

Over and over again Raffles expressed his thanks and enthusiasm repeating, "Thank you, sir" and "I'll do my very best, sir."

We know you will Raffles", said Ramsay, "because we know how hard you work and how serious you are in all that you do. One day, in the not too distant future, you may have the opportunity to become Secretary of the Presidency and always remember - governors may come and go but the Secretariat goes on forever.

"You know our philosophy about Penang. The

Dutch look like monopolizing the islands; the French are contesting with us from Arabia to the South China Sea. Heaven help England if the French and the Dutch should combine. They could drive us out of India and cut us off completely from the China trade.

"We are giving Penang the resources it will need to become a great British naval base between India and China and in creating it a free port we are directly challenging Dutch monopoly in the Indies.

"Study what can be made of Penang, study what else we can do in the area, find out what the Dutch and French are up to and let us have your reports. It is no overstatement to say that the fate of Britain's trade in the Far East may hang in the hands of Penang."

Raffles left Ramsay's office with his head reeling. His future was no longer filled with ledger columns and pensions but with helping to collect priceless economic and political data which would be use to formulate policies on which the Company's and Britain's fortunes depended. This was the kind of role for which Raffles felt he had been born!

When he told his family the news of his appointment Mrs Raffles was predictably upset, but the prospect of an income of £400 a-year which Raffles proposed to settle on her plus the promise of an early return to England eventually accustomed her to the temporary loss of her son.

Although she certainly had never said as much, it was clear to Raffles that Olivia had journeyed to Britain to look for a second husband. Born in India, and never welcomed by her father's Irish family, Olivia would just as soon have stayed in India forever. She had clung on in Madras for four years until it became clear that her best prospects lie in England. While Olivia was searching for a husband but dreaming of her opulent life in India, Raffles was also fantasizing about India and a conversation with the Ramsays convinced him that, as a young man, if he was serious about living in a remote location overseas, he had best do it in company with a wife. European women were in short supply in Penang and Raffles life there would assuredly be the more comfortable if he could share his life with a female companion.

Raffles proposed to Olivia at her aunt's house telling her how he delighted in her company and extolling the virtues of a life together in the Indies. Six days after his promotion was gazetted, Raffles and Olivia married quietly at a spired and collonaded church in London much favoured by the Comany, St George's Parish Church, Bloomsbury. Raffles' mother and sisters attended but none of Olivia's parental or ex-husband's relatives were invited and, instead, friends from India acted as witnesses on Olivia's side.

"You will be my love, my bosom friend, my confidante", he whispered to Olivia on their wedding night.

"And you shall be my knight in shining armour", said Olivia, her great brown eyes dark with passion.

Raffles was not a shy young man and he had lived with sisters yet he had never seen a female naked before and had only an intuitive idea of what to do with her. Fortunately, any first night jitters were painlessly smoothed by Olivia who had not only become accustomed to the delights of the conjugal bed for seven years but had been deprived of them for four! After the initial awkwardness of removing all his clothes in front of a curious woman Raffles had·found himself guided smoothly but urgently to an objective they both shared. The consummation took place in his room at his mother's house, since there was no money for separate lodgings and, in any case, no point in renting them because he had been told officially that within 30 days they would be sailing for India.

Olivia fitted easily into the Raffles' household becoming a worldly older sister to the four young girls who, from the outset, did not dissolve into embarrassing giggles at the thought of what Raffles and Olivia might be up to behind his closed bedroom door but, on the contrary, behaved with great maturity and as if the whole thing was nothing more than nature taking its course. Olivia shared the diversions as well as the chores of the home and went with them on many an outing. Her brightness and breeziness soon overcame an element of seriousness she found in all their characters until the five of them were the closest of friends with not a secret between them. The girls became so close that Raffles' favourite sister, Mary Anne, even decided to join them on the trip to Penang, partly as a companion for Olivia and partly in the hope that, in the Far East, she might at least marry a successful officer, much as Olivia herself had done in marrying in Madras.

Many were the tears shed as Raffles, Olivia and Mary Anne sailed from London in April, 1805 of aboard the East Indiaman 'Ganges'.

"God keep you", sobbed poor Mrs Raffles, all but collapsing into the arms of her three remaining daughters, each wishing secretly that they could go with Mary Anne.

No man would have been happy to be leaving a city as vibrant as London at that time. But Raffles was enormously pleased to be embarked at last upon a course which seemed to promise an end, in effect, to apprenticeship and a beginning of a time when he could make his own mark upon the world, enjoy it and be paid handsomely for doing it. What thoughts of the future raced through his mind as he sailed that day at the age of twenty four, the very age at which Pitt the Younger became Prime Minister! The 'Ganges' sailed slowly down the Thames in company with two naval vessels, HMS 'Blenheim' and HMS 'Warley' - fear of attack by the French, from the Moors off the coast of West Africa or by privateers, never far from the minds of ocean travellers. Forests of masts stretched for miles along each bank of the great riverine highway of trade while the hordes of ferries and wherries which linked each side and carried passengers up and downstream dodged before and behind them. When, at last, the English coast was receding Raffles and Olivia stood on deck, he with tears in his eyes, she smiling contentedly.

"Goodbye, old England", said Raffles quietly. "Some day we'll come back to you in glory."

The two of them stood for many minutes, in company with a jostling crowd of others lining the rail, staring in silence at the English coast sinking lower and lower on the horizon.

Raffles sighed. "The deed is done now", he smiled and, turning, held Olivia close to him. "I only hope that I can be successful".

She looked lovingly into his eyes and clasped him back. "You will, my darling, you will" she whispered.

Olivia's mind was, if anything, even more made up than Raffles'. She was thirty four. It was crucial that her marriage and her husband should be a success. As she clung to his arm, she vowed silently to herself that nothing within her power should be left undone to assist and advance him.

Raffles had the extraordinary good fortune to be sailing in company with the new Governor of Penang, Philip Dundas, a man reputed to have made a fortune from the operations of the British naval dockyard in Bombay. Ships were not only to be repaired but built in Penang from

Burma teak and who better to mastermind the development than a man who already had a record of unbroken success in India. The 'Ganges' was small and even though, on land, Philip Dundas may not have thought it right to spend much time with a mere assistant secretary, on ship board, betters and inferiors mingled more freely and Raffles found himself uniquely placed not only to get to know the new governor but also to impress him, en passant, with his own talents.

The voyage from London to Penang took an incredible six months, south from England, around the Cape of Good Hope and across the Indian Ocean to the islands of the eastern seas. Conditions on board were cramped for all those less august than the new Governor, with deck space having to be shared with other people.

Half-a-year cooped up, without privacy and in intolerably uncomfortable conditions was enough to sour even the strongest relationship, yet alone a new one like that between Raffles and Olivia. But both were good natured and generous and bore their privations with typical English stoicism and good humour.

In moments of acute boredom and frustration Raffles rushed about the upper deck, telescope in hand, searching for even the merest speck of interest. Olivia was a seasoned traveller able to explain much to the eager-eyed Raffles to whom everything he saw en route was completely new. Born aboard ship Raffles was a good sailor and even in the violent storms which they encountered rounding the Cape he was unaffected. The voyage was tough and rough enough that two junior clerks actually died en route from the sea sickness.

Life and attire aboard ship was casual and dress clothes were locked away for the duration of the voyage to be replaced by breeches and stockings, short, dark jackets and shallow crowned hats for the men and long, but non-flouncy and practical dresses for the ladies with wide brimmed hats to shade their delicate complexions from the sun.

There was little to do to defray the boredom and Raffles could not bare to be idle. Anticipating the jitters such a long trip would give him and jealous of the time potentially to be wasted he pushed himself to learn the language of the Malay islands so that by the time the 'Ganges' reached Penang he was fluent, Olivia having tested him on virtually every word and phrase. This was no idle exercise because Raffles knew from his long years at Leadenhall Street the difficulties and even financial losses that occurred throughout India because officials did not bother to learn the local language. Many times linguistic deficiency made them more victims than masters of any particular situation. And how better to obtain the information sought by Ramsay and the Board of Directors than to talk to the local people in their own language.

Olivia was a romantic at heart and busied herself with reading and even composing poetry, which she read in the evenings with moving dramatic embellishments. The two of them had brought a veritable library of books aboard and whereas Raffles had selected those likely to inform and assist him in his new life Olivia had selected authors who could entertain as well as inform.

The three masted 'Ganges' sailed within sight of Penang, known officially as Prince of Wales Island, in September 1805 and how eagerly the passengers and crew alike scanned the shore. Six months at sea, touching briefly at only two ports, was a lifetime to a landlubber and a penance even for those who made a living by it. There was little possibility of any of those posted overseas being able or of wanting to make a voyage home in a hurry so necks were craned to see what their new 'home' looked like.

It was soon after dawn and the light was still grey and indistinct as Raffles stood with his arm around Olivia's waist, looking eagerly to landward. They passed to the north of the island and into the Strait of Malacca, the channel separating Penang Island from the Malay mainland. Gradually the mist cleared and the sun climbed higher in the sky until the two could see jungle covered land on either side, skirted by sandy beaches, shining brilliant white. In the distance, on the mainland, great mountains could be seen and all of Penang seemed to rise up in a succession of rugged peaks to the centre. On a point of land at the end of a wide, curving bay, partly but charmingly hidden by trees, stood the little settlement of Georgetown, dotted with red roofed houses, gay with flowers, native huts and, close to the shore, Government House and the British fort over which flew welcomingly, the Union Jack.

In the harbour bobbed an assortment of shipping the like of which Raffles and Olivia had never seen before. Chinese and Thai junks with strange lateen sales looking like the wings of prehistoric birds, triangular sailed Bugis prows from Macassar, British merchantmen, country ships from India, Dhows from Arabia, a huge, triple decked man-of-war and an assortment of smaller craft ferrying passengers and goods to and from the busy town jetty.

Olivia almost danced up and down on her toes, pointing out new sights to Raffles.

"I see it or I see him", Raffles responded excitedly, immediately barraging her with a stream of questions.

As he heard the ship's anchor hitting the water with a splash, Raffles was eager to get ashore. Naturally, almost everybody else had the same idea but protocol dictated that the Governor and his party, he in full dress uniform, must be the first to depart by a long boat sent out from the Fort. Raffles, Olivia and some merchants went next, all the men looking very much alike in black breeches with light stockings and buckled shoes and black tail coats with high, white, starched collars over cravats. The baggage would come later.

Even though Raffles was not the first to land, as the rowers pulled for the shore, his romantic nature suggested a mental picture of himself as a plenipotentiary about to disembark in a strange land. He was seated in the stern of the boat, in front of the helmsman, and looking over his shoulder he could see the Company's great standard fluttering at the stern, almost brushing the surface of the water shimmering in the early morning sun. The Governor's boat had not yet landed and he could see a welcome party of troops drawn up on shore. Cannons boomed in salute. Were they for the Governor or were they for him. The great adventure had begun!

CHAPTER TWO

Raffles' consuming passion was to begin his official duties as soon as possible. The thought of what he might be called upon to do, in whose sight and where took precedence even over finding accommodation for himself, Olivia and Mary Anne. A clerk had met them at the jetty in the shadow of the guns of Fort Cornwallis and escorted them to the Company's guest house, overlooking the sea. Without even waiting for the luggage, Raffles had insisted on an immediate appointment with his new chief, William Pearson.

Olivia had kept house before and needed no instructions about what to do to secure their baggage and arrange for their immediate creature comforts and needs. Temperamentally like Raffles, Mary Anne was a willing and capable assistant. The government guest house was almost a home coming for Olivia, not only because of its high roof, wide eaves and verandahs but because many of the staff were bewhiskered, turbaned Indians.

Unbeknown to Raffles, until they met, Pearson was also a new appointee to the post of Secretary.

"I'm afraid there's not much I can tell you, my dear chap. I'm as much in the dark as you are. My advice is, go and have a look around the town today. Everything will be known tomorrow after the Governor's address.

Because of Penang's elevation to the status of a Presidency, a whole new government had been appointed at the island, effective from the date of its leading member's arrival from Britain. The company's headquarters was smaller than Raffles had expected and he was surprised to see virtually no signs of activity. He asked Pearson about it.

"All the senior people are upset about being pushed aside to make way for the new governors. A lot of them have been with the Company all their working lives and they feel that some of the newcomers are stronger on titles and decorations than on experience. It's a difficult situation."

Raffles was disappointed at not being able to get his teeth into some work right away but at the same time pleased that there was almost a whole day in which to look around Penang and make enquiries about permanent accommodation. Whereas earlier he had rushed to the Secretariat, on his way back to the guest house he walked in a more leisurely manner, as Pearson had suggested, taking his time to look around.

While Georgetown could in no way be compared with the City of London, its appearance struck Raffles as vaguely similar to a developing British provincial town but with less substantial buildings and swathed and overhung by tropical foliage. The sun was by now at its height and the streets were less crowded than they were earlier or would be by evening but Raffles smiled with pleasure as he passed pigtailed Chinamen with loads slung across their shoulders on poles, turbaned Indian Hindu and Muslim peddlers, Indian merchants in colourful tunics and muslin trousers, Arab traders dressed from head to toe in flowing cotton robes. Raffles' heart sang with the romance of the scene. At last he was in the very heart of Asia. Though he could not have know it on that first day passers-by included not only Indians, Chinese, Malays and Arabs but northern peoples from Burma and Thailand and islanders from Java and Macassar. He was not only overjoyed to be in Asia but ecstatic at seeing so many different races attracted by commerce to the Company's newest settlement. Raffles had been told in London to expect a population of about 10,000 of which the European contingent was small, perhaps 10 per cent. Most of the European accents were British but here and there he recognized an accent from continental Europe. Raffles knew instinctively that bringing people together like this from around the world and around the region was the very essence of trade. Just seeing them all in Penang deepened his optimism about the island's success. Arriving back at the guest house he found that the Indian houseboys had prepared lunch and so the family sat down to their very first meal ashore in the Indies.

"Do you think you will like it here", Olivia smiled.

"I love it all already", said Raffles excitedly, "and I've barely seen one street!"

"I'm so glad, my dear."

"Government has pretty well come to a stand still pending Mr Dundas' speech to Council tomorrow so, after lunch, let's go and see the town. You'd like that wouldn't you Mary Anne?"

"Oh, let's. I can't wait," said Mary Anne stamping her little feet with anticipation.

Never-a-one to stand on ceremony Raffles gave scant thought to the propriety of the Council's Assistant Secretary walking through the town. Anyway, as yet, he knew virtually no one and virtually no one knew him. It was all smiles and excitement when they left the house feeling happier than they had ever felt and exhilarated at being able to walk on dry land after six months at sea. The guest house was to the west of Fort Cornwallis, among a cluster of the spacious mansions of wealthy merchants and high officials. Between it and the little town was the encampment of the Sepoys or troops of the Company's Indian army and, of course, the fort itself. There were no paved roads or sidewalks and in the absence of rain the streets were dry and clean. Beyond the Fort they came first to row after row of Company warehouses or godowns and then, leading away from the godowns, to a maze of small streets arranged in a grid around a principal thoroughfare called China Street. Sure enough most of the shops were run by Chinese but some were also run by Indians and in other streets most of the shops were run by Hindus or Muslims. Some of the mainly white buildings with red tiled roofs were of one storey, others two. The shop fronts were open and the dark interiors crammed with goods or produce. In the town proper there were many houses built in the Chinese or Indian style and on the outskirts Raffles' little party glimpsed great gardens containing some of the bungalows and mansions of wealthy European residents, usually with atap or coconut frond thatch atop an eclectic blend of European, Indian or Malay architecture.

"Good heavens. Look at that" squealed Mary Anne, as they neared the western extremity of the urban area.

In front of them the town seemed to end in a picturesque Malay settlement where all the houses were built of wood and raised on stilts above the sea.

"Imagine. Living above the sea like that." said Olivia. So romantic."

The sun burned down fiercely on the party in their heavy European clothes and, on the return, they sheltered often beneath trees or awnings, Mary Anne and Olivia several times complaining of thirst. Sweat poured down inside Raffles' stiff clerical collar but to him this was no tourist walk, no idle past time. His active mind was already surveying the settlement, cataloguing its contents, appreciating its strengths, noting its weaknesses. Once again they passed close to the jetty where they had landed and Raffles cast a lingering sidelong glance not at the busy shipping in the Penang Roads but far across the narrow strait to the mainland. Just as he had wondered about the traffic outside his schoolroom window in Hammersmith, today he wondered about the fabled lands to the East. Already, even on this first day, he knew that one day soon he must set foot in those lands and see what potential they offered for trade. The party arrived home around five'o clock to find another meal already prepared. As they dined, a growing stream of carriages and horse riders passed their open windows until Raffles asked one of the houseboys what could be going on.

"Nothing special sahib", replied Mahmud, the chief houseboy, in heavily accented Indian-English. His hair was oiled neatly into place above a bushy mustache which was so perfect it looked waxed. He wore a white short tunic with metal, crested buttons over a long white sarong. Like the other house staff he went barefoot.

"But there are so many people. When we were out the streets were almost empty."

"Too hot before, Sahib. Now the sun has gone so everyone is coming out. The Europeans love to walk or ride in the cool of the evening and local people always take their food about now. If you walk back into the town now you will find that all the Chinese, Indians and Malays are making their food. A happy time Sahib."

Although the Raffles party did not leave the guest house again that night, Raffles felt that not a moment

41

had been lost. Since landing in the morning, he had checked on his duties and he had explored the town. He stood poised, as it were, to commence whatever the Company asked of him, as fully primed as a man in his position could be.

September 20, 1805 was an historical day in Penang. On the 19th crowds of the inhabitants had watched the pomp and ceremony of the arrival of the new Governor, seen the honour guard, watched him shake hands with Company officials and leading dignitaries, seen him and his lady disappear in an open carriage in the direction of Government House. What did it mean? What was going to happen? The very air was expectant. Today, the atmosphere was electric, throbbing with anticipation. Soon after eight o'clock the Governor's carriage appeared with an escort of light cavalry clattering along beside. Sepoys lined the driveway to the modest Council Chamber with its classic columns lining a deep portico, today jammed with local merchants eager to hear the news - news which might mean even more money in their pockets.

Governor Dundas took almost three hours to read a 74 paragraph statement of policy to Penang's governing Council, which Raffles and the Company's other staff took as a blueprint of all their future exertions. First came the announcement of the elevation of the government of Prince of Wales Island to the status of a Presidency. Since administration cost money the merchant's reaction to this was subdued. Governor Dundas spoke sombrely about the threat to Britain's Far East trade of war with France, renewed earlier in the year. His broaching of concern about the limitations placed upon English trade with the eastern islands by the monopolistic policies of the Dutch drew loud shouts from the assembled merchants. The shouts turned to hoarse cheers when the Governor went on to say that because of these concerns Penang was to be built up into a major trade centre, levying no fees or taxes on all who used the port which in addition to its role as a major regional entrepot was also to be made a centre for the construction of British warships and for regional defense. The defences of Georgetown were therefore to be improved and, as a corollary, a new arsenal built. The hoarse cheers almost drowned out his direction that the Port of Malacca, captured recently from the Dutch, was to be physically destroyed and the inhabitants induced to remove to Penang. Also, the Company's only base in the Indies, at Bengkulu, was to be closed down.

"For the first time", said Dundas, "Britain will have a trading and naval base in eastern India without which other European powers will not only force us from the region but may also threaten our trade with China. Today, during the north-east monsoon the French have the ability to drive us from the Indian Ocean and the Bay of Bengal. And if a single ship needs repair between Bombay and China it will have to throw itself on the mercy of a Dutch port. This is intolerable and from this very minute I announce to you that British power is now firmly established east of the subcontinent."

Cheers upon cheers greeted this news and many a glass was downed that night in celebration. Even navy tars and the military linesmen joined in the celebrations creating such a racket of shouts and curses that half the town missed its sleep that night.

Raffles felt as elated as a man who has been told that he is about to be given enough money that he need never work again. If he'd had a hat he would have tossed it in the air. After the speech the excitement among even the most junior company employee was fantastic. A great lunch was laid out on trestles on the lawn behind the Council Chamber and for two hours a steady procession of dignitaries passed by the Governor, shaking his hand and murmuring congratulations. Pearson stood to the Governor's left and on the Governor's right stood the Commander of the land forces, Colonel Norman Macalister. Soon after two o'clock the Governor departed and the guests began to drift away. Raffles stayed unobtrusive but close to Pearson throughout and with Dundas safely in his carriage Pearson turned to him with a wide smile.

"Well, Raffles, a great day for us eh!"

"Indeed, sir."

"And a great load of work for you and me to get everything set up and running well."

"Yes, sir."

"Go home now but tomorrow we set the world on fire!"

Set the world on fire! What a phrase! Yet reflecting so accurately how Raffles felt. What a far cry Penang was from the drudgery of Leadenhall Street. Here he was on his first day already involved in planning extensions to the town, building a shipyard, an arsenal and new defences, expanding trade and, most of all, extending trade into areas hitherto hardly touched by British traders and right under the noses of their European competitors and enemies. Raffles had listened to all the details about costs and revenues, about coinage, about laws about the mundane, day-to-day running of the colony. But his mind remained riveted on the Company's overall purpose in the Indies and fantasized what his role might be within it. Visions of himself treading where no European had ever trod, going as a plenipotentiary to foreign rulers who had never before had treaties with the British, bringing freedom and enlightenment to the enslaved world of the east or hoisting the Company flag where no British flag had ever flown danced before his eyes that sunny afternoon. When he arrived home he was barely coherent with excitement and almost failed to grasp Olivia's several times repeated:

"I think I've found us a charming little house. The price is high because good accommodation is in short supply but if you like the house I think we should snap it up."

"What are we waiting for? Let's go. The sooner we're settled in the sooner I can concentrate on work."

Olivia was right. The house was utterly charming. West of the fort, at the base of a low foothill overlooked by a substantial peak, soon to be named on official maps 'Mount Olivia' the house was made entirely of wood and built on stout wooden piles, Malay style, above the ground. The roof was atap and each, large window had a large awning which could be opened or closed depending on the position of the sun. A covered brick staircase led up to a verandah in front of living and sleeping rooms, which were large and airy.

"I like it. I like it", Raffles said immediately. "And it's big. We can relax on the verandah in the evenings, I can have a study and there are plenty of spare rooms for guests."

"What are those outhouses at the back?, asked Mary Anne.

"The servants quarters," said the always knowledgeable Olivia. "The servants work in the house but they sleep out there."

The house had belonged to one of the Company's servants who had died just before Raffles had arrived and needed a good deal of cleaning up. But it stood in its own grounds, surrounded by mature trees. It was beyond the wildest dreams of any of them.

"You are a Nabob already, my dear", laughed Olivia, swinging Raffles round and round in the great dining-cum-living room.

September 20, 1805! What a day it had been! A new mission. A new house and, tomorrow, a new life!

Within a few hours of starting work Raffles was brought to realize two crucial facts:- His superiors really were were more decorative than effective and there were very, very few able people to undertake the complex and extensive work of reorganizing and running the Penang establishment. This realization represented both a burden and an opportunity. Much though he disliked working with superiors who perhaps lacked qualifications or merit but who owed their appointments to powerful patrons, he decided to sublimate these feelings into the infinitely less fractious and more rewarding course of pursuing opportunity. Pearson was an amiable and good natured man who certainly knew his job. Nevertheless, he liked to delegate and so from day one Raffles found every decision of Council passed directly to him for its implementation. Raffles did not want to complain too soon to London but it was immediately very clear that the scale of Penang's new government and the ambitious nature of the plans for expansion would require more than just himself and he made a note to see that Leadenhall Street was asked to augment the establishment of clerks.

Meanwhile, as day followed day, Raffles again found himself veritably chained to his desk from which he had no sooner cleared one file than a mound of others immediately appeared. Details of government proceedings, rules and regulations and even the dispatches to head office all either passed through his hands or originated at his desk. Whenever something needed to be done but lacked a body to do it Raffles could be counted on. Merely by virtue of doing so much of what had to be done there was a constant stream of visitors to his office from among the councilors, from Company employees, from military officials and from the merchant community. All were met and welcomed with civility and interest partly because Raffles knew that his promotion in the Company depended on him doing a good job and partly because, from such meetings, he learned a great deal not only about the problems and opportunities represented by Penang but by the region as a whole. Unlike his position at Leadenhall Street or at Hammersmith there were, as yet, none to be jealous of him and from every quarter he heard only expressions of the most sincere respect for his prodigious abilities and energy. Within sixty days of landing he felt bound to write to his old chief, William Ramsay, to let him know how he was getting on and to convey his optimism about the likely success of the Company's plans for the island, even including the possibility of it making money through the sale of opium to the east, pepper to the west, local land regulations and the Company's monopoly over marine stores.

Olivia was invaluable to Raffles in being able to undertake alone all that was necessary to establish their new home. Some servants came with the house; others had to be interviewed and employed. Domestic help was cheap and the house was soon filled with a cook and helpers, bearers, cleaners, washers and gardeners with other staff being added as required. Olivia persuaded Raffles that the key to a well run house was its major domo and that it would be helpful if they could secure the services of Mahmud. Raffles duly sounded out Pearson informally before submitting an official request. Within a few days Mahmud's tall and familiar figure appeared as if by magic to fulfill even the smallest need or solve the most trifling problem. Olivia had proved adept at finding local suppliers of everything from daily food to furniture, which she had managed to have made to European standards but at incredibly low cost.

Raffles had emphasized to her that of all the furniture she planned to order the dining table and chairs would be the most important.

Within less than a fortnight their dining room was dominated by a beautiful teak table and high backed carved chairs capable of seating eight. And virtually from the first day of the table's arrival it was in use. Raffles needed to get to know people and he hoped that society would want to know him. Every week, sometimes twice a week, guests were invited to join him at a table loaded with game, fish, rice, vegetables and fruit with beer and wine to wash it down. The hospitality of the Raffles' household was soon known not only in Penang but among visitors from as far afield as India. Obtaining news was slow and difficult in those days and Raffles lost no opportunity of adding to his knowledge and therefore adding to his power by the information he gleaned even from social contacts at his house in the evenings. Olivia, assisted by Mary Anne, planned the meals and the entertainment - few evenings ended without singing - and while Olivia was as busy as a bee during the day, during a soiree she appeared to give each guest her relaxed and undivided attention, endearing her to them.

"What an absolutely charming couple the Raffles are", was a refrain forever on the islanders' lips.

Working hard for the Company and, in a sense playing hard in the evenings, Raffles also made time to follow up the strategic interest in the surrounding region recommended by William Ramsay. Although, because of his unfinished schooling, he always thought of himself as an untutored fellow, less than six weeks after arrival at Penang he was lucky enough to be able to offer accommodation at his house to Dr. John Leyden, on convalescence from Madras.

Leyden was a driven spirit like himself who

believed that a man could achieve anything he put his mind to - especially a Brit.

"Isn't the world full of self made and successful men", he told the eager Raffles, convincing him that his talents were inferior to no man's.

Being a brilliant linguist as well as an irrepressible student, Leyden decided to use his three months in Penang to learn Malay. Who better to teach him than Raffles! Leyden was a trained and accomplished scholar and during his stay he introduced the Assistant Secretary to disciplines and procedures Raffles' wide but random study had never known before.

There was no doubt that through ability and drive Raffles was very good at his job and like so many other Englishmen were doing at the time, he longed to explore where no Englishman had yet explored, longed to accumulate, collate and submit knowledge which would be of value to the Company, to Britain and perhaps even mankind, longed to be able to do valuable things in the right way so that he could enjoy the widest respect. This was by no means foolish thinking because men with worse education than him had already made a name for themselves as explorers and navigators. The age of Darwin and modern science was just beginning. Buoyed by its fortuitous early start in industry, everywhere in Britain men were eager to delve scientifically into the why and the way of everything.

Soon after his arrival, Raffles engaged several able Malays to introduce him to Malay manuscripts and assist with their translation. Through this work he hoped to arrive at an accurate understanding of Malay laws and customs of the adjacent mainland and, eventually, of the entire Malay island world.

Although Oriental studies were only beginning in Britain they were well under way in India and Leyden enthusiastically encouraged Raffles in his efforts, an encouragement which, from such a formidable scholar, Raffles felt was praise indeed. Always able to spot an opportunity, he could see clearly that no one other than himself was taking a serious interest in the Malays and that, if he chose, here was a field that he could dominate.

Knowing his interest, Governor Dundas honoured him by asking him to gratify a request for information about the Malays from the renowned British Orientalist, William Marsden. Raffles was delighted. He could hardly believe that what he still felt were his poor skills and observations should be wanted and valued by leading scientists in the home country. When he replied to that first fateful letter Raffles could hardly know that it would be the first of many or of the great stimulus Marsden's questions would give to his interest in the eastern isles and in his ability to marshal data.

Leyden wanted to see all over the island and so did Raffles. There had been so much to do during the first two months in Penang that there had been little time for sightseeing outside the town. Within days of Leyden's moving into the Raffles' household, early one morning, Raffles returned from the office soon after he had arrived there with syces (grooms) and four mounts.

"Come. Let's take a day off and see the island," shouted Raffles bounding up the front steps and into the living room and provoking the recently acquired family dogs to a frenzy of barking.

No one was ready and momentarily there was plenty of female prevarication.

"What! Now!" said Olivia. "Why didn't you warn me?"

"I'm not dressed", wailed Mary Anne.

Yes, yes, now," insisted Raffles pushing and

pulling the harassed ladies into their rooms to change into riding habits and thence down the steps to the waiting horses. Raffles and Leyden wore riding boots and Olivia and Mary Anne sat side saddle. Each horse was accompanied by its own mounted groom who also carried umbrellas and water. Fired with boyish excitement the men led the party off at a cracking pace, the dogs barking at the horses heals.

They stopped first at the spectacular waterfall roaring in a storm of white spray through a steep gorge at the back of the settlement, approaching across the huge boulders as close to the precipice as they dared. Their next stop was the 'Great Tree', at its widest, an incredible 200 feet tall and 35 feet wide. Only a fragment of a single exposed root was enough to dwarf a man.

"It's surely one of the wonders of the world", gasped Leyden. "In all my travels I have never seen anything like it."

"If the forests of the Indies contain monsters like this the British navy will never want for timber," smiled Raffles, tapping the tree meaningfully.

On they went, their pace slowed by the rocky, winding trail, and the intense heat of the day until they reached the top of Penang Hill, with its magnificent views of Georgetown and Kedah. A naval signal station had been built on the peak and Raffles had already arranged for the party to take tiffin here while they drank in the view.

"I do believe I can see our little house", said Olivia pointing down at the base of the hill from which the mansions of the islands wealthy spread out across a triangle of land cleared of forests on the tip of which had been built the town. As usual the roads were dotted with moored vessels while bum boats or lighters darted to and from the shore.

51

"One of these days it will be nice if we can afford to build ourselves a house on the North Beach", said Raffles, pointing at the still largely empty shore. "The development has all been to the eastward but a house on the beach to the west of the fort would be more or less on its own with uninterrupted views across the Strait. We could sit on our verandah and watch the shipping coming and going."

"You should have a house up here", joked Leyden. "The air is so fresh. This is the place to recover one's health.

They sat on rocks for almost an hour, drenching their senses in the wonderful view over blue-green hills, the gay red roofs of the settlement and the busy shipping in the port. They ate their lunch from hampers brought by the grooms but everyone was reluctant to tear themselves away.

We must go back," said Raffles, at last. We don't want to risk being out in the jungle when it gets dark."

After a jolly and bracing day out, the party wound its way slowly back down the mountain arriving exhausted at Raffle's residence.

Life in Penang for Raffles was like a dream come true - a whirlwind of work, meetings, honours, opportunities, soirees, banquets and balls. Olivia found herself restored to the head of a family, married to an energetic and ambitious man who had already proved he could achieve success. Unlike in London, here Mary Anne found herself with the pick of a hundred beaux. Soon after the glittering King's Birthday Ball at the Prince of Wales Island Club she married Quintin Thompson and the entire Raffles family felt so optimistic about the prospects in Penang that Raffles impulsively sent to England for two more sisters, Harriet and Leonora.

"They can find husbands too and they will love

the life here."

Mary Anne and her husband took a house at the foot of a hill adjacent to Mount Olivia. As if to crown his happiness during his first year in Penang, Secretary Pearson took an abrupt six months leave and Raffles found himself promoted to Acting Secretary, a position to which he was soon confirmed. He could hardly believe his luck. With still a month to go before he could celebrate even one year on Prince of Wales Island he had become 'The Boss' in the sense of head of the Secretariat.

In practice, discharging his new duties seemed very much like discharging the old because so much delegation had left Pearson with little enough to do and the reins of power very much in his assistant's hands. It was in his new capacity that, accompanied by Olivia, he had the good fortune to attend a feast provided by the wealthy Malay merchant and businessman, Syed Hussan.

Seeing the expansion of British power in Penang, Syed was not unnaturally interested in positioning himself to try to take advantage of it. From their point of view the British were keen to befriend a powerful Malay merchant who could, perhaps, advance their interests. From Raffles' point of view the very special magic of the evening was the way in which it brought Malay culture to life. He had seen Malays around the island, he had read about them but this was the first time he had attended a cultural event.

Syed occupied a large house and grounds in the suburbs and, on this night, Raffles was astonished to see that not only the house and its grounds but even the streets round about were all illuminated with gaily coloured lights. Large numbers of ordinary people had gathered outside the low perimeter wall to watch the carriages and riders arrive. A huge marquee had been erected on the lawn to which guests were escorted upon arrival. Chairs were arranged on three sides of a square with one side open and with the side facing it reserved for VIPs. Syed himself, wearing a dark, patterned sarong with a bejewelled kris or short wavy dagger tucked into the waist band and a short black tunic with gold braid stood beneath a great ceremonial umbrella to meet and shake hands with each guest. Syed had short black hair and a close cropped mustache and his eyes were warm with welcome. Raffles knew enough of Malay etiquette to merely touch the proffered hand with his finger tips. A beautiful Malay girl, also dressed in sarong and kebaya and with flowers and gold jewelry in her black hair, escorted each guest to their seat. They treated each charge like an old friend, not speaking unless spoken to but then smiling broadly with warmth and hospitality.

At six o'clock there was a storm of sound as a Malay orchestra in maroon trouser suits with black waistcoats and pill box caps struck the gongs and xylophones of the traditional gamelan orchestra. At that moment His Excellency, The Governor, entered with his Lady. Syed bowed to the Governor; the Governor bowed to Syed. A fresh musical salute, like the tinkling of a thousand hammers on metal interspersed with scores of sonorous gongs, greeted the arrival of each VIP. Syed sat down only when all guests were seated and after being formally introduced to the assembled company he pronounced a few words of welcome in Malay and in English.

Immediately there began a fascinating entertainment in which bare shouldered, gold skinned, Malay girls performed a selection of traditional dances. Between each dance there was an interval so that costumes could be changed. Tonight, foreigners saw Malays as they had never seen them, not as farmers or fisherman nor even as merchants or dignitaries but as the possessors of an ancient culture in which they took great and obvious pride. Raffles thought that the dresses and make-up of the young girls were like a scene from some fantasy medieval palace in Europe. Their faces wore fixed expressions yet their eyes flashed like points of fire. They did not move quickly yet from the beginning of the dance 'till the end each nerve and muscle was strained to produce the desired posture and movement. Even fingers and toes were disciplined to the rhythms of the dance. Black eyes flashed dramatically, golden head dresses bobbed and swayed, gold belts glittered in the bright lights. Raffles was entranced and absorbed. He enjoyed the much more spirited dances of a troupe of Malabar maidens from India but the Malay panorama he was seeing meant so much more to a man of his interests.

Later that night he was to say to Olivia: "Before I came here I had no idea that these people had such a deep and ancient culture; they are not savages, living in trees. They are very cultivated. I wish so much I had time and opportunity to get to know them."

After the entertainment in the marquee, the party was led into Syed's mansion to a sumptuous feast of Malay foods laid out on glittering white cloths, some of the food came from the fields and some from the sea, some was served on leaves, some in baskets, some on shining brass trays, some cooked, some cold. And there were wines aplenty to please the foreigners. After dinner toasts to a total of nine were drunk to His Majesty the King, to the Sultan of Kedah, to the Honorable Governor, to the Commander of the Forces, to VIP visitors and, most important of all, to long lasting friendship and mutually beneficial prospects. Each toast was accompanied by an appropriate tune struck up by a naval band specially lent for the occasion by a warship in the roads. By nine o'clock the official programme was ended, tables and chairs were cleared and the whole party danced with great enthusiasm until the early hours of the morning.

Syed's banquet and entertainment had made Raffles more than ever determined to escape from the confines of Penang Island and see for himself conditions on the Malay mainland. He was genuinely interested in the Malays and everything about them and he was also conscious of Ramsay's encouragement to assess realities and possibilities in the region - something his heavy work load had until now precluded. Like so many of his time Raffles pursued work with near religious zeal. After all, wasn't hard work the making of the British! But, like so many others, high and low, excessively hard work coupled with excessively little exercise or fresh air and numerous late nights at social functions where too much was frequently eaten or drunk eventually took its toll on Raffles' health.

Raffles was well aware from his work at Leadenhall Street that there were great dangers to the health of Europeans in the tropics. After a prolonged stay, if they ever reached home again they were lucky. Only a few weeks after Syed's dinner Lady Dundas died in Calcutta where she had gone to try to repair her health. A few months later Governor Dundas himself was dead and Raffles' friend Pearson became Acting Governor. Feeling ill with overwork himself Raffles was suitably alarmed. In view of deaths, retirements and postings and with no replacements being sent by the Company from Britain Raffles found himself heaped with ever more responsibilities. In April 1807 Mary Anne's young husband died, bringing the ghastly spectre of death into Raffles' own family. Mary Anne moved back into the Raffles' home with her infant daughter, Charlotte. Olivia could not have children and was delighted to have the little Charlotte to coo and fuss over. Raffles took over Quintin's job as Naval Agent. Raffles' friend Leyden had come to Penang for the sake of <u>his</u> health and two years in the Far East was more than enough for Raffles to know how inimical the climate and conditions could be to the health of Europeans. When he was working he enjoyed every minute of it but he knew that his mind and body protested at the strain. In the tropics, there were the added challenges of a hectic social life, inadequate sleep and the recurrent stomach upsets suffered by all Europeans no matter how hard they tried to be clean and eat wisely.

Olivia was more used to the climate than Raffles and suffered less. But she was not only a devoted wife but an unremitting companion to Raffles in all that he did with the result that she, too, became tired. Perhaps, not being able to give him children, she had worked even harder to please. She was now aged thirty seven and her unrestrained commitment to life and to Raffles had taken an irredeemable toll on the bloom of her youth.

Raffles applied for leave and, taking into account two hectic years in which his labour had been prodigious and far beyond the call of duty, leave was granted. As he and Olivia set out, Raffles looked rather stooped in his long, black clerical coat and, preoccupied as usual with the coming opportunity to explore the mainland he hardly noticed that Olivia, though dressed distinctively and even a little eccentrically, looked worn beyond her years. But, in the hearts of both optimism burned bright.

At last Raffles would have the chance to visit the Malay mainland. Freed from the chains of daily clerking and excited beyond measure by the prospect the happy pair sailed down the Strait to the town of Malacca.

Napoleon had installed his brother, Louis Bonaparte, on the Dutch throne in 1806, sending shivers of alarm down the spines of every Englishman needing to pass through the islands of the now Franco-Dutch controlled

Indies. Raffles remembered what William Ramsay had told him in London at the time of his appointment: "Heaven help England if the French and the Dutch should combine!"

As they sailed, the threat to Penang still seemed no more than normal in seas where French and English squadrons made regular encounter. So long as the British navy was active in the Bay of Bengal Penang was safe.

"The Strait of Sunda is another matter," Raffles told Olivia reflectively. "If the French and Dutch are now strong enough to close it our ships from India will be cut off from China."

Thank goodness Admiral Pellew was sent out," smiled Olivia.

"Thank goodness," echoed Raffles grimly.

Soon after the French acquisition of Holland, the Penang Brits had learnt of the defeat of a Franco-Dutch fleet in East Java by Admiral Pellew, one of Nelson's former captains. When the Admiral arrived in Penang such was the feeling of relief that he was given a war hero's welcome.

"At least we shan't meet any French ships here," Olivia joked.

"Hopefully, not", smiled Raffles, never a man to take anything for granted. "Hopefully not."

The Raffles spent a very pleasant Christmas at the home of the British Resident in Malacca, Major William Farquhar, from whom Raffles learned much about current realities and opinions in the ancient territory.

It seemed to Raffles that almost no sooner had he arrived in Malacca and intensified his studies of the Malay people than he was recalled urgently to Penang by the new Governor, Colonel Norman Macalister, a man Raffles had known since he landed at Georgetown. Macalister's note said,

"We shall not be able to make up any dispatches for the Court (of Governors of the East India Company) without your assistance".

The summons was obviously urgent and, never a one to put comfort ahead of duty, Raffles raced back to Prince of Wales Island in the tiny converted long boat of an East Indiaman, in doing so risking the violence of tropical storms which wracked the region at this time of year. Olivia returned a week later in the Portuguese ship 'Theresa' transporting the Governor of the Portuguese colony of Macau to another of Portugal's colonies at Goa, India. Upon his welcome return Raffles found a huge backlog of work and the need to compile the dispatches mentioned by Macalister for which ships were already waiting in the roads.

Deaths, retirements and postings continued and Raffles found himself Clerk of the Crown, Registrar of the Court and Licenser of the Press. A fire wiped out a substantial part of the commercial section of Georgetown, greatly adding to Raffles' burden as he wrestled with the problems of temporary housing in a colony already seriously short of housing. Crime was rampant yet there were insufficient police to enforce what little law there was.

By mid-year, when he was not only Secretary but Assistant Secretary as well, due to the leave of a subordinate, Raffles was again so seriously overworked that he was obliged to once more request leave and for a second time proceeded to Malacca where he again stayed with the British Resident.

Shortly before his departure he wrote to a friend: " I am convinced my health will never permit my holding this office for many years. I am afraid they will work the willing horse to death."

But he didn't die. And after a short voyage he found himself virtually holding court at Farquhar's house in the manner of an Oriental potentate. The chains again having fallen from his body, doing what he liked doing made a new man of him and soon restored him to the vigour and energy for which he was famous.

"We must use this time to find out all about the importance of Malacca," Raffles had told Olivia on the voyage down.

Raffles had good reason to want this information. The great projects announced almost four years ago, in 1805, had barely got off the ground in Penang either for want of investment capital from the Company or from the Government. One 1,200 ton ship was under construction but no other work was being undertaken, including the permanent docks, the naval arsenal and improved fortifications. Penang had certainly grown, more land had been cleared, more commercial premises and homes built, civic improvements made but the Company felt that the trade passing through Penang in no way justified the earlier optimistic plans for expansion.

The initial premises on which Penang had been founded and upgraded had seemed sound to Raffles but even in his mind there was now a large question mark over why the trade and prosperity of the colony was developing so slowly. Resident Farquhar had his own ideas but being an infinitely painstaking man Raffles interviewed British and Dutch merchants and Chinese, Bugis, Malay and Arab captains so as to enable him to piece together a picture of his own. He was almost as busy with visitors and dinners at Farquhar's house as he was at home in Penang.

The Resident's domicile was the old Dutch State House, a sprawling mansion at the foot of what had once been an intensively fortified hill. Britain had taken Malacca over from the Dutch to prevent the port falling into the hands of the French. When Penang had been elevated to a Presidency the British Government and the East India Company had taken the decision that Malacca was to be razed to the ground so that no one would wish to or could live there. By this means, even if Malacca was restored to the Dutch at the conclusion of the war with Napoleon, it was hoped to force the Indies trade into Penang so that the new Presidency could enjoy both the Europe-India-China trade and the island trade. All those of means at Malacca were to have the option of moving to Penang. The squat, thick walls of the great Portuguese fortress of La Famosa which had skirted St Paul's Hill were especially targeted for destruction to deny their use to others. When Raffles arrived, except for a single gateway, the Porta de Santiago, the fort had been duly destroyed but, on his own authority, Farquhar had stopped the destruction of all other buildings.

"Too many people are to long established here to quit", Farquhar told Raffles, with a tone of uncontradictable certainty peculiar to Scottish accented English. "Even if we pull down every public building they'll still stay and shipping from the eastern islands will continue to stop here instead of going on to Penang."

The more Raffles researched, the more his impressions resembled those of the astute Resident.

"The decision to raze Malacca is hopelessly wrong," he told Olivia at the end of weeks of exhaustive enquiries. He was sitting behind the Resident's large oak desk with his head thoughtfully in his hands.

"We are getting the India and China captains in Penang because with their large ships they can't use the Strait of Malacca and they benefit from the advantages of Penang before or after crossing the Bay of Bengal. But, the island trade we are missing completely. Small prows come to Malacca from Riau, Java, Borneo, Bali, Sumba, Macassar and the Moluccus but they can only sail before the wind and most can only make it this far before the Monsoon changes. More importantly, the market for the goods the prows bring from the eastern islands is at Malacca and not at Penang. The captains want to sell to the Malays but there are hardly any Malays in Penang. And whatever they need they buy here because everything is readily available."

"After the news has presumably spread about our destruction of Malacca, are the island captains still coming at all?" asked Olivia.

"They are, because, despite the decision from London, Farquhar halted the destruction of the city and the population has refused to move. There's been virtually no change. While we hold Malacca at least we can share in the trade from here. If we wipe out Malacca we'll lose the trade altogether!"

Farquhar had been delighted to learn that Raffles agreed with him.

"It's been a one man battle until now," he smiled like a man who had long known he was right but could never persuade anyone else. "The Company mean well but they don't understand the situation. You can't just destroy a community that's been in existence and expanding here since the 15th century! There are 20,000 people here and their ancestors go back generations."

Many a businessman told him: "We cannot move Mr Raffles. We cannot take our houses and our lands with us. It's impossible. And if we went there, what could you give us to match what we have here. If you want the people of Penang to move to Malacca that's fine because they are all adventurers and newcomers but we have been here for generations."

"All this sows the seeds of the most vital question of all," Raffles had told Farquhar with a rivited glance. "If the people of Malacca cannot move, if the island trade captains cannot sail further north and if we want access to the island trade........."

"Can we ever hand Malacca back?" broke in the Resident.

"Exactly", said Raffles. "Can we afford ever to give Malacca back to the Dutch!"

Raffles had yet another concern. While Olivia watched, he leapt up and looked keenly at the chart on the wall behind him, with its many islands strung out across the route from India to China. He moved the tip of his finger southward down the Strait of Malacca.

"Suppose the Strait of Malacca turns out to be a more efficient route for large ships bound for China than via the Strait of Sunda?"

"That would be very good for Penang, wouldn't it?"

"It should mean very good times not only for Penang but for Malacca too but not necessarily for Britain if a rival or an enemy comes to occupy Malacca or sets up a new post further south. That would be a disaster because they could cut us off at Penang whenever they like."

"Has anybody tried to sail a large ship through the Strait," asked Olivia.

"Not as far as I know", replied Raffles thoughtfully. "But if the prows and junks can get through it may be possible for bigger ships too."

Then, the sooner you can find out the better."

"Quite so, my dear. But I have to be careful. If I recommend that a ship explores to the south I must not give Penang the impression that the results will in any way undermine the new Presidency. If they think that, probably they won't co-operate at all."

Concerned about his career prospects, Olivia agreed. "We don't want to make trouble before we've hardly arrived."

"We don't, "agreed Raffles, "but the fact remains that relinquishing Malacca is the wrong thing to do and I can prove it. Do you think the Company will thank me if I don't speak out and they lose thousands of pounds as a result of failure to plug in to the island trade? What I have to say may be unpopular and certainly provoking but better to face the truth now than disaster later."

"Be very careful, my dear. I know you. You are so direct. In this case I think the utmost diplomacy is called for."

With typical energy Raffles set about preparing a detailed report for the Company. The first words of what would inevitably be a controversial document were:

"Very incorrect information appears to have been received by the Honourable Court of Directors (in London) respecting the trade and advantages of the settlement of Malacca."

Raffles' visits to Malacca had enabled him to reach two important conclusions. First, he argued that Malacca must not be razed. And, contrary to all the political realities, his second argument was that Malacca should never be handed back to the Dutch or to anyone else!

"Nothing commands the Strait of Malacca like Malacca. We now have the command. Why give it up, unless we are forced?

Raffles noted the settled population, the richness of resources and crops, the prospects for increased trade and even the possibility of the enclave running at a profit before concluding that, if retained, Malacca would be complementary instead of competitive to Penang, the former being a growing centre for the trade of the eastern islands and the latter a base for ships engaged in the Europe-India-China trade and using the Strait of Sunda. Because Malacca had once been an independent Malay capital and because of the traditional regard for it among mainland Malays Raffles foresaw that whoever held Malacca held their allegiance too.

"You see," Raffles said confidently to Olivia, "I have avoided any criticism of the Company's decisions but instead concentrated on the idea that our information was inadequate, that I have discovered that Penang and Malacca each performs a function and that both should be retained."

Olivia smiled. "You've made your point but you will not antagonize them and jeopardize your career.

Raffles smiled in agreement.

"But I haven't yet mentioned the prospect of the Malacca Strait being navigable by large ships because I don't know. I have to find a way of sending a ship to explore. Should we discover a safe route to the Far East for even the largest ships, then, as I said before, the very existence of Penang will be called into question."

Raffles lost no time returning to Georgetown and within two days of his arrival at the Secretariat his revolutionary report was in Governor Macalister's hands. The response from Macalister was immediate. Raffles was right! All action to destroy Malacca was ordered suspended!

"But," warned Macalister, "Just because I agree doesn't mean that London will!"

Raffles sensed the truth of this and he had already taken the precaution of dispatching another copy to his friend John Leyden in Calcutta asking that it be shown to the new Governor General of India, Lord Minto.

"I am absolutely certain that London will not appreciate the importance of Malacca," Raffles told Olivia. "I remember from the time I worked at Leadenhall Street how new the Indies was to the Directors and how little they knew about it. If they ask Lord Minto for advice he may not know either so it is essential that he has a copy of my report in his hands."

"Did you mention the possibility of the Strait of Malacca being an alternative to the Strait of Sunda?"

"I did indeed. Because Lord Minto can take a more strategic view that our colleagues in Penang. He will understand the potential long term importance of Malacca. He may even give me the ship I need to explore the channel to the south."

CHAPTER THREE

Raffles' return to Penang coincided with a new house being completed that he had commissioned at North Beach and which he very significantly named 'Runnymede', the name of the English field upon which King John had been compelled to grant the Magna Carta or first charter of an Englishman's rights. Steeped, as he now was, in Malay culture, though simple, the house was very much in Malay style - single storey with atap roof and built on the traditional pillars with louvered wooden window shutters, carved balconies, deep, cool, eaves and large, relatively open living spaces within. Compared with his mother's humble house in London's increasingly congested East End 'Runnymede' was paradise.

By now he was a past master at every aspect of the Company's business in Penang and what, four year's ago, had been new and challenging, had now become routine. His oft repeated pleas for additional staff had at long last been respected and he now had more hands among whom to share the work. After a day's labour on the Company's account he spent most evenings working at his burgeoning unique collections of Penang flora and fauna and to the compilation of a work on Malay laws and customs, stimulated by Marsden and encouraged by Leyden. If he hadn't had to work for a living, his life at 'Runnymede' would have somewhat resembled that of an English country gentleman, a lifestyle very much in vogue among the nouveau riche. No opportunity was missed in Penang for public or private festivities and, being relative newcomers, eager to widen their social circle, Raffles and Olivia hosted more than their fair share of dinners and entertainments - even though they could barely afford them.

But contentment per se was anathema to Raffles and the more idyllic life was the more restless he became.

"It's wonderful here; I know it", he told Olivia many times. "Yet it is like living in a gilded cage. We have everything we want and we are happy but I can't go on like this, year after year, doing the same old things."

Olivia knew only too well her husband's restless spirit. She knew his ambitions. She knew his impatience in seeing things continue which should be changed, knew his driving ambition to see the whole of the trade of the East opened to Britain and, indeed, to all comers in a free and competitive way.

"Maybe the Company has something else in mind for you," she said consolingly. "You've been here nearly five years now so it's time for promotion."

"Yes, but promotion to where? I don't want to go to one of the presidencies in India and, other than Malacca, where else is there for me in the Indies? "

News was very slow to travel and it had been fully six months after the Battle of Trafalgar, at the close of 1805, that Penang had learnt about Nelson's victory over the French fleet. What rejoicing there had been! The whole European community went wild and there was drinking and dancing for two days. Britain fought many battles with the French but somehow, this time, there was an underlying feeling that perhaps French sea power had been irreversibly smashed.

Now, disturbing news arrived in Penang of the arrival of French war fleets at Reunion and Mauritius with the intention of commanding the Indian Ocean. Clive had pushed the French out of northern India but they were still entrenched in strategic bases along the Malabar Coast at which their warships could refit and replenish prior to harassing British shipping in the Indian Ocean and across to the vital sea lanes to China via the Indies. Now they could be reinforced from Mauritius and Reunion! Despite Clive's gains, there were pessimists aplenty who foresaw the forecast William Ramsay had given Raffles of the British being swept out of India altogether!

In the Spring of 1808 the appalling news had arrived in Penang that Napoleon had appointed a new, aggressive Governor General to build up Franco-Dutch strength in Java! As if this wasn't bad enough still other news arrived that the French were planning to establish a naval base at the northern tip of Sumatra at Aceh, a move that could allow them to dominate the sea channels eastward through the maze of thousands of islands which make up the Indies. With the French in Aceh <u>and</u> Java all channels could be closed to British shipping leaving no viable route to China.

Alarm bells rang in London, at the East India Company's Far East headquarters in Calcutta and in the mind of Thomas Stamford Raffles. No-one was more sensible than Raffles to the fact that the last thing the East India Company could afford was loss of revenue caused by new French threats to the sea lanes. Month after month the Government of Penang fought to run the post at a profit and month after month, in his capacity as Secretary, Raffles was exposed to the chill winds of corporate displeasure about how little profit the Company was making and about the need to keep expense to an absolute minimum, including his entertainment bills. They even quarrelled with him about the way in which he drew his salary, which he did in such a manner as to take into account fluctuations in the currency and inflation.

"I can't believe that the Company even begrudges you your salary", commiserated Olivia. "After all that you've done".

Raffles' usually bright eyes were, for once, vacant and dull with depression.

"They just won't realize that the expenses involved in building a new post are very high nor that Penang can never hope to enjoy the revenues of the island trade which are going to Malacca, Raffles said thoughtfully, his long fingers picking reslessly at the leaves of a manuscript. "I wish there was some way that I could get them to address this fundamental underlying problem."

"I suppose the problem is money again!"

"Money again. The Company don't want to spend money and now that I have told them that we should keep Malacca they will assume that they must incur the expense not only of Penang but of Malacca as well."

"But there will be extra revenue from the island trade."

"A reasonable assumption for us here," said Raffles. "But, so far, the Directors in London probably feel that they have been given more promises than profits and they will be very, very reluctant to take on board more costs."

"There is still the political dimension."

"Indeed there is. Only the British Government can decide whether or not to hand Malacca back to the Dutch."

"If London won't listen to sense there's no

point in them nagging you about expenses. You can't make Penang profitable if the facts are totally against it."

Territories in the Far East that merchants and farsighted administrators feared might now be lost to the French were at one and the same time both a source of revenue to the Company as well as substantial new liabilities. Making a profit was essential under circumstances where the frontier of new liabilities, represented by fresh and often unapproved acqisitions, moved relentlessly forward. And, even if turning to the national government was an option for help shouldering some of the ever growing burdens, after the disastrous loss of the colonies in America and almost five years of war with the French, Westminster was also severely strapped for surplus cash.

In the face of the French threat throughout the Indian Ocean and the Indies and despite its slender finances, the British Admiralty instructed Admiral Drury to impose a close blockade of Java and other Franco-Dutch controlled islands in the Indies to keep the channels of trade open.

Far from being welcomed, the blockade frightened the Penang and Malacca merchants more than ever lest it deterred the Malays from traversing the island waters and depressed revenues still further! All too soon news was flooding in to Raffles' office of reduced trade at Malacca and even of whole Bugis fleets sailing home again rather than cross the British blockade. Raffles' routine tranquillity was suddenly ripped apart by an explosion of protests about the blockade and dire prophesies of widespread bankruptcy.

"The Government's gone mad," Raffles frankly told the protesters. "It only needs one of our warships to mishandle one of the native prows and all our relationships with the Malays will be at risk.

"If we blockade the Indies we harm our

friends. What we should be doing is driving out our enemies."

Time and time again, Governor Macalister and the Company's Court of Directors in London protested vigorously about the blockade, soon able to give examples of just the kind of mishandling Raffles feared. After a great deal of avoidable aggravation which would take years of patient diplomacy to repair, eventually, the British Government called off the blockade. Everyone in Penang and Malacca heaved a huge sigh of relief.

"Common sense at last," observed Raffles acidly.

All of Raffles' friendships with and knowledge of the Malays were now put to the test as he spent day after day, night after night, in a feverish, crisis-filled atmosphere either writing letters to prominent Malays or receiving delegations from the Malay mainland and from the islands. Far into the night the meetings went on, with the ever helpful and solicitous Raffles patiently explaining that the naval blockade had not been aimed at anyone other than French or Dutch ships.

Napoleon's new Governor General, Marshal Daendels, and his troops were quickly active in Java and their influence was soon felt on Company balance sheets in Penang and Malacca. Reports followed one after another about the number of island vessels visiting Malacca continuing to decline in the face of Franco-Dutch pressure. Even more alarming, Marshal Daendels was said to be building a military road across Java linking a chain of strong new forts which could be used both to close Indies ports to enemy shipping and also as bases from which to intensify pressure on Indies captains not to trade at British controlled ports.

Raffles watched events unfolding not only

with increasing concern but with a sense of self worth greatly heightened by the realization that perhaps he alone knew enough and was willing to risk enough to avoid the looming threat not onlt to Penang but to Britain's entire Far east trade.

"We must push the French out of the Indies," he fumed to any who would listen.

While there were few who, in principle, disagreed with him, by the same token there were equally few willing to recommend a new war in the Indies to cash and resource strapped London.

"Every day the situation can only get worse,"Raffles told his staff at the Secretariat. While we do nothing the French grow stronger in the Indies by the hour."

Had Raffles but known, hardly a day passed without Marshal Daendels pacing up and down in his office in Batavia fuming:

"We must push the British out of the Indies."

In a process intensified by the war with France, Holland had witnessed one territory after another fall into the hands of the British until all that remained was their base on Java.

"If we lose Java we have lost the Indies", Daendels told his staff with a deeply furrowed brow.

In Calcutta the new British Governor General, Lord Minto, a close friend of the quietly aggressive Admiral Nelson, was fortuitously more clear than anyone about the urgent need to deal with the problems of India and the Indies by administering a crushing blow to the French in the Far East. If they were given the opportunity to build up, either at sea or on land, British power in the East might come to a sudden and historic halt, just as it had in America. Like many a British leader, Minto was determined that Britain should suffer no more losses! It was not a matter of acquiring territory. If lands were increasingly closed to Britain its vibrant, industrializing economy would stagnate. Above all Britain needed widening markets and free trade.

Gradually, after a veritable bombardment of letters and dispatches, Leadenhall Street came round to the view that a swift, successful, punitive action against Napoleon's Far East forces, followed by an equally swift withdrawal would serve the purpose. Whitehall had no wish to antagonize Holland, which they hoped to have as an ally in Europe against France. Accordingly, there was no willingness to occupy former Dutch territories permanently and therefore no support for spending money even for occupations of the shortest duration.

"The Company would rather raze Malacca than pay for it and risk the French getting back into Java rather than pay for an occupation," grumbled Minto who had his own strong views either about the wisdom of making Holland and ally or of a swift withdrawal from the Indies. He gambled that if he could only launch a successful attack against Franco-Dutch forces in the Indies what followed could be worked out later.

Raffles listened to the reports reaching him from the island world to the eastward with rapidly mounting anxiety. His sixth sense told him that there was no time to lose either in bringing peace to the Indies or in interrupting the military preparations of the French on Java. All of the Company's posts in the Indies were at stake - Penang, Malacca, Bengkulu and scattered establishments extending to the Spice Islands in the Banda Sea. As had been the case from his school days, Raffles was not one to passively await the unfolding of events. His focus was riveted not only on what had to be done but also on what role he could play in doing it. More of a statesman than a clerk, much as he had used to do with his mother in London, he nightly paced the outer verandah at 'Runnymede', weighing up aloud what action he could take. Now that Admiral Drury's blockade had been lifted, and with mounting French threats to shipping, surely there was little alternative than the full scale invasion of the Franco-Dutch Indies!

"There just isn't any choice," Raffles told Olivia. "The war in Europe has reached us here and if we don't fight we risk losing everything".

Olivia was worried. War meant fighting and fighting meant death or imprisonment. This was not what she had in mind when she encouraged Raffles to come east. On the other hand she had been around the British all her life and she knew their mettle. She rocked to and fro in her bamboo and rattan rocking chair without responding. Raffles was saying that if the British invaded Java and the islands they would need a Malay expert. Who could be better than himself!

"Distinguished scholars such as Mr Marsden have asked for my advice about the Malays and about the Indies and last year I was honoured when Lord Minto recognized the value of my work and views at a public address.

"They have no-one who knows the Malays and realizes the importance of the Indies as I do", Raffles told Olivia. "I really think I must step forward."

"Be careful, my darling. Don't go too fast. There are plenty of people jealous of you and you don't want to tread on too many toes."

Raffles was not so green that he did not already know the power of jealousy but he recalled the words of William Ramsay in London:

"You know our philosophy about Penang. The Dutch look like monopolizing the islands; the French are contesting with us from Arabia to the South China Sea.

Heaven help England if the French and the Dutch should combine. They could drive us out of India and cut us off completely from the China trade.

"We are giving Penang the resources it will need to become a great British naval base between India and China and in creating it a free port we are directly challenging Dutch monopoly in the Indies.

"Study what can be made of Penang, study what else we can do in the area, find out what the Dutch and French are up to and let us have your reports. It is no overstatement to say that the fate of Britain's trade in the Far East may hang in the hands of Penang."

Was this not a brief for him to act the role more of statesman than clerk? Who could be jealous of him for merely doing what he had been told to do? Nevertheless, Raffles agonized for many days and nights about the best course of action. He was not a governor but only a secretary. Superiors might resent his going round them or above them. Olivia was right. Whatever he decided to do must be done carefully and diplomatically so as to give no one offence.

"If there is an invasion I hope that you won't have to go with the troops," said Olivia, her face and voice full of worry.

Raffles smiled broadly. "Even if I do my love, have no fear. They are British troops and I don't doubt that they will be victorious."

"Maybe so", said Olivia with typical female scepticism, "but in war people always get killed and I pray God that it won't be my husband."

While Raffles and the entire Penang and Malacca establishments were fretting about the activities of the French among the islands news arrived that the British had seized the Malukus from Franco-Dutch forces.

"It's a small victory," commented Raffles, "far removed from the major offensive we need."

Raffles was horrified to see in dispatches copied to him that, knowing his expertise, Admiral Drury had asked Lord Minto if he could take civilian command in the Malukus - the much fought after home of cloves, nutmeg and mace.

"Even if they offer it to me I must not accept the Malukus," he said to Olivia.

"But it will be a step up."

"Yes, but maybe only a temporary step up. What happens if I accept, lose my seniority in Penang and then the Malukus is handed back to the Dutch? Then I would end up with nothing."

"It's very risky", Olivia agreed, sensing an opportunity while, at the same time, knowing it was perhaps not the right one.

"In any case," said Raffles, "the Malukus have only commercial value, not strategic value. They are a backwater and becoming more so as the price of spice keeps falling. The front line is here.

"We cannot solve the problem in the Indies in this piecemeal fashion," Raffles told her. "We will face a huge crisis if the French begin to mount aggressive naval actions against us from Java or Aceh or if Malacca is returned to the Dutch. The question the Company and the Government must address is how to solve these problems in the long term. There is only one way and that is by the invasion of Java and the conquest of all Franco-Dutch territories in the Indies before the French have time to make their military deployments and complete their build-up."

"The Company will never agree", snorted Olivia with feminine practicality. "It's asking too much. It will cost too much. They will never agree."

"Maybe. Maybe not", said Raffles with a twinkle in his eye. "The key to what might happen is Lord Minto. If it is what His Lordship wants then, ambitious or not, it can happen. I hear he is contemplating driving the French out of the Indian Ocean!

"Think about it, my dear. The Company have already accepted my views on Malacca."

"Macalister has," interrupted Olivia.

"If Lord Minto acts to drive the French out of the Indian Ocean, from what I hear of him, he may also be prepared to drive them from the Indies. After all it's two sides of the same coin. If the French threaten the Company at Mauritius they also threaten it in the Indies."

"And if we win but after the war with France the Indies are handed back to Holland? Where will that leave us?"

"Where might it leave us if the Indies are not handed back?" asked Raffles mischievously.

"It's a pity that you don't know Lord Minto and that he's so far away", said Olivia.

"I could apply for leave and go there! Macalister is as worried about what's happening as anyone else. Farquhar doesn't know what to do in Malacca. Someone has to go to Calcutta before too much damage is done and convince Lord Minto that we should seize the Indies!"

Raffles was as excited as if he'd just conquered a high mountain. His eyes shone with enthusiasm.

"This is the biggest chance I have ever had, my dear. Who would I rather be? Governor General of the Malukus or Governor General of the Indies!"

Olivia was still circumspect. She smiled fondly at Raffles as she sewed quietly. His plan was huge and audacious and, despite the cogency of his arguments, something she could never imagine the conservative, penny pinching, East India Company agreeing to so long as it lasted.

Olivia put down her sewing, stood up and embraced her husband.

"You've been successful so far, my love, and there's nothing to lose by trying. If we win in the Indies but they have to be handed back, with your record, I feel sure you'll be able to get a very senior post at one of the Indian presidencies."

"You're right. The risk to us is small. I'll do it. I'll apply for leave and I'll go to Calcutta to meet Lord Minto."

If anything, Governor Macalister was delighted with Raffles' initiative. He could describe the French threat in the Indies with graphic detail and if Malacca was retained it would surely only complement the revenues of Penang as well as extend Georgetown's administration to a new dependency! Though Raffles would be missed, other officials were on hand now to take on what he must set down. As with his rapid return from Malacca to Penang three years before, on learning that no reputable ship was available to immediately transport him to Calcutta, Raffles risked life and limb in a frail vessel departing at once for the sub-continent. Olivia knew her husband too well to try and stop him. Raffles had suggested that she remain behind and she agreed. Ship travel was no fun, especially across the tempestuous Bay of Bengal and, anyway, she had visited Calcutta before. Also, there were a host of other reasons why she should stay behind at Penang. The couple felt that it was important that Raffles should be represented in the island during his absence, if only by his wife. He didn't want people to think **he** was spurning Penang! And then there was his sister Mary Anne and little Charlotte. They would miss Olivia if she accompanied him. And finally there was the expected arrival of two more sisters from England. Both felt it essential that a member of the family was on hand to welcome and orientate them.

"Be careful, my dear and good luck", Olivia smiled bravely through her tears as Raffles prepared to depart.

Mahmud carried his box to the ship and, seeing its poor condition, the whites of his eyes rolled in horror in his black face.

"Please, master, wait for another ship," he wailed.

Raffles smiled benignly. "Don't worry Mahmud," he said with confidence bordering on bravado. "It's good enough."

With a cheery wave Raffles and Abdul, a Malay houseboy inherited from Quintin Thompson, departed in the decrepit craft. On his return Raffles terrified his family with the story of how the ship nearly sunk on the sand banks at the mouth of the River Hooghly, along the banks of which stood India's capital, the city of Calcutta!

Raffles had decided to take Abdul because it was obvious that he would need all sorts of help during the trip. Though still young and small, Abdul was fiercely loyal and no one had even the smallest chance of hoodwinking him. Abdul was an orphan and, through Raffles numerous Malay contacts, he had found him for Quintin while he was almost a child. When Quintin died he moved to the home of his benefactor with Mary Anne, where he was as much family as a domestic helper.

Raffles' vulnerable looking conveyance sailed with quiet state up the Hooghly, a tributary of the River Ganges. Even from a distance the eager Raffles could already make out the taller spires and cupolas of the city which had been India's capital since 1772. Ships of seemingly every shape and size crowded the river on the approach to Calcutta, especially the country ships built in India and used mainly for coastal trade. Raffles loathed the cramped conditions of ocean travel and had himself rowed ashore almost before the ships's anchor had been dropped. He left young Abdul to look after his luggage. The river was a frenzy of activity along the length of the stone bastions and redoubts of Fort William, right up to his intended landing place in the heart of the European quarter, looking every bit as much like Greenwich as Calcutta. Boat loads of bluecoats and marines were being ferried out to a veritable fleet of warships anchored in the channel.

"What's going on", he asked the helmsmen.

"No idea, sir," replied the man, as new in port as Raffles himself.

Water was churning all around the stone jetty where a dozen boats were vying to get in or get out.

"What's going on mate", Raffles' helmsman shouted to a counterpart in one of the outgoing military longboats.

"We're off to beat the French", he shouted as his boat glided out with shipped oars from a spot where Raffles could glide in.

To beat the French, Raffles repeated to himself. To beat the French where? Off Pondicherry? At Trincomalee? In the Indian Ocean ? In the Indies? Great things were obviously afoot! What a time to arrive in Calcutta!

Raffles heart was almost bursting with pride as he stepped ashore at a stone jetty which lead directly into an enclave of grand buildings adorned with columns, porticos and domes. He could see at once how Calcutta had earned its reputation as the 'City of Palaces'. Its buildings were like a vision of the ancient world of Greece or Rome.

This was his town, a company town, founded by the East India Company as long ago as 1690.

In addition to the embarking troops the jetty was seething with Indian porters all shouting at once and all offering either to collect his baggage, to find him accommodation, to locate an address or to do anything else which might please him. Not knowing the city, Raffles hired a palanquin carried by four coolies to take him the short distance to Government House. The dusty streets were crowded with coolies, peddlers, sedan chairs and palanquins, open and closed carriages and an unbelievable animal with a large hump on its back, the camel, used for everything from carrying heavy loads to the immaculate lancers of the camel corps.

Raffles' palanquin was halted by Sepoy guards at one of the huge stone entrance gates and, having no carriage, Raffles walked the fifty yards or so to the imposing main entrance, a veritable forest of Doric columns. He asked for Lord Minto's adjutant and found himself being chaperoned along seemingly endless high ceilinged, wooden floored corridors, turbaned Indian orderlies standing politely to one side to let him pass, European civilian and military personnel looking as curiously at him as he at they. How much more he would prefer to work here than at the Company's offices in Penang, offices which by comparison looked more like an outhouse than the Company's headquarters in Prince of Wales Island! The adjutant was expecting him but welcomed him in a purely formal manner, passing on crisply the instructions left by Lord Minto pending Raffles' arrival. Within minutes Raffles found himself directed to walk back along the echoing corridors, but, before doing so, he had felt determined to find out what was going on in the port.

"May I have the honour to know what's going

on at the quayside?" he asked the adjutant.

"By all means, sir. His Excellency has ordered the French cleared from Mauritius and Reunion and the fleet sails tonight."

Raffles thanked the adjutant and returned with his escort but while his face betrayed no emotion his mind raced over the possible implications of the news. In his trunk was a memorandum of policy which he would present to Lord Minto on the morrow. Was it already out of date? Did the invasions strengthen his case? Should he have to make changes? Was there time between now and tomorrow morning? Raffles was told to get himself accommodated in the usual way at the Company's guest house pending the allocation of a temporary bungalow of his own. A carriage was at his disposal for the collection of his luggage from the ship. More importantly, he had been told that a room in which to work had been set aside for him at Government House.

While he commandeered the carriage, collected his trunk and Abdul, and moved into the guest house, Raffles went about the chores mechanically, all the time thinking about the implications of the invasion of Mauritius for the Indies. By early afternoon, while Abdul unpacked, he was hard at work taking into account the news he had heard and sharpening up the memorandum which he would present to Lord Minto. He broke off to join a press of excited, cheering spectators lining the quay as the war fleet weighed anchors to the sound of pipes and drums and a thundering salute from the guns of Fort William.

One, two and three decked ships, the positions of their cannons picked out in white bands around the black hulls, each ship carrying from 30 to 80 guns. The Company standard flew from each topmast, Britain's merchant flag at the stern. As each vessel sailed slowly past Fort William its cannon returned the fire from the fort. Contingents of blue coated marines were drawn up to attention on both sides of each bow. And on each raised stern, pipes and drums played stirring tunes. Scores of native craft swarmed around the vessels together with the skiffs and wherries of the crew's families and friends. Such a sight Raffles had never seen. Great white sails billowing against the blue sky, the roar of the guns, the sound of the music, the shouts of the crowds afloat and ashore. Surely there was no force on earth that could stop such a fleet, his fleet, the Company's fleet.

Too excited to sleep early Raffles went to bed rather late, working into the night by candle light. But he was up and about soon after dawn next morning and in plenty of time for his eight o'clock appointment with the Governor General. Raffles drove in style through one of the four tall stone archways of Government House, his closed carriage, bearing the Company crest on the doors, pulled by two sprightly black horses beneath the carved lions and sphinxes adorning the gate. Today, he was welcomed by one of Lord Minto's European aides and escorted to His Lordship with the utmost deference and civility.

If Raffles was slight, Lord Minto was a frail man, past middle age, white haired and soft skinned yet with bright blue eyes which, while they could look kindly, could also be piercing and implacable.

"Welcome, welcome, welcome, my dear sir," Minto told Raffles, walking towards him across the cavernous, sparsely furnished reception room and shaking him many times by the hand. "It is such a pleasure to meet you at last."

The two sat opposite one another in high backed, leather, winged chairs at each corner of a large hand-knotted Persian carpet. Another chair was occupied by a European male secretary. In the centre a high, round, wooden coffee table was adorned with a silver vase of fragrant blossoms. Elderly Indian retainers sat around the walls tugging with hands or feet on cords attached to cotton covered, wooden, punkahs which were moved persistently too and fro to stir the sweltering air. Cold tea was served.

The Governor General told Raffles that he appreciated very much his concerns about the threat to Company ships in the Indies, a similar threat to the one in the Indian Ocean that Lord Minto had yesterday ordered eliminated.

Initially, Raffles listened in respectful silence, now and again murmuring his concurrence and all the time trying to get the measure of the man.

Minto thought that he had disappointing personal news for Raffles inasmuch as he was not to be offered the civilian command of the Malukus but no sooner had he imparted the decision than his eyes took on a new brightness and he bent forward in his chair with enthusiasm.

"Never mind about the Malukus. That is a small affair. The most important thing is the Indies as a whole and I have no one in Calcutta who knows about the Indies as you do, Raffles."

Raffles knew instantly from his words and demeanour that Minto was on his side. And he could see that he was a man who liked standing on ceremony and beating about the bush as little as he did. It was still early days and Raffles replied in a self deprecating way that he was sure that on his return to Calcutta either John Leyden had been able to help or perhaps former officials of the Penang Government. He added that he was in no way disappointed about not being posted to the Malukus. But sensing the mettle and drift of his man he plunged ahead boldly to say what he had risked life and limb crossing the Bay of Bengal to impart.

"I agree with Your Lordship. It is not the Malukus which have strategic importance in the Indies, sir, but the Straits of Sunda and, perhaps, Malacca and the islands of Sumatra and Java. Java is especially important because the Franco-Dutch regime is extending its military activities there, threatening our shipping using the Sunda Strait. Our small post at Bengkulu, in Sumatra, is no match for the Franco-Dutch forces on Java!"

"I quite agree, Raffles," smiled Lord Minto with obviously heightened interest. But what can we do? I shall be happy to receive any information you can give me."

Raffles felt that he would never in his life forget the look of searching scrutiny and anticipation directed at him by Minto at the mention of Java and he was emboldened to respectfully present his long and well argued memorandum. Instead of passing the document to the secretary Lord Minto kept in his hand.

"I will read this line for line as soon as I am able, Raffles. I want to meet you as often as possible during your stay in Calcutta and my secretary will advise you of the appointments. Before you leave there is one thing I must ask you."

"Please do, sir."

"What about the Strait of Malacca? Is it navigable for large ships?

"I must say honestly that I don't know the answer to that," replied Raffles. "But the Bugis fleets and Chinese junks reach Malacca through the Strait so I don't see why our ships can't use it to."

Lord Minto looked at him more piercingly than ever.

"We must find out Raffles, we must find out. We think we must drive the French out of Java because we want access to the Sunda Strait. But what if the Malacca

Strait is also a practical route to the Far East?

"What indeed, My Lord."

"You must send a ship to the south Raffles and report to me your findings as soon as possible."

"I understand, sir."

"If we are successful in Mauritius and Reunion other things may become possible and I must be prepared. I need more information."

When he left Lord Minto that morning Raffles was well pleased. He had been correct in his estimation that Calcutta would need a man with his unique knowledge of the Indies. The gamble was paying off. He was the right man in the right place. And in essence, an important new commission had already been hinted at - the exploration for large, European ships, of the Strait of Malacca.

Raffles was now faced with a hiatus while Minto read his report. He had also to await news of the allocation of a bungalow. He decided to become a tourist for a few days but only tourism strictly related to his work. As Secretary to the Council in Penang and on his first visit to Calcutta it was understandable that he should want to see the nerve centre of the Company's activities.

His first stop, therefore, was the enormous Writers Buildings, constructed thirty years earlier to accommodate the Company's burgeoning clerical work force. Raffles shared the opinion of many others that it was an ugly, barrack-like structure with its rows and rows of office windows in an unadorned facade. The Company's headquarters in Leadenhall Street would have fitted into one tiny corner. But, ugly or not, how he wished he had even a small version of it in Penang! And especially that he could have a handful of the many clerks.

His second visit was almost a pilgrimage to the house at Alipur of former Governor General, Warren

Hastings, the first governor general of Bengal and a man who had fought with Clive in clearing the French from northern India. Hastings was a man from a similar humble background whose approach to native affairs was well known to Raffles and whom he admired very much. Hastings had come in for severe censure from the Company for his handling of the Indian rulers and Raffles felt that he had been much misunderstood. Hastings had been impeached for corruption and took seven years to clear his name. In Raffles' mind the accusations had been brought about largely by London's ignorance of Indian culture rather than by any mistakes of Hastings'.

While his visit to Alipur was an indulgence, his tour of Fort William, on the other hand, directly related to the ongoing possibility that Penang's fortifications would be improved and extended and that the long promised arsenal would be built. While Company personnel welcomed him with open arms he found the military's reception somewhat cold, believing as they did, that civilians had no part in military affairs. Be that as it may, Raffles was determined to arrive at a better estimate of what should be done in Penang, and its cost, and so he spent a day in the company of very formal officers touring the gigantic fortifications. Within a day or two a bungalow was put at his disposal, like so many others, situated within its own huge garden, behind low walls. A rectangle of uninspiring rooms, the house was plain enough yet its Doric portico, beneath which his carriage could draw up, and the white stone balustrade around the perimeter of the flat roof gave it an imposing presence. A small army of bewhiskered, white robed and turbaned staff had been assigned to look after him, making him feel very grand.

From the outset, Raffles enjoyed a privileged relationship with Lord Minto. They worked together more as colleagues and even collaborators than as chief and subordinate. Both were gentle, good humoured men. Both were liberal in their political views and humanitarians and both shared similar far sighted views about the future of the Company's trade in the Far East. There was never any argument, never any irritating challenging of the facts by Minto, never any of the penny pinching quibbling so typical of the Court of Directors in London. The two men got on so famously that when Raffles thirtieth birthday arrived the Governor General insisted on inviting Raffles to a gathering in the great colonnaded ballroom of Government House with its glittering chandeliers. The up and coming young man was introduced to the cream of Calcutta society. Many a matron with one or more daughters in tow smiled at him to know whether he was married?

"I'm afraid so, ma'am, Raffles would always reply with a gracious smile and the utmost politeness.

Actually, Raffles was, as the saying goes, married to his work and in many senses it had suited him that Olivia could not bear children and that the two of them should have been business partners as much as husband and wife. But, in Calcutta, there was absolutely no doubt that he was regarded as the 'catch' of the season. Still young and a favourite of the Governor General's, with almost open access to Government House, any mother would have thought her daughter privileged to marry him.

Olivia wrote to him constantly to tell him of her sadness at being left alone in Penang and about her fears at being ill at a time when many Europeans in the East expected to survive only two years at the most! How he wished she could be in Calcutta with him or that he could be in Penang to comfort her. But she wasn't and he couldn't. In their hearts both knew that what Raffles was doing had to be done because in their hearts they were one and what

Raffles could achieve was achieved for Olivia also.

Meanwhile, the hectic and glittering social round, at which so many potentially valuable acquaintances were made, had to go on. Not only the social round and his meetings with Lord Minto but his scientific work as well, because Calcutta was the hub of scientific enquiry in India. Raffles made his academic debut by having the signal honour of reading before the Asiatic Society his erudite and fact packed paper 'On the Malayu Nation'. When he finished describing the history, characteristics and wealth of the Malay people and sat down he was given a standing ovation.

Within a week of taking up residence in his new house Raffles had the pleasure of again making the acquaintance of his good friend and mentor, Dr John Leyden. Along with a stream of missionaries, prominent scholars and Orientalists, Leyden was a frequent visitor to the house and, by correspondence for which he had more time than Raffles, he kept Olivia fully informed of her husband's progress in the Indian capital. He described his old friend's relationship with Minto as "cordial", his 'star' as having "risen" and his health and even appearance vastly improved as he was feted by the society of the town - especially the young ladies! Raffles was having a great time!

Raffles provided His Lordship with the most detailed facts and analysis he had about Franco-Dutch power and activities in the Indies yet he kept the main lines of his arguments simple, repeating over and over again what threat existed and how it could be removed. Knowing now that if Minto felt strong enough to authorize a move against the French in the Indian Ocean it was certainly possible he could be induced to do the same in the Indies, Raffles stressed what he perceived to be the deceptive strength of the Franco-Dutch grip on the islands.

"They control only four kingdoms in Java and virtually no other part of the huge archipelago," he said with enthusiastic confidence.

He dwelt on the restlessness of the traditional Javanese rulers in being deprived of their powers by Marshal Daendels and of the bitter unrest among ordinary people who were dying by the thousands to built his new military works as well as starving in the teeth of the Dutch East India Company's monopolies. With links to Europe interrupted or severed by war, Raffles drew a picture of Franco-Dutch officials out of control in the Indies, lining their pockets with corrupt practices which were a further heavy yoke for the suffering people. The enemy's military strength he disparaged telling Minto that, in addition to small numbers of Europeans, the armed forces were made up of slaves and convicts.

If all of this didn't make the invasion of the Franco-Dutch controlled Indies attractive enough, Raffles lured the trader and company man in Minto by extolling the incredible richness of Java and the likely revenues and profits to be derived from the sale of coffee, pepper, cotton, tobacco and indigo - if only the cruel and inefficient monopolies established by the Dutch could be dismantled and free trade put in their stead. And he played upon Minto's humanitarianism by emphasizing the benefits to the islanders of enlightened British rule in freeing them from their sufferings and restoring not only their economic freedom but personal dignity. Eventually, Lord Minto was so convinced of the black nature of Franco-Dutch rule in the islands that removing them for humanitarian reasons appeared to carry as much weight as removing the military threat to the Company's trade throughout the islands and the Far East. When it came to corruption this was an accusation about which the Company was especially sensitive having only recently put its own house in order at the instigation of William Pitt. Like Raffles, Minto believed in fair play and free trade and in keeping with the reforming spirit of the time their's were swords not long to be resisted!

These were exciting days as Raffles informed and persuaded Minto of his views but also frustrating days because he knew no decision would be made about the Indies until news was sent back from the war fleet to Mauritius and Reunion.

After what, to Raffles, seemed an interminable wait the day came when a lone ship of the invasion fleet was spied in the Hooghly. The cry went up and a large crowd gathered at the jetty. The wait was agonizing as a long boat pulled for the shore. Then the news was out! The French had surrendered at Reunion and Mauritius! Boys ran through the streets carrying the news to every corner of the city. Horsemen and crowds dashed hither and thither with excitement. Again the guns of Fort William boomed salute and the streets around the European settlement were gay with revellers. A quiet man, Lord Minto was ecstatic.

Raffles seized the opportunity to beg the favour of knowing whether His Lordship had yet formed any definite plan for the Indies, news of the current victory seeming to point to the present time being most auspicious.

"I couldn't agree more," Lord Minto told him with a broad smile. "You want me to fire the starter's pistol, don't you? What orders do you think I should give you?"

Raffles couldn't have been more delighted. He was being asked to draft his own orders! He could hardly believe his luck. After long weeks of the most friendly discussions Raffles plans for the Indies had now become Minto's plans. Just as Raffles needed Minto to authorize and enable the solution he proposed to the Indies problem so Minto needed Raffles to guide and implement the plan. The two men were a perfect team.

Before submitting a draft of his 'orders' Raffles advised Minto that because of contrary winds nothing could be attempted east of Calcutta for at least four months and he urged that he should be allowed to go ahead as an advance courier to spy out the land. A crucial part of his job would be to feel out which leaders would support the British should they invade Java.

"I know that we are not supposed to meddle in military affairs," said Minto, "but you should also try to gather information of interest to the army and navy and perhaps even indicate where you feel to be the best place of attack. Of course, the sea route to Java is of critical importance. If you discover that our ships can use the Malacca Strait it will cut weeks off the voyage and take the enemy by surprise."

But the tortuous waiting was still not over. Raffles was clear that Minto wanted to use him as a special agent in the Indies to prepare for an invasion of Java but Company protocol had to be observed and, first, Minto had to request his release from the Government of Prince of Wales Island. A ship had to be sent and a ship had to bring back the reply. At the same time a formal blessing had to be obtained from Leadenhall Street and the Company's bureaucratic wheels rotated with infuriating slowness.

The wait tortured Raffles as he bubbled with excitement and energy at the thought of the tasks and challenges ahead. There were so many ifs and maybes over shadowing his hopes that there were many days when he felt that his entire trip to Calcutta was wasted. It was one thing to enjoy having Lord Minto's agreement and to bask in the adulation of Calcutta society. But it was quite another to secure all the complicated approvals to their plans. Again, his luck held and, while there was still no news from

Leadenhall Street, word was received from Penang that he was released!

"Good old Macalister," Raffles smiled to himself.

The drab monotony of his clerking in Penang faded before his eyes as Lord Minto created him Agent to the Governor General with the Malay States.

Minto had paid Raffles the greatest compliment he had received to date. Leyden wrote to Olivia: "If he succeeds in his present objects he will have a much finer game to play that he has hithertoo had."

Not that Raffles left Minto without concerns. London has still not given the go ahead and without it all their talking, scheming and planning could come to nothing! He was to be relieved of his clerking in Penang but this meant that he was to be an official with no territory! Privy as he was to Lord Minto's most secret thoughts about Java, he was gambling that with the Franco-Dutch expulsion from the Indies the islands would remain under the Company's influence and that he may have a part in their future, perhaps even governor general! But suppose they weren't? What would his future be then? Would Penang want him back? Would he want to go back? Could he find a post in India? Would he want that? And what if Lord Minto was pushed aside or resigned. Would his successor 'look after' Raffles? In the end the potential prize of the Indies was simply too great to worry unduly about what might or might not happen and Raffles accepted his new appointment with alacrity.

Nearly five months after quitting Penang and thanks to a smidgen of audacity denied to what he saw as his pedestrian colleagues, the boy from London's East End, the boy too poor to finish school, the young man who had endured ten long years of clerical drudgery and subsist-ence pay, the man who had arrived in Calcutta as Secretary to the Council of tiny Prince of Wales Island, this man departed for 'home' in the Company ship 'Ariel', full of achievement and full of pride as the newly created Agent to the Governor General of all India, the cordiality and praise of Calcutta ringing in his ears and his life's greatest prospect before him!

CHAPTER FOUR

Even before his feet touched the jetty in Penang, Raffles eyes searched the crowded jetty for Olivia.

"There, Tuan," shouted Abdul, pointing excitedly. "There she is, behind the Sepoys."

Raffles raced up the steps, his frank, open face, boyish with happiness. Olivia ran towards him along the jetty clutching him in her arms as if her life depended on it. Raffles hugged and squeezed her to him, at the same time whispering in her ear, "We did it, we did it." And then there was Mary Anne and little Charlotte and, the biggest surprise of all, his two sisters Harriet and Leonora, who he had not seen for a decade.

"When I left London you were only girls", he laughed "but now look at you."

Like him the girls were fair skinned with large blue eyes. Their thick tressess flowed from beneath wide sun hats. Leonora was pulling a youngish man along after her by the hand.

"Tom, this is John Loftie," she announced proudly and I am no more Leonora Raffles but Mrs John Loftie!"

Raffles was aghast! It was true that in bringing his sisters to Penang he hoped for a good marriage for them but who could have imagined that one would find a husband even before he returned from Calcutta!

The Raffles' house at North Beach was jammed in every nook and cranny with members of the Raffles clan. Raffles' only regret was that his mother and youngest sister could not join them to complete his happiness. That evening the house rang with laughter, not least at the news brought by Raffles from India that he was now Agent to the Governor General!

It was next day when Raffles called upon the Governor and he quickly discovered that the innocent joy of his family was by no means shared in official circles. His friend Macalister had departed and Charles Bruce, a brother of the British diplomat Lord Elgin, had replaced him. Having just taken over the government, Bruce was, perhaps understandably, more worried about who he could find to undertake the prodigious work load previously shouldered by Raffles, than interested in Raffles' intended adventures in the Indies. Knowing that Raffles had not only been discussin the retention of Malacca but the conquest of the entire East Indies, Bruce saw an infinitely larger and less optimistic picture than his predecessor - one in which, instead of being built up, Penang would be eclipsed by a new Company administration in Java!

Thus, Raffles detected a strong thread of resentment about his initiative to Calcutta as well as, he suspected, envy even of his scholastic achievements. Criticism came couched either in outright denigration or the behind the hand comment that he was "getting above himself". Raffles outstanding abilities were extremely unusual in the clerical service of the British East India Company. His humble background was known and, while there were many who respected and admired him, his enemies and detractors saw in him someone from the lower orders barefacedly gate-crashing society's upper echelons. Successive governors of Prince of Wales Island were never to forgive him for his perceived opinionated and misplaced adventures "to the eastward." While there were many in Penang eager to shake his hand, especially merchants who looked forward to new markets in the Indies, Raffles' reception in government circles was decidedly frosty and an anti-climax to the new title and responsibilities he had lately been given.

Luckily for his peace of mind, Raffles felt that Malacca was a much better base from which to gather intelligence about the Indies than Penang and Minto had authorized him to set up a temporary headquarters for himself there. Everything that he was about to do required money and supplies and the Council of Prince of Wales Island was extremely upset to discover that, in addition to losing their Secretary, they must pay the cost of his activities to the eastward - which were no business of theirs!

"We will leave these paltry people behind us", Olivia said grandly on hearing Raffles' description of the reaction of Bruce and the Council. "Anyway, all here is dullness and stupidity. It is high time we moved on".

And move on they did. As if to underline his expectations after any invasion of the Indies, within a few days 'Runnymede' was put up for sale! Impetuous or not, Raffles believed that not only could there be no turning back for him but that there would be no turning back on the thinking and promises of Lord Minto in Calcutta. It was near Christmas and it might have been tempting to any other man to spend the festive season among friends in the relative comfort of Penang. But, for Raffles, duty came before everything and a fortnight before the holiday he and his large family departed in a Company cutter for Malacca. The faithful Mahmud went with them as major domo and Abdul too. In addition, he took with him one European translator, Merlin, and his most trustworthy Malay translator, Ibrahim.

Raffles may have arrived in Calcutta with only a single box but he had returned laden with many large trunks and boxes and these were now shipped on to Malacca.

While he needed plenty of space for the work he must now do, Raffles had also to maintain as much secrecy as possible. Rumours were rife in the community that a British attack was imminent against Franco-Dutch forces in the Indies but, unless Raffles or anyone else in authority confirmed them, they remained only that - rumours. Instead of staying at Farquhar's residence, Raffles accepted accommodation at a spacious house owned by the son of Malacca's Captain China, Baba Cheng Lan, situated on an estate at Bandar Hilir.

Each ethnic community in Malacca had its own leader or captain and Cheng Lan headed the community of Chinese who were born in Malacca and had even adopted major elements of the Malay life style, hence the appellation 'Baba'. Raffles held no particular brief for the Chinese and thoroughly disliked the manner in which the Dutch allowed them, as he saw it, to prey on the Malays throughout the Indies. He guessed that, knowing this, Cheng Lan had offered him the house to win favour. The Chinaman was very aware that Raffles had virtually single handedly saved Malacca from the fate the Company intended for it and that he and all Chinese businessmen there owed their survival and future to Raffles. In accepting Cheng's offer Raffles removed himself from the spotlight occupied by the local British authorities and isolated himself from prying ears. Few could guess what was going on within the walls of his new bungalow and none succeeded in getting passed Mahmud unless properly authorized.

The house at Bandar Hilir was a dream for Raffles. Whereas 'Runnymede' had been built in modified Malay style his house at Malacca was Baba Chinese. It was divided into two parts, living rooms to one side, sleeping rooms to the other with an open courtyard between with a Chinese gate at one end leading to the outside. The living area was still at first floor level with the servants quarters beneath. The cool, dark rooms inside had high ceilings and plenty of ornately carved doors, windows and furniture, some of it brought from South China. Many of the walls were wood panelled, carved and gilted. All of the dark, wooden furniture struck Raffles as oversize, apart from the four poster bed he shared with Olivia, which was rather small and incredibly hard. Refreshing breezes blew through the open doors and windows in front of which bamboo chics hung down to keep out the sun. Potted plants seemed to bring the verdue of Malaya into every corner of the house.

The house staff were mainly Hokkien Chinese, who spoke little English and boosted Raffles' security from the dangers of loose gossip. Outside staff were Malay or from the sub-continent. Abdul and Mahmud were virtually supernumeraries so Abdul acted as a kind of personal helper to Raffles and Olivia while Mahmud took up the role of butler cum guard, his tremendous black mustaches frightening away any who had no business to be there.

During the first days after their arrival, Raffles went about his life with all the leisure of a wealthy English dilettante, evincing little interest in politics or even trade but to all appearances continuing his well known concentration on Malay customs as well as the local flora and fauna. Farquhar knew full well why he was there but the two colleagues thought it prudent to portray Raffles' visit as a private one with the objective of continuing his studies.

Raffles met his many guests in a reception room at the front of the house, where none could see his staff at work in a room at the rear, or guess at its nature. He himself worked in the room at the rear, at a great, black wood, writing table in the company of Martin, Ibrahim and others that he came to employ for translations and clerical duties. Raffles spread the word of his studies throughout Malacca and within days he had employed four more men to scour the shore and jungle for specimens that he wanted. One man he sent to gather leaves, flowers, fungi, mosses etc., another for worms, butterflies, grasshoppers, beetles, cicadas, centipedes and scorpions. The third he sent to collect sea shells, mollusks, oysters and fish. The fourth was sent to capture wild animals such as jungle fowl, birds, deer and small quadrupeds. Some of the specimens Raffles pinned to file cards, some he immersed in spirit, some, like wild flowers, he pressed between the pages of books, others he instructed to be drawn by a Chinese artist from Macau.

For many such objects he paid, and there was a constant stream of people in and out of the reception room bringing items they thought may interest this strange Englishman in their midst. In addition to wild life, Raffles was also interested in Malay history and culture and other streams of people brought him even the most priceless books and manuscripts, numbering hundreds. Those not given to him in perpetuity he instructed his five clerks to copy. To many local Malays it seemed as if the whole of their literature was either copied by or sold to Raffles. Aside from his scientific interest, Raffles loved animals and now the grounds of the house began to look more like a menagerie than a residence. Monkeys, an orang-utang, tigers, bears and many other animals were brought for him to study. There was nothing phony about this interest of Raffles. As yet, very few in Britain knew even a small amount about the Malay world and, despite his many other responsibilities, Raffles never abated his energy in building up a comprehensive study of the places in which he found himself.

101

He acted on the principle that since nothing was known everything might be relevant and collected large numbers of specimens and huge amounts of data. As he made his findings, these were conveyed in dispatches to Calcutta.

In addition to Raffles, the Company man, there was also Raffles, the intense individual, and as he shipped the voluminous data to India, Raffles thought he saw another opportunity to boost his name and reputation. After all, even his prospects within the Company should, in theory, be improved by a heightened reputation in society at large. Hadn't the Asiatic Society in Calcutta given him a warm welcome? Plans began to form in his mind for more scientific papers and even for a series of books. And he made time to form a Malacca branch of the Asiatic Society to help ensure that the ground breaking investigation into all things Malay that he had begun would go forward.

When she wasn't flitting about the house making sure that everything was in order and that everything was being done, Olivia shared Raffles' interest in Malay culture and even language, augmenting her vocabulary by asking the translators for the names of all objects unknown to her and joining with her husband in the fun of purchasing his many specimens from those who brought them to the door, some wholly reputable, others not so reputable. Raffles always asked her advice about what price he should pay and, more often than not, deferred to her. Not that Raffles was mean. On the contrary, no one could be more naturally open handed. A shrewd political animal, it pleased him to be seen to be generous and to know that his behaviour was being sharply contrasted by the community to the tight fistedness of the Dutch. Whatever finances he needed he indented for to the Company treasury in Penang, ostensibly as part of the researches he had been instructed to undertake by Lord Minto. Each time he received a new cash requisition from Raffles Governor Bruce fairly choked.

"Jumped up little clerk. Who does he think he is," he was heard to fume with as much regularity as the arrival of each indent.

There were still merchants and plantation owners of Dutch origin living in the city but most non-Dutch Malaccans fervently hoped that, after the end of the war with Napoleon, Malacca would not be handed back to the Dutch but could remain under the benign rule of the English.

Raffles took time to visit mosques, schools and even the humblest home, to see for himself how the inhabitants of Malacca lived. It gave him a headache to be cooped up in the dark house for too long but it was impossible to do anything out of doors in heavy clothes, under the burning sun. The solution was for himself and Olivia, often with one or more of his sisters in tow, to take a carriage around the town. Mary Anne had married her second husband in Malacca, Captain William Flint of HMS Teignmouth, but there was still Harriet to keep them company and Abdul nearly always rode on the outside of the coach.

Malacca was hot and dusty and the streets narrow so they rarely stayed long. The crowded Chinese houses in the town were extremely quaint with their gay colours, louvered shutters, carved doors and ornately hand-decorated stucco facades. And the many Chinese and Indian temples bearing testimony to the longevity of settlement here were fascinating.

"It would have been such a pity if all this had been destroyed", he said. "How could the Company give an order from London to destroy the town when they know absolutely nothing about it?"

Instead of remaining long in the town, Raffles preferred to drive out and see the beautifully carved, wooden, Malay houses on their stilts beneath the coconut palms. He loved to pause for a while at one of these houses in the more restful country districts around Malacca and many times he and his lady would be invited inside. They would remove their shoes and sit with their hosts on the floor while they ate fruit and sipped cool but boiled drinks.

"Terimah kasih banyak", (thank you very much) Raffles would always say in departing.

"Terimah Kasih, Tuan", (thank you, sir) would invariably come the respectful reply.

Raffles always treated the Malays as his equals and they liked him for it. When he spoke with them, he was always very unhurried and full of interest.

Some evenings they took the carriage to watch performances of Chinese opera at temporary mat sheds made from woven bamboo and rattan and in which all the parts were played by men - even if they were meant to be women. Other nights they watched Malay puppet shows. Luckily they were in Malacca to watch the celebration of Chinese New Year with its feasting and fire crackers and also the end of the Muslim fasting month, Hari Raya, marked by massive Muslim celebrations.

If Raffles' and Olivia's days were spent in the apparently harmless pursuit of gathering data and specimens of local flora and fauna or cultural sight seeing, what happened in the house after dusk was very different! Not that there were the exciting dinners or glittering and noisy parties of Calcutta or Penang! On the contrary those who came by night on foot, by horse or in closed carriages were few and far between. Yet their meetings with Raffles were long and the letters they brought and took away were of the utmost urgency and importance. By day a generous smile never left Raffles' face but at night he was transformed into a tiger of energy, his eyes glittering with purpose above his hollow, overworked cheeks.

By night he had time hardly to rest, keeping a small bed close by to his desk upon which he occasionally threw himself down - but not to sleep so much as to ponder the exact wording of some sensitive dispatch to a Malay ruler. His orders from Lord Minto were to find out in close detail which of the Malay rulers would support the British in the event of an invasion of Java. From his room messengers came and went in the strictest secrecy in the dead of night, to carry his enquiries and promises to the rulers of the islands by prow or ship. Though the pace of his scholastic studies on view to the public surely didn't reflect it, at night Raffles was working feverishly against time. He knew that Minto <u>did</u> intend the invasion of Java and was only awaiting the go-ahead from London. Haste was of the essence, before the French and the Dutch could consolidate their hold on the Indies and, worse still, mount attacks against British shipping. Just as messengers raced to and from the islands others were sent post haste to Penang, sometimes more than once in a single day, so that his advice could get quickly to Minto in Calcutta.

During his letter writing sessions to the rulers of the Indies, Raffles often became carried away by his dislike of the Dutch colonialists, not only because, thanks to French conquest, they were enemies, not only because they were monopolists in a dawning era of free trade but because they were cruel to the Malays and despised them. Many of his hand written letters to Malay rulers began with British concern at the way in which the Dutch colonialists had "broken through and destroyed long established customs and the rights and dignity of your majesty". By his correspondence Raffles aimed to let the Malay rulers know that the English were ready to eject the Dutch and to restore lost "rights and dignity". In this way Raffles' plan was to detach as many as possible from the Dutch colonialists and to ensure that if the British invaded they would enjoy the fullest local support.

Spies or emissaries were sent to Borneo, Riau, Sumatra, Java, Madura and Bali to carry Raffles' letters and also to gain first hand intelligence about the military deployments of the enemy. Raffles worked constantly on a map he kept locked in his desk on which he marked the military strength and dispositions of the enemy as well as indicated the loyalty of native kingdoms. His deductions and recommendations were rushed urgently to Penang for onward shipment to Calcutta. Raffles was afraid that any delay in the transmission of military information could lead to disaster and grew increasingly frustrated with the disinterested and, therefore, slow assistance of Penang. On more than one occasion he was obliged to order a ship direct to Calcutta, once in the record breaking time of twenty one days.

Raffles and Farquhar found public pretexts to meet more often so that, in secret, they could assess the military intelligence being gathered and make their recommendations. The Franco-Dutch colonialists were strongest on Java and, since Raffles' visit to Calcutta, there had never been any doubt that if a strike against the enemy was to be launched in the Indies it would be against Java, primarily the city of Batavia, the enemy's headquarters in the Indies. If the fortifications of Batavia and its environs could be overcome, Franco-Dutch garrisons elsewhere could be mopped up relatively easily. In any case, many of these were small posts, often manned by local troops, sometimes with and sometimes without European officers. Based on reports the two men estimated Franco-Dutch strength at Batavia on the north coast, Surabaya in the east and Semarang in the south at no more than 14,000. They recommended that a force of

3,000 Europeans, 6,000 native Indian troops and 500 cavalry would be sufficient for victory.

Because of Dutch monopoly, the Indies trade had long been a big secret to the British. Raffles now more fully understood the trade and prospects of the Indies than any Englishman living. He had traced the habitual practice of the Bugis fleets in sailing westward from Macassar in Sulawesi and the Malukus to Java where the Dutch controlled and restricted all island trade to the port of Batavia, he had come to know the importance of Java both as a staging point for the fleets and as a rich centre of trade in its own right. He knew that all of this island trade plugged directly into Malacca where it linked up with the other great trade route from China, through India and all the way to Arabia and Europe. The more he came to know the more he came to detest the way in which the Dutch colonialists imposed monopolies throughout the Indies. The more his fury grew the more determined he was to work not only to kick out the French but to exclude the Dutch as well!

His first concern, Lord Minto's concern and the Company's concern was that no enemy should disturb or control the trade through the Indian Ocean and the South China Sea to China. Raffles and Minto both realized that if the Franco-Dutch were ejected from the Indies and the British did not make a permanent commitment, there would then be nothing to prevent hostile native rulers emerging or augmenting their power and nothing to prevent current enemies or other European powers from moving into the Indies once the British had withdrawn. The military threat by enemies in the Indies could be restored almost as soon as it had been removed. And if peace was declared in Europe there would be nothing to prevent the Dutch from returning and reimposing their exclusive monopolies, so limiting to British trade.

Both men found it impossible to believe that any sensible person could agree to a British withdrawal from the Indies once conquest had been effected. Plus, it would give Britain and the East India Company not only the bonus of access to the island trade, but also to the direct trade between Java and Europe, until now monopolized by the Dutch. As information built up in his note books, it seemed to Raffles that the Company should seize the chance it was being providentially offered and that all the Company's possessions in the Indies would best be incorporated into a new unitary structure, centred on Batavia or Semarang in Java. His precipitous removal from Penang underlined how few doubts he had that if such an administrative entity was created he would be its first governor general, just as Warren Hastings had been the first Governor General of Bengal.

Raffles admired very much Hastings' way of working with indigenous rulers. Knowing the Company's conservatism and the lack of financial resources either at Leadenhall Street or in government, Raffles was reluctant to hope for direct British rule in the Indies. What he had in mind and, as his correspondence to the Malay rulers clearly showed, was a pattern of alliances in which local kingdoms would be allowed optimum freedom within the protection of the British East India Company, represented at strategic posts throughout the Indies. Naturally, even this modest scenario would involve expense, but, from what he knew of the island trade and the potential of the Indies, especially Java, Raffles was convinced that the Indies could make a profit for the Company over and above the cost of any establishment it was required to maintain.

Raffles had emphasized to Lord Minto in Calcutta the tenuous nature of Dutch claims to the Indies, pointing out that they really only had influence over the kingdoms of Java.

On the other hand the Malukus had already fallen into British hands, there was a British post at Ambon, the gateway to the Malukus and at Makasar, the home port of the powerful Bugis fleets of south Sulawesi. Britain had what counted as a major post at Benkulu, in Sumatra, plus several others scatters around Sumatra, including at Aceh, a strategic port fronting onto the Indian Ocean and the Strait of Malacca and important even for shipping bound for the Strait of Sunda. Padang, the gateway to the little known kingdom of the Minagkabaus had also fallen into British hands. In Borneo, there was a British post at Banjarmasin and Raffles had sent leters to try to establsh commercial relationships with several other rulers, notably at Pontianak.

Over and over again Raffles used a pen to circle the handful of Dutch possessions remaining in the Indies, circles which even penetrated his dreams and disrupted his sleep. He had told Minto:

"Once we drive the Franco-Dutch forces out of Java the prospect before us is of the acquisition of a second India!"

Despite the huge numbers of letters and dispatches written, everything concerning a possible invasion of Java remained on paper only. No decision had been received from London. No action could be taken. Once again, in the dark of the night, Raffles was assailed by doubts and fears which Olivia knew gnawed at him. What if permission was not granted? What would happen to him then? What would happen to his family? The stage was set for a great achievement for the Company and a personal victory for himself but would the Company understand the opportunity?

As the year 1811 opened with brave promise for the future, dramatic news came from Calcutta. In February, Raffles received a top secret dispatch from Lord Minto. He could have jumped in the air for joy. Leadenhall Street had finally approved a punitive invasion of Java! Raffles ran from his work room to find Olivia.

"Its on", he cried excitedly. "The invasion of Java is on and Lord Minto will personally lead the force."

"Sh", smiled Olivia. "Should you be telling the whole world. Even walls have ears you know."

Minto would lead a force of 4,500 European infantry, cavalry and artillery plus a similar number of Indian infantry. There would also be a contingent sent from Fort St George at Madras. The same dispatch announced to Raffles that he was to be promoted.

"During the campaign I am to be Secretary to the Governor General! I can't believe it. A second promotion within five months. My life must be charmed. We are so lucky."

"Well done, my dear. Well done," Olivia repeated over and over to Raffles as she hugged him at the tidings. "All your hard work has paid off at last."

Although the people of Malacca still had no confirmation of their suspicions that Raffles had been sent to plan an invasion of Java, their certainty increased as increasing numbers of Dutch ships arrived at the port. Raffles had given the order that all boats or ships flying the Dutch flag were to be arrested and brought to Malacca. The certainty was intensified when English ships began arriving with tents, wagons, artillery pieces, guns and ammunition. All of Malacca society from the highest to the lowest now began to seek out Raffles to try to find out what was really going on. Were the inhabitants of Malacca to be forced to remove to Penang at gun point or were troops coming which would be used to evict the Dutch from the Indies? Mahmud now ceased his guard duties at the Raffles residence and was replaced by police guards supplied by Farquhar.

Based on his spy network and replies to his many letters, Raffles wrote encouragingly to Lord Minto:

"I am well satisfied that there will be very little serious opposition. Were the English now to appear off the coast (of Java) in any number, the whole of the native population, with the exception of those in the immediate pay of the Dutch, would declare in our favour."

Day by day in the coming weeks Malacca was transformed into a hive of military activity the scale of which the old fortress city had never seen before. Sometimes a single sail was seen on the horizon, sometimes three together, sometimes six or seven. Some flew the blue merchant flag of Britain with the Union Flag in one corner, others flew the white flag of St George with its bold red cross, all the Company's ships flew its pennant and standard. Slowly there assembled a huge fleet of war ships large enough to completely fill the shallow bay in which Malacca was situated, their masts like one continuous fence, stretching along the shore in an unbroken line for miles from Limbogan to Tanjung Kling. Crowds of local people gathered to watch as unit after unit disembarked from the ships. And what a spectacle it was! Some of the troops were European, some Muslim, some Hindu. The crowd had never seen people like them. Many of the English officers wore tiger skins, hats with birds feathers or trousers made from the skins of other exotic animals from India. All along the shore a veritable town of white and red tents sprang up in orderly lines.

For days on end the troops trained on the flat land around Penang, discharging their muskets, firing their heavy cannon, pulled by bullocks, and practicing cavalry manouvres. The crowds particularly liked to watch the great Arab mounts of the cavalry put through their paces. At the end of each session, during which the horses were made to move with clockwork precision, one officer regularly entertained them by jumping his horse effortlessly over a ten foot high fence. The crowd always gasped at the display of skill and control and there were many who whispered:

"That man is surely not human to be able to do such a thing. He must be a ghin!"

For the first time, Raffles had access to large ships and, using Lord Minto's authority, he determined that one should be sent to explore the Malacca Strait forthwith. If passage could be made to Java via the Malacca Strait rather than the Strait of Sunda many, many days at sea would be saved and the implications for the long term value of the Malacca Strait known conclusively.

It was by no means easy to find a captain willing to risk his ship among the numerous uncharted rocks, shoals and islands and at constant risk of attack by the bands of ferocious pirates who made their homes among the forest covered islands.

"It's a treacherous channel, Mr Raffles," the captains told him, one after another. "Water depths vary enormously, there are islands and rocks everywhere and if that isn't bad enough the locals have built fish traps which we can't see in the dark."

The prize for the captain who successfully explored the Strait was the very making of history and, eventually, Captain John Birkin agreed to take the Company ship 'Scavenger' to find a safe way to Java through the thousands of islands. He was instructed to proceed cautiously, during the hours of daylight only, and to be especially diligent in confirming the positions of islands and taking depth measurements. The 'Scavenger' had 12 heavy guns, numerous smaller pieces and a detachment of armed marines was put aboard.

"It'll take a daring pirate to attack me," said Birkin knowingly.

Several nights in a row Raffles took Olivia by carriage to St Paul's Hill where they climbed in the cool of the evening to the ancient stone church of St Paul's with its massive tomb stones. From here they could see up and down the Strait of Malacca, a narrow strip of water, even now so vital for country ships, that more blood had been shed to control it than almost anywhere else in the Indies. They stood together, Raffles' arm round Olivia's waist, gazing in awed silence at the huge fleet which was the living embodiment of Raffles' genius and energy. Sometimes, in the cool immediately after dawn, Raffles went alone, on horseback, to the hill top, scanning the horizon for any sign of the 'Scavenger'. Even a cursory glimpse at a chart revealed immediately how helpful it would be to the fleet to be able to navigate the Strait of Malacca through to Java. And what would it do for Raffles' reputation if he could be the first man to confirm safe passage for large ships! As the days ticked by Raffles became more and more tense lest Lord Minto arrive before Captain Birkin had time to complete his exploration. One morning Raffles returned home disappointed from St Paul's Hill, not knowing that among the forest of masts the 'Scavanger' had quietly anchored at first light. It was almost eight ' clock in the morning whan Captain Birkin reported to Raffles at Bandar Hilir. Raffles met the captain on the steep steps leading up to the house and, before he could say more than "Good morning, Sir," he held his fingers to his lips to indicate the need for silence. Raffles led the way to the back of the house and very politely asked everyone to leave the room so that he alone should learn Captain Birkin's tidings. Birkin had hardly time to complete his report before Mahmud rushed into the room selaming and apologising but with crucial news.

"Excuse me, Sir, sorry, Sir", he muttered over and over again as he approached Raffles. "Lord Minto's ship is in the roads."

Raffles and Birkin were completely surprised and it showed on their faces. They swung round to Mahmud like thieves or conspirators caught in the act. Birkin's eyes were wide and his mouth still open from speaking to Raffles. Raffles jerked up his head and darted a swift glance at Mahmud holding his eyes momentarily while he absorbed the news. His mind raced. Days of tension suddenly exploded as the arrival of Birkin and Loird Minto brought the days of waiting to an abrupt end.

"My carriage, my carriage, bring the carriage", he shouted, jumping up from the chair.

Striding around his desk he clasped Captain Birkin by the hand and by the arm and shook his hand vigourously and warmly.

"My heartfelt thanks, Captain Birkin", he said, with a broad smile. Please excuse me if I rush to meet his Lordship but what you have reported this day shall never be forgotten."

Sitting inside the enclosed carriage, waiting impatiently for it to sway its way to the shore, Raffles wished he could take over the reins and, whipping the two horses, tear through the little streets in a cloud of dust so as to greet His Lordship all the sooner.

The morning sky was cloudless, the sea was blue, the host of ships in the roads a riot of sails, rigging, flags and uniforms. On shore the huge guns of Fort Malacca boomed and boomed their salute to the Governor General of all India as he arrived in the roads aboard the Company ship 'Modeste.' Thousands upon thousands of people of all races had gathered on the shore to glimpse the great man. No impediment was put in their way by the British authorities and the curious sightseers included farmers, fishermen, shop keepers, coolies and even the very poor. A column of red coated troops a thousand strong with flags flying high and led by pipes and drums formed up in ranks of three on either side of a long pathway between the shore and the great, white, house of the Resident, the old Dutch state house, in its way quite as imposing as Government House, Calcutta. Every officer wore a brand new uniform. At the command of a bugle, a column of three hundred magnificent cavalrymen thundered into position behind the proud infantry.

From beside the 'Modeste' a pinnace pushed off, her Indian oarsmen dressed in red tunics and turbans. Behind it came two long boats and in the stern of all three vessels sat men in black. Raffles joined Farquhar and other dignitaries close to the waters edge to await the arrival of the boats. As Lord Minto stepped ashore the guns from the fort again commenced firing and were answered by every ship in the fleet. The smoke from so many cannons, fired so often, formed a cloud in the clear sky.

When Lord Minto landed the infantry snapped to attention and the cavalry presented arms. He was a kindly man and, as he walked, he tried to glance in every direction, keeping his hand permanently raised in salute and occasionally bowing slightly. Unpretentious, in a black tunic and breeches, with white stockings and black buckled shoes, the hearts of all the poor Malays, Chinese, Indians and Eurasians went out to him because they recognized a fine character and a man who knew how to earn the affections of people.

Within seconds another boat ground ashore bearing the Commander of the Land Forces, Lieutenant-General Sir Samuel Auchmuty, as big, broad and bullish as Minto was slight. He too was dressed entirely in black with a single great medal upon his chest.

In the third boat came Sir Samuel's deputy and the commander of the Madras contingent, the heroic Colonel Robert Gillespie, unruly dark hair swept by the sea breeze across a distinctively open Irish face.

No man dared to approach this august trio except Raffles. After greeting the three leaders and introducing them to Farquhar, Raffles led them towards the Resident's house, the Governor General stopping frequently to make some new acknowledgement. Dignitaries in the crowd raised their hats and bowed as he passed. As the party reached the steps of Farquhar's house, the infantry fired three times in succession with enough noise to shake the foundations of all the houses in Malacca.

After lunch Lord Minto immediately called a council of war consisting of himself, Auchmuty and Gillespie, Commodore W. R. Brougham, who had taken over command of the fleet on the death of Admiral Drury, Raffles and Farquhar and their respective civilian and military secretaries.

Raffles revealed that Napoleon had ordered the replacement of Marshal Daendels by the Dutch General Jan Janssens, an appointment which encouraged everyone since it had been he who had earlier surrendered the Cape of Good Hope to the British! There was loud laughter around the conference table at this news! Despite Daendels' extensive building of new fortifications Raffles told the leaders that about the only wall surrounding the Franco-Dutch forces was one of hatred and passive resistance by the population of the Indies. He reiterated that he was certain that the entire population of Java would not help the Franco-Dutch forces.

"Whether Europeans or natives most of the population are longing for us to invade!"

Moreover, said Raffles, the raising of the French flag in the Indies had alienated the Dutch from the French as much as the cost in suffering and human lives had poisoned the minds of the natives. To cap it all, Daendels' defense works had bankrupted the country! The less cash it had the more the regime tried to levy funds from the natives. The greater their efforts, the greater the resentment. In the end Batavia was forced to issue sack loads of worthless paper to make even a pretense at solvency!

"Out timing couldn't possibly be better", Lord Minto beamed.

No detailed military plans were discussed that day but Lieutenant-General Auchmuty stressed that time would be needed for the troops to fully recover from the arduous ocean voyage from India and also to become accustomed to functioning as a single military unit. The command structure and the troops would benefit from at least two weeks of exercises.

In view of this it was decided to the war ships 'Leda', 'Bucephalus' and 'Baracouta' to Batavia to reconnoiter the enemy port and naval positions. Furthermore, the leaders decided to try to calm any fears among the local population by circulating a proclamation in advance of the invasion assuring them of the good intentions of the British.

"We leave this to you, Raffles," said Lord Minto.

Commodore Brougham described the proposed route to Batavia, from Malacca back to Penang, along the southern coast of Sumatra past Bengkulu, through the Sunda Strait, past the fortified port of Banten and on to Batavia on the north coast of Java.

Raffles looked at Lord Minto, Minto looked at Raffles. What mere civilian dare presume to advise the commander of the navy.

"Raffles," said Lord Minto casually, turning to his Secretary, "Were you not telling me in Calcutta that you thought the Malacca Strait might be navigable for large ships to the south.

"Indeed, My Lord and I have the honour to report that a route has been explored and soundings taken which show that it should be perfectly possible to pass through the Riau and Linggan islands and out into the Java Sea, following the south coast of Borneo."

"Stuff and nonsense," exploded Brougham. "Unless it was one of His Majesty's ships that tested the route I don't believe it."

"It was the Company ship 'Scavenger', answered Raffles politely and softly. "But I have every confidence in Captain Birkin and in the accuracy of the exploration."

"With the greatest respect, Mr Raffles, you are a civilian. These are matters best left to the experts."

Brougham was planning to take the invasion fleet on a long and circuitous voyage, wasting time and risking life and limb to the terrible, unpredictable storms that regularly raked the area.

"Might it be that, with a little caution, in view of the unknown nature of the waters, our objective can be achieved much more quickly and effortlessly merely by sailing south through the Strait of Malacca," Lord Minto said thoughtfully.

" I can assure Your Lordship that the Strait of Malacca is unsafe for ships larger than a prow or a junk," said Brougham tersely.

"They seem to get through all right", observed Lord Minto quisically.

"Because they're small and prepared to take

the risk but I am not", said the red faced commodore.

Lord Minto knew Raffles extremely well because of the months Raffles had spent in Calcutta. He knew Raffles thoroughness and he knew that Raffles would not make such a suggestion unless absolutely certain that he was right. Still, over-ruling the navy commander was not a step to be taken lightly.

"We must not put the fleet at risk", Minto observed to the meeting at large.

"There will be no risk, my Lord", said Raffles confidently. "There is absolutely no doubt that the Strait of Malacca is a viable seaway for large ships bound for the the East provided that the route is well researched. If there is a risk it will be not so much from the waters as from pirates but no brigand in his right mind will attack a war fleet."

As always, Raffles had a suggestion, a compromise which might please everybody.

"May I suggest, Your Lordship, that, just as we are sending the ships in advance to reconnoitre Batavia, we send one of His Majesty's ships through the Strait to take soundings anew and establish its complete safety for the fleet?

"Capital idea," Mr Raffles, said Lord Minto with a slight smile. "What do you think Commodore? Will you be satisfied with a report from a captain in His Majesty's Royal Navy?"

Brougham stuck to his guns that the fleet should not be put at risk but it would have seemed irrational not to agree to even one ship proceeding ahead to reconnoitre.

The 'Minto' commanded by Captain Greigh was delegated to explore the passage, a task which would made very easy by Greigh's being able to collaborate closely with the pioneering Captain Birkin.

"That's settled, then," said Lord Minto quietly. "We'll wait for the report."

Thus, the first meeting of the war council broke up.

No British Governor General of India had ever set foot in Malacca on the Malay mainland before and, while awaiting the tidings of the ship named after him, Lord Minto was keen to see the district. Accordingly, with the advice of Raffles and Farquhar, every day, he drove out in a carriage to see as much of the country as time permitted. He showed no offensive pride and wore no ostentatious uniform but just a plain black business suit.

Knowing the reputation of the Dutch for cruel and unjust punishments, on the very first day of his tours, he expressed the wish to inspect the prison. Upon entering the gates and alighting from his carriage the prisoners broke away from their guards and rushed forward to throw themselves at his feet. Within the day Lord Minto had ordered the release of all prisoners as an act of clemency. The prison, with its windowless, barren cells with no furniture and bare earth floors, he ordered destroyed and a more humane place of detention built. Later he saw the torture instruments used by the former Dutch governors of Malacca.

"Tear all these down and burn them", he told the jailer. "Do not leave a single one."

In a short time, by his good and humane deeds, Lord Minto endeared himself to the population of Malacca, poor or rich, and, wherever his carriage went, he was obliged by the crowds to stop and exchange greetings, taking off his hat, which he waved in salute.

Several times His Lordship visited Raffles' house at Bandar Hilir and did not feel himself even slightly demeaned in talking either to Raffles' staff of translators and clerks or even to the house helpers. Many an evening he stayed to dinner, sharing a rich table with the entire Raffles family, and often, also, with John Leyden, whom he had brought with him from India. As the first senior representative of Britain ever to be seen in this place, Lord Minto's kindness toward everyone was long remembered.

Other meetings of the war council took place and, instead of long dispatches to Calcutta, Raffles was now able to argue face to face his case for the permanent debarment of the Dutch from the Indies, except as traders on an equal footing with any other nation.

At the outset Minto had told him sadly:

"I agree with you wholeheartedly but achieving such an objective will not be easy. I must tell you in confidence that, although I have received the sanction of the home Government for this expedition, the views of the Directors do not go beyond the expulsion or reduction of the (Franco-) Dutch power, the destruction of their fortifications, the distribution of their arms and stores to the natives and the evacuation of the island by our own troops."

Faced with the disappointing news that Leadenhall Street would not, at this stage, countenance its rule being extended in place of that of the Dutch or their conquerors, the French, Raffles wracked his brains to find some middle way. Knowing that Minto agreed with him and was in persistent correspondence with the directors of the East India Company in London, Raffles made a point of ensuring that His Lordship was well armed with every sort of information about the wealth of Java, the commercial prospects, the nature of Dutch rule "contrary to all principles of natural justice and unworthy of any enlightened or civilized nation," and the extreme danger either of the Dutch returning after once being driven out or of another European power moving in.

Every night he told Olivia with growing exasperation:

"I must persuade Lord Minto to convince the Directors to make the expulsion of the Dutch as rulers of the Indies permanent. Not to do so is madness!"

Olivia agreed:" Not to do so means that everything that we are doing now is a total waste of time", she said with grim perspicacity.

Sensing that the resistance of Leadenhall Street to permanent British posts in Java was probably based as much on the expense of retaining them as upon Britain's relationship with Holland, Raffles sought to minimize the cost of getting and keeping the Dutch out of Java as a monopolizing power. Fearing that, in the end, his arguments might fall on deaf ears, Raffles added that, even if the Dutch <u>were</u> allowed to return to Java and elsewhere in the Indies at the end of the war with Napoleon, many local sovereigns with whom Holland currently had no treaties could be tempted into alliance with the British East India Company and this, by itself, could break their territorial monopoly.

"We shall secure such a footing among the Eastern isles, and such a favourable regard among the bravest races, as will baffle all the attempts of the enemy to dislodge us", Raffles told Minto at one of the many soirees at his house.

Raffles' strategy was to do everything possible to promote the Malays to control their own ports with all foreigners, including the Dutch, being allowed equal access.

"The Dutch must not be allowed to exclude all powers except themselves," he thundered. "And the benefits which the Malay nations may derive from a close connection with the British are such that there is no possibility of their ever deriving from the French or Dutch."

Minto wrote repeatedly to the Directors in

London, conveying Raffles' arguments and expressing hopes that the Company would change its mind about the immediate departure of the invasion fleet once its work was done. He hoped that, if his force was victorious in Java, the Company could be convinced of the benefits of a continued presence. And, after all, conquest was one thing but withdrawal would take time and, from a military point of view, could not happen at all without peace with Napoleon!

"Any withdrawal until Napoleon is defeated will only allow back the French and renew the threat that we are now invading to eliminate," he wrote.

"Don't worry, Raffles," His Lordship would say so often. "It's a fair gamble that we'll stay there. You'll be governor general of the Indies yet!"

Captain Greigh returned to Malacca in the 'Minto'. Just as Captain Birkin had done earlier, he brought news that safe navigation was indeed possible to the south, through the Strait of Singapore and along the south coast of Borneo to Java, provided, as he put it, 'the captain is always on deck with both eyes wide open". Still, the conservative Commodore Brougham had doubts! When the time came for the first ships of the fleet to sail from Malacca he insisted that a ship should go on ahead at all times to triple check! Nevertheless, Raffles was well pleased because once again his advice had been unique and right!

News came from Batavia that the squadron sent there had captured a Dutch cruiser and about fifteen flat bottomed boats used to ferry cargoes from ships anchored in the roads to the city. Guarding the port of Batavia were three fortified islands, chiefly, 'Onrust' (Restless Island), a base for ship repair as well as defence. The squadron reported that armed resistance in the islands had been crushed, the fortifications severely damaged or destroyed and many of the buildings burnt to the ground.

"The port of Batavia is open", the dispatch ended.

All the news flowing into Malacca was positive. Raffles' intelligence seemed faultless and the ground appeared to have been laid well. Lieutenant-General Auchmuty and his commanders had hammered out a plan of battle promising the quickest success at the least cost. Lord Minto accordingly fixed a secret date for the invasion of Java.

Knowing that he must depart soon and taking advantage of the incidence of the King's Birthday during the first week of June, Lord Minto threw a great ball at the Malacca State House, attended by his officers and the cream of local society from which His Lordship wrote to his wife that he had "mustered the whole female community." It was a ball long to be remembered in Malacca, not only because of the very important people who were there but also for its sheer magnificence. Officers wore their full dress uniforms and although there were not many European wives, perfumed Eurasian ladies, descendants of the Portuguese or Dutch, with their brown skins, their gold ear rings, necklaces and finger rings, their off-the-shoulder ball gowns and flowers in their hair, splashed the ballroom with colour and gaiety. Lord Minto opened the Ball by doing Raffles the signal honour of leading off with Olivia. It was a night without end. Even in the early hours of the morning there were still those who sensed that battle was near and who therefore squeezed every last lingering moment of happiness from the occasion. The troops had their own celebrations in the lines and, if anything, these were even noisier and longer than those at the ball.

Within a day or two, Lord Minto held an open air levee, under awnings in the grounds of the State House, to which all the local male dignitaries were invited along with officers of the invasion force. The Malay, Chinese, Indian and Arab communities sent their leaders and visiting merchants from Borneo, Sulawesi and China also attended, hopefully to be impressed by the Company's magnificence and power. What an incredible sight it was. So many cultures, so many costumes, white skins, yellow, black and brown, pigtails and fans, robes and trousers, turbans and helmets. To Raffles, the crowded guests were the living embodiment of his dreams of a great emporium of eastern trade. He and Lord Minto went out of their way to be gracious to everyone and tried to meet as many people as they could. Many a toast was drunk, not least to success in Java!

"These are great days my love", Raffles told Olivia after the levee in the privacy of their bedroom at Bandar Hilir. We have been blessed."

"Be happy my dear", said Olivia hugging him to her and gazing lovingly into his eyes. "I have no doubt that you will succeed."

CHAPTER FIVE

On June 11, 1811, the ships sailed - the largest British war fleet ever to pass among the islands of the East Indies. Again, crowds thronged the shore and again the shore batteries boomed their salute. War ships, troop transports, horse transports for the cavalry, gun boats and supply ships hoisted their pale sails against the blue sky and moved slowly southwards, ferrying 12,000 soldiers to the battlefields of Java. The ships moved off in small squadrons, one squadron at a time, each in the charge of a frigate. Whistles shrieked and drums beet as sailors swarmed up the rope ladders and into the rigging of each vessel, edging their way out along the swaying spars to lower the sails. The fleet took several days to disperse entirely and after the first day Raffles went about his work without watching the remainder depart. Only the heaviest transports were left when Lord Minto himself embarked in the fast 'Modeste' and Raffles and his family were invited to share the ship. Raffles had plenty to do during these few days. The boxes he had brought from Calcutta had to be shipped on to Batavia. His own personal possessions and by now very extensive scientific collections had to be packed and sent to the ship. As he stood with Lord Minto on the poop of the 'Modeste', Raffles had no idea whether he would ever return to Malacca again and no certain idea of what lay ahead of him in Java. Olivia and he had prayed the night before and now their fate was in the hands of God.

Although the 'Modeste' was swift, generally the ships made a slow passage, tacking constantly against contrary winds and making the best use they could of squally weather or winds from the land. Rendezvous points had been set by Commodore Brougham and in the interests of safety and security the entire fleet was obliged to assemble at these points. Obviously no commander could risk any part of his force arriving late at the battlefield or, worse still, not arriving at all. Many a Malay, high born and low, gazed in awe from the shore as the great armada passed down the Strait toward Singapore, flags and pennants flying. Off Singapore the sky became dark with huge clouds and a violent tropical storm swept through the fleet with torrential rain, thunder and lightening, so severe that even the heavy horse transports were tossed in the air like children's toys. Fortunately there was no damage and when the sun shone again the hereditary ruler of the southernmost state of Johore and his followers watched the fleet reassemble from atop a hill on the island of Singapore. Could the ruler have seen in detail who was doing what on the decks of the ships he might have noticed Raffles staring searchingly toward Singapore.

"This must be the very tip of the Malay mainland", my Lord, he observed to Lord Minto as they stood, as usual, on the stern deck, marking their progress carefully on a chart.

"If we had a post here, My Lord", said Raffles, "we would be at the very centre of the entire Far East trade."

"Assuming traders switch from the Sunda to the Malacca Strait," said Lord Minto advisedly." For the moment most vessels use the Sunda Strait to sail to and from China so, if we gain Java, we shall also be at the centre. We shall see to it that one else will occupy Singapore while we have control of the Indies."

The 'Modeste' sailed on and, while Lord Minto went to his cabin, Raffles continued to look thoughtfully at Singapore's jungle covered coastline. Lord Minto was right but what if Java had to be returned to the Dutch? Raffles' had always thought the islands of Bangka and Beliton also ideal as bases for commanding the vital sea routes to China. Coincidentally they were rich in the tin for which China's appetite was insatiable. But Captain Birkin's voyage and the progress of the expeditionary force had proved for the first time that large ships could safely navigate the Strait of Malacca - even against contrary winds. He sat for a long time, stroking his chin and watching Singapore receded over the horizon.

For once in his busy life Raffles could afford to relax. He had no need of writing voluminous dispatches because all the key players were with him on this voyage and he could talk to them face to face. Now that he was working directly for the Governor General the Government of Penang suddenly and thankfully ceased to concern him. It didn't matter now what Penang thought or did. As for London, this was Lord Minto's concern. Never had Raffles felt better. No longer overworked by the drudgery of clerking, and doing things that he loved, he was a new man, brimming with health and optimism. Like him, Olivia now looked forward only to a victory over the Franco-Dutch forces at Batavia and the almost certain promotion of Raffles to Governor General of Java. Surrounded by scores of warships bearing thousands of battle hardened troops who would not have felt confident!

As usual, Raffles had the members of his large family around him, Mary Anne and Captain Flint, Leonora and John Loftie and his unmarried sister, Harriet. As usual Mahmud was there and Abdul, now practically a veteran of the sea and looking prouder than a boy could ever look. And, of course, his dear friend John Leyden, who, despite or perhaps because of his scholarship, seemed to treat the whole invasion like an episode in college theatricals. Lord Minto had made much use of Dr Leyden in Calcutta, because of his knowledge of the Malay language, and both he and Raffles were optimistic that the scholar would play a leading role in the administration of Java after the expected conquest. Since the Company's occupation of Java was to be temporary Lord Minto had not been able to bring with him the administrative staff a permanent post would require. Knowing that whoever governed Java, even for a short time, would need all the assistance he could get he had simply called on all those he could to help out.

The route to Java was oustandingly beautiful, dotted with large and small islands, each covered with jungle and encircled by rocky coasts and occasionally sandy beaches. At the fleet's last rendezvous, close to Pontianak, on the south coast of Borneo, the ships anchored off one such sandy beach for almost a week. Watering parties went ashore, fresh fruits were gathered, carpenters and their gangs felled trees for spars and planks, clothes were washed, smiths' forges set up and many of the men were able to cook their food on terra firma and cavort naked in the sparkling sea, black and white skins together, united by a common flag and uniform. Several groups went out hunting fresh game.

Departing reluctantly from this tropical paradise, the ships proceeded onward through the Karimata Strait and across the Java sea to Batavia. Apart from the storm off Singapore there was only one scare throughout the whole voyage when sails were spotted on the horizon which turned out to be a fleet of Bugis prows from Macassar heading for Malacca. Even by a shorter route, the trip from Malacca to Java took almost two months but vessel by vessel the great fleet ponderously anchored off Batavia - a low, uninspiring, jungle covered coastline where the roofs and spires of the Dutch settlement could just be made out.

The behaviour of soldiers and sailors daily became more sombre as they cast glances at that fateful shore. How strong was the enemy? How many of them would die? How many would fight their way to glory? For those who survived what kind of land was this 'Java'? Reconnaissance parties were sent to probe the shore in several places and small craft approached as close to the land as possible while officers looked hard through their telescopes for signs of military preparations Raffles and the force commanders had been tipped off in advance that they might meet resistance from forts along the north west Java coast, especially Merak, but not a single shot had been fired as they sailed past. One reason could be that, having made the unprecedented decision to sail to Java via the Karimata Strait, weeks had been clipped from the travelling time and the fleet had arrived off Batavia much earlier than the enemy could have expected. Spies had reported that, whenever they arrived, General Janssens' strategy was not to oppose the British at Batavia and, indeed, from the ship's decks, no indications of military preparations could be seen. Certainly, not a single gun battery had opened fire since the fleet began to anchor. There was an element of uneasiness among the commanders that their arrival had perhaps been too easy! Janssens must have known of their presence since they arrived off the Java coast. Was he up to some trick? Was a trap about to be sprung? But the reconnaissance parties all returned with the news that the coast was deserted and no evidence of any trap could be found.

As the day selected for the invasion neared, the commanders met to make their final reviews and to give and receive final orders. Raffles was extremely concerned that the British troops fully understood that their enemy was the French and the Dutch and that no harm should be inflicted on any Malay or other local person. If natives were harmed during the assault the British cause in the Indies would be finished. Raffles hoped that he had won the rulers' acquiescence in the invasion and also their future support by his emphasis on the humanity, justice and good intentions of the British. Every leader in Java would now be studying the actions of the troops. One mistake, and British occupation of Java might not only be made so much more difficult but may not be able to take place at all. It was one thing to attack a relatively small European force but quite another to be at total war with all the people of Java and the islands. This was a war that the British could not win with their present forces.

The day came when the invasion was planned for the morrow. Lord Minto gave one final dinner in his candle lit cabin, with its great windows at the stern of the 'Modeste'. Auchmuty, Brougham, Gillespie and Raffles attended and, in view of the apparent absence of the enemy around the town of Batavia, the evening was a jolly one. But, for the final toast, faces were stern and eyes were hard as Lord Minto stood up and raised his glass to "Victory."

At dawn on Sunday, August 4, 1811 'Raffles' army' began to disembark onto the soil of Java. There could be no part in this for Raffles and what a frustrating time he spent, confined for security reasons to the "Modeste' but itching to get ashore and begin whatever work fate would ordain. The wind was high and the sea so rough that any attempt to regulate the departure of the troop- filled longboats from their mother ships was soon doomed. Instead the boats came and went at will. But not to Batavia! The capital city of Java was built on mud flats at the mouth of the River Ciliwung, with the principal buildings about a kilometre inland. The land to east and west of the estuary was low and marshy and, on the west bank, spies reported the location of a quarter housing Malay and Javanese people, the very people Raffles was so concerned not to harm. If the army advanced directly into Batavia the Javanese would be in the enemy's front line!

Although the British knew that Marshal Daendels had completely destroyed the great fortress of Batavia, which until two years previously had occupied the east bank, the commanders could not believe that new defensive works had not been put in place to halt the invasion nor that substantial forces had not been rushed there. Lieutenant-General Auchmuty reasoned that it would be folly to throw his force at what might turn out to be the enemy's strongest point. During his wait for the fleet to assemble in the Batavia roads, Auchmuty sent patrols along the coast to search for a place where there was a firm beach instead of mud and marsh. This he found at Cilincing, fifteen kilometres east of the capital, and it was to this place that the long boats headed. Although the port defenses at Onrust had been disabled by Sir Edward Pellew and the three ship advance squadron had cleared the bay of enemy shipping, nevertheless, frigates and gunboats took up positions on the left and right flanks of the landing force to guard against surprise attack.

The army was divided into four brigades, one forming the advance, two the line and one the reserve. Colonel Gillespie led the advance. There was a hard beach at the landing area but because the hinterland was marsh and salt pits, intersected by streams and rivers, it was miraculously unguarded. The month was August, the sun at its highest and the ground could not have been drier or firmer. Despite the high sea and the difficult terrain, before nightfall, all infantry had been safely landed, formed up and marched to defensive positions to the north and south of the village of Cilincing. The enemy had even obligingly or thoughtlessly left bridges standing over the rivers!

From Cilincing one road led to Batavia in the west and another to General Janssens new fortress at Meester Cornelis in the south. At first, the doors and windows of the little village houses were slammed firmly shut, their occupants terrified inside. Once again, a Malay language proclamation signed by Raffles was handed out explaining that no harm was intended to the local people so long as they did not support the enemy. On the second day the cavalry and artillery were landed followed by a continuous flow of munitions and supplies. Spies and patrols reported an enemy column about ten kilometres to the south but by the time Gillespie reached there the place was deserted. The road westward to Batavia was reconnoitered to within two kilometres of the suburbs but also found to be deserted. At night, enemy cavalry patrols probed British positions several times, keeping Auchmuty's force on its toes in case of sudden attack. But as the hours lengthened into days not a glimpse was had of any significant defences or of any main body of enemy troops. The British were puzzled and more wary than ever lest they step into a trap. On the third night the dark tropical sky over Batavia was lit up by a pall of flame. A patrol of European dragoons returned to the lines shouting:

"They're setting fire to the town."

The commanders met each morning and evening in Lord Minto's tent and were meeting at that very moment.

"It's scorched earth," growled Auchmuty,

"that's what it is. They don't want to come out to fight us and they're hoping that if they leave us nothing we'll be so weak that they can defeat us easily. Look at the countryside! No food, no water. And now they're burning the town! Gentlemen, there's only one way to go and that's forward! Order the advance!"

The advance was planned for the following night to give the navy time to bring long boats up the Ancol River which separated the British forces from Batavia. A bridge of boats was formed and by midnight the entire advance party had crossed over, marching unchallenged to about two kilometres of the town. Batavia was known to be criss crossed with Dutch-style canals and Colonel Gillespie was ordered to wait until the following morning before advancing further. Even then he was only to send a small party to feel out the way ahead. Minto and Auchmuty knew from intelligence sources that a large enemy force existed in the vicinity of Batavia or not more than a few kilometres distant. Where exactly they didn't know because no one they sent could find it!

One British and one Indian company advanced cautiously through the suburbs, occasionally spotting enemy cavalry, which immediately galloped of. They found every substantial house empty or the occupants locked fearfully inside. The advance party noticed that conduits bringing fresh water into the city had all been destroyed. There could be no doubt now that Janssens' policy was indeed scorched earth! The party was led by Major William Thorn and using a map previously supplied by spies it reached the city hall or government house, where leaders of the local community had assembled and quietly surrendered. Another proclamation drafted by Raffles and translated into Dutch was distributed informing the Hollander population that no harm would come to them so long as they gave no support to the French.

Elements of the party made their way north a short distance to the flag staff at the main city wharf and there hoisted both the British colours and the standard of the East India Company. To deprive the British of any valuable goods or stores, the Franco-Dutch commanders had ordered all godowns opened and from many of them they had even stripped the tiles from the roofs. En route to the wharf, large parties of natives were found looting the apparently abandoned properties and the streets were strewn with the coffee and sugar which was part of the life blood of the trade of the port. On being informed, Auchmuty decided that in the best interests of the whole community the city should be put under martial law. The response to the hoisting of the British colours was the din and smoke of a massive royal salute from each of the more than 100 ships in the Batavia Roads. By evening Colonel Gillespie had entered the town with more units of the advance which were soon drawn up in parade order on the great square in front of the town hall.

"Brave soldiers of Britain," he shouted to lusty cheers from the assembled men. "Batavia is ours."

The first night in Batavia was not a peaceful one. Knowing that the enemy knew that the British strength in the city was still only very small, Gillespie and his men were in a constant state of alert. So much so that after dismissing his men to temporary quarters, Gillespie called them out again under cover of darkness and bade them sleep on their arms in the square. There had hardly been time to regain the square when enemy units appeared out of the darkness, firing as they came. Gillespie had ordered his men not to return fire but to instead use their bayonets only, thus making it extremely difficult for the enemy to spot his forces in the darkness. The British were already in command of strategic canal and river crossings which could not be passed and Gillespie himself led a flanking column out of the city to the west where his small forces savaged the head of a long Franco-Dutch column. Meeting unexpected fierce resistance the enemy retreated. It was a nerve wracking few hours but no more was seen of the enemy that night!

But nothing was settled until Auchmuty's force had met and defeated Janssens' army and next day his forces pressed on without pause to where they thought his army might be. General Janssens strategy had indeed been one of scorched earth. He had counted on the marshes, the rivers, the canals and above all the heat to decimate the British invaders. Batavia was a stinking, pestilential and altogether unwholesome place where death could occur after only a day ashore. Majority of wealthy people had long ago abandoned the city for airier and healthier suburbs. Unaccountably, looking for all the world as if they were built in China, the cramped shop houses of the Chinese, lining the stagnant canals, were busy night and day!

To anyone who knew Batavia, Janssens' gamble was a reasonable one. If the intense sun didn't do for them, the British would be weakened by thirst and hunger. Hoping that lack of water would become a major problem Janssens had even plied many of the Chinese inhabitants of Batavia with beer to give to the British soldiers who, it was well known, were heavy drinkers, if they were given the chance. But, such was the discipline of Gillespie's troops that no beer was accepted let alone drunk. And so rapid was the British advance and so abundant the stocks of food and water that they had been able to collect en route through the Karimata Strait that not a man suffered the deprivations anticipated by General Janssens.

Janssens never intended to fight the British at Batavia unless he could encounter smallish units cut off from the main body. To offer battle in the streets of the city where, thanks to Marshal Daendels, there were no longer any fortifications of any kind, would have been madness. Daendels had not torn the fort down on an idle whim. The Dutch, like the Portuguese and the Javanese before them, had built on the marshy ground around the mouth of the Ciliwung and had even added canals so as to make it even more riverine. Unfortunately, in the tropics, water attracts mosquitoes and although no one realized it the mosquitoes carried malaria. To malaria had to be added the complete lack of sewerage and the filthy state of every waterway, natural or man made. The result was that Batavia became known as the white man's grave, so unhealthy that it was unlikely that you would meet a dinner guest more than once! Funeral processions were a daily occurrence! Malaria, dysentery, cholera and typhoid guaranteed that few would survive there more than a matter of months. Marshal Daendels had ordered all of the military and as many of the civilians as possible to move to drier terrain a few kilometres inland. New barracks and fortifications were built in this healthier location and a new market established. It was in these new facilities that Janssens' troops awaited the arrival of the British. In capturing Batavia all that the British East India Company had won was an unhealthy, dying, city!

Intending no let up in the pace of the advance, early next morning Colonel Gillespie led a force of 1,500 men up the very road along which the Franco-Dutch forces had retreated only hours before. The road was wide and tree lined and, on either side great, deserted, mansions stood in groves of trees behind low walls and wrought iron palings. Eventually they came to a huge open space known as the Kings Plain adjacent to the new government headquarters. There were tall trees on all four sides and patrols reported only the empty buildings of an extensive, new military cantonment at a place called Weltevreden. These buildings were in no way suitable for defence and no enemy forces were found there.

As the British commanders knew well, the massive new fort built by Marshal Daendels was about two kilometres further on at what had once been the country estate of a plantation owner named Cornelis. Reconnaissance patrols reported that General Janssens' forces were concentrated there. Trees had been felled to block the road and no approach was possible on the flanks due to the presence of rivers. A deep trench lay across the front of the fortress which was strongly palisaded. There were numerous tiered redoubts defended by hundreds of cannon. Meester Cornelis looked to be a formidable fortification!

When he replaced Daendels with Janssens, Napoleon had told the general: "Your second chance is your last chance", so Janssens was under no illusion as to his fate if, in addition to his earlier defeat by the British at the Cape of Good Hope, he lost Java. Unfortunately, he had inherited the defence plan of another and inherited an army which was quite different from that now assembling in the field before his gates. Before him stood many of the victors of Mauritius and Reunion, in bold spirits and with excellent equipment. Lord Minto had successfully ended a mutiny by Sepoys in India and the units of the Indian Army he led held him in high regard. There wasn't a soldier on the field who did not feel proud to be where he was. On the other hand General Janssens had inherited a force consisting of extremely reluctant islanders, some of whom had been recruited in chains! The Dutch among them were only there because Holland had been conquered by Napoleon. And among the relatively few French troops there were former deserters and convicts and even the best of them had already been spoiled by the climate and the impact on discipline of being thousands of miles from home. Few of his officers from any source possessed qualifications for commissions. Thus he was forced to fight from a base such as Meester Cornelis since there was no possibility of such a hotchpotch of troops being used in open battle. Janssens gambled that if it came to a question of 'do or die' only then might they fight reliably.

During the advance to Meester Cornelis, Colonel Gillespie encountered his first opposition. Enemy infantry occupied two villages running along each side of the road to Cornelis making it impossible for the British troops to pass. A number of horse artillery pieces also threatened the column. Gillespie summoned his own artillery to intimidate the enemy, told off sharp shooters and launched two flanking attacks during which, again, no shots were fired, instead the men relying solely on the sharp points of their bayonets. Repeated use of bayonets in this way often terrorized hostile troops who knew that, if defeated, they could count on a gruesome and agonizing death. A successful defence of the access road was obviously important to Janssens and, during the fierce battle to clear the road, Gillespie captured no less a person than the recently arrived French Chief of Staff, Brigadier Alberti, lying seriously wounded and unable to move. Other senior French officers narrowly escaped with their lives to Cornelis. At the head of a squadron of European dragoons, Colonel Gillespie himself led the pursuit of fugitives until right under the fortress walls - no mean feat for a man aged fourty five!

The major part of the British army now stood before the redoubts and batteries of Cornelis or at least were concealed in thick jungle about a thousand metres away. The two brigades of the line had by now joined the advance and the reserve brigade had moved from Cilincing to Batavia. Almost 7,000 troops now stood poised before

Cornelis.

The advance had been swift not really because of any outstanding achievements of the British but because Janssens had decided against attack and had instead concentrated a 13,000 strong force at Meester Cornelis, the only fortress in the area following the razing of the castle at Batavia. Now the British invaders faced their first and most important test. Before them was a heavily defended fortress in which it was known that the bulk and the cream of the Franco-Dutch forces were concentrated. There could be no British conquest of Java unless this force was vanquished!

The British commanders had a daunting task before them. Storming Cornelis must involve large numbers of casualties and everyone naturally wanted to avoid this. Cavalry could not be used. An artillery bombardment would have limited effect on the massive bastions, bristling with cannon of their own. Worse still, from the heights of the fort, every move the British made could be observed and every attack plan therefore countered.

"We haven't come thousands of miles to give up beneath the walls of this fort," Auchmuty acidly told his commanders.

Reconnaissance patrols consisting of, at the most, only two trusted officers, were sent to the three concealed sides of the fort to try to spot some weakness or at least to recommend what seemed the easiest place for an attack. Larger patrols would have excited enemy interest and, if a position was chosen in this way, perhaps even give away its choice to the enemy. During this hiatus, during which the two armies faced each other without a shot being fired, envoys arrived from the French under a flag of truce requesting the exchange of prisoners. Auchmuty sent his reply back to General Janssens under his own truce flag. In this extraordinarily amicable way prisoners were duly exchanged. All the while Auchmuty continued his reconnaissance and Janssens augmented his works.

August 15, 1811 was the birthday of the Emperor Napolean and a huge cannonade was fired by all the hundreds of guns in Cornelis, a symbol not only of celebration but of proud defiance.

"This is insufferable, Auchmuty growled. They think that we can't beat them and they're letting us know it."

Auchmuty positively ground his teeth with frustration as he helplessly watched the enemy heighten and widen their defenses before his very eyes, watched them fly their flags, heard them beat their drums, saw the huge birthday barrage. And all the time, while he ached to storm the fort and tear the enemy to pieces, he had to wait and wait and wait until he had enough of the right information upon which to make a careful decision.

He instructed units of the advance to dig trenches leading to the front of the fort to give cover during any subsequent storming of the ramparts but General Janssens promptly ordered them flooded from the ditch surrounding Cornelis, fed by waters channeled from each of the two flanking rivers. Again Auchmuty ground his teeth. In the lines his men suffered under the blazing sun and from the discomforts of being always outdoors in rough, mosquito infested country. While no voice was raised against him, as they days passed, his officers relayed to him the restlessness of the troops.

"It's very hard on the men, Sir."

"I know it, I know it," said Auchmuty with exasperation. "But they must wait a little longer. Better to wait a while than to die quickly."

Auchmuty's patrols reported and he sent them out again. They reported again and reconnoitered again until the British commander felt sure that he was in a position to make a decision about attack which would involve the least loss of life. The entrenchments and redoubts at the front could clearly not be taken except at terrible cost. A path around the fort along the bank of one of the two rivers could only be used be men walking in single file so Auchmuty judged that he could make little impact in this direction. His patrols left no doubt that the rear of the fort was as well defended as the front. This left the west side.

The river on this flank was, in fact, a man made canal which had been bridged to enable access to the city to the north. Although strong redoubts guarded the bridge, the mere presence of an entrance road at this point inevitably weakened the fort's defences. Here, there was no unbroken perimeter but fortifications through which a determined force might fight its way into the very heart of the defences. The country fronting the fort at this point was flat and reached through plantations of betel nuts and hops which could afford excellent cover to troops. Auchmuty's thoughts were greatly assisted by the information obtained from an enemy sergeant who had deserted to the British from a point on the fort's right flank.

A plan began to develop in Auchmuty's mind and he ordered cannon, howitzers and mortars to take up positions to the left and right at the front of the fort, their weapons adjusted to different elevations and targets within the enemy's works. The work was undertaken at night but eventually General Janssens discovered what was happening and a furious fire was opened from the artillery in the fort, inflicting unwelcome casualties on the British soldiers. Seeing that, despite the bombardment, work continued on the British batteries, two large enemy columns launched a night attack from the left and right, the one from the right arriving late at the scene after getting lost in the dark! Nevertheless the surprise attack was so successful that before the enemy force could be repulsed at least one British forward post was temporarily occupied.

To the right of the fort was the very side Auchmuty was considering for his own attack. He was electrified by the fact that the French force lost its way there¡ Surely this would be the side from which they would least expect any attack! His only guarantee of his own troops not getting lost was the French deserter but with Janssens's fortifications being daily strengthened, his men falling beneath the bombardment from the walls, and, now, with determined enemy assaults against his positions, there was little more time to lose. Auchmuty ordered the attack!

On August 24, his artillery opened up to be answered by a fire from the fort so devastating that much of the tree cover beneath which the British had been dug-in was shot away! Nevertheless, night and day for two days Auchmuty's artillery maintained an incessant bombardment, which it could be seen damaged many of the enemy's batteries and dismounted the guns.

On the night of August 26, the indefatigable Colonel Gillespie was ordered to lead an advance to the right, to take the bridge across the river and to try to enter the fort. Gillespie flew to his duties like an unchained bloodhound. Before setting out, again and again, he went over hand drawn maps with the deserter to be sure that, unlike the French attackers before, his troops did not get lost! If they arrived in front of the fortress walls too late and with daylight approaching they could be cut to pieces. The French sergeant was taken along for added insurance.

Sharpshooters, riflemen, grenadiers and other infantry crept stealthily from the British lines and headed into the trees and plantations to the right of Cornelis. In the dark, the route through the groves and plantations was triply difficult, with frequent entanglements with fences and near falls into shallow ravines. Many a silent curse fell from the lips of the soldiery! There was no moon and the column moved at a snail's pace. The terrifying result was that it was almost dawn before the lead troops completed the circuitous trek and arrived before the walls.

Gillespie was an officer of exceptional bravery and daring with a string of victories behind him in India and a reputation for being able to successfully storm any defense. A short man but of bull-like proportions, even he felt his neck muscles tighten with the tension of knowing that approaching daylight could mean death for him and his men. It was almost too late to go back but had enough men arrived to go forward? What to do! Ahead was the river and the bridge and, beyond, strong redoubts had been built to the left and right in front of the fortress walls. All was still silent! Gillespie knew that the whole British campaign could be made or broken at this place on this night. The entire success of the British expedition was up to him! All the preparations, the sailing of the fleet, the landing, the hopes for the future - the success of everything was in his hands. There was only one thing to do. He remembered those immortal lines from Shakespeare: "Forward unto Heaven or hand in hand to hell". There was no choice. Time had run out. He ordered the attack.

There was no sounding of bugles or beating of drums. Instead his still small force moved forward toward the bridge in as much silence as possible. Suddenly, enemy pickets shouted a challenge to which the French deserter replied "Patrole" and the troops advanced. Before the sentries knew what was happening Gillespie's men had quietly overwhelmed them. The Colonel was sweating. He looked up at the greying sky. They had to move fast if not to be caught. Against the pale light of dawn he could make out a strong redoubt at the other side of the bridge, close to the river. Again, in response to a challenge, the French deserter shouted "Patrole" and again all of the guards were either bayonetted or taken. But Gillespie's luck had run out. Something had alarmed the fort and blue flares began shooting up everywhere as the enemy tried to pinpoint his force and determine its number. A murderous discharge of grape and round shot flew, mercifully, over the invaders' heads. His troops now faced batteries of cannon on either side of the road but his advance was so swift and unexpected that these too were miraculously overcome. There were now loud shouts coming from the fort and large numbers of enemy troops advanced toward the British along the road linking the river bridge to the fort. Three regiments of Gillespie's grenadiers had hurried forward at the sound of the firing and cut through the French with fixed bayonettes but under a withering fire from the fort. Two huge redoubts now guarded the entrance to Cornelis.

"Go on, go on", Gillespie waved on the charging Grenadiers. Within minutes the captains of each regiment and many of their men could be seen silhouetted against the light of the flares, locked in hand to hand combat atop the crucial redoubts. Then, from the right, there was a blinding flash and a thunderous roar amid which the captains and their men disappeared in an instant, blown to fragments by a massive explosion. Shells and rockets whined into the air and a sulfurous black deluge of ashes, smoke and fragments rained down on the invaders. Inside the ruined redoubt the ground was strewn with bloody, mangled limbs of men who, seconds before, had been gallant soldiers! The sight of their dismembered leaders drove Gillespie's men to a fury which no mere flesh and blood enemy could withstand.

Later, it was discovered that two enemy soldiers, in a last act of defiance, had fired the redoubt's magazine. Unknown to Auchmuty, General Janssens had ordered his men to fight to the last man!

The French were pouring their fire down onto the bridge across which British troops were still streaming and artillery was directly pounding Gillespie's force. Gillespie took a column to the left, ordering Colonel Gibbs and the grenadiers to the left. Gillespie moved around the perimeter, knocking out one redoubt at a time until, strengthened by reinforcements, he felt strong enough to attempt to silence the guns located off the walls in the central artillery park and which were keeping up a constant bombardment of his men. Massed British infantry drove back a charge by enemy cavalry and the way was clear for Gillespie's men to attack through the flank of the artillery, laying waste to everything in their path.

Gillespie saw large numbers of the enemy fall back before him, attempt to regroup and fall back again. French reinforcements were being prevented from being brought up by the heavy artillery fire from British gunners on every side of the fort. British troops now poured across the bridge opened by Gillespie and the enemy could soon be seen streaming out of the back gates of the fort towards the south.

Until now the British attack had been made by infantry but cavalry now galloping into the fort, Colonel Gillespie, sword in hand, put himself at the head of the dragoons and with a detachment of horse artillery chased the enemy for almost fifteen kilometeres to the south. They rallied several times but were driven out of pitiful positions by artillery and cavalry. Eventually, the road was littered by arms, caps, accoutrements and pouches as the French-commanded forces threw away their arms and tried to run away. Six thousand prisoners were taken that day including generals, colonels, majors, lieutenant colonels, captains, lieutenants and cadets. Nearly three hundred cannon were captured. One entire French regiment simply laid down their arms without even leaving the fort! Unfortunately General Janssens and a small detachment of cavalry escaped!

General Janssens first fled fifty kilometres to a strongly fortified position in the mountains at Bogor (Buitenzorg) but, finding that so few troops joined him there, he fled onwards across the mountains to Cirebon, on the north coast. Immediately he left Bogor local troops mutinied and the fort soon fell into the hands of the British. From Cirebon he was obliged to flee again from a squadron of British frigates, armed with marines, sent along the coast from Batavia. His troops which arrived in Cirebon after he rode hurriedly away were captured by the marines. Forts all along the north coast surrendered easily to the naval task force.

Spies reported that Janssens was headed for the port of Semarang, a major Dutch centre of trade and administration, on the south coast of Java. Auchmuty himself decided to pursue the enemy commander there and he ordered troop transports and war ships promptly around the coast via the Sunda Strait. Lord Minto repeatedly called upon Janssens to surrender but, with Napoleon's words ringing in his ears that a second chance would be his last, the general steadfastly refused. When Auchmuty arrived at Semarang, as at Batavia, he found the fortress abandoned, with Janssens having taken up a strong position in the hills at the rear. But not so strong that a determined British assault could not dislodge him, and, once again, Janssens was on the run! Auchmuty chased him mercilessly across Java until eventually he surrendered unconditionally at Salatiga. The whole of the island of Java and its dependencies was now in British hands!

CHAPTER SIX

Neither Raffles nor Lord Minto could do much until the Battle of Java was won - or lost. During the first few days they did not even sleep ashore and, until Lieutenant General Auchmuty's final victory, no permanent arrangements concerning themselves or society dare be made. The civilians in the invasion force spent almost ten days wallowing in the heavy swell aboard ship in the Bay of Batavia. With the fall of Meester Cornelis Lord Minto made his headquarters at Batavia City Hall, a smaller scale version of the Dutch East India Company's sprawling headquarters in Amsterdam.

Martial law had been in force in the ancient city since the commencement of the attack but, with the victorious storming of Cornelis, Lord Minto ordered it lifted.

When British troops had first occupied the century old City Hall they had discovered dark, waterlogged underground dungeons crammed with prisoners from the local population. Many were found to have been accused of trifling offences. Adjacent rooms were equipped with hideous instruments of torture. As at Malacca, Lord Minto ordered all prisoners released and the paraphernalia of torture destroyed. From these acts the indigenous people of Batavia came to see that the British regime was quite different from that of its predecessor and seemed to mean them no harm. Minto reassured the leaders of the Dutch community that no harm would come to them either so long as they cooperated with the new rulers.

Captured official buildings all had to be investigated and military guards had relocked and guarded the Dutch East India Company's go-downs. As the entrepot not only for trade from the eastern islands but also from Arabia, India, Thailand, Vietnam, China and Japan the godowns were full of valuable commodities and merchandise. Among other things, Company officials and British troops reported finding coffee, sugar, pepper, cloves, mace and nutmegs, opium, tin, copper and precious metals from Japan, China trade goods, Indian fabrics, cinnamon from Sri Lanka, Java cotton and large quantities of timber. It was not only a question of preventing their destruction or theft. These goods represented the only available backing for the local currency. Without them it would be worthless and many a merchant would be bankrupt. The British knew that the Franco-Dutch regime was already on its beam ends. The last thing they wanted or could afford was that the merchants should be bankrupted too.

Because of the climate, the bodies of those killed in action had to be buried immediately but, with the return of Auchmuty to Batavia, a huge commemorative parade was held on the Plain of Mars at Weltereden. A colour party was present from every unit that had suffered losses and after prayers had been said the flags were lowered until the point of each standard touched the ground, artillery fired a salute, officers doffed their hats and the entire parade stood with bowed heads and in silence for two minutes. No crowds thronged the great field but the dark eyes of local people peered curiously from behind trees and the enclosing walls of the mansions of the rich.

Raffles stood behind Lord Minto at the ceremony and both men felt doubly sad because this was their second funeral. The brilliant John Leyden had died of malaria within a few days of landing. Both were present at the death of the young man that each could still see in his mind's eye, full of youth, full of life, full of talent and full of enthusiasm for the part he was to play, at Lord Minto's request, in assisting Raffles with the government of Java. Now he was gone and Raffles missed him as if he had been one of his own family. In Leyden he would have found a valuable professional resource and, just as he had stayed with the Raffles' in Penang and become an intimate friend, Raffles had looked forward to having the doctor near him in Jakarta as one of the very few people to whom he could lay bare his private feelings. His death might have been more acceptable had he been killed by enemy bullets but it seemed doubly cruel that he had been snatched away at the very summit of victory by a climate that seemed unremittingly cruel to Europeans.

With the return to Batavia of Lieutenant General Auchmuty, Lord Minto read out a proclamation that he and Raffles had prepared in the event of victory. The captains and leading members of all the local communities which made up polyglot Batavia were invited to attend - Dutch, Eurasian, Javanese, Sundanese, Balinese, Ambonese, Madurese, Bugis, Arab, Malay, Portuguese and Chinese. Awnings had been erected in the centre of the square in front of the City Hall to protect the participants from the hot sun and a thousand infantry and cavalry were drawn up on each side, leaving people free to come and go from the south and north. Europeans tended to congregate together standing at one side while many of the local people squatted on their haunches on the other. Chinese in colourful silk gauze gowns and black skull caps and Arab merchants in long, white robes and turbans stood close to the Europeans and Eurasians, with most of the latter wearing native dress. Lord Minto knew it was customary for Dutch officials to address the public from the first floor balcony at the front of the City Hall but, instead, he chose to stand at the top of the wide stone steps leading to the main entrance, from which he could see above the heads of the crowd and all could see him. He had no wish to be associated in the public mind with the hideous sentences which had been read out from that bloody balcony. Merchants and community leaders had been coming to the city hall for days asking how they were to be governed and by what rules so, in fairness, Minto felt a statement should no longer be delayed.

"People of Java," Lord Minto began. "The British Government sincerely wishes to promote your prosperity and welfare. We want to work together with you for mutual advantage, in a spirit of kindness and affection. Providence has at last brought to you a protecting and benevolent government."

It took time for everyone to understand His Lordship's words because some knew English but many didn't and had to rely on translators. When the words of the great English lord were understood they were like none that had been uttered in this square before. Here people had been tortured and even impaled, their screams lingering horribly for hours on end while their stern judges looked on from the balcony above His Lordship's head. No one had spoken of kindness and affection! Could it really be true? It was certainly hard to believe! But Lord Minto was an old man, approaching sixty, with a soft kind face and mild manner. Surely, he would not lie!

Lord Minto's words were soft and brief but, as he continued, their meaning was momentous and shattering!

151

As if to underline the humanity shown by his freeing of prisoners and the destruction of instruments of torture, Lord Minto's first command was that the torture and mutilation of criminals was henceforth banned. And there would be no more capital punishment except with the permission of the soon to be appointed Lieutenant Governor.

"You have been subject to the grossest military oppression and tyranny and to a system of forced loans and levies that have destroyed every shadow of security, either for person or property. From this day forth all that is ended. We shall make the law fair and every person shall be subject to it equally."

Local people looked at each other in amazement at these signs of enlightenment, honesty and leniency. They were already shocked by the fact that the British troops insisted in paying in full for all supplies that they were obliged to request and for every service performed. Many of them were used to being treated like slaves, whether they were or not, and this fair play seemed too good to be true.

Lord Minto and Raffles were implacable opponents of slavery and they had been horrified to discover that fully twenty per cent of the population of Batavia were slaves. As a first step, Minto now ordered the freeing of all slaves employed by government and a prohibition on replacing them with others.

Also, the Javanese were much addicted to card games and to cock fighting which the British rulers believed to be immoral. In addition they were subject to taxation by rapacious Chinese or Javanese who, in turn, remitted a portion of their receipts to the Dutch authorities. This system was also abolished by Lord Minto.

Next His Lordship turned his attention to trade, immediately electrifying his listeners.

"His Majesty's subjects in Java will have the same privilege and freedom to trade as British born subjects"

"And we intend to revise the oppressive, vexatious and inconvenient system of monopoly, not only as it affects trade but also the health and morals of the people."

To those with a vested interest in monopolies it was as if the heavens had fallen. To others it was as if the prison gates had been flung open. Minto had declared free trade.

Lord Minto had been careful not to point a public finger at the Dutch when he spoke of he oppressive nature of former regimes, although no one could mistake that they were responsible. Dutchmen in the audience knew well that Britain was moving erratically toward free trade while The Netherlands had traditionally preferred monopoly. As in Britain, in these times of change, the Dutch community at Batavia was divided, with some aligned with the progressive ideas of the new century and some clinging to the past. Of course, being so far from the centre of their own culture and society there were many who didn't care what system was followed so long as there was money in it. Such people Minto and Raffles particularly disliked because their amoral attitudes were frequently the source of iniquitous corruption.

The more enlightened Dutch among the crowd were relieved and interested to hear that they were welcome to participate in the new government and, indeed, in all positions of trust. Everyone in the Dutch community was relieved that there were to be no reprisals either against people or property.

Money makes the world go round and the British, as much as every race and class of local people, were critically concerned about the large quantities of inadequately backed paper money in circulation, money which Daendels and Janssens had issued in a desperate bid to raise cash to defray the regime's expenses, escalating upwards because of massive military expenditures. Would the notes be honoured and if not what was intended? Poor people simply wanted to know when the inflation would stop! Minto described the steps taken to secure the godowns, urged the whole community to get trade moving again immediately, reassured those holding the old regime's paper that it <u>would</u> be honoured and revealed that an urgent enquiry was in hand to identify ways of stabilizing the currency and reducing inflation, which he knew to be onerous upon the poor.

All the while Minto was speaking Raffles stood behind him while Colonel Gillespie and Sir Samuel Auchmuty stood on either side. Now the Governor General turned and with his right hand brought Raffles forward, between himself and Colonel Gillespie. Looking at Raffles he didn't notice the look of pained incredulity on Gillespie's handsome face.

Minto realized that the public was eager to know how they were to be governed, who would be in charge, which institutions and offices from the Franco-Dutch regime would be allowed to continue, which persons would be removed from office, who the new office bearers would be etc., etc. Standing side by side with Raffles, Lord Minto said that Java would be ruled by a new Council headed by a Lieutentant Governor.

Colonel Gillespie prepared to step forward. In situations like this the senior military man would always be invited to take command.

" On this day I am pleased to appoint the Honorable Thomas Raffles the new Lieutenant Governor of Java", Lord Minto declared.

Gillespie covered a gasp with military correctness. Raffles stepped forward, as usual in black clerical suit with a high white collar and cravat. He smiled and bowed slightly but did not speak. Lord Minto had already covered all the points they had agreed before hand. At thirty, Raffles was half Minto's age and his hair was still dark. His face still had something of boyish optimism about it. He was young to have risen so high but then he had started young, almost fifteen years ago in the dark offices at Leadenhall Street. Raffles was well pleased. He had achieved the objectives which had been crystallizing in his mind since his first fateful journey to Malacca where he had uncovered the secrets of the Indies trade. The French had been driven out of Java. The Indies were now entirely under British control. Free trade had been declared. Restrictive Dutch monopolies were to be reviewed and, where desirable, dismantled. Most satisfying of all, he was in charge!

From the brave face put on at City Hall that day, few could have guessed the agonies running through the minds of Minto and Raffles. They had behaved as if the British East India Company had arrived in Java to stay. But was this true? Could it be made to be true? Minto had been told clearly by the Company's Directors in London that he had permission to do what he had achieved but that then he must withdraw! On his own authority he had not only decided not to withdraw but to confirm the Company's rule by appointing a Lieutenant Governor and Council along the lines of the administrations in all the others of the Company's permanent posts.

"No one must know our true position here except you and I," Lord Minto told Raffles, privately and confidentially. "If the Dutch or anyone else thought we were about to pack up and leave we'd never get cooperation!"

"Much less get anything done," added Raffles.

"Our strategy has to be to behave as if we're here to stay."

"Agreed."

"You must reform the economy and make it strong, providing the revenue for me to be able to convince the Directors that if the Company stays here it will make money."

"You know that I will do my very utmost, My Lord."

"I know you will Raffles but remember this. In their present mood neither the Company nor the Government will agree to Java or other parts of the Indies being ruled as a British Crown Colony. Do not pursue territory. Do not create expense. On the contrary you must keep your costs to the absolute minimum."

"But we can make treaties? ."

"Yes, we can make treaties. I know that you have long favoured treaties with the native rulers to bind them to the Company and to Britain. That's the way to go. It costs us nothing and the potential benefits are huge."

"Plus, it continues to keep out the French, the Dutch or any other power," added Raffles.

Lord Minto smiled knowingly.

"Quite so," he said looking Raffles directly in the eyes and repeating part of what he had said.

"Treaties with the rulers will keep out all other foreign powers, including the Dutch, so long as the Company or Britain is prepared to stand by them. Even if there is peace in Europe, London will still have to decide whether to break the treaties you make or to stand by them and usually we British prefer to stand by our treaties."

"Dutch colonial rule here has been an abomination and if we can keep them from coming back it will be a job well done," Raffles said passionately.

It was still early days but the British command now felt secure enough to formally occupy the new glittering white barracks and government buildings south of Batavia in the beautiful park land setting of Rijswij and Weltevreden. The British knew well the reputation of Batavia as the white man's grave yard and Minto and Raffles had already suffered a personal loss because of it - John Leyden. Quite apart from the fact that Rijswij and Weltevreden were now the right places to be, no one wanted to spend longer than necessary in the old part of Batavia, close to the port.

With his usual curiosity Raffles had toured the old city a few days after arrival and was amazed to see the terraces of airless and cramped European style Dutch houses and Chinese shop houses and temples lining the sides of stinking canals. The area north of the residential quarter, close to the sea, was basically a foul marsh on which godowns and fortifications had been mistakenly built. A strong aura of decay and death hung over the northern part of the old city as much as life and optimism was exuded by the almost Calcutta style stone buildings of Rijswij and Weltevreden. The new town was reached through pleasant groves and plantations, buildings were large and in spacious grounds and the living environment seemed altogether healthier. Both European and Chinese style mansions dotted the still rural looking suburbs to the south and Raffles and Minto each moved into palatial houses, formerly occupied by Dutch officials on the edge of the King's Plain, close to Government House.

As in Malacca, so at Batavia, there was many an hour when Minto and Raffles were cloistered conspiratorially together. The issues were so sensitive that making others privy to their discussions would only have favoured confusion and instability. Minto felt himself highly fortunate to have been appointed Governor General of India at a time when Thomas Raffles was up and coming in Penang. There were very few matters on which the two men failed to agree. Far from Raffles having to push Minto to endorse his views, Lord Minto was only too grateful to be able to turn to someone who empathized with him.

In the first place, both men felt that it would be absurd for the British to now quit Java. Britain was still at war with France and the French could simply return. Or some other power might move in. Or the Indies leaders themselves might take over but not favour British trade interests. Then there was the whole question of the Dutch. Now there was a chance to overturn their monopolies and establish free trade. But if the British left and the Dutch were free to continue as before their territorial and trade monopolies would once again threaten British interests from Calcutta to Shanghai.

Minto and Raffles were both humanitarians of their time and while neither may have undertaken a rights campaign per se, when the opportunity arose in the natural course of events, each was keen to do what could be done to alleviate human suffering and distress. But neither would have denied that self interest wasn't also uppermost in their minds. Minto told Raffles:

"To make the people of Java richer, happier and to give the people a feeling of independence which they are now totally without, is the best recipe for making this country less accessible to European invaders."

Following the loss of the American colonies a great debate was raging through the English corridors of power as to whether colonies exited for the benefit of the mother country or vice versa. Raffles and Minto both took the view that a healthy colony was essential for the mother country. They believed that the healthier and more prosperous the people of the Indies, the better for trade and, therefore, for the Company and for Britain. Their first priority was to restore economic health to the Indies and neither would have shrank from admitting that their object was to secure a fair slice of it for the Company and for Britain.

To Minto and Raffles, it seemed that the Directors in London were chronically out of step with what was required by the events of the day, and with the opportunities offered by the Indies. A large part of their problem was that the men in London hardly knew where the Indies were on the map. Raffles had done his best to address this ignorance with his frequent copious reports but lack of knowledge and scepticism remained in the Director's minds. To them, new responsibilities meant new costs more than new opportunities. Both men also knew that the times within which they were forced to act did not favour them. Britain was not only at war with France but with the thirteen American colonies whose forces were threatening British Upper Canada. International alliances were in a state of constant flux.

On the other hand, in this uncertain situation, Britain's Industrial Revolution had unleashed ship loads of merchants upon the world searching for new markets and, as in India, this search was frequently accompanied by the establishment of trading posts.

In 1811 the British Government was besieged with requests for funds during a time of intense uncertainty, change and even loss. At the same time the East India Company was confronted by men from its own ranks who seemed more determined to increase its liabilities through the establishment of new trading posts than to do their utmost to increase its profits.

"My chief concern", Minto told Raffles, "is

whether you'll be able to manage here if the Company don't soon approve a proper permanent establishment. The troops can't stay forever and then you'll almost be alone. Now that I've been here I can see that Java isn't the Prince of Wales Island. It must be almost as large as England! And then you have Sumatra, so the two together are about the size of France!"

"Many of our Residents manage entirely alone, My Lord, but in fact I shan't be, because of the colleagues we brought from India and Penang."

"Less than a dozen".

"I had less than a dozen in Penang. In fact, sometimes it seemed as if the whole government devolved upon me!"

"I'm afraid it will here too. I know how conscientious you are and how hard you work. I don't want you to kill yourself. Nothing's worth that. "

"Neither do I, My Lord, " said Raffles with a grin. "But hopefully, these difficulties are only temporary. The crux of the matter is what the Company will do if there is peace with France. Will we hand the Indies back to Holland or will we keep them. If we keep them, surely London will increase the staff. Meanwhile, I dare say I can persuade one or two more colleagues from Penang to join me."

"Be careful with that Raffles. You don't want to antagonize Penang further."

"No. Of course. In the short term it's not going to be easy here. But I'm confident that we can succeed, especially if, instead of trying to run everything ourselves, we work through others."

"You'll have to".

"We must call on reputable people from the former Dutch regime. Much though we despise their general attitudes to the natives and their trade policies the Dutch have not been our enemies."

"You may have difficulty selling that to Gillespie. I'm sure that the military will feel that every non-Brit in the government here is a potential threat."

"We have no choice, My Lord. Later, maybe some of them can be replaced but to begin with we have to work with them."

After days of brain storming, the two leaders decided that Minto would support Raffles to the fullest of his powers and funds. In exchange Raffles must work might and main to make the Company's presence in Java a profitable one. Only cash in hand was likely to change the hard headed Director's minds.

During the hectic days of the first month, the new Council was in almost permanent session at the huge, barrack like Government House, newly built by Daendels in Empire style.

Raffles ordered that all Dutch or European people in Java must register with the British authorities. Meanwhile, Herman Muntinghe, formerly President of the Supreme Court of Batavia and the former President of the Board of Aldermen, Jacob Cranssen accepted invitations to join the Council. Muntinghe had been brought to the Indies by Marshal Daendels. He had been partly educated in England and had been greatly influenced by French modernism. Muntinghe favoured an end to feudalistic land and labour practices, with personal ownership of the land and wages paid to workers. Cranssen was so pro-British that he once said that until his dying day he would be proud to always think of himself as both Dutch and British. In these two men Raffles could not have made a better choice. While Lord Minto was in Batavia the Council's meetings were cordial and, after understandable initial hesitation, the Dutch members played their parts to the full.

Colonel Gillespie was appointed commander of whatever forces were to remain in the Indies after the return to India of the main invasion fleet and, naturally, he was a senior member of the small Council. Gillespie was delighted to be appointed Commander-in-Chief but deeply resented Raffles having ultimate authority. Again, while Lord Minto held the chair, the Council's meetings were friendly enough but behind the scenes Gillespie was bubbling with rage.

"It's outrageous", he secretly fumed to army colleagues. "Tell me one place in the Company's domains or throughout the British Empire where a civilian rules the military?"

Minto had felt that since Java and the Indies were not a British Crown Colony a military officer should not be put in charge. He wanted to make it clear to the world that the invasion of Java was not undertaken by the British Government but by the private British East India Company. In Gillespie's soldier's mind a British invasion had taken place, led and carried out by the military, with an occupation now guaranteed by the military. There was no doubt in his mind that he should be in charge. Gillespie hardly knew Raffles at this time but it also rankled that despite all that he had achieved, repeatedly risking his life on the field of battle, the Lieutenant Governor should not only be a civilian with no fighting experience or honours but a man fifteen years his junior.

"It's intolerable," he choked. Utterly intolerable."

Yet orders were orders and although Minto sensed Gillespie's disappointment, when he left Batavia for Calcutta, Raffles was definitively in command. Not only was he deputed to run Java as head of the Council but, bearing in mind the Dutch members of it and, to Gillespie's further fury, Raffles was given ultimate authority to make laws or regulations out of council as well as within it. He also held secret powers of which he had no call to inform anyone.

Just as, sixty days earlier, Auchmuty's first military task had been to secure Batavia so that he could have at his back the sea and his supply ships now, in the third month of occupation, the civilian task of Minto and Raffles was to secure the political loyalty of Batavia as a base for governing the Indies.

This was an objective by no means left to bureaucracy alone. Dinners and balls launched the European community of Batavia into an hysteria of bon homie. Individuals hosted social functions, the civilian government hosted social functions and the military hosted social functions. Chinese compradores were rushed off their feet to procure all the food and wine required. The economy of Batavia boomed as never before. Servants were in big demand, carriages and drivers were wanted everywhere. To the non-European residents of Batavia whatever else the arrival of the British might mean, for the time being, at least it meant plenty of work, money and an end to the dark days of living in the shadows of torture and execution. This was a time of getting to know you among the British and the residents of Java, a vital time during which Lord Minto did everything possible to win the hearts of the people the Company were now governing in Java.

On his last night in Java Lord Minto threw a state ball at the ornate former residence of the Dutch Governor General - a house which had been captured by the British with all its decorations to celebrate the birthday of Emperor Napoleon still intact. Knowing that Lord Minto was about to depart for India everybody who was anybody attended the glittering dinner and ball. The huge ballroom was a sea of military uniforms, red, blue, black, gold with cummerbunds, epaulettes and yards of braid, gleaming brass buttons and side arms, polished leather boots. If the uniforms of the military were brilliant the billowing, the multi-coloured gowns of the ladies were like a field of flowers. Many of the Dutch had married local women and the dark skins of their wives and daughters contrasted richly with their dresses, hair adornments and gold jewelry. Despite the heat the music was lively and the dancing energetic. More was achieved at social functions to seal the indispensable new friendship between the British and the Dutch than at any meeting or committee.

While some of the Dutch may have felt uneasy about the modern economic ideas hinted at by Lord Minto and elaborated on privately by Raffles, there were none who preferred the French. For the time being this was the East India Company's trump card. So long as Holland remained under French rule the Dutch were in no position to do anything but welcome their British benefactors in Java and the Indies.

Important though his base at Batavia was, Raffles was sharply aware that the Company's ultimate prospects in Java did not depend any more on the Dutch but upon the indigenous people of Java, upon their rulers inland whom it was now urgent that he meet. There had been no local ruler left in Batavia but Raffles knew he had to move fast to prevent any encirclement of Batavia by potentially hostile native rulers. The rulers could be reliably expected to be mostly concerned with their sovereignty or about what they may receive in lieu of it. News from Batavia had already begun to suggest to the rulers the type of men they would have to deal with.

The principal kingdoms of the Indies were Yogjakarta, and Surakarta (Solo) in the centre of the island and Palembang in Sumatra. Yogjakarta and Solo had once been one, ruled by a single emperor. Auchmuty had already sent emissaries to all three informing them of the surrender of the Franco-Dutch forces and promising no threat or harm provided they did not either oppose the British or support their enemies. He had told them that a British Resident would soon be posted to each court to represent the East India Company's interests. Marshal Daendels had held hostage a prince each from Solo and Yogjakarta but these were both freed by Raffles and sent home with kind words.

Nevertheless, Java and Sumatra were lands foreign to either the British or the Dutch and it was natural that with the defeat of General Janssens their rulers mind's should be feverish with possibilities. Must things go on under the British as they had under the Dutch? This was the crucial question and the reply obviously had many unknowns and possible variables.

Spies watched with interest and expectation as they saw at least half the British invasion force return to their warships in Batavia roads at the end of October and hoist sail for India.

With them went Lord Minto, Lieutenant General Auchmuty and Franco-Dutch prisoners of war, including General Janssens, who was taken to England.

Lord Minto's last official comment to Raffles, before departure for Calcutta, revealed his heart to watching Javanese spies. His words: "While we are here let us do as much good as we can," were subsequently carried from royal court to court.

If the princes were now excited beyond bounds at the new possibilities opening before them, Raffles and Gillespie were concerned beyond measure. They knew that, given the attitude of the British East India Company in London, Minto had no choice but to take a substantial part of the army back to India. But, what would be their fate if the powerful rulers of Java and Sumatra now decided to seize the chance to move against them? Was there a long term future for the Company in Java or would they, too, soon be forced to take ship and quit the island forever, with all the catastrophic repercussions this could have for Britain's Far East trade?

CHAPTER SEVEN

With fewer than a dozen other British administrators to help him govern the Indies Raffles had plenty on his plate. Partly for this very reason, with the departure of Lord Minto for India, he decided to immediately move his residence from Rijswij near Weltevreden to the former palace built half a century before by the Dutch Governor General, Willem van Imhoff, among the hills of Buitenzorg (Bogor). Raffles felt it somehow appropriate that van Imhoff had been a zealous reformer; it was an association he enjoyed since he, too, was a reformer.

Unlike at Batavia, the living environment in the grand new suburbs of Rijswij and Weltevreden was extremely congenial. But Raffles had to run the Government and he needed peace and quiet to undertake the prodigious amount of paper work involved, which largely only he could instigate. Bogor promised this, whereas the house at Rijswij was a magnet for society. During the day there was a constant procession of people on official business and at night there was an equally constant round of offical dinners and receptions. Raffles found it tiring, Olivia found it tiring and, most importantly, Raffles felt he could rarely snatch the time required for concentrated work.

There were other factors influencing the move.

Despite the apparent salubriousness of Rijswij and Weltevreden, like all Europeans, Raffles had a fear of not achieving fame or making fortune in Batavia so much as dying there of the kind of awful disease which had carried off John Leyden so quickly! No one knew why Batavia was so unhealthy but the fact that it was built on marshes was thought to be a major cause. Then there were the canals, which looked so picturesque in Holland, but which in Batavia were repositories for every kind of offensive garbage, including the carcasses of dead animals. They also provided the only flushable lavatory in town. Confronted with living tortuously and probably dying quickly in this stinking, rotting environment Marshal Daendels had also made his home first at Rijswij and then at Bogor. Raffles decided to follow suit. His home would be Bogor while he would retain the house at Rijswij for official business and entertaining.

Mary Anne and Captain Flint and Leonora and John Loftie had each taken deep-roofed houses in Weltevreden so Raffles and Olivia set out for Bogor with only his unmarried sister, Harriet, from the immediate family. On the day of the move, as they made their way by carriage across the hot plains on which Batavia and its environs were situated, Raffles and Olivia felt a profound sense of escape as the horses drew them higher into the cool mountains of the Preanger to the south of the city. They had a small military escort of mounted hussars and a convoy of ox carts brought on their possessions in the rear.

Batavia was surrounded by coconut groves and rice fields with sleepy looking villages dotted among them. En route to the heights of Bogor, they passed through acres of emerald green paddy and shady coconut groves, then through pepper and betel plantations, passed fruit orchards and fields of cotton, before coming to the thick jungle which cloaked the lower reaches of the mountains. Herds of cattle grazed unexpectedly on land specially cleared for the purpose. Thanks to Marshal Daendels the road to Bogor was excellent. It passed in an almost straight line through numerous villages and markets before turning sharply to make the ascent into the mountains. Here the road wound is way upwards through a forest of exotic trees and shrubs until Raffles' party reached the river in front of van Imhoff's white palace. The carriage had to be taken across the river on a bamboo raft which a single boatman pulled along by means of twisted rattan lines attached permanently to each bank. On the other side, the four horses pulling the carriage were re-harnessed and whipped up a short incline until before them, like a heavenly vision, stood the palace.

"It's perfect", sighed Olivia, holding Raffles' arm in the privacy of the carriage and leaning her head on his shoulder.

Behind the rather squat and symetrical, two storey house with flanking towers, a row of blue, cloud capped, mountain peaks rose against the noon sky, like dragon's teeth.

The nearer they approached, the more fairy tale the appearance of the shimmering white palace became. A grand driveway swept round a large pond in front of the house, huge green lily pads dotting its still waters. There was a porticoed main entrance beneath a regal copula which they soon found lead into a magnificent high ceilinged and chandeliered reception room with other public rooms to left and right. The residential accomodation was in the wings of the building, tentacling out on each side and by their very modesty flattering the mass of the near classical main entrance. The porticoed verandahs along the front of the wings were shaded from the sun by striped bamboo chicks or blinds.

"Do you know what the name Buitenzorg means?" asked Raffles with an affectionate smile.

"No, what."

"It means without a care," said Raffles.

"Let's hope we shall be," laughed Olivia.

In front of the house were rice fields which, in the morning and evening, were full of bent backed farmers and water buffalo. The people dressed so colourfully in their hand painted sarongs and kebayas that they looked like living flowers among the green fields. At the earth coloured river they had crossed, fed by myriad streams from the mountains above, under shady, overhanging trees, women washed clothes in the mornings and in the evenings whole families walked down to bathe. Small boys jumped in and out of the deliciously refreshing water with shrill cries of delight. Men stripped off to cleanse away the dirt of the day. Girls and women clustered together, sarongs drawn up under their armpits bathing inconspicuously and decorously, squatting down in the stream. Harriet giggled at the sight of naked men bathing unconcernedly in the river as their carriage passed.

"If there's a paradise in Java this must be it," said Raffles happily.

"What a splendid hill station this will make," said Olivia. So close to Batavia, easy to reach and yet another world entirely."

Though he had spent his days in noisy, bustling towns Raffles longed for the peace and beauty of country life and he and Olivia found the most perfect happiness in unspoiled rustic Bogor. Once they were settled the family took the carriage higher to the crest of the Puncak from which, just as in Penang one could view Georgetown, from here they could see Batavia far below, shrouded in a transparent haze. This was the Preanger country and scattered round about were the mansions of Dutch farmers and coffee plantation owners, often with high roofs propped up on slender pillars shading an open verandah on all four sides.

On that first day and on many a subsequent day, as his carriage rose higher through the foothills to the peaks of Bogor, Raffles felt like a man from whose shoulders a great weight was slipping. On the plain he felt as if the world controlled him. On the peaks of the Preanger he felt as if he controlled the world. He, Olivia, others of his family and friends went for many a walk in these hills with their magnificent views, bubbling streams and waterfalls and cool, cool air. Surely none of the evils threatened by the fetid air of Batavia could possibly find their way here!

But Raffles had not moved to Bogor only because he was busy at Rijswij or to safeguard the family health. With Batavia secure his urgent priority was to confirm the support for the British of the indigenous rulers of the Indies and two of the most important of them were at Yogjakarta and Solo in Central Java - much closer to Bogor than to Batavia.

'Without a Care' was a spacious official residence, with servants quarters, stables, rooms for clerical assistants and a separate block for the billeting of troops. Aside from his family, Mahmud and Abdul, Raffles had with him two aides de campe and the Company Secretary. He had met one of his aides, the Irishman, Thomas Travers, five years ago in Penang where he was an officer in the local garrison. Such was the shortage of British personnel that Travers also had to act as Mayor of Batavia and kept a permanent establishment there from which he commuted to Bogor as the need arose. Raffles had appointed as Secretary to the Council his old friend William Robinson, also from Penang, where he had been senior civil servant. The brilliant Charles Assey was Assistant Secretary. Aside from his second aide, Captain Robert Garnham, Raffles' key colleagues and those he felt he could most trust were people he had known since his first years in the Indies at Prince of Wales island. Bogor Resident Thomas McQuoid was also from Penang. With this slender personal staff Raffles planned to undertake the governance of the five million people of Java.

"I have no idea how you're going to accomplish it," Minto had said before returning to Fort William, Calcutta. "The Dutch East India Company's treasury is bankrupt, the whole administrative and economic machinery is on the point of collapse, around the country people are starving and the rulers could revolt at any moment."

"I don't know how you're going to manage it either," Olivia had told him, her brow creased with concern about his health. "You must try to delegate as much as you can otherwise all this work will make your poor head ache again."

Raffles knew that he was confronting the most formidable task he had ever faced, under conditions of utmost uncertainty and starved of resources. But he was a man of his time as much as he was a man of ambition. Fate beckoned to him and to him alone and he must answer the call. Perhaps the challenge of Java was the special purpose that he had dreamed about long ago in his mother's house in East London. It required administrative skills amounting to genius for one man to attempt to sort out the complex mess he had inherited. Raffles was not a proud man but, in his heart, he knew he had genius and it was this knowledge that enabled him to go forward boldly and optimistically even in the face of the most damning criticism or awesome difficulties.

He had decided to make Bogor his command centre. Although he was no military man, he saw himself as being at war, fighting fiercely against time and adversity to turn Java from a simmering hot bed of discontent and misery into a commonwealth of free and prosperous men who would one day be proud of their association with the justice, humanity and moderation of the British.

"We have rescued these people from tyranny and oppression," Raffles told Olivia. "Now it is my duty to lead them to self improvement."

While suffering from no pride in himself, Raffles was keenly proud to be an Englishman, a member of what he felt to be the greatest nation on earth at the time; a nation which alone was developing the thinking which could lift men and women everywhere from the dark pit of ignorance and poverty to the high peaks of enlightenment and prosperity.

"It is my mission", he told Olivia. "If I fail, my life will have failed."

In the quiet of many an evening and in the privacy of their bedroom, Olivia ran her fingers through Raffles' brown hair and massaged his aching brow whispering, as if to a child, "There, there, my dear. There, there."

'Without a Care' was swiftly turned into the nerve centre for all that Raffles must achieve. A large room was commandeered and clerks were brought up from Batavia and Weltevreden to help. Since he spoke fluent Malay and Javanese Raffles could work with many local people easily. He amazed those who came to know his frantic work habits by dictating letters to two people at a time. All day long every day he kept three clerks busy with his correspondence, often signing off an incredible two hundred letters in a single day. But the adrenaline flowed. He was happy doing what he wanted to do. He would have worked all day and all night if it would have guaranteed the achievement of his objectives. Throughout the day a tra-

ditional Javanese orchestra, the gamelan, created a soothing ambiance of sound, like the breeze gently tinkling the
hollow tubes of a wind chime.

His first act was to write to the rulers of
Yogjakarta and Solo and to dispatch new Residents there to
take over from the Ministers appointed by the Dutch. Even
from casual conversations with his many friends in Java he
knew that rulers throughout the island were daily weighing up their chances of once more becoming free of foreign
rule. This was something that the politics of the day could
not permit. If the British were not in Java someone else
would be and this someone else was more likely than not
to be an enemy of Britain.

On the other hand, he knew full well that the
Javanese had suffered terribly both under the colonial Dutch
and the French. Forced extractions of commodities, exorbi-
tant taxes farmed out to Chinese collectors and, finally, ten
thousand Javanese lives lost building the military works of
Marshal Daendels had left the rulers little, if any, reason to
feel well desposed toward Europeans. Some of the rulers
had even been imprisoned and put in the public stocks and
all had seen their prerogatives removed. Residents had been
appointed to their courts whom they were ordered to obey
"without variation." To proud men, this loss of face and
prestige was insupportable. Death itself would almost have
been preferable. Looking at the British the rulers asked themselves:

"Will these men behave any differently? Whatever they say, why should we trust them? And finally they
asked: "This is our country. Why should we have to bow
down before these foreigners at all?

Raffles knew all this but at the outset, before
he had time to bring about changes and improvements,
Raffles had no choice but to accept the Dutch administra-

tive structure in the Indies as he found it. He sent Colonel Alexander Adams as Resident to the royal court at Solo and John Crawford as Resident to the court at Yogjakarta. Charles Jackson he sent as Resident to Palembang in Sumatra, a major trading port and once the seat of the wealthy and powerful empire of Sriwidjaya. With him went Alexander Hare and Willem Wardenaar, a former member of the Dutch ruling Council of Batavia.

Pacing too and fro in his private study, lined with shelves crammed with books, manuscripts, weapons and specimens gathered for his scientific studies Raffles briefed his emissaries.

To all three new Residents he announced that the Dutch system of allowing their court representatives to gain their salaries through trade and commissions was not acceptable to the British. Instead they would be salaried officials, responsible directly to him. The three were told to dismiss their Dutch predecessors and in low key ways "feel out" the rulers as to what they expected from the British. Above all, he emphasized, they must be diplomatic.

"At Palembang," he told Jackson, "if the Sultan seems amenable, please try to see how we can get hold of the island of Bangka."

Even as he planned the permanent presence in Java and throughout the Indies of the British East India Company, Raffles could not be sure that after peace with Napoleon the Indies would not be handed back to the Dutch - especially Malacca. If so, British possession of the island of Bangka would be crucial to the free passage of British shipping through the Sunda Strait to China. Raffles realized that he must go himself to each of the strategic courts but first he must have intelligence, and not the sort brought by spies but direct impressions from people he knew he could trust.

While the emissaries were away Raffles commissioned a kind of Javanese Domesday study. Just as William the Conqueror had wanted to know all about Britain in 1066 so Raffles wanted to know all about Java. Not having enough staff of his own the task was given to three Dutchman, Rothenbuhler, Knops and van Pabst but reporting to Colonel Colin Mackenzie.

The journey from Bogor to either Yogjakarta or Solo could be undertaken relatively quickly and in a day or two Adams and Crawford had returned couriers.

Raffles was extremely alarmed at the news from the powerful kingdom of Yogja. The ruler deposed by Marshal Daendels had murdered the incumbent and recovered his throne. Crawford interpreted this act as hostile to the Company, which had several times mad it known through proclamations and letters that all arrangements and laws made by the Dutch must remain in force until changed or cancelled by the British. Crawford had even threatened the ruler with troops. Raffles fumed with exasperation.

"What in God's name is the man doing! I told him to tread on egg shells and he's threatening war!

Raffles knew and understood that the Javanese rulers would prefer freedom to foreign rule. But foreign rule had come to Java and it would not go away- except by force. And force was the thing he feared most. Under the command of Colonel Gillespie, Raffles still had 7,000 European and Indian troops on Java as well as frigates, transports and gun boats. Slightly less than two thirds of these were hardened and well equipped British troops but the population of Java was five million and the sultans could mobilize four or five times his force! No. War with the sultans was the very last thing he wanted to happen. There was no worrying news from Solo but Raffles always had it in mind that Solo and Yogjakarta had once been united. What if they buried their historical differences to combine against the British? The result could be catastrophe for the Company.

"I must go at once", he told his aides. "But to Solo first. All seems well there and if I can sign a treaty with the ruler of Solo first, at least I won't have to worry about the prospect of having to face two hostile rulers."

Speed was of the essence. With Thomas Travers, two clerks, two secretaries and the faithful young Abdul to look after his personal he set out from 'Without a Care', his carriage escorted by a small guard of Hussars which Colonel Gillespie had allocated him. They drove only as far as the port of Batavia where Raffles had invited Herman Muntinghe to accompany him to provide intelligence as well as to give continuity to his dealings with the rulers. From Batavia a frigate took them round the island of Java to Semarang, a short ride from Solo.

At Semarang Raffles collected a force commanded by Colonel Watson to provide him with the style befitting a Lieutenant Governor. Raffles knew that among the Javanese form and impression was everything. If he arrived in Solo, with only an aide and in travel stained clothes his cause would be lost. Nothing was more impressive than cavalry. The British horseman rode horses, not ponies and one horse was about twice the size of an Indies pony, with great strength and pounding hooves. The Indian cavalrymen looked particularly fierce with their luxurious, twirling whiskers and magnificent turbans. Whether European or Indian each cavalryman had a rifle slung across his back, two huge pistols on either side of his saddle and a sword or lance - swords for the Europeans, lances for the Indians. One horse and rider together rose as tall as two or three dismounted Javanese. Raffles also requested four field guns. Immediately on landing he dispatched a polite letter to the ruler of Solo informing him of his arrival. After a night's rest, soon after dawn next day, Raffles and his party set out. Raffles was mounted on a black charger supplied by Colonel Watson. European dragoons rode before him, next came the guns and after that Indian lancers, flags and pennants flying.

The king of Solo was known as the Susuhunan and word had spread to him fast that the English governor of Java was approaching. He sent some of his senior officials and detachments of cavalry to meet his guest as the state border and escort him to the kraton or palace. This was Raffles' first visit to a Javanese royal capital and, as he rode, he looked around with keen interest.

The city was surrounded by the incredible lush verdue of coconut groves, rice fields and fruit orchards. For several miles his cavalcade passed through tree shaded farming villages with little houses made with interlaced bamboo walls and atap or palm thatch roofs. Rivers and irrigation channels glittered in the early morning sun and the fields were full of working families, the young children all naked, the men in only a rolled up sarong and head covering and the women in the long sarongs. Many of the women's mouths were crimson from chewing betel nut. Any whom they met along the road shrank back at the approach of the column and squatted down in respect, all the time looking at the ground. Raffles meant them no harm but it was clear that they were mortally afraid, not only of the strange looking foreigners but also of their own Susuhunan's arrogant and heavily armed riders.

As they approached the suburbs of the city they passed by several colourful morning markets selling fruits, vegetables and meats from ramshackle looking stalls. At Raffles' instructions Colonel Watson led the British force slowly and with dignity through the narrow streets until they arrived at a large open field in front of some substantial buildings the roofs of which could be made out above high whitewashed brick walls.

In front of the walls a special pavilion had been erected before which many dignitaries were seated on the ground. Raffles guessed that the party seated on the raised platform were the Susuhunan and his principal officials. More native cavalry was drawn up on the flanks of the pavilion and a guard of infantry, armed with wavy daggers Raffles' knew were called krises stood behind and to the rulers' sides. Several thousand townspeople, dressed in colourful batik, had gathered to watch. Raffles and Colonel Watson noted that many of the men wore krises stuck into their waistbands.

With the arrival of Raffles' party the crowd was quiet. There was a look of tense anxiety on every face. Raffles dismounted and with Travers, Herman Muntinghe, Colonel Watson and two dragoons with drawn swords, allowed himself to be escorted through the ranks of seated spectators to the presence of the ruler. Though his mission was deadly serious Raffles did not allow himself to appear serious. He smiled affably and nodded to all whose eye he caught. As he arrived in front of the pavilion Raffles was startled by cannon fire from the kraton in the rear. The Susuhunan honoured Raffles with a salute of 19 guns, the number formerly fired for the Dutch Governor General of the Indies. The royal troops saluted.

Chairs had been provided in the pavilion. Raffles and his party sat to one side with the Susuhunan's leading officials on the other. The Susuhunan sat in the middle with his lesser officials seated cross legged on the floor behind and to the sides. Raffles led his delegation and sat in the first chair, close to the Susuhunan. Opposite sat the ruler's Prime Minister, heading his 'delegation'. Raffles noted that with each seated on a chair and more or less in a circle no-one took precedence over the other. Raffles looked at the Susuhunan and the Susuhunan looked at Raffles. Neither man had met and there were now only a few seconds for each to weigh up the other and to decide what might be possible and what might not. The Susuhunan greeted Raffles with a faint smile but no bow or even inclination of the head. Though he was studying Raffles closely and cataloguing in his mind every tiny nuance of the British leader's behaviour he gave no sign of it. Slender Javanese girls in tight intricately patterned sarongs fell to their knees in front of the VIPs, placing a cool drink and little sweet meats before each.

"Makan and minum", said the Susuhunan softly, waving to the refreshments and himself setting an example by sipping his drink.

Cleverly, he invited Raffles to speak first. While Raffles was not Javanese he was a politician and had noticed immediately that he had not been invited inside the palace and that while the Susuhunan had preserved the forms of respect by ordering a salute he had not shown any deference to Raffles in his personal demeanour. Most importantly he had not indicated any sharing of his power with Raffles by inviting him to sit next to him. Raffles realized that the Susuhunan was not afraid of him and had probably agreed to the meeting today only because it had been requested and because he had nothing to lose by listening to what Raffles had to say.

Raffles was no philosophical friend of the traditional rulers of the Indies. In private to Olivia he had often described them as "despots". He disapproved deeply of their arrogance and forced extractions from their subjects. However, they ruled a feudal society in which they enjoyed the love of people who saw whatever happened to them as their just and unavoidable lot. Fate had created ordinary people poor and stupid just as it had created the Susuhunan wise and great. He deserved to be their father and they deserved to be his children. Raffles knew he could count on no popular uprisings against the traditional rulers. He also knew that they tended to have large families producing many sons so that if one ruler was deposed another would swiftly take his place.

Matching the dignified reticence of the Susuhunan, Raffles, too, spoke in a quiet but confident and friendly manner, opening by telling the Susuhunan of the recent British defeat of the Franco-Dutch and reminding him delicately of British power. He hoped the Susuhunan could accept that British rule and sovereignty was now permanent and that the British East India Company should in all respects be regarded as the legitimate heirs to the Dutch East India Company, enjoying all its rights and privileges. The fact that Herman Muntinghe was with him signalled to the Susuhunan that the Dutch had already accepted the British hegemony and inheritance Raffles described.

Despite the presence of Muntinghe, Raffles went on to talk about the iniquitous, forced exactions and unfairness of the Dutch which he said the British hoped to rectify. Even as they spoke, he said, his headquarters staff were gathering all the information necessary to make a comprehensive review of Dutch policy in Java and throughout the Indies.

He assured the Susuhunan of his deep respect and regard for Javanese culture and traditions, including the position of His Highness. He promised the Susuhunan that as long as he was Lieutenant Governor of Java he would do everything in his power to make his life comfortable and trouble free. Mindful of both the Susuhunan's despotic power and the British East India Company's urgent need of revenue, Raffles sought the Susuhunan's permission to transfer the right to collect all duties from himself to the Company. But, so that the Susuhunan should suffer no loss, he proposed that the Company should pay him an adequate stipend in lieu.

When he finished speaking, Raffles looked carefully at the Susuhunan but in a kind and solicitous manner. He had no idea what the ruler's response would be and in the back of his mind was the disquieting remembrance that the Susuhunan had dispatched over a thousand men to support General Janssens in his last days! He hoped that the impression he had created was that the British were now the legitimate successors to the Dutch but that the Susuhunan could expect much better treatment by the officials of Leadenhall Street than he had received from those of Amsterdam and The Hague.

At the conclusion of his address Raffles made a request to Travers who signalled troopers to bring forward some of the boxes which Raffles had brought from Calcutta. All the while Raffles spoke the Susuhunan sat motionless, knees splayed under his rich sarong, palms of his hands resting on each thigh, his head upturned slightly to give his expressionless, almond shaped, eyes a look of haughty majesty beneath a black fez or pillbox hat. Raffles personally handed him one priceless gift after another and the Susuhunan smiled slightly and even seemed embarrassed as he passed them to aides. Herman Muntinghe studied his boots! Such gifts would not have been made by his Company! Finally, Raffles had brought with him a treaty, in English and Javanese, which he told the Susuhunan he hoped he would sign.

To Raffles, whatever was agreed that day was binding so long as the treaty remained in force. To the Susuhunan it might be binding or it might not. It depended on circumstances and whether these were favourable or not.

Listening to what the new Lieutenant Governor had to say the Susuhunan felt that there was no point in making any military challenge to a power that had just demonstrated its superior strength by defeating not only the Dutch but the French as well. A challenge might come later - or it might not. If there was a chance to regain sovereign control over his kingdom he would certainly take it but any steps toward self determination must depend on the risks involved. At the moment these seemed high. And after all, although a few trifling changes had been made, life was to go on much as it had before, except that now he was to be given an income by the new Company. Raffles seemed a likable man and had brought many presents of a kind impossible to find in Java. Clearly he attached importance to his friendship with the Susuhunan. At all times he had behaved and spoken with respect and the Susuhunan felt that Raffles was a man he could work with. But paper was, after all, only paper and he could see no disadvantage in signing whatever it was the Englishman wanted. Accordingly and without any questions or discussion the Susuhunan said: "Saya setuju (I agree) and the first of the treaties so critical to British rule in Java was signed.

More substantial refreshments were brought and, in the early afternoon, Raffles indicated that he must depart. As he was led through the seated ranks of court officials and local dignitaries, at the perimeter of the grass square in which the meeting had taken place, he caught sight of a European. He went up to him and shook hands. The young American introduced himself as Dr Thomas Horsfield, a naturalist. He told Raffles that he had lived in Java since 1800 and quickly described his researches. Raffles was already preparing his own "History of Java' and was highly interested in seeing more of Dr Horsfield.

"If you can come to Bogor come and see me",

he said with utmost cordiality.

After this brief exchange with Horsfield, Raffles' force returned the way they had come, slowly, affably, with dignity and feeling more secure than when they had arrived. Raffles was eager to complete the fifty kilometre journey to Yogjakarta before nightfall and once away from the environs of Solo the cavalry tried to maintain a gruelling pace. As they rode, their air was thick from the smoke of fires being used either to clear land or to burn off unwanted crop residues. The sound of gamelans tinkled seductively as they passed close to villages. Very soon the gigantic mass of Mount Merapi loomed to their right, smoke drifting lazily from the cone of the still active volcano.

Raffles had already sent Colonel Colin Mackenzie and a Captain Phillips from Semarang to restrain Crawford and ascertain the lie of the land. At Yogja's Fort Vredeburgh they reported that the Sultan was willing to meet Raffles and even to reach a satisfactory agreement. Against the background of his experience at Solo, Raffles slept well that night, perceiving little reason to worry. The main point which impressed him was that the Sultan wanted a settlement. With his arrival in Yogja Crawford was back under his immediate command and could be prevented from doing anything silly.

It was Christmas Day, 1811 and, for the first time in his married life, Raffles celebrated Christmas without Olivia. Not that it was much of a celebration. Cautious about what may transpire on the morrow, officers and men were moderate in extremis and after an ordinary supper they went to sleep early. Raffles could have slept in the Resident's house, a short distance away, in front of the main gate, but Gillespie convinced him to remain in the Fort. British personnel were unobtrusively called from the house to join them behind the thick protective walls.

Crawford had discharged his intention of moving troops into Yogja and, with Raffles' cavalry, almost 1,000 British troops slept enclosed by the fort's great stone walls that night, about eight hundred metres from the Sultan's fortified palace.

By daylight Raffles felt that the view of the kraton bore an uncanny resemblance to Solo. Between the fort and the palace was a large open space and, as at Solo, rooftops could be seen above a high whitewashed wall of enormous length. Before leaving for the palace Raffles requested that the entire garrison parade just outside the fortress walls, facing the kraton - infantry, cavalry, artillery, Europeans, Indian Sepoys. As he rode out of the gates the parade snapped to attention in salute. Raffles took with him an escort of about fifty mounted dragoons. Herman Muntinghe rode at his right with Travers on one side and John Crawford on the other.

The massive dragoons went first, their great horses forming up in front of the palace in two lines, huge hooves restlessly stomping the ground. As at Solo, courtiers came to meet Raffles and escort him into the presence of the ruler. But, this time, there was no temporary pavilion outside the walls. Instead, Raffles was taken up a flight of shallow but wide steps to an immense royal audience hall, an open pavilion with an intricate and brightly decorated roof supported on huge teak columns. The Golden Pavilion had wide, tree shaded, space on every side and thousands of the Sultan's soldiers were assembled in their shadow. To the eyes of Raffles and his party the royal troops looked angry and insolent above their black bristling mustaches. Raffles was painfully aware that only two years before Marshal Daendels had been obliged to use force to suppress a violent uprising here.

The Kingdom of Mataram, with its seat at

Yogjakarta, was the most powerful in Java. The Sultan's army made the Susuhunan's seem minuscule. His armed followers outnumbered Raffles party by ten thousand to one. While Crawford's suspicions that the Sultan's seizure of power was a deliberate insult to the British were probably not true his other suspicion that the Sultan wanted to regain his sovereignty probably was. Of all the kingdom's of Java Yogjakarta was the most fearlessly jealous of its sovereignty. But then, understandably, all the Indies rulers were at heart. To Raffles this was nothing new! The burning question was only whether the Sultan was willing to negotiate or whether he intended war. The meeting did not begin auspiciously. Immediately he approached the seats which had been arranged he could see that the chair intended for him was placed in a position obviously and greatly inferior to the Sultan's. He was being tested! The Sultan watched him as a cat watches a mouse. Would he accept the Sultan's sovereignty by taking the seat artfully prepared for him or would he challenge it? A courtier waved Raffles to sit down. Javanese guards armed with swords, krises and pikes stood along all four corners of the audience room. The scores of court officials seated on the floor were also heavily armed. Raffles knew that he could not let the Sultan force him to take the seat offered. On the other hand his knowledge of Javanese culture warned him that if he insulted the Sultan he could be killed. The room was still, the atmosphere tense. Thousands of pairs of resentful, dark eyes were fixed on him. Raffles stopped dead in his tracks and as he did so he heard the rasp of hundreds of daggers being slipped from their scabbards. Raffles did not refuse the chair but smiled broadly. Using his fluent Malay to maximum advantage he explained that it would be more companionable if he and the Sultan sat together, on the same level, side by side. There was a moment of terrifying silence. Then the Sultan agreed, the daggers were heard slipping back into their scabbards and the chairs were rearranged.

With the experience of Solo behind him Raffles felt strongly that as he delivered more of less the same speech he had given the Susuhunan, the Sultan, like the Susuhunan was trying to get the measure of him. Perhaps for the same reason as the Susuhunan the Sultan also agreed easily to all Raffles proposals and after cordial refreshments and the presentation of more of Raffles' gifts brought from India, a treaty was signed. Raffles was now formally master of all Java! He quit Yogja immediately, riding fast for Semarang where he took ship to Batavia. He arrived at 'Without a Care' on New Year's Day, 1812 - just in time to celebrate with Olivia and wipe any anxiety about his safety from her tired face.

But for Raffles the first day of the New Year brought no let up in the pressure. The news from Palembang was black.

A dispatch from Charles Jackson informed Raffles that all the Dutch at Palembang, including women and children had been killed by Sultan Badru'd-din. And the Sultan was quoted as having said:

"I am not like other native princes. I fear nobody and I shall listen to nobody."

Raffles threw down the dispatch with uncharacteristic vexation.

"They should not have murdered the Dutch", he fretted to Travers and Garnham. "Palembang is now under British protection and whatever my feelings of friendship to the Malays I can't let this pass. No British government would be worthy of the name to allow this man to go unpunished."

Raffles knew that Badru'd-din's capital lay up a long, winding and heavily defended river which would require a significant force to reach and overcome. Despite his new treaties with the rulers of Solo and Yogja he was concerned at the prospect of perhaps having to send a major part of his standing army and his ships. On the other hand, to show any weakness toward Palembang might be to court disaster from the rulers who had just sworn to him their loyalty but who could so easily retract it.

"Difficult, difficult," he muttered to himself as he paced his study.

It was not only the peace of the islands and the sovereignty of the company that was at stake. Badru'ddin had flatly refused any deal involving Bangka island.

"There's no choice. He must be dealt with."

Raffles summoned an emergency meeting of the Council which took place in the conference room of the City Hall, Batavia. As expected, the decision to move against Palembang was unanimous. The Dutch members of the Council were particularly enthusiastic! Colonel Gillespie was only too pleased to take personal command.

"The bayonet and the boot is all anybody understands East of Gibraltar", he growled, slamming his fist down onto the heavy table.

Four transports, two warships, a sloop, two of the Company's cruisers and two gun boats were ordered to prepare to make sail. A dozen companies of European and Indian infantry were marched north from Weltevreden and within a few days the invasion fleet was on its way the short distance to Palembang.

"We'll soon see who the Sultan listens to", Gillespie muttered to the world at large as the fleet left Batavia Roads.

Unfortunately, the winds of the Western Monsoon were now against the British and it took Gillespie a month to reach the Musli River on which Palembang was situated, fully eighty kilometres upstream. Gillespie was a hot tempered man, used to winning, and the Sultan's disdainful rejection of his initial overtures was not calculated to improve his patience. Gillespie had read the dispatches and heard the verbal reports of Sultan Badru'd-din and it took little to convince him that the "bayonet" was the only effective policy.

The fleet anchored for a week at Nanka Island where work gangs were put shore to build special boats for the trip up the winding Musli. From mid-section to stern, each boat had a bamboo awning to shelter the crews and fighting men from the burning sun. Each vessel could accommodate about fifty armed men. Floating platforms of bamboo were constructed for the field guns. The navy warships and troop transports had too much draught to be able to get over the mud bar across the entrance to the Musli River but, after two days work, all the smaller ships were safely floated over and the formidable, if mixed, fleet was ready to proceed.

As far as possible, the boats sailed in line abreast across the seven hundred metre wide river. Look out boats went first, followed by the lighter craft and gun platforms. The sloop, gun boats and cruisers brought up the rear. Gillespie received several messages from the Sultan in which he claimed innocently not to understand why the British task force was moving against him.

"As if," Gillespie observed sarcastically to his officers. "He's the butcher of Palembang yet he says that he can't understand why anyone should want to punish him!"

Getting up the Musli proved to be easier said than done as violent storms and rain and changing tides and water depths made their progress painfully slow. Eventually the war fleet was close enough to Palembang to run into potential serious resistance. The river ahead was blocked by an armed Arab ship, flanked by floating batteries, in turn flanked by heavily fortified shore batteries. Piles of wood, driven into the river, defended the approach to the armed prows.

Yet another messenger arrived from the Sultan offering to abandon the defensive boom across the river if Gillespie would proceed to Palembang alone to discuss matters with him face to face.

"For sure," smiled Gillespie, with even heavier sarcasm.

The messenger invited Gillespie to inspect the floating fortifications as a token of sincerity.

"Fine. Let's put him to the test," Gillespie said, ordering the units of his advance to move forward.

Predictably, almost the minute when the British boats moved toward the blockade they were turned back.

"That's no surprise", said Gillespie, recalling his boats. "Nothing a murderer like Badru'd-din says can be trusted.

Gillespie now sent a message but not a messenger of his own, to the Sultan.

He said that he intended proceeding forthwith to Palembang, despite all obstructions, and that, once there, everything would be made clear to the Sultan.

Without waiting for a reply Gillespie led a squadron of formidably manned light boats supported by gun launches and field artillery against the Arab ship, the floating batteries and the shore defences. The large dawn raiding party took the entire garrison by surprise and, incredibly, as the British soldiers and sailors overran the installations the enemy gunners melted away, either into the jungle or in small boats kept hidden for just such an eventuality.

During the afternoon and even on into the

evening the fleet clawed its way further upriver. Suddenly, out of the dense tropical darkness points of flickering light were spotted which quickly turned into huge fiery conflagrations.

"Fire rafts", was screamed from one boat to another.

The rafts were extremely dangerous, even to small craft, and if they floated in amongst the bigger ships and fired their rigging Gillespie knew that he could face disaster and defeat. Several of the rafts were strung together across the river and the heat was intense. Hot or not, the rafts had to be approached and driven to the shore and time and again the small boats darted in while tired tars with long poles fought to push them away. Even as the last of the rafts became safely ensnared in the river banks or drifted harmlessly downstream an Arab merchant arrived by canoe with urgent news.

"The city is being destroyed," My Lord, he yelled from the boat. Everything is being burnt, people are being killed and the Sultan has fled.

With characteristic daring, Gillespie decided to take a chance. The Arab could be baiting a trap yet both he and the news seemed probable and genuine enough. After all, the enemy had already abandoned their strong river defences before even one British soldier had set foot in them. Now that they were getting close to Palembang it might well be that the Sultan had decided upon a tactical retreat. He boarded the Arab's canoe with an interpreter, Captain Meares as an aide and seven grenadiers. Another ten grenadiers were told off to another canoe. Ordering the advance boats to make all speed behind them the canoes paddled toward Palembang. Long before they could see the houses of the town they knew that the Arab was right. Lurid flames lit up the night sky, the fired bamboo of the homes of the rich was exploding on every side like fire crackers, and frightened screams filled the air. Burning and screaming filled the city for almost ten kilometres along both banks of the river. Terrified shadowy crowds could be seen hurrying this way and that. The Sultan's followers were looting and burning the homes of all the foreign merchants and wealthy Chinese they could find.

At the fortified palace large numbers of armed Malays crowded the bank. Without hesitation Gillespie, his seven grenadiers, his two aides and two seamen stepped boldly ashore and pushed through the threatening throng. A Malay sidled up to the Colonel and Captain Meares saw one of the crowd pass him a double bladed knife.

"Watch out, Colonel," he cried.

Gillespie had seen the knife too and himself helped the grenadiers to seize the man and disarm him.

The scene at the palace was unbelievable. The floors and walls were covered in the blood of the Sultan's innocent and helpless victims, every room had been stripped of its valuables and, as the messenger had said, the Sultan had fled, loaded down with his ill gotten treasure. The nightly thunder storm now began to rage, dousing the fires but illuminating the city with shafts of terrifying lightening. Another ten grenadiers swiftly joined the Colonel and Gillespie ordered all entrances to the palace sealed in case of attack. He had taken possession of the Sultanate of Palembang with a force of less than twenty men and it was to be three hours more before the main party caught up.

Fortunately for him, with the Sultan fled and the palace abandoned, Badru'd-din's men were leaderless and undirected and quickly melted away into the darkness. On April 28, 1812 the British flag was hoisted over the palace. Gillespie and Raffles had heard only positive comments about Badru'd-din's brother and this meek and benign man,

Ahmad Najimu'd-din was therefore appointed Sultan. Bangka Island was ceded to the British together with nearby Biliton.

When the news of the victory reached Raffles at Bogor he was elated. By treaty or bayonet the Indies was his! Or was it?

Raffles had all along suspected that the treaties signed with the Susuhunan of Solo and the Sultan of Yogjakarta were worth very little and represented largely an effort by the rulers to buy time to consider their options in the light of the British conquest. Just as he had feared Solo and Yogjakarta combining he feared even more their combining while Gillespie and substantial forces were away in Sumatra.

From Solo, Adams reported that the Susuhunan was evasive and would not meet him. From Yogja, Crawford reported that the Sultan was more hostile than ever. Worse still, his Residents said that, in flagrant defiance of the treaty they had signed with Raffles, both men were secretly plotting the overthrow of the British regime. The rulers had choked at signing away their rights to yet another foreign power and from the moment Raffles returned to Bogor until now they had looked for his weaknesses and plotted his ousting. Now, with Gillespie and a large part of the army in Sumatra, troops were being mobilized. Raffles knew that time was running out. Could he afford to wait for Gillespie and the return of the army from Palembang? And, if he did not wait, could he be defeated by the combined forces of the rulers?

Gillespie had still not returned on May 23 and Raffles felt that if he waited longer there was a real danger that the Company and the British would be driven from Java. Quite apart from the British lives that would be lost, this was not a defeat he relished on his record. Prepared to wait no longer, he departed again for Semarang, this time taking Olivia with him. Raffles was not the kind of man to panic and he had every confidence in the few troops at his disposal. But he did think that Olivia would feel safer with him. Despite the tension and pressure of the situation, in Semarang, he hosted a ball to celebrate the birthday of King George III. The dancing was opened by Olivia and the Semarang Civil Commissioner, Hugh Hope, to a specially composed tune called 'The Fall Of Cornelis".

Raffles was no military man but, as Lieutenant Governor, he had the same powers as Gillespie to request the compliance and cooperation of military commanders. Calling a war council he explained the problem, listened to their advice, and took his decisions without an ounce of fear.

When the Javanese rulers learned that Raffles had arrived at Semarang with no additional forces they scoffed arrogantly and openly. However, the very next day after the ball, the Commander in Chief of all land Forces in the Indies arrived like a bolt from the blue in Semarang. Finding Raffles gone from Bogor, and learning of his intentions, Colonel Gillespie had ridden poste haste across the island, through dense forests and across range after range of mountains. The journey took several days and, at night, his pillow was his saddle, his mattress a pile of leaves. Gillespie came from a wealthy family and had chosen soldiering because he liked it. For him, there could be nothing better than another chance to ride to the attack! Covered in dust when he leapt from his horse at Semarang, Gillespie instantly reported to Raffles and heard what arrangements were planned. Without rest or even food he ordered the troops at Semarang to prepare for war!

Units were ordered to the vicinity of Solo to create fear in the Susuhunan's mind by giving the impression that an attack was imminent there. At the same time he sent Hugh Hope with a message to the Susuhunan telling him that if he sued for peace the Lieutenant Governor might be prepared to suspend the attack. Hope was also instructed to demand all those proved to have been conspiring with the Sultan of Yogjakarta for the overthrow of the British. Once again Raffles' luck held. Threatened with force, and fearing even for his own life, the Susuhunan agreed. Moreover he agreed to pay the British an indemnity of $200,000 and to reduce the size of his well armed so-called bodyguard. He ceded a number of territories demanded by Raffles and agreed to cede any others requested. And he accepted fully and in full the terms of the treaty he had signed before.

Whether all this was genuine or not Raffles had no means of knowing but at least it meant that the Susuhunan would not send his guards and militia to support Yogjakarta. Raffles was extremely relieved. He told Olivia:

"I'm so glad we didn't have to fight. I hope very much that we won't have to shed blood in Yogjakarta either. I don't want to harm these people. I want to help them."

Whatever his private feelings, prudence directed that Raffles now turn his attention immediately to Yogjakarta. He and Gillespie galloped away from Semarang with three detachments of Indian light infantry, artillery and two full troops of dragoons. Lieutenant Colonel, Alexander McLeod was ordered to follow at top speed with a large force of additional troops and more artillery. More than five hundred guns had been captured from the French at Weltevreden and Cornelis so there was no shortage of weaponry.

Gillespie and Raffles found the city of

Yogjakarta seething with military activity, with large bodies of cavalry and irregular troops in front of the kraton and round about. Immediately Raffles' arrived, the Sultan positioned a force in their rear to cut them off from reinforcements. The troops set to work destroying bridges and tearing up roads so as to put every obstacle in the way of McLeod's advance. A fifty strong reconnaissance patrol of dragoons led by Gillespie and Crawford took casualties and had difficulty even in regaining the fort!

"There may be too many of them," Gillespie told Raffles. "I'd feel a lot better if McLeod was here."

Gellespie called for a volunteer to ride through the enemy lines and warn Colonel McLeod to make more haste!

With the fort surrounded, the Sultan sent a note demanding the unconditional surrender of the British force! Never had Raffles faced darker days!

Gillespie was defiant. "No man under my command will ever surrender," he said.

In front of the main entrance to the palace a double row of cannon had now been placed with flanking batteries to left and right. The British estimated the perimeter wall at about five kilometres in length, bristling with cannon and with about 11,000 troops inside. Gillespie estimated that there were forces outside the kraton numbering up to another six thousand men. And, from the surrounding suburbs and villages the Sultan could call on a further hundred thousand armed militia. Gillespie and Raffles were huddled in the fort in front of this mighty host with a mere twelve hundred men! Even though his soldiers were armed mostly with sling-shots, pikes, swords and daggers, of course, the Sultan scoffed!

Events moved fast. Throughout the day of their arrival the Sultan's forces maintained a periodic bombardment of the fort, setting fire to several buildings and killing a number of men. Gillespie responded by constantly sending out patrols here and there to keep the enemy forces guessing and in play. Towards evening the messenger he had asked to ride to McLeod was dumped, dead, at the fort gates. The British commanders were not afraid but they knew that they had to think quickly and not make any mistake. One false step and the Sultan's hordes would be upon them.

"We'll have to send a force to McLeod," said Gillespie. It's a small risk because I doubt that they will attack us inside the fort. Anyway, it'll be dark soon."

Gillespie dispatched a strong force of dragoons to hack their way, swords in hand, to link up with the reinforcements. With the fall of night he ordered all his patrols into the fort so as to give the Sultan the impression that no further attack was intended. Lest the Sultan's forces try to rest however, the British cannon kept up a furious bombardment until about three o'clock in the morning when, at last silence descended, lulling the enemy to sleep.

"The sleep of death, I hope", said Gillespie as he looked enquiringly toward the enemy positions.

Gillespie was calculating that his dragoons would get through where the lone messenger had failed. it was one thing to pull a single rider from his horse and kill him and quite another to go up against a heavily armed body or huge dragoons on their enormous and powerful horses. And he suspected that the Sultan now thought that, having sent for reinforcements, they were desperate and in no situation to mount any attack against such overwhelming forces. The fact that all the British patrols had been recalled seemed to confirm his suspicions. It was true that Fort Vredeburgh was noisy with cannon fire but the Sultan was wily enough to realize that the British were just trying to unsettle him.

"It is the snarling of a toothless tiger," he told his chiefs.

Inside the fort, no-one was sleeping. Could he have seen, the Sultan would have been amazed to see every man and boy of the small British force turned out for battle! Every man knew that their lives depended on winning. Tomorrow they might be dead or prisoners! When Gillespie gave the order to attack, at about four o'clock in the morning, his heavily armed troops stormed out of the relative safety of the stone fortress not like toothless tigers but like ravenous tigers who had smelt the blood of the kill!

Lieutenant Colonel Dewar led a column to the north gate at the rear of the palace. Major Grant led his troops to the south gate. Lieutenant Colonel Watson led his Sepoys and grenadiers directly into the heavily defended main gate. The palace was surrounded on all sides by a deep ditch which the attackers crossed in complete silence. The palace walls had to be taken by escalade and so swift was the British approach that the troops had what ladders they had been able to make against the palace walls before they were spotted. In places where there were no ladders the soldiers stood upon one another's shoulders.

Once the alarm was raised a hail of grape swept through the invaders. British sharpshooters returned a withering fire to the embrasures making it nigh impossible for the enemy to stay there long. Inside the palace all was pandemonium as the sleepy defenders ran hither and thither in the darkness, men without their weapons and units bereft of their commanders. Meanwhile the grenadiers were up and over the walls and along the rampart to the point where they could open the main gate and let in Colonel Watson's column. The Javanese fought fiercely, but, surprised, and with their inferior weaponry they could not stop the British troops running all along the perimeter wall to open the north gate for Lieutenant Colonel Dewar. The British made no attempt to hold ground because their force was too small. Instead, three compact columns of British troops marauded inside the palace, turning captured royal cannons on the Sultan's own troops with such effect that they were savagely dispersed. Outside the palace, Gillespie's dragoons cut off the retreat of many and eventually captured the Sultan himself. Unfortunately, the Colonel was wounded in the arm by a blunderbuss fired from the milling crowd.

In less than three hours the Sultan's great host had been defeated and in less than three days the Sultan was sent as a prisoner to Prince of Wales Island. His son, Prince Hamengkubuana, agreed to accept the throne in his father's place. He also agreed to honour the treaty his father had signed earlier. The victory was marked by a grand parade of all the British troops, who also stood witness to the installation of the new Sultan. Raffles and Gillespie had never been closer or more proud. They stood together and, for once breaking with stiff propriety, raised their hats in joyful salute to the courageous fighters.

"It was death or victory, my friend", Gillespie smiled at Raffles. "Death or victory."

Upon his return to Bogor, Raffles opened a letter from London with trembling fingers. It bore a royal seal and was from the Prince of Wales, the Prince Regent, the man who would be King of England after the death of George 111. The letter was not to Raffles but a copy of one sent to Lieutenant General Auchmuty. It conveyed thanks "in the strongest terms" for the distinguished gallantry and spirit" displayed by the British Army during the conquest of Java and authorized that medals be struck and presented to the most outstanding combatants.

Raffles wished that there could have been something for him, something which at least recognized his immense role in the undertaking to push the French out of Java and to bring economic freedom and prosperity to the Indies. But he could not complain. Lord Minto had conceived the invasion plan, not him. At that time, little did he know that Minto had also received no thanks. Meanwhile, the unstinted praise from the Prince Regent at least told him that what had been achieved in Java was a job well done and led him to dream about achievements and honours yet to come.

CHAPTER EIGHT

Neither Raffles nor Gillespie were under any illusion that the Company's treaties with the Indies rulers had much hope of being maintained without force. Raffles would have preferred agreements with the rulers reached through amicable and peaceful negotiations but he could not afford to ignore the politics of the day. If the rulers could not be induced to take the British side the danger that had to be averted at all costs was that they would themselves become enemies or support enemies of Britain's trading interests. In two kingdoms Raffles and Gillespie had placed their own nominees on the throne but in Palembang, Sultan Badru'd-din was still on the loose, and at Solo both felt that no steadfast reliance could be placed on the ruler to keep his word.

"There's still no time to lose", Raffles told the Council. "We have to show the rulers and their people that we want to help them. It's essential that we reform the set up here as fast as we can."

The pressing need to introduce reforms forced Raffles to work harder than ever. Given the tropical climate, which never seemed to bother Raffles as it harassed other Europeans, observers were amazed at his punishing schedule, maintained from early in the morning until late at night.

Of necessity, all decisions began and ended at his desk and there were few in Batavia who were not impressed by his energy.

"Name me one other country as large as Java being basically run by one man," his aide, Travers, was often heard to say proudly during mess discussions with colleagues.

A storm of new rules and regulations poured from Raffles' Secretariat.

His experience in coming to terms with the native rulers highlighted to Raffles the need for the comprehensive legal system, binding upon all, promised by Lord Minto in the proclamation he made at the time of the conquest of Batavia. He set up a Supreme Court of Justice with Herman Muntinghe as President and he established a Board of Magistrates headed by Jacob Cranssen. Knowing how deeply the traditional rulers resented their humiliation by the Dutch, local district governors, called Regents, had their powers restored and augmented to enable them to work in concert with British Residents in operating regional and circuit courts and police. Lands and income sufficient for their needs were also restored to them so that they could once again enjoy the dignity their people expected. Other courts were established in Semarang and Surabaya. A police force suddenly appeared on city streets to help ensure that all obeyed the new courts and the changing laws of the land.

The war with France had totally disrupted Java's trade, which the Dutch had financed largely from the export of spices. The Malukus, where the spices grew, had also fallen into British hands but the post reported directly to Calcutta and its valuable spice cargoes all bypassed Batavia. Raffles wrote urgently to Minto to ask permission to have these cargoes brought to Batavia from where he could send rice in return, thus enabling Java to enjoy the proceeds of the lucrative spice sales in India. Without waiting for a reply he unilaterally abolished the duty on rice to the Malukus and encouraged native prows to take Java rice there in exchange for spices. While opening Batavia to all comers he was forced to impose duties to finance his government and a new Customs House was established to collect them.

Slavery was an issue about which Raffles felt very strongly. While he had no direct experience of it, because his father had been in the West India trade, Raffles had heard many stories about the treatment of black slaves snatched from Africa and forced to work in the colonies of America. Slavery worried him immensely. Even though he realized that there were no Javanese slaves, he felt diminished at the sight of people serving him on their knees. He wanted to blurt out to them to "For Heavens sake get up". He believed passionately that slavery was morally indefensible, personally offensive and, also, against the new economic doctrines of leaders like Adam Smith. Smith argued, and Raffles agreed with him, that it would be to the benefit of every nation for the people to be free, fully developed and industrious, trading together around the world for mutual gain. He knew that the Directors of the British East India Company were still of the old school and didn't give a tinker's cuss about slavery but he was determined that, under his stewardship, something should be done in Java.

"Slavery", he wrote to Minto, "is repugnant to every principle of enlightened administration."

But, finding a remedy did not seem as easy as Raffles hoped. Slaves were shipped to Java from Bali and islands to the east, such as, Sulawesi and Timor, for sale mainly to Dutch colonialists. Pending investigation, and with his father's stories in his mind, Raffles feared that the sale might generate such substantial revenue for the eastern chiefs that they would be reluctant to forego it. He guessed that to outlaw slavery completely could only be achieved by the use of force and not only were his forces limited but he knew the Directors in London would never sanction payment of the costs.

Raffles also discovered that, by and large, slaves were not harshly treated and received food, clothing and shelter from their masters. Raffles described slavery in the East Indies to Minto as "regulated domestic servitude rather than the detestable and inhuman system practiced out of Africa. Pretty girls, especially, were encouraged to dance and entertain and could thus live in conditions of relative wealth. When taking soundings among slaves employed by the government to ascertain their reaction to being given their freedom he found that none would find it economically worthwhile to accept it!

In 1807, the British had outlawed trading in slaves between Africa and the Caribbean and while Raffles would have liked to immediately do the same thing in Java, not yet understanding the political repercussions, his first step was to make slave trading more difficult by doubling the duty payable at destination and to fix the age at which a person could be sold into slavery as fourteen.

Then, as a matter of urgency, he investigated the identities of the slave traders and the importance of the revenue to the eastern chiefs. To his relief and delight he found that the eastern chiefs were hardly interested in profits from slavery and that, in fact, the trade was almost entirely in the hands of Europeans. By the close of 1812, Raffles was able to bring to reality one of his greatest gifts to humanity in the Indies. He prohibited the importation of slaves into Java or into any of its dependencies under his control. And he insisted that existing slaves should enjoy the fullest human rights - they should be transferred only with their own consent, punishment should be codified and limited, wrongs to a slave were civil wrongs, no slaves could be used outside the home unless they were paid a full wage and, finally, slaves could purchase property and, if they wished, their freedom!

'Before I leave Java I want to emancipate every man, and woman the Indies", Raffles told the governing Council. "I don't want another child born into this world who is not free."

The Lieutenant Governor's next target was the forced services imposed by the native rulers and he instructed Muntinghe to look into the reaction of the rulers to outlawing these services.

Raffles was the closest thing to a democrat his age could produce and while dreams of universal emancipation raced through his mind so also did such important corollaries as universal freedom to own land and property. Javanese society was feudal and Raffles front line, European, modernist thinking burst upon it like a bomb shell. Not a Dutchman in Java agreed that he could dismantle feudalism overnight or even soon. And many an Englishman agreed. Yet private ownership of land and property by free people was no dream to Raffles. He wanted it and he wanted it now. He was prepared to work 'till he dropped to achieve it. He had a dream and he was also a missionary, a man of Jesuit-like will and determination to put it into practice. His biggest fear was that he wouldn't have time to do all the things he wanted before the Dutch returned and everything carried on the way it was.

Forced services were not only unjust but disturbed production on the land. And not only interrupted production but cut directly across a concept which Raffles held to be as important as abolishing slavery. How could a man be genuinely free if he was obliged to give unpaid labour whenever it was requested, by the Dutch colonialists or by their feudal rulers. And how could a man be genuinely free unless he owned the land he worked and enjoyed the profits of his labour.

By the winter of 1812, with Napoleon's grand army streaming homeward through the murderous snows of Russia, Raffles was more afraid than ever that peace with France was close and that his time would run out. Now, every minute of his waking day was lived at fever pace. Countless meetings had to be attended, more research commissioned, reports to be studied, policies agreed, regulations framed. He had so few competent and reliable Europeans to help him that some officers held two or even three portfolios.

In addition to running the government, Raffles also had two ferocious battles on his hands. The priority was to placate local people by rapidly introducing reforms from which they would benefit. The second was to continue to work with Lord Minto to convince an ever sceptical London that the Indies were worth keeping - whatever happened after peace with France. Meanwhile, the uncertainty over British tenure in the Indies cast a shadow over the permanence of all his policies and, Raffles was sure, blunted their efficacy. There was also another ramification which he sensed was beginning to carry more weight with Colonel Gillespie. If peace was made with France but Britain retained the Indies as a British colony it was usual for such colonies to have military commanders. What then would be the role of Raffles? Gillespie drew strength from this knowledge while the community at large was confused. Should they back Raffles or Gillespie? And if the British handed the Indies back to the Dutch it wouldn't matter anyway!

Raffles was thrilled beyond words with all that

he was able to do and sent detailed dispatches to Calcutta and London setting out his policies and actions in comprehensive detail. Except in the case of opium, upon which the revenues of India substantially depended, Lord Minto was behind him all the way.

Despite the fulsome praise of the Prince Regent, far from being pleased, Leadenhall Street was horrified that Minto had so far exceeded his instructions as to set up an administrative establishment in Java. His brief had been only to clear out the French and withdraw. But with no end in sight to the war with France and a threat to the Company's trading vessels therefore still latent, with extreme reluctance, the Directors agreed that an establishment had to be maintained until such times as Java could be handed back to the Dutch. They insisted that it should be run at the very least cost and preferably from funds generated in Java. Unlike Minto and Raffles, none of these conservative men had a vision of Java with a Company presence in perpetuity; none understood the vast potential of the Indies; all were concerned only to spend the least amount of money as caretakers of the Indies and to get out as soon as was politically possible.

Buoyed by confidence in the likely success of his economic reforms - boosted still further by thousands of Chinese immigrants pouring into Batavia to take advantage of the myriad new opportunities - Raffles wrote optimistically to London that he could foresee no obstacle to Java being financially self supporting. Though the directors were sceptical, unless and until proved wrong, they were pleased to have the assurance of Raffles' forecasts. After only three months in Java, Raffles had felt confident enough to predict to Calcutta that Java could henceforth support itself.

But then had come the wars with Palembang

and Yogjakarta and, instead of being able to repatriate majority of the troops of the invasion fleet, necessity decreed that these be detained. Sensing that early promises might not be met, Lord Minto told London that he doubted that Java could be profitable in the first year. He argued that the security gained for the Company's ships and trade routes through the conquest of Java should be ranked at least as important as profitability, perhaps more so. With no profits in hand and regular reports from Raffles about schemes so extensive as to amount to the total remolding of government and society in Java Leadenhall Street quickly attacked Raffles for recklessness.

Raffles was utterly convinced that a healthy and profitable economy could be created in Java. His free trade policies had already resulted in Batavia Roads being busier than ever with trading ships from throughout the islands, Vietnam, Thailand and China. Batavia was a hive of business activity and the merchant community were prospering as never before. Public breakfasts, balls, dinners and races followed each other in daily succession.

He had freed trade and created revenue through duties. What he needed now was revenue from the land.

Raffles unveiled a revolutionary land policy which would transfer ownership of all land, other than portions specifically reserved for them, from the native rulers to the British East India Company. With strict respect for traditional rights of cultivation among the people, all land would be available for lease from the government and, with the exception of certain coffee plantations, any crop could be grown, excluding the poppy, which Raffles abhorred. Not only was the land policy revolutionary but so also was the complete dismantling of the Dutch system of monopolies which forced farmers to grow only approved crops.

The Company earned huge profits from the sale of opium but, despite the risk to his career, Raffles argued with the Directors for months to limit opium imports into Java. To satisfy the need for revenue among merchants in London and Calcutta he agreed to keep the price high.

"Opium rots a man's very fibre" he said sternly to the Council in Batavia, to Minto in Calcutta and to the Directors in London.

"While I am Lieutenant Governor only the least amounts of this pernicious and evil drug will be sold here."

Raffles won his point but the Directors were not pleased at being cheated of what they thought would be a handsome revenue from the Indies.

Under the new system of land ownership government would obtain income from a capitation tax with payment accepted in cash or kind. Government collectors would be appointed to facilitate payment. The scheme was aimed only at the Javanese, to turn them into independent cultivators like England's Yeoman. Foreigners were not allowed to rent land although existing ownership would be respected. Pilot schemes in Central Java, close to Mount Merapi, on land ceded by the Sultan of Yogjakarta, were put in hand forthwith. Within less than a year a commentator was writing:

"I beheld old watercourses under repair and many fields under irrigation for the purpose of receiving seed, while the hoe wielded by the brawny arm of industry rooted out noxious weeds and briars from the fertile soil of the wilderness; the clouds of smoke which obscured the sky showed that the impenetrable thicket must recede from its ancient limits and give way to luxurious crops. These are the visible marks of increasing industry cherished by the dawn of liberty rising on the debasing feudal system of oppression and tyranny."

Raffles could not have put it better himself. He was ecstatic about his experiments and fidgety to extend the land scheme to all Java. In this mood he wrote to the Board of Directors in London:

" Whatever must be the eventual fate of Java, whether it is decided that the Colony be attached to the Company's possessions, transferred to the Crown or even given up at a peace to a foreign power (which God forbid), the inhabitants of Java will have the happiness to bless the day which placed them under such a system of Government."

But these gargantuan reforms took time and, meanwhile, not only were revenues insufficient but inflation threatened the solvency of the entire economy.

With characteristic speed and boldness, Raffles took the decision that some of the lands newly acquired by government must be sold to raise money. He sensed that buyers might be reluctant because of the fear that if the Dutch returned the whole new land ownership scheme would be rescinded. To give encouragement and boost prices he bought a parcel of land himself. Such was the confidence of the market that within a month all of the territory's devaluing paper money had been redeemed and the treasury was again solvent.

Raffles was delighted with the result and told the Company so. Java had been on the brink of financial ruin and he had been obliged to act fast. Lord Minto acknowledged this but was forced to inform Raffles of the displeasure of merchants in India that there had been no time for them to bid. When he heard this, Raffles regarded it as a trifling criticism bearing in mind the result obtained. He was equally delighted with his land policy which, in the pilot areas, had already seen rents double. The prospects seemed better than ever. Out of adversity victory was being born before his very eyes. As usual Leadenhall Street took exactly the opposite view and criticized him heavily for undertaking anything as monumental as the total reform of land ownership and also for his precipitate land sales which they felt the Dutch would disapprove.

The Directors irritated Raffles to distraction.

"They accept that there is no choice for us but to be here but they don't want to pay", he complained privately to Olivia "If I try to raise money they criticize me. If I try to introduce a little humanitarianism and decency into this society they say it's not my business."

"My poor darling. They are short sighted, stupid men. Whether they approve or not at least you can be proud that everything you are doing is wise and well meant."

"Yes, but if they disapprove it may all be for nothing. The nub of the whole thing is that despite everything they don't want Java and they don't want the Indies."

"You must keep trying to convince them. All they understand is money. If you can make them a profit they'll soon come round to your way of thinking."

"I can. I know I can. But it takes time. I must have time."

Busy though he was with the governance of Java, Raffles wore himself out writing long descriptions, explanations and exhortations to Lord Minto in Calcutta and direct to Leadenhall Street, all with the single intent of showing the basis for his optimism, which he was convinced, time would thoroughly vindicate.

To secure backing for his reforms from the community at large Raffles was as active socially as he was officially.

At social gatherings Olivia was an important

partner, obtaining information he might otherwise not have known and enabling him to convey messages perhaps inappropriate for himself. Of course, it was Olivia who bore the burden of the very extensive preparations state and private entertaining involved and with the management of a large house and a busy social programme she felt her life to be almost as hectic as his.

Olivia had been very tired during the first months of landing in Batavia but the fresher air at 'Without a Care' had been good for her and her old spirits had returned. Although the social round was not nearly as arduous as it had been at 'Runnymede', at Malacca or at Rijswij, not a week passed without at least a formal dinner. Occasionally there were card games or theatricals. Sometimes the guests were important or interesting visitors, sometimes members of the English or Dutch communities, sometimes Chinese, Indian or Arab businessmen and more occasionally local dignitaries. As at the Ramsay's home in London, at Bogor, conversations ranged from health and climate to affairs of state, politics and scientific matters.

Dr Horsfield was an early visitor, after his chance meeting with Raffles in Solo, and Raffles thought so highly of his studies that he provided him with a Company allowance to ensure that he could continue. After this Horsfield was a regular visitor to the house in the hills where he and Raffles spent hours together poring over maps, reports and specimens.

Raffles had also been fortunate that his Chief Engineer, Colonel Colin MacKenzie, had an unquenchable interest in curiosities and antiquities. Raffles encouraged MacKenzie to record everything of historical note in Java and Mackenzie and his Indian assistants set too with a will.

To carry forward the scientific work of the community as a whole, Raffles breathed new life and dynamism into the moribund Batavia Asiatic Society, which now commenced regular meetings culminating in decisions and projects. The Society had been the first of its kind established in the Far East with a distinguished membership and record of achievement. But as a result of quarrels with the Dutch authorities and the impact of the war with Napoleon it had fallen on hard times.

One of Raffles' and Olivia's few genuine relaxations at Bogor were the walks and rides they took through the surrounding countryside. There was not the interesting domestic architecture they had enjoyed around Malacca but they found the simple and peaceful rural life of the Preanger fascinating in its own way. While the country around Malacca had been flat and hot, in the mountains around Bogor the climate was by turns hot and cool and every night a thunderous storm deluged it with life giving water.

"It's so fertile here that even if I planted my walking stick I think it would grow", Raffles joked.

Wherever they went they saw literally hundreds of strange and exotic trees and plants.

"We must find out all about these plants," he said one day, tapping a huge frond with his walking cane. "We have plenty of land around us so I think I shall establish a garden for research and experimentation. Whose knows, maybe the Company can make money exporting some of these plants or their produce."

"There could be something as valuable as the clove or the nutmeg under our very noses yet we don't know about it," said Olivia.

Raffles hated thought that was not followed by action. The very next day he instructed Dr William Hunter to establish a botanical garden and began putting it abroad that he welcomed receiving a specimen of every kind of tree and plant. Hunter was Superintending Surgeon of Java. As at Malacca, there was soon a constant stream of people bringing plants for the apparently eccentric Englishman's garden.

Raffles was no more a scientist than he was a military man, yet he had the thorough and systematic approach of the scientist and was so fascinated by everything he saw in his new land that he wanted to at once probe it and catalogue it.

Not only did Olivia play the fullest part in Raffles' hectic social life as a delightful and informed hostess but also as a trend setter in fashion, which the English felt had seriously deteriorated among Dutch Batavians. Many of the so-called Dutch inhabitants of Batavia were not really Dutch at all, having either been born in the Indies or being Eurasian. The population of the offspring of mixed marriages was large and the wives and daughters of these families had adopted Indies dress. By her example, Olivia changed all that and very soon these ladies arrived at functions in English style apparel.

Because of the long war with France very few new Dutch immigrants had settled in Batavia and this not only distanced the community from the manners and styles of Europe but also accounted for some of the weakness of the Franco-Dutch regime when the British arrived. A significant number of the old regime's troops and servants were of the worst kind and the venality even of merchants and farmers was well known. If they wanted something they just bribed someone and usually got what they wanted.

Olivia's unceasing work to support Raffles in all that he did, plus her extraordinary warmth and charm, which broke the ice with strangers so quickly and rapidly, endeared her to all who met her gave her a position in the colonial community in which she was greatly admired and respected. She was flattered beyond words when, at a dinner Raffles had arranged to celebrate their seventh wedding anniversary, Herman Muntinghe rose from among their family and close friends to propose the toast:

"To the First Lady of Batavia".

Realizing the importance of enabling the community to mix together, get to know one another and exchange views, Raffles allocated funds for the completion of a building begun by the Marshal Daendels at Weltevreden - the Harmonie Club. The Club was open day and night and within a few months became the very heart and soul of Batavian social life. And realizing that not all news could be passed by word of mouth he launched the 'Java Government Gazette' so that the community would at least have a reliable and timely source of official news.

Raffles' administration had been in place for only two years but its activities seemed equal to a century of those of its predecessors.

"If only they allow me enough time Java can be the richest island in the Indies," Raffles repeated over and over to Olivia with frustration.

Despite constant sniping from Leadenhall Street and the pessimism he deep down felt about the Company remaining in Java, Raffles was heartened by the news that the Sultan of Banjermasin, in Borneo, agreed that the Company should inherit all the privileges previously enjoyed by the Dutch, thus extending the Company's sphere of control from Java to Borneo. Alexander Hare had now returned from Palembang so he dispatched him to Banjermasin as the new Resident.

Piracy was the scourge of honest traders throughout the Indies and he dispatched ships to try to root and destroy some of the worst nests while at the same time supporting local rulers in efforts of their own.

Leadenhall Street's constant nagging to cut costs was in his mind night and day. He had even received an unusually cold note from the Secretariat in Calcutta about it.

"We have observed with much regret that your drafts upon this Presidency have been very considerable (Raffles had previously drawn cash from Fort William to enable him to get set up) although the estimates and explanations received from you gave us recent to expect that, far from requiring aid from resources of India, a very large surplus revenue would be realized by your Government."

When he received this note Raffles sat behind his desk for a long time staring vacantly into space. It depressed him and distressed him. The letter made him seem a liar and an incompetent yet he knew himself to be neither. If he had not painted a prospect of riches from the Indies Leadenhall Street would not have supported him as far as it had. But it took time. Riches were only beginning to be generated by his reforms yet the Company not only already had its hand out but was thumping the table for payment!

The words "profit, profit, profit" and "costs, costs, costs", rang in his ears night and day and turned his sleep from rest into a nightmare of restless tossing and turning.

After a lot of thought, Raffles saw a way of at least cutting costs, pending the realization of the expected profits. With peace now established in the Indies it was possible that he could bow to the remorseless pressure from Leadenhall Street by taking steps to reduce troop levels. The troops were expensive and if most of them could be safely repatriated costs would come tumbling down overnight. Lord Minto was under equally heavy pressure from London and, like Raffles, felt that anything that could be done to appease the Directors should be done.

Accordingly, Raffles officially relayed to Colonel Gillespie that he had decided to agree to headquarters' repeated demands for troop reductions. After all that they had gone through together Gillespie's response stunned Raffles and established their relationship on a course which greatly added to his already immense burdens. Suddenly, while he was struggling to balance the interests of the Company, the Dutch and the Indies' rulers, fighting to introduce his social and economic reforms, striving might and mane to convince London that it should hang onto Java, worrying about the island being handed back to the Dutch and even beginning to be anxious about his own future, in Gillespie he suddenly discovered, not a friend, but an implacable enemy!

"I am the commander of the troops", he told Raffles with anger and arrogance. "It is up to me to say whether and when it is safe to reduce troop levels."

The conflict between Raffles as a civilian and Gillespie as a military man, under circumstances where it was normal for a military man to be in charge, now burst into the open.

Gillespie's response to Raffles' proposal that troop levels should be reduced, primarily by repatriating European units such as the guards, dragoons and horse artillery, was a towering rage that an "upstart clerk" should have the temerity and cheek to think he could give orders to the military!

"Who does the man think he is", he choked to brother officers.

Generally speaking, the military were a law unto themselves and Gillespie's reaction reflected this. He had been equally choked at Raffles' appointment as Lieutenant Governor, as he thought, over his head. But now, for Raffles to actually intervene in military matters was the last straw! Minto had given Raffles the power to do so but in attempting to exercise it Raffles now found himself up against an intractable foe. His suggestion had been received as if it was an enemy attack. Worse still, with no decision yet from the British Government as to whether Java would be made a Crown Colony, governed by a military man, Gillespie suspected that Raffles was maneuvering to slash his powers and make the confirmation of his own appointment the more certain. If there were few troops and no threats to security Raffles could argue that there was no need for a military governor!

It was true that Raffles had been obliged to manoeuver but by no means in order to reduce Gillespie's powers. Time and again he had to mollify members of the Dutch community in the face of high handed and unreasonable behaviour by Gillespie - in whose mind all Dutch were sworn enemies deserving to be treated as such. Gillespie's attitude made Raffles' operation of his Anglo-Dutch coalition very difficult indeed.

Gillespie's military arguments were, in fact, strong and had it not been for the determination of the East India Company to save every penny Raffles might never have proposed troop reductions in the first place.

"The garrison is already small", said Gillespie. "We don't want to run the risk of losing what has been so recently won at a cost of over 600 British lives.

"And remember, my friend, the strength or weakness of the civil government in Java is a direct reflection of the strength or weakness of the armed forces. If we are weak, you are weak!"

The Colonel allowed himself the one luxury that poor Raffles could not - he totally ignored the financial aspects of keeping so many troops in Java and instead chose to look only at military considerations.

Raffles insistence that the troops should be removed seemed to Gillespie hopelessly wrong and to bolster his case against the Lieutenent Governor he now began to throw into the attack complaints that Raffles had neglected military quarters and pay. In fact, such matters were always discussed by the Council of which Gillespie was a member so there was little chance of making these charges stick! Without committing any indiscretion, Raffles had appointed his relative, Captain Flint, to an official position and this in turn was seized upon and attacked by Gillespie.

Gillespie ceased to attend Council meetings so that the increasingly acrimonious debate between the two leaders had to be conducted in writing. Perversely, he then criticized the long suffering Raffles for not discussing all the various points of contention with him face to face! Next he moved his residence from close to Bogor, on the southern slopes of the mountains, to a hill station on the other side at Cipinas. There he caused more trouble and severely angered the Regent of Buitenzorg by forcing local people to build a house for him without wages - the very practice Raffles was trying to stamp out. Raffles was obliged to be seen to reprimand him or lose important political ground with the native rulers as a whole.

Gillespie was enraged to the point of madness and fired off dispatches to Calcutta and London seeking clarification of his powers and denigrating Raffles wherever possible. In India, Gillespie had been used to working with lieutenant governors who, as a class, were regarded as expensive and ceremonious know nothings. If at any time he put Raffles in this category he had massively misjudged his man! He shared with Raffles' enemies in Penang the belief that Raffles was an opinionated fellow acting "far above his station" and with scholastic pretentions calculated only to impress.

The two former friends had arrived at an impasse: Raffles could not give way because of the intense pressure to cut costs; Gillespie could not give way because he believed that in military matters his advice must be paramount and that, in any case, troop reductions would imperil civil security and stability.

At the conclusion of weeks of wrangling and sheaves of dispatches Raffles' friend, Lord Minto, unsurprisingly, upheld his decision that certain military units should be returned to their permanent bases in India! And, far from supporting Gillespie, Minto very soon followed up with the news that the argumentative colonel was to be sent home to India himself! His replacement would be Major-General Miles Nightingall.

"It's a bloody plot," roared Gillespie, when he read the news. "We'll see what happens when I get to India."

No longer on speaking terms with his commander-in-chief and, fortunately, not needing to be, Raffles proceeded with the work of government. But, also, he wanted to show Gillespie that not all the cost cuts were falling on the military. He issued a minute to all the Company's staff which said: "The strictest economy is at present urgent, proper and unavoidable." On the civilian side he took urgent steps to amalgamate all departments of his government and moved the Secretariat to his capacious premises at Bogor. The savings were so great that, once again, he was able to tell India that he did not expect to require new subventions in the coming year.

It was plain for all to see that it was not only the military who were 'suffering'. Raffles and his tiny staff were already seriously overworked and either these new cuts must interrupt his ambitious programme or someone must work even harder. Raffles fitted the latter category!

Raffles joked with his Secretariat staff that now they were all at Bogor they were more like a family than a government. Although certain protocols were observed the staff and the Lieutenant Governor became close friends as well as colleagues.

Despite his increased burdens and, almost free of the irritant of Gillespie, as Raffles awaited the arrival of his commander's replacement, he pressed ahead at top speed with other projects dear to his heart.

The incidence of disease among the native population depressed him, particularly since, as a modern man, with extensive scientific interests, he knew that certain of them could now be eradicated by the use of vaccines. He instructed the Superintending Surgeon, Dr Hunter, to draw up a programme under which all the inhabitants of Java and Madura could at least be protected against smallpox and syphilis.

One morning, at his office, he was amazed to receive a messenger with a dispatch from Palembang informing him that the murderous Sultan Badru'd-din had been returned to the throne by his new Resident, Captain W. Robison. Raffles was incredulous and read and re-read the dispatch several times.

"I don't believe this," he said. "I just don't believe it. Robison must have been out in the sun too long and gone mad".

In fact the position of Raffles' nominee at Palembang had always been weak. After Najimu'd-din's enthronement his brother's influence continued strong - plus he had run away with all the state treasures and funds. Najimu'd-din was both afraid of his brother and lacking in the cash he needed to retain the loyalty of regional chiefs. He had the throne, but, his brother had the power.

A meeting of the governing Council was called which even Gillespie deigned to attend. The Council took the view that they could not allow the return of a man who had murdered all the Dutch inhabitants of Palembang. Lord Minto's son, Captain Elliot and Lieutenent Colonel McGregor, heading a force of four hundred Europeans, were ordered to Palembang to oust Badru'd-din. With them went a replacement Resident, Major W. Colebrooke. Fortunately, their objectives were rapidly achieved in full and Captain Robison was brought back under arrest to Batavia.

Just as he was solving the crisis in Palembang, Raffles felt himself forced to take the unprecedented step of dismissing his Acting Secretary, Charles Blagrave, for misconduct. He had not known Blagrave previously but met him in Batavia en route from the British controlled Malukus. Chronically short of manpower, Raffles had invited Blagrave to take over from William Robinson while he went on leave. Now his behaviour had turned out to be so unacceptable that there was no choice but to dismiss him. The very capable Charles Assey replaced him, but taking him away from other valuable duties.

Raffles took his argument with Gillespie and the problems with Robison and Blagrave in his stride. It was common for colonial officials to be at loggerheads, common for mistakes to be made and common for rotten apples to have to be plucked from the barrel. His quarrel with Gillespie was unfortunate and stemmed largely from the special powers given him by Lord Minto but, as Lieutenant Governor, whether he liked it or not, it was his job to discipline and correct.

Toward the close of 1813, Raffles breathed a huge sigh of relief. By an incredibly happy freak of circumstance - largely the infrequency of vessels plying directly between Batavia and Calcutta, Gillespie, Robison and

Blagrave were all able to depart aboard the 'Troubridge'. Once their ship was safely over the horizon Raffles lent back in his chair with a happier smile than he had allowed himself for some time.

"Thank God for that", he said softly several times to no one in particular. "Thank God."

He was now in unchallenged command of Java and its dependencies in Madura, Sumatra and Borneo. Despite the retreat from Moscow, the war in Europe with the French continued and there was no sign of an early peace. Every extra day of war was an additional day for him to extend and entrench the position of the British East India Company in the Indies. If only Lord Minto could now convince the Company that it was worthwhile to stay, whatever the outcome of the war with France, Raffles world would be utterly perfect.

Consistent with his view that the East India Company could best further its interests through treaties with local rulers, Raffles continued to dispatch emissaries to islands throughout the archipelago, inviting collaboration. He had large Admiralty charts which he liked to spread out with Travers, from time to time, excitedly jabbing his finger here and there.

"Look at it Travers, " he said with excitement. "If you look at the whole East Indies, the Dutch possessions are just a pin prick. Even if they come back what will they really have - part of Java, one city in Sumatra, the Malukus and a city or two in Borneo. The Indies is a region of traders and we must get access to that trade. We can try to negotiate treaties wherever any other European power doesn't have them.

"That's a big area, sir."

"Not big. Huge! Not only the Indies but all the way up to Thailand, Cochin China and Vietnam. It's vast

Travers, absolutely vast.

"Now the British have the chance of permanent ascendancy in these seas. I wish I could convince London that if we lose this opportunity it may never again be recovered."

"I'm sure you will, sir."

"And the beauty of it its, Travers, that if we can establish treaties with local rulers, even if the Dutch are given back the Indies, these treaties can remain in force.

"We'll have posts and they'll have posts."

"Exactly."

For three years Raffles had worked at the pace of a forced march, through night and day, sunshine and rain. He was tired. Olivia was tired. But it was a happy tired. The tiredness of feeling that all their labours and sacrifices would be worth it in the end. Their happiness was only marred by the death of Leonora's husband, John Loftie, but within six months she had remarried Dr Thomas Brown of the Indian Medical Service, then working for Raffles in Batavia. It had been a sad time but the circle of happiness was once again complete.

Despite his happiness, there were many nights when Raffles lay awake wondering about the fate of the Indies and wondering too about his own future. As is the wont of insomniacs, Raffles mind involuntarily ran over all that had happened since his audacious but fortuitous trip to Lord Minto in Calcutta. There the two men had only dreamed about the Company displacing not only the French but the Dutch, too, from the Indies. Now their dream had come true. Surely, now they were in a much stronger position than ever before. Wasn't ownership nine tenths of the law! There remained the final hurdle of convincing Leadenhall Street and, of course, the British Government. Raffles was unsure how the campaign was progressing because the dispatches he had sent and received of late dealt almost exclusively with dollars and cents matters. But, if anyone could persuade London, it was Lord Minto. Raffles felt that Minto had brought the Company nothing but benefits and that his recommendation was bound to win through in the end.

One morning, after a night of unusually heavy rain and a pestilence of mosquitoes, Raffles was hard at work on administrative and scientific matters when a dispatch arrived from Calcutta bearing Minto's unmistakable seal. The moment he read its first lines the bottom dropped out of Raffles' world. Lord Minto was to retire! Worse still Minto, the visionary civilian, was to be replaced by Lord Moira, a stiff backed soldier!

"Terrible, terrible news", Raffles told Travers. "What an earth can we do now?

Travers told him that perhaps the changeover would not be as bad as he feared and that they would simple have to wait and see. Whatever he said Raffles smiled faintly and repeated over and over again: "Terrible, terrible news".

In the same letter Minto revealed his fears:

" The final decision concerning Java may not be known during my Government and there will certainly be difficulty if, after I am gone, we decide to quit the Indies and some other appointment must be found for you."

But he added with mysterious optimism: "If you should be superseded I trust and believe that you will be taken the best care of that circumstances permit and that you will always be kept harmless and free from cost.

"You will carry with you the credit of having been selected for a great trust, and of having justified the choice down to the latest period. You have many years of action and energy before you, and I trust that you may yet build a fair superstructure upon the foundation, which I have had the honour and pleasure of laying."

The most depressing paragraph in the letter read:

" I say this, however, on the suggestion of my own mind, having received no advice from England."

In an instant the rosy picture before Raffles' eyes changed to a sorrier prospect. His loyal friend and supporter, Lord Minto, was out! Henceforth, he would, in all probability, have no champion in Calcutta. The danger that the Company and the British Government would return the Indies to Holland in the event of peace with France was now very acute! And then, what of Raffles? What job would be found for him? On Minto's own admission there was no promise from London! And what of his dreams to bring free ownership and production to an Indies through which all ships could sail in freedom? What of his dreams of expanding he Company's influence throughout the Indies? What would happen to Malacca? What would happen to Penang? All the old problems that he and Minto had wrestled with years ago could now be right back on the table!

Minto was aware that Raffles had known all along that the Company's activities in Java might not be permanent and he wrote:

" I have only to hope that the possibility of the Company quitting the Indies which existed from the beginning will have so far prepared you as to soften the possibility of any blow.

"There is a great division of opinion on the question of permanent settlements and their extension under the Presidency of Bengal which has, in a great degree, been carried out during my administration."

This dispatch left Raffles with a deep sense of impending doom!

"It seems that nothing I tell them of the abominable behaviour of the Dutch out here or the threat to our trade posed by their monopolies bears any comparrison to London's determination to make a friend of Holland against France," Raffles told Olivia gloomily.

Feeling depressed beyond words his earlier happiness was further eroded by news from two of his sisters, Mary Anne and Harriet that they would be returning to England in the ship bringing Major General Nightingall. It was no more than a coincidence but the phrase "rats deserting a sinking ship" ran immediately through Raffles' mind.

His depression was considerably lifted by the arrival at Batavia of Nightingall, a man he took as much instant liking to as he had found Gillespie difficult. But, Nightingall could shed no further light on developments in Calcutta and was simply looking forward to his new command.

Raffles did him the honour of meeting the Commander and his wife at the dock in Batavia and gave a public breakfast at Government House so that Nightingall could quickly meet senior colleagues and members of the Council of which he was sworn in as Vice President. Next he invited the couple to stay with him at Bogor where they joined in the farewell party Raffles gave for his sisters.

Never in his life had Raffles felt so uncertain about the future and, when the next urgent dispatch arrived from Lord Moira, he hoped would put him out of his misery.

"Let's hope it's good news", said Travers as he handed him the sealed package.

"Let's hope so", replied Raffles with his usual friendly smile.

After only a second or two of reading, Raffles

face froze and his heart missed a beat. He stared at the paper in disbelief.

"Something wrong, sir?" asked Travers seeing the smile disappear from Raffles face.

"I'm being impeached," was all that Raffles could manage to say, his mouth open and his eyes bulging.

Looking back on events, he could see that his delight at seeing his three enemies sail away on the same ship was misplaced. They had used the time to concoct charges against him which were now set out in the form of the enclosed impeachment. He read them quickly to Travers.

"The villains," said Travers. "Unspeakable villains."

"It's ridiculous," said Raffles, "utterly ridiculous. As if we haven't enough to do, now I'll have to answer every charge."

"Perhaps Colonel Gillespie feels that if he can get you removed from the Government he can take over himself," said Travers.

"With Nightingall here, it's too late for that," said Raffles. "No. This is pure malice."

Once he had become accustomed to the idea of being impeached, Raffles looked serious but not grim. He gave a large sigh.

"It's all too ridiculous for words," he said. "Come on Travers, ridiculous or not, we'll have to answer everything."

Raffles almost smiled as he went down the list of accusations. He was being called to account for selling government lands, which he had to do if the post was not to be bankrupt. He was being accused of corrupt practice by buying lands himself, but, it was well known, that he had been obliged to do this to boost confidence. It was asserted that the land sale was not undertaken for the declared objective of propping up the increasingly worthless paper currency of Java - when, in fact, this was the only reason. He was accused of violating regulations by employing the same person for more than one job - under circumstances where less than a dozen men were struggling to govern a country the size of England. He was accused of manipulating coffee growing and sale for personal gain when he had acted only to free farmers, except where harm would result. He was deemed to have undertaken military works without proper permission even though Colonel Gillespie knew about or approved every such decision. He was accused of further undermining the traditional rulers when, in fact, he had striven to achieve the reverse. Finally, he was accused of personal indelicacy toward Gillespie because he would not permit him to build a house for himself, free of charge and using forced native labour.

"This is pathetic, absolutely pathetic," Raffles repeated as he read the charges again. "It's even more pathetic that we should have to waste our time wading through such a mass of absurdity and trash!"

Blagrave also accused Raffles of committing irregularities in regard to land purchases but based on incomplete information which Raffles was, of course, very happy to supply. Robison was motivated purely by hatred of Raffles for being removed from Palembang, and his contribution to the impeachment was a general attack on Raffles' government in Java in which he said there was " little honour, justice or prudence and that public interests had been sacrificed to vainglory and the splendid profusion of the Lieutenant Governor." He accused Raffles of lording it in "two splendid palaces" employing messengers in "Royal liveries" and of never going out on the road without a troop of expensive European dragoons. He also accused the Lieutenant Governor of using forced labour to build a road to his house at Bogor.

"As if!"

Raffles and Oliva, who could only live by penny pinching, whose staff "liveries" were of the simplest, cheapest and oldest roared with laughter at reading all this. It was true that Raffles always went out with a guard of hussars or dragoons but, initially, it was the military who had insisted on it because they were concerned for his safety! Colonel Gillespie had been more insistent than anyone else. Robison also charged that Raffles unfairly helped members of his family by finding them positions but, at a time when this was universal common practice, no one would be even slightly concerned about the very modest assistance given by Raffles to the men his sisters had married. In any case, he was genuinely chronically short staffed.

Perhaps inevitably, given their source, some of the allegations were pure fiction. For example, Robison accused Raffles of forcing the Susuhunan of Solo to travel to Semarang to be taught whist by the "Lady Governess." As Raffles replied, the Susuhunan had never been to Semarang in his life, not for whist or for anything else.

Inspired by jealousy, vengeful and evil minds, trash though the allegations were, they succeeded in creating in the minds of Calcutta, and the Directors of the British East India Company in London, the impression that perhaps Raffles was not the saint that he always purported to be. Even before any investigation into Raffles conduct had been mounted let alone completed the Board was writing to Moira that:

"Whatever may be the result of the investigation of the charges preferred against Mr Raffles, we are of the opinion that his continuance on the Government of Java would be highly inexpedient."

Messrs Gillespie, Blagrave and Robison had

handed them a Heaven-sent opportunity to rid themselves of a man whom they had come to regard as causing nothing but trouble for them. He and Minto had led the Company into an adventure in the Indies which the pair had promised would make profit but which had done nothing bust cost money! If Raffles had made money their attitude might have been very different. It was not the morality of one of their servants that was in their minds so much as the lack of cash in their corporate pockets.

Lord Moira was jubilant at the Director's attitudes. There was nothing he wanted more than to avenge Gillespie by getting rid of Raffles. Moira had never met Raffles or waded through the library of files containing his impressive reports on his progress in the East. But he had met Colonel Gillespie and the opinion of another military man was good enough for him! Nevertheless, form required that he instruct Company officials in his Secretariat at Calcutta to examine minutely Raffles' replies to the many charges.

Whatever the soldier Moira's hopes, his senior civilian officials, led by Chief Secretary, Neil Edmonstone, who had known Raffles since he first met Lord Minto, were adamant that Raffles' character was unstained by the charges brought against him. Edmonstone wrote:

"After a scrupulous examination of all the documents, both accusatory and exculpatory, and an attentive perusal of the minutes of the Governor General and of the other members composing the Council, we think it due to Mr Raffles, to the interests of our service and to the cause of truth, explicitly to declare our decided conviction, that the charges, inasfar as they went to impeach the moral character of that gentleman, have not only not been made good, but that they have been disproved to an extent which is seldom practical in a case of defense."

The bureaucrats of the Indian service not only gave Raffles a clean moral slate but, since, as Company officials, they could so easily empathize with his economic problems, an attached memo from Archibald Seton, who had served in Penang and was now a member of the governing council in Bengal added:

"That Mr Raffles has not succeeded in his endeavors may, I think, be attributed to the exhausted state in which he found the island, to the annihilation of its export trade, to a want of specie, and under the great disadvantage of these difficulties, to the fatal necessity of engaging in early and extensive wars with the sultans of Palembang and Yogjakarta."

Unable to fly too far in the face of truth, the Directors in London described to Raffles Edmonstone's minute as "elaborate and able." They concluded:

"Whatever judgement may ultimately be passed on the various measures of the Government of Java , which underwent review in the course of the investigation into the conduct of its head, we are satisfied, not merely that they stand exempt from any sordid or selfish taint, but that they sprung from motives perfectly correct and laudable."

But Raffles' purchase of land was described as a "grave indiscretion" - even though there was no regulation forbidding colonial officials from buying land within their own jurisdictions and that, indeed, officials were often encouraged to do so!

More ominous for the future of British involvement in Java, the Directors forbade him to crack down on piracy which was described as "interference" in the affairs of the Indies rajas. Furthermore, all embassies to native rulers throught the region must cease at once!

This was in direct contravention of the policy

and thinking of Lord Minto and signalled unequivocally to Raffles that the former governor general's dreams were not at all shared by Moira. Minto had sketched out a picture in which Java would remain British, the Malukus and probably Bengkulu would be put under rule from Batavia, other "out-stations" would be established and, in the interests of the safety of commercial shipping, the seas would be cleared of pirates. Raffles had done no more than carry out his instructions! Now Moira was ordering a complete halt!

Raffles allowed himself to draw consolation from what he learned subsequently became of his accusers. The brave but misguided Colonel Gillespie died a month after the Company reached its verdict, gallantly, or perhaps foolhardily, leading a charge in India. The terms of Blagrave's complaint against Raffles were strongly condemned by the Company as being "unbecoming and reprehensible". Captain Robison went on to be court martialled for general insubordination.˜

CHAPTER NINE

Raffles' impeachment, and the Directors' other admonishments, made him feel more than ever that, far from being the Company's 'golden boy' he was under attack. Instead of concentrating to the full on the government of his enormous territory he found his mind again and again wandering to the fate of Java and to his own fate. And now that Lord Moira had replaced Lord Minto, he opened dispatches from Calcutta, not with the old excitement but with dread. To relieve his mind he decided on a tour.

"Let's take a few days off and go out and see the results of what we've done," he said to Olivia with a smile. "For all we know my achievements are only words on paper. It's time to go into the field and see what's happening."

Olivia was still tired and was not too delighted about an exhausting and bumpy carriage ride around the island but she knew how deeply Raffles had been hurt by his impeachment and how the trip might restore some of his old optimism.

Leaving Major-General Nightingall in charge at Batavia, Raffles set out with Olivia in the Lieutenant Governor's carriage with Captain Travers and a small guard of British dragoons. Supply wagons brought up the rear. The cavalcade wound its way over the beautiful mountains of the Preanger and passed Colonel Gillespie's former home, which had caused Raffles so much trouble. The Regent was pleased with Raffles' policies and greeted the Lieutenant Governor with a sumptuous lunch. Raffles felt gratified. As the party rode into the coastal kingdom of Cirebon they were met by crowds of people carrying signs which read: "Welcome to the English who have made us free and happy."

"I hope I truly have," smiled Raffles to Olivia.

"You have, my dear," she replied with a squeeze of his arm.

For many miles they travelled via Java's northern coastal road, courtesy of Marshal Daendels yet, sadly, at the cost of so many of the lives of local people. The tree lined road passed through a hot, flat, plain with great mountains on the right and the incredible blue of the ocean to the left. Here and there the jungle had been cleared for farming and here and there on the sea they could see brightly painted fishing boats with huge eyes painted on the bows. At night, they camped under the stars. Abdul prepared their beds and sleeping clothes while Mahmud marshalled the cooks he had brought from Bogor to make dinner. Olivia liked this part of the day best of all. The jogging and jolting of the coach had at last stopped; they could stroll in the still warm but faint afternoon sun; lap up the fresh air and beauty of the countryside and dine, alfresco, with the moon and the stars overhead.

"I'm glad we decided to come," she told Raffles. "It's perfect, just perfect."

Raffles nodded and smiled contentedly.

A man of unrestrainable curiosity, Raffles decided that, to reach Solo, they would strike out over the mountains along a track he had been told no European had ever traversed.

"Are you sure it's safe", asked Olivia.

"We are always safe with the dragoons," he told her confidently.

The party rode through thick jungle and forests of huge bamboos, the trees sometimes closing in a canopy over their heads and so dark that even in daylight flaming torches were required. Jagged mountain peaks and sugar loaf hills rose on either side at what they took to be the centre of the island. To Olivia the green of the jungle seemed endless but Raffles was entranced by the hundreds of trees and shrubs he saw and mesmerized by the incredible beauty of the sunlight filtering through the patchwork of leaves. Their porters eyed the forest depths nervously, sure that spirits or tigers were watching their every move. Fortunately, the weather was dry and after several days they succeeded in making the crossing of nearly six hundred kilometres of wild and uninhabited country. They emerged from the rain forest at Magelang, a former Dutch station, where they were welcomed by the British Resident, William Lawrence.

"My dear sir, you made it," he congratulated the crumpled and dusty Lieutenant Governor and His Lady." He was almost jumping up and down with delight. "Many, many congratulations. You must be exhausted. Come in to the house, wash, eat, rest."

British troops had recently discovered ancient, jungle encrusted, remains nearby at a place called Borobudur and the very next day Raffles insisted on going there. Because of the tangle of trees, from a distance, there was little to be seen. Few visitors could have guessed that they were looking at one of the largest Buddhist temples in the world, wrapped around an entire hill for a distance of two hundred square metres.

"This is incredible", exclaimed Raffles, once he

was standing amid the ruins, "absolutely incredible."

"Be careful of snakes, sir," Lawrence called.

In his excitement, Raffles took hardly any care but poked and prodded his way around as much as he could of the six platforms which ran around the structure before ascending to tree top height where it was crowned with dozens of stone Buddhas. In fact, the whole complex seemed to consist of nothing but hundreds of stone Buddhas, interspersed with thousands of carvings showing scenes from centuries past.

"This must be documented for science," he told Lawrence. "I shall order a survey party here from Semarang. Meanwhile please arrange to have the whole sight cleared of trees and bushes so that we can see everything better. But for heaven's sake be careful. Don't let the men damage anything."

Olivia had remained in the carriage because the stone steps linking each platform were steep.

"I can see just as well from here," she had said. Raffles stood by himself for a long time at the highest point of the temple. It was like being at the top of a mountain in Wales, or overlooking Georgetown or at the Puncak. Yet it was much more. As he had climbed, he noticed that the pictures of earthly life sculpted in stone reliefs gradually diminished until at the final level there were none - only the Buddha himself. Just as the structure seemed to ascend from clutter and tribulation to nothingness so Raffles felt his mind gradually empty and relax. He looked at the peaceful, motionless Buddhas. Buddha was a god - maybe this was what it would be like to find God, to know Heaven! His gaze took in the endless inanimate trees and thrusting peaks, as yet untouched by the hand of man, as still and peaceful as death. The tension in his jaw subsided, the focus of his eyes became ambient, his ears heard nothing,

nothing, nothing...............

"Sir, sir", called Lawrence. "There are still some other monuments to see and time is short."

Instantly Raffles was called back to reality but as he left Borobudur he felt a lingering regret which it was impossible to explain but which it had been beautiful to experience.

"There is no distance too far, no journey too tiring, that would have prevented me seeing that", Raffles told Olivia.

A few kilometres further on, the party began seeing the crumbling stones of what had clearly been a huge Hindu temple complex. Several were still extant and, at Prambanan, one reared up out of the forest in a mighty tower of carved stone. Whichever way he walked Raffles stumbled upon more stone debri, not only of other Hindu temples but of Buddhist shrines as well.

"Incredible. Absolutely incredible", he muttered over and over again. "It must be recorded before it is lost. We must have drawings and measurements. Maybe it's a lost city."

"Local people used to believe that the Hindu gods lived at the top of the mountains through which you passed, sir."

"Really", said Raffles. "Something like Mount Olympus?"

"Same sort of idea, sir, yes."

"Is there anything up there? Any temples?"

"We don't know, sir, Nobody's been up. The jungle's very thick."

"Fascinating," said Raffles, gazing at the cloud capped peaks to the north. "I'd love to have time to go and find out."

Raffles' party were frankly rather bored. Even

to Olivia they were just piles of old stones. None could understand how Raffles could see delicacy and beauty in this crumbling, rotting mess. No one had felt what he had felt as he stood at the highest point on Borobudur, gazing out over limitless forest tops.

They stayed another night in the comfort of the Residency at Magelang before moving on to official business at Solo. Before leaving, he instructed his escort to take time to clean their uniforms and polish their leather and equipment. Close to Solo, he ordered the colours broken out so that they could enter the city full of spit and polish and with flags flying.

What a difference there was between his arrival at the royal capital this time and the last? Not that the Susuhunan had given up his desire to once again be independent but he recognized in Raffles a strong and principled leader whose power, for the moment, ruled. Raffles' land experiments were in his area and his own lands and revenues had already been guaranteed in perpetuity plus a generous annual stipend.

On the outskirts of the city they were not met, as before, by a party of cavalry alone but by all the chief military and civil authorities instructed to convey the Susuhunan's congratulations and homage! An artillery battery fired a salute of nineteen guns. Shielded from the sun by a huge yellow parasol, the proud ruler came to meet Raffles in person! Raffles smiled to himself!

A procession was formed and crowds of Javanese stood or squatted down lining the route, along which gamelans were placed at intervals to honour the visitors. Raffles noticed that they were not heading straight for where he remembered the palace to be and soon they stopped at a spacious residence he gathered was the Susuhunan's private country house. They were greeted by three volleys of rifle fire from two hundred royal guards and by the thunderous playing of the state gamelan. Here they met the Susuhunan's consort and ladies of the Court and also the British Resident, Colonel Adams. The Colonel was accompanied for the visit by a detachment of hussars. The colour and pageantry of the scene was something Raffles and Olivia would never forget. Tunics of so many different solid colours, sarongs beautifully decorated with all the richly variegated colours and motifs of nature, gold jewellery adorning men and women alike, weapons encrusted with precious stones in every official cummerbund. Raffles had never felt happier. How far from Leadenhall Street he was now. How close to his dreams of the Indies.

In a large and richly decorated pavilion the Susuhunan, his queen, their princes, the Prime Minister and all the officers of the royal court entertained Olivia, Raffles and his officers to a luxurious lunch served, as usual, by Javanese girls. It seemed hardly possible that, here in the midst of the jungles of Central Java, food could be so abundant or dishes so various.

After lunch, the Susuhunan and his queen conducted Raffles and Olivia each to a special state coach which looked like the coronation coach of the Kings and Queens of England! Six ponies drew each carriage and each pair had a liveried groom. The drivers and pillion riders wore plumed three cornered hats like 17th Century English gentlemen. Led by Javanese cavalry mounted on ponies which seemed tiny beside the stallions of the British dragoons and hussars in open file and with drawn swords, the coaches moved off. Another infantry volley was fired as they drove slowly toward the royal palace in the centre of the city.

More crowds of Javanese were waiting to catch sight of them in the wide open square of grass in front of the palace gates. Upon arrival a second salute of nineteen cannon was fired in Raffles' honour. Last time he was here Raffles had not even been invited into the palace! They alighted from the coaches in front of the main entrance, with its ornate wrought ironwork and stone giants, one on each side. As a symbol of equality and friendship, the Susuhunan walked arm in arm with Raffles through double lines of native infantry. Wearing hats like Nelson's sea captains the guards stood to attention, long pikes of seemingly unmanageable length towering above them. Passing through the main entrance they were escorted to a huge open pavilion which, like the Susuhunan's guards, was an interesting and eclectic mixture of Javanese and European styles with Chinese influence. The very tall, pyramid shaped roof was supported by scores of carved and decorated pillars while the glass of enormous lit chandeliers glittered like diamonds.

Inside the pavilion Raffles now found himself seated next to the Susuhunan. Refreshments were brought to them by servants who approached on their knees and dared not look up at the Susuhunan. Raffles and the Susuhunan toasted their mutual success and the Susuhunan invited the Raffles to spend as many days as they wished at his palace. The royal gamelan crashed into life and the toasts were followed by graceful traditional dances, including some danced only for royal rituals and never before seen by foreigners. The bewitching young ladies even included some of the Susuhunan's own concubines! No greater honour could have been paid. More sumptuous refreshments were served and the Susuhunan brought the evening to a close with a spectacular display of fireworks. Raffles felt that, here in Java, at last he had reached the very heartland of the Malay world he had been seeking since his early days in Penang.

Raffles sensed, and almost feared, that he was being treated with the full honour a Javanese ruler would have felt demeaned in not providing to a respected guest, and he harboured no illusions about the Susuhunan's long term loyalty. Yet, after his impeachment, and the critical reaction of Leadenhall Street to his policies, it was certainly nice to be feted for once! And it would be nice if he could believe that, protocol aside, the Susuhunan genuinely appreciated the merits and fairness of his policies.

His entry into neighbouring Yogjakarta, a few days later, was similarly totally different from his first visit. From their point of view, the royal family and people of Yogjakarta had little reason to like Raffles. Only a few months ago he had been here at the head of a punitive military force. Yet, on this day, when he arrived with Olivia, the welcome was every bit as courteous and respectful as it had been at Solo. Here, too, he was met by all important officials while still many kilometres from the town. Here, too, the ruler came to meet him beneath his great yellow umbrella and here, too, there was a rich greeting of military salutes and parades, feasting and toasts to mutual success. The sheer pageantry of the processions was breathtaking. There were palace staff in sarongs and tunics with their distinctive Java hats (Belangkan Jawa), scores of military units dressed eclectically in styles influenced equally by local traditions and foreign invaders, sometimes in sarongs and bare feet, sometimes in coats, trousers and cavalry boots, sometimes in breeches and all wore an astonishing assortment of hats ranging from the fez to something akin to the headgear of nelson's captains. Numerous marching bands included drums, gongs, pipes and trumpets. Most of the troops carried the familiar long spears, krises and swords but some had bows and arrows and even muskets. The colours of the uniforms were kaleidoscopic including blues, black, gold, yellow, grey, red and white.

"It's like a fairy tale," Olivia whispered to Raffles, who nodded but gave a tight smile.

Few Europeans were as fascinated by Malay culture as Raffles but, on watching the parade, he made a mental note that the standing armies of all the Java sultans would be better reduced if no significant new threats to his expedition were to emerge later on.

The Sultan was dressed very grandly in a flowery top with a violently clashing and equally flowery sarong. Walking slowly and with grave dignity, he took Raffles and Olivia on a tour of the palace that they had last seen in flames and littered with bodies. It seemed to the Raffles more like a small town than a palace, with many pavilions, and state offices, royal apartments and quarters for the hundreds of people who looked after or assisted the ruler's family.

While he had last seen it more as a fortress than a royal residence, today he saw an enormous royal enclave, reflecting not only centuries of artistic synergy, but, also, the role of the palace and its regal owners as the cultural and moral heads of a large and thriving community. Raffles was shown the royal heirlooms and a library full of books including many written on lontar leaves in which, the Sultan explained, the entire history and philosophy of the Javanese people was set out. Seeing them, plunged Raffles into frustration. Here was all that he needed for his history of Java but, despite his accomplishments he could not yet read Javanese!

"I hope Your Highness will do me the honour of allowing me to translate some of the more important works, Raffles offered, thinking feverishly of their contribution to his 'History of Java.'

Raffles was amazed at the engineering of a water castle built within the portals of a stone fantasy which gave the royal family complete privacy. Beneath the waters was a maze of stone chambers, connected by tunnels, where the family could meditate or pamper themselves in complete seclusion and coolness, while the tranquil waters of their artificial 'lake' lapped above them. During this trip, which he had made at one of the lowest points in his career, Raffles gave thanks that he had been privileged to be allowed to enter the innermost sanctums of the Javanese people. His eyes had been opened to the antiquity, richness and sophistication of Javanese belief and culture as no other European before him.

When the time came to leave Yogjakarta, to return to Batavia by ship from Semarang, Raffles was consumed with impatience and itching to get back to his study to work again on the unique history he was painstakingly piecing together. Olivia, especially, felt that the trip had made Raffles into a new man. She almost wished that she could be left behind to rest while her husband bounded energetically ahead!

Back at Bogor, the enthusiasm of the trip was maintained. Major-General Nightingall had reviewed the military establishment and fully agreed with Raffles that some units could be repatriated to India, especially the expensive European cavalry and artillery!

If Nightingall can reach such a conclusion why couldn't Gillespie," Raffles' said to Olivia.

"It was a personal matter with him," said Olivia. "He wanted to be in charge and would have done anything to strengthen his position or undermine yours."

"Life is so short. Why make it so difficult?" observed Raffles' rhetorically.

While his policies unfolded around him, Raffles threw himself into a vicious programme of scholastic endeavour. His days now commenced at four o'clock in the morning and ended at midnight. Guests were frequently present at 'Without a Care' for breakfast, lunch and dinner. His public duties were immense. Yet he now found time to compose thousands of pages of notes about the origins, history and culture of the Javanese, with many an erudite and shrewd insight into the history of the peoples of the region as a whole. His specimen collections mushroomed and now required several helpers to put in order and adequately label.

Mid-1814 brought good news for the Dutch inhabitants but worrying news for him. Holland had declared its independence and, by a treaty with England, Dutch shipping was to have unimpeded access to British ports. No mention was made of Java or the Indies but Batavia was now also a British port!

Raffles held an urgent, informal, 'summit' meeting with his senior British staff at the Secretariat, his 'Family' - William Robinson, Travers, Charles Assey. His imagination and determination had been fired by everything he had seen during his long three month journey around Java. Now his deepest fears were ignited by the new Anglo-Dutch shipping treaty. The British Government was befriending the Dutch at a time when Napoleon seemed to be weakening. Suppose peace with France was close? Then, the fate of Java must also be close!

"We must keep Java," he told the meeting, pacing up an down restlessly. "It will be a sin to see it returned to the Dutch. We have brought the bright hope of freedom, justice and prosperity to the Indies. It is our sworn duty to do everything humanly possible to ensure that it isn't allowed to go back to the dark days of Dutch rule. Theirs was a more cold blooded, illiberal and ungenerous policy than has ever been exhibited to any country. When we arrived here people were starving!"

Otho Travers was dispatched immediately to

the Court of Directors of the British East India Company in London with a long and detailed dispatch from Raffles arguing passionately in favour of British retention of Java and the extension of the Company's posts and influence throughout the Indies. Charles Assey was sent off with the same message to Lord Moira in Calcutta.

"They are not listening to me", Raffles fumed with frustration. "For all I know maybe they are not even reading my reports. You must each go to London and Calcutta and make my case for me, push my files to the top of the pile as it were."

Raffles was careful that both the British and Dutch colours were displayed at the ball he gave at Government House to mark the birthday of King George. It was a long journey down from Bogor to Rijswij and his heavy programme had prevented Raffles leaving the day before. Olivia had been tired on arrival at the house he still kept there but she lay down to rest and Raffles thought she looked fine when the time came to go to Government House.

"The rest obviously did you a lot of good, my dear," he said fondly.

As usual, the First lady led off the dancing but a little later, while dancing with Raffles, Olivia asked to return to their table for a while.

"I must be getting old", she joked. "One dance has worn me out."

She fanned herself while Raffles stood behind her before being taken aside by some of the Dutch merchants, eager to know what changes might be in the wind, now that all the signs were beginning to point to the defeat of Napoleon and peace in Europe. Raffles was still telling them his thoughts when he heard a crash and a horrified and concerned gasp rise from the crowd around him. Still speaking he looked round and had to adjust his vision downwards before being able to see that Olivia had fallen sideways out of her chair and was lying senseless on the floor!

Officers rushed forward to help her and Raffles dropped to his knees at her side shouting for brandy to be brought. He held Olivia's head while she sipped the strong liquor.

"I was just so tired", she mumbled as the men helped her back into her chair.

"I know, my dear, I know", said Raffles lovingly. "We'll get you home."

Without a thought for the ball, Raffles immediately rushed Olivia back to their town house by carriage mopping sweat from her brow as they drove. Sir Thomas Sevestre, the family doctor, had been at the ball and accompanied the couple. At the house, he examined Olivia thoroughly and prescribed complete rest.

"You're working her too hard, Mr. Raffles. She's only a woman, you know."

Raffles was not unduly alarmed because he knew Olivia had been tired lately. The journey round Java had been exhausting and, on their return to Bogor, they had resumed their heavy social life with a vengeance. Olivia rested for a week at Rijswij where Sir Thomas Sevestre could look in on her every day. But she longed for the cool air of Bogor and, at the weekend, their carriage made its way more slowly than usual to their happy nest in the hills.

Almost at once Raffles had to return to Weltevreden and convene a full meeting of the Council. A dispatch had arrived informing him that four months earlier peace had been proclaimed in Europe and Louis XVIII had been proclaimed King of France in place of Napoleon! The Dutch members of the Council immediately resigned. Muntinghe and Cranssen were long standing friends of

Raffles for whom they had the greatest respect and, although Raffles had received no word either officially or through Travers or Assey, they sensed more than he did that the days of the British East India Company in Java might now be numbered! It would not be good for their careers to be seen to be backing the British unnecessarily.

The news happened to coincide with the birthday of the new ruler of Holland, the Prince of Orange, and to Raffles embarrassment, the celebrations organized by the Dutch community were as much a salute to him as to the royal prince. Cranssen gave a public breakfast at his mansion in Weltevreden and Olivia was once again well enough to accompany Raffles to the house of their loyal friend. Upon their arrival, a military band struck up the royal salute! In the evening, Batavia was ablaze with illuminations, the streets busy with the carriages of spectators. At Government House, Raffles staged a fireworks display followed by a champagne supper for five hundred people. Herman Muntinghe proposed a toast to the Lieutenant Governor:

" The most fortunate day that Java has ever known was that on which Lord Minto selected Mr. Raffles as the Governor. There are no words enough to express our gratitude for the many benefits we have received from his benevolent administration."

Raffles smiled with embarrassment and looked down at his feet. Public praise always made him feel very uncomfortable.

"Whatever I achieved was due only to the excellence of my advisers", he replied.

Raffles' embarrassment was not yet over. No sooner had the toasts been drunk than brawny Dutchmen picked him up, chair and all, and carried him shoulder high around the ballroom to the loud cheers of the assembly.

The birthday celebration happened to fall on

the anniversary of the conquest of Meester Cornelis and Raffles had one more toast before the evening was done. Mentioning this concurrence, he called solemnly for a final toast to the man who had made Britain's presence in Java assured - (now) Major-General, Robert Rollo Gillespie, the officer who had achieved more than any other to destroy Raffles reputation and career!

Soon after, back at Bogor, Raffles was again depressed to learn that Lord Minto had died trying to get back to the home in Scotland which he had not seen for so many years and where he dreamed of a peaceful retirement. Minto had retired and gone from his life but he had been not so much a superior as a good friend. Raffles could see him still, in his mind's eye, in the reception room of Government House in Calcutta, at their many meetings where they had planned the conquest of Java, at their conspiratorial tete a tetes in Java and at the many pleasant dinners he had attended at Raffles' various homes. Always smiling, always gentle, always kind and generous and always a far sighted man, completely free from the ignorance and prejudices of most of the others who had power over Raffles life.

"We shall miss him greatly," Raffles told Olivia.

Olivia was now much better. At Raffles' insistence she left as much as possible of the management of the house to Mahmud and the staff. She sewed, she drew, she went for short walks and Sir Thomas confidently predicted that with a continuance of this relaxing regime she would soon be on her feet again. But there was, he warned, such a thing as recurrence.

"Don't overdo it."

With peace in Europe Raffles felt strongly that the probability was that Java would be returned to the Dutch.

"If Java is returned to the Dutch let's go home

to England for a while", he suggested to Olivia.

"That would be so nice", she said. "I can see my family again and so many old friends. Oh, please, let's do it."

"It's ten years since I've seen my mother," Raffles told her. "Harriet and Mary Anne are there now but I should be too."

"Maybe next year we can go", Olivia said, looking out of the window at the idyllic view, down toward the stream in front of their house.

She rose from her chair and walked with him hand in hand to the window.

"We have been so happy here, haven't we my darling?"

"Very happy."

"I couldn't have married a kinder, more intelligent husband," she said affectionately looking him in the eyes.

Raffles smiled his embarrassed smile.

"And I couldn't have married a more charming soul mate", he said, kissing her lightly on the lips.

"You have worked so hard to bring nothing but good to these islands."

"So have you, my dear, "so have you."

"I hope with all my heart that Travers and Assey are successful. There's still no decision about Java so there's still hope. I wouldn't want to feel that all we did has been wasted."

Raffles had his arm round her shoulders, squeezing her to him. The evening shadows were beginning to lengthen. Villagers were making their way to the river for their evening bathe and they could hear the joyful screams of the children jumping in and out. An ox cart moved heavily up the river bank and disappeared slowly through the trees.

"What we've done won't be wasted, my dear. Even if they come back I doubt very much if even the Dutch can overturn everything."

"Let's not think about it," she smiled gaily. "Let's hope we can stay here together forever."

Next day Olivia was dead!

Feeling tired, she rose a little after Raffles had left to begin work, completed her toilet and lay down again "for a few minutes." She never got up again.

That first day was the worst in Raffles' entire life. No member of his immediate family had ever died and although, in the East, death was an ever present companion, he had never seen it at such close quarters. Not that death per se scared him. Not even the sight of Olivia's peaceful face, looking younger than it had ever looked. It was the loss of Olivia which moved him; the knowledge that she would never again be his companion. Sir Thomas Sevestre came, and, between him and William Robinson, arrangements were made for the funeral. Raffles was distracted, his face set into a stony mask. Throughout the day he popped in and out of the bedroom to look again at Olivia's familiar face, a face that would soon be hidden from him forever. Robinson apologized repeatedly for troubling him but he needed to know Raffle's wishes for the funeral. Olivia was laid out and placed caringly in an open coffin, to lay "in state" in the reception room of 'Without a Care." The bustle and gaiety of the great house came to a halt. The rooms and corridors fell silent. The local house staff stared at each other with faces filled with pain and sadness. Raffles' 'Family' at the Secretariat whispered among themselves and did whatever they could to ease their chief's pain. Not all were present. His loyalist aide and closest friend, Otho Travers was in London and Charles Assey was in Calcutta.

That night, Raffles lay down alone on the bed where only yesterday he had kissed Olivia good night. He lay on his back with his left arm covering the spot where she had been. He lay there until dawn, tears streaming from his open eyes but with his lips sealed tight. Raffles had eaten nothing all day and his head started to throb. His brain couldn't accept that she was dead. She was only 43! They had years and years ahead of them. Only yesterday they had been talking about going home to Old England. Throughout that terrible night, the faithful Abdul squatted on his heals by the door, anticipating any need and preventing all visits. Raffles regarded him almost as a son and was grateful that he was there. Next day Leonora was able to rush to Bogor from Rijswij and, at last, Raffles had a member of his family with him.

All through the long hours of the second day first the entire house and garden staff, then the Regent of Bogor, the Resident, Thomas McQuoid, local military and then mourners from Batavia came to pay their respects. The most touching scenes of all were of the barefoot Javanese staff in their simple sarongs wringing their hands and covering their eyes in heartfelt grief at the loss of their mistress. They touched the coffin lightly with the tips of their fingers as they passed. Raffles had been adamant that she should not be taken to her final resting place until all those who loved her could pay their respects.

On the third day she was taken in a closed carriage, with a military escort, to the European graveyard in Batavia where a plot had been readied close to that of their young and much valued friend, Dr. John Leyden. The entire society of Batavia crowded the mournful cemetery that day where they listened in stunned silence to last words which told of a heart glowing with the most generous affections and a mind guided by the purest principles of friendship and kindness. In Bogor, where they had spent so many happy days, Raffles ordered a cenotaph to be built to her undying memory. On the grave, Raffles had inscribed Olivia's full name and the words: "My beloved companion".

Back in Bogor, Raffles could not concentrate or rest. And his head ached unbearably. He tried lying in a dark room. Doctors bled him. But all to no avail. He had no appetite and looked more slight than ever. The whole weight of government fell on his long time friend William Robinson, who had sailed with him from London with Olivia in the 'Ganges' to Penang. Knowing the harmful affects of the tropical climate friends began to fear for his life. A short sea trip was arranged for him to Sumatra and his health seemed improved.

On his return to Batavia he learnt that Robinson was also dead! Once again he found himself standing among a large body of mourners in the graveyard of Batavia, his wife and his best friend nearby!

Olivia dead, Lord Minto dead, Robinson dead. The sheer weight of disaster numbed his brain. Remembering the tranquillity of Borobudur he decided that high mountain air might do him good. Behind 'Without a Care' was a mountain which he had been told no European had climbed. Even in his weak and sad condition, Raffles climbed it. Abdul walked in front of him with a bag containing food and water and squatted down on his haunches from time to time while Raffles caught up. Raffles was only thirty three and still in the prime of life yet years of tropical sun had dried his tanned skin, anxieties had put bags under his eyes and etched deep lines in his face and the string of recent tragedies had stripped the meat from his bones. At almost ten thousand metres, Raffles sat on a rock at the peak and looked down across the plains to the Bay of

Batavia, with it's many ships riding at anchor. The day was so clear that they could see the southern tip of Sumatra. Turning round to face the south they could see beaches and surf. Raffles sat a long time and no one ever knew what thoughts passed through his mind about his wonderful adventure with Olivia. He always loved mountains and, mysteriously, he felt better and his headache cleared. He wrote to a friend in England:

"I am now a lonely man, like one that has long since been dead."

In this condition Raffles went about his work of government at Bogor. His spirits were not much lifted at the appearance of Travers and Assey toward the end of August 1814. Neither had any news, good or bad. There was simply no decision about either Java's or his own fate. Both were shocked at Olivia's death and at the change in Raffles' appearance.

Raffles had built yet another hideaway at Cisarua, deep in the Bogor mountains. Now, most days he spent there, his beloved gamelan tinkling gently throughout the day while he read, wrote and discussed aspects of life in Java with Javanese confidantes.

But then came wonderful news! Napoleon had escaped from his prison on the isle of Elba and war was again threatening in Europe. Sad or not, sick or not this was an opportunity not to be missed! He wrote again, not only to the Company in Leadenhall Street, but to the British Government in Whitehall, urging upon them the desirability of confirming a permanent British establishment in Java. He revealed that during the tour of Java he had made with Olivia he had encountered universal horror at the thought of a return by the Dutch. He wrote:

"Are we not in some measure bound to the native population to secure to them by every means in our power the enjoyment of that liberty and independence we allowed them to taste - or is the cup to be dashed from the lip as soon as it is touched?"

He acknowledged that Java had not lived up to the initial optimistic financial projections of himself and Lord Minto but he attached pages and pages of data to prove that the tide had now turned in the Company's favour.

Still suffering from poor health and haunted at "Without a Care" by the ghost of Olivia, Raffles moved to the hill station retreat of a Dutch friend where he spent most of his time reading and translating and preparing what he hoped would be the first and most definitive work on Java. Raffles was meticulous and strove to leave no question unanswered. Assey had replaced Robinson as Secretary and tried to worry the Lieutenant Governor as little as possible. Still, it was necessary for Raffles to devote a few hours a day to official business. In the late afternoon he broke off to walk, resuming his scholastic efforts in the evening. There had been too many deaths and too many disasters in succession for him to completely regain his health and, to staff and friends, he seemed but a shadow of his former self.

A major part of his listlessness was having to soldier on, month after month, neither knowing the fate of Java nor his own fate. Many times he asked himself if there was any point in attempting new things and many times he gave his own answer, "no!" If London would agree to his plans for the Indies he could go ahead with his dreams, extend his land scheme throughout Java, take further measures to improve the lives of the local people, boost production and trade, quash piracy, extend the influence of the Company as far as possible throughout the archipelago. Now he lived in a twilight world of indecision. He couldn't go forward and he couldn't go back. All he could do, every day, day after day, was wait. Wait for the pleasure of Directors in London whom he was coming to despise for their ignorance!

He wrote to the British Government in London:

"It is not possible to conceive the real injury to the public service, to the public character and to the national interest by the state of suspense, the indecision which has been connected with everything concerning Java affairs."

In May 1815, at last, the suffering was over. News arrived from William Ramsay's son in London about the Directors' decision regarding his own future. Raffles was thunderstruck. He was sacked!

In a sense, Raffles was almost past caring whether he was fired or not! He had been in Java nearly five years and after so much tragedy he was ready to go home. His aides and staff were appalled by the injustice. It was not as if Java was to be handed back to the Dutch! Raffles was to be dismissed while Java was British and, presumably, another put in his place. Until now, Raffles felt that he had been exonerated of all the ridiculous charges levelled against him by Gillespie, Blagrave and Robison, but now his political nous told him that the slur on his reputation had stuck. To a man of his ambition reputation was everything. Much more than the Lieutenant Governorship.

"I must go to Calcutta and talk to Lord Moira", he told his staff.

A rider was sent poste haste to advise Major-General Nightingall, who had become a devoted admirer of Raffles and shared many happy times at Bogor with him and Olivia. In Raffles' absence he must take command. Nightingall was away from the capital and, on receiving the message the Major-General rode night and day, covering five hundred kilometres in a record four days, to reach

Raffles' side. As a soldier, he knew the military bias of Lord Moira and he advised Raffles strongly not to waste his time and health going all the way there. Instead, Captain Garnham was sent, not only to Calcutta, but to London as well, with letters protesting the decision.

To the Earl of Buckinghamshire, President of the Board of Control at the India Office and a division of the British Government, as opposed to the Company, Raffles gave free range to his hurt. He wrote:

"I learn that in the month of April (1815) the Court of Directors came to a resolution, in consequence of some communication from the Earl of Moira, to direct my removal from this government. It is scarcely possible to conceive a greater degree of injustice than what I have thus received at the hands of the Earl of Moira."

He added:

"Calculating on the same spirit of hostility being continued against all the measures of the late Earl of Minto, which has hitherto distinguished the administration of his successor, at least as far as the interests of this Colony have been concerned, it will be in vain for me to attempt more in this country than my personal justification" and, he might have added, complete exoneration.

Two weeks later the British in Java learned of the defeat of Napoleon at Waterloo.

"It is almost too late for us in Java", Raffles said when he heard the news. And his instincts were right. In November, 1815, dispatches arrived at Batavia providing details of a new Anglo-Dutch Treaty under the terms of which Java was to be restored to the Dutch!

Raffles received the news calmly because, as the months had passed, he became more and more convinced that the window of opportunity which had opened for the British in the Indies with the Napoleonic Wars would be allowed to close again. Despite his best efforts, he had not been able to convince the Company of the importance and merits of the Indies. Even if he had, politics had clearly ruled the day, with London unwilling to offend the Dutch, risking a new war in the process. The treasuries of Europe were empty and everyone wanted peace.

"We have lost Java", he told his staff quietly and, after a pause, "We must write to the Susuhunan and to the Sultans at once."

Throughout 1815, Moira was working to oust Raffles from Java and, bearing in mind the slow pace of sea transport, it was January 1816 when Raffles received official confirmation of the news of the dismissal conveyed informally to him by Bill Ramsay. The delays had not bought him any useful time, but merely dragged out his agony of suspense and paralysed his Government from undertaking new initiatives.

The official documents, brought by military courier, seemed almost to gloat at the confirmation that the British East India Company was not interested in new territories eastwards of its existing posts in India, and, in this context, disapproved all Raffles policies in Java. Raffles was not surprised because the one was the concomitant of the other. But he was deeply disappointed. And the language of the correspondence, signed personally by Lord Moira, hurt him immeasurably.

He wrote that Raffles' Government had been "consecutively injudicious" and that he had "launched out into endless and costly undertakings" with "persevering imprudence".

The final insult came in the final paragraph where he wrote that there was no reason why Raffles "should not be employed in a situation of minor responsibility and of more strictly defined duties such as at the Residency at Bengkulu."

"The smallest British post in the Indies", said Raffles quietly as he dropped the letter onto his desk. "The very smallest post!"

Moira was determined to punish him for his perceived slighting of Colonel Gillespie and, although he could not go against his own officials by denigrating Raffles ethically, the decision to restore Java to Holland enabled him to pull down everything Raffles had built up. Had there been no peace in Europe, he would in all certainty have succeeded in having Raffles replaced by a military governor. Indeed, Lieutenant-General, Gerald Maitland had been mentioned so many times that many in Java actually expected his arrival!

The terms in which Raffles' dismissal were couched were so casual as to make his tireless labours seem unimportant in the extreme. The letter said:

" The Honourable Court of Directors, having ordered the removal of Mr. Raffles from the Government of Java, and the selection of some person from among the civil servants of the company to whom the charge of the colony can in confidence be entrusted, the Governor General (Moira) proposes to find some suitable person to succeed Mr. Raffles."

"They make it sound as if anyone could do what I have done," snorted Raffles.

Following on the heels of so many disastrous and depressing events, his dismissal as Lieutenant Governor pushed Raffles down to the very depths of depression and brought back the blinding headaches from which he suffered so much. Sir Thomas and other doctors thought it might be his stomach or his liver or simply too much anxiety. Once again he took to his room and lay there in the dark for several days.

Sir John Fendall, a middle aged civil servant from Bengal, duly arrived in Batavia to take over the government. Travers felt that Raffles looked too ill to leave his bed but Raffles insisted on meeting Fendall at the quay. Although unable to stand unassisted, he hosted a breakfast for the new Lieutenant Governor at Government House. Fendall, his wife and his daughters were all very distressed by Raffles' condition and the news that was soon broken to them about the death of his beloved wife. Out of respect for Raffles, Fendall made it known that he would continue to enjoy the title and style of Lieutenant Governor so long as he remained in Java.

Raffles' last letter from Java to the directors in London said:

"At the close of an arduous and extensive administration, which will be admitted to have commenced at a moment of peculiar financial difficulty, and to have been attended by embarrassments unusual to a new government in consequence of the bankruptcy of the preceding government, time only was wanting, and a perseverance in principles of liberal and extended policy, to render (Java) equal to the extend that has been contemplated or reported."

He wrote to young Bill Ramsay that:

"My character and my future happiness require my presence in England."

Clearly, there was no point talking to Lord Moira!

Alone, at 'Without a Care" the task of packing up all his, and Olivia's, belongings was sad in the extreme. Some things he sold but majority of his personal effects, books and specimens were crated up to go with him to England. Before leaving Bogor for Rijswij, Raffles walked alone around the now silent rooms which had once been such a hive of activity. In his mind's eye he could picture Olivia laughing with guests or pottering about in her herb garden. There was the window where he and Olivia had stood for the last time. There had been so much happiness, so much achievement, so much optimism.

His departure from 'Without a Care" seemed as much like a funeral as the day of Olivia's lying 'in state'. With tears in their eyes, his Javanese staff filed past him, lightly touching his fingers in farewell. Instead of Raffles going to him, the Regent of Bogor and his dignitaries came to Raffles to say goodbye for the last time. Raffles asked one of the Javanese chiefs he knew what he thought of the return of the Dutch. The old chief replied:

"Can't you fancy a young and beautiful widow, who has been joined to a harsh and withered old man but has lost him and is wedded to a liberal and gallant young bridegroom - can't you fancy how she will rejoice when she finds the old man returned to life again and come to claim her?"

Raffles left Bogor for Weltevreden with many a backward glance. At Government House, John Fendall gave Raffles a farewell dinner, ball and supper at which, one by one every native, Dutch and British organization in the city requested to pay him their most sincere respects.

At dawn, on Monday, March 25, 1816, Raffles prepared to leave Java for the last time. From Government House his carriage with its familiar military escort drove slowly along the tree lined road from Weltevreden to Batavia City Hall. As he drove into the great square drums and bugles announced his arrival. There, where Colonel Gillespie had stood at the scene of the first British victory in the conquest of Java, representatives from every unit of the British army in Java were paraded for his inspection, the troops under arms and with colours flying. He stood beside Fendall on the steps of the City Hall while an address was read on behalf of the British merchants.

"We, the undersigned inhabitants of Batavia, request to approach you on your departure from this island and to offer you the warmest expressions of our thanks and attachment. Placed as we have been during your administration of this extensive and valuable colony, we have had the opportunity of observing the eminent talents of your Government and the virtues of your private character; and we feel ourselves fully warranted in expressing our admiration and acknowledgment of the ability, justice and impartiality by which you have been guided in the intricate and peculiar circumstances attending this colony ever since it came under British Government. While we regret most sincerely the state of your health which renders your departure from India necessary, we confidently hope that your recovery may be complete, and that your life may long be preserved for the exertion of those talents and virtues which have distinguished your career in Java. As a lasting memorial of our esteem we request your acceptance of a service of plate which we shall cause to be presented to you as soon as possible after your arrival in England."

Raffles was pleased that, not only the British, but the Dutch merchants also bade him farewell in the most flattering terms.

From the square, Raffles took carriage again for the quay, to which he was led by army and navy bands, European and native infantry and a small cavalry escort. At the quay the procession drew up in parade. A longboat with shipped oars was waiting to take him to his ship in the Batavia roads. His long time aide, Captain Otho Travers walked beside him, in full dress uniform. Sir Thomas Sevestre walked behind. Then, came his sister Leonora and her husband Dr. Brown. Raffles already foresaw that he could use the months aboard ship profitably and persuaded his best two Javanese clerks to accompany him to London - Ali and Muhammad. Abdul and Mahmud brought up the rear. They had served Raffles so long that he could not bare to leave them behind. To leave them would have been like leaving a part of himself.

There were many other boats at the quay that day. His remaining close staff from the Secretariat at Bogor, the "Family", were rowed out to the ship behind him. So was every one of his close friends. So were all the leaders of all the communal groups including Malay, Javanese, Bugis, Ambonese, Balinese and Chinese headmen. None would let him go until they had seen him safely on board and wrung his hand in farewell. When the time finally came to hoist sail every armed ship in the roads joined in a thunderous nineteen gun salute.

As his boat approached the side of the ship which was to carry him to England Raffles noticed that the name was 'Ganges". He gave a tight faced and sickly smile, saying to his party at large:

"The 'Ganges'. The same name as the ship which brought me to Penang. Everything changes yet everything is the same. Has it all been a dream? Have a I really achieved nothing!

As he stood on the poop, watching the low coastline of Batavia recede, Travers handed him a short letter from the "Family". It read:

"Among the varied and distinguished proofs of regard and veneration which you have received from all classes and descriptions of people in this island, on your approaching departure, we hope you will accept from us a more silent, but not less cordial, assurance of the regret we feel at losing you, of the grateful and pleasing remembrance we shall ever entertain towards you; of the respect and affection, in short, which can cease only with our existence...

"Whatever may be our future destination, and however it may be our chance to be scattered, when we return to our different fixed stations in life, we can never forget the time we have passed in Java. The public sentiment has expressed what due there is to the energies and value of your administration, which the more it is examined the more it will be admired. It belongs rather to us to express what we have witnessed and felt - to bear testimony to the spotless integrity and amiable qualities which shed a mild lustre over your private life. These we acknowledge with gratitude, and these are imprinted on our hearts too strongly to be ever erased.

"You will not receive these expressions of our regard until you have left us; and when, perhaps, it will be long ere we meet again. Accept them then, dear Sir, as the genuine feelings of our hearts."

Raffles looked overcome with emotion.

"It's too much", he said with characteristic embarrassment. "Much too much".

He ordered a message sent back immediately by fast boat.

"This last and unexpected proof of your attachment and esteem is too much for me; it is more than, in the shattered state of my existence, I can bear without an emotion which makes it impossible for me to reconcile my feelings with the ordinary feelings of consideration. You have struck chords which vibrate too powerfully, which agitate me too much to admit of any attempt to express to you what my feelings are on the occasion of your address.

" You have been with me in the days of happiness and joy - in the hours that were beguiled away under the enchanting spell of one, of whom the recollection awakens feelings which I cannot suppress. You have supported and comforted me under the affliction of her loss - you have witnessed the severe hand of Providence in depriving me of those whom I held most dear, snatched from us and the world, ere we could look around us! You have seen and felt what the envious and disappointed have done to supplant me in the public opinion and to shake the credit of my public and the value of my private character; and now that I bend before the storm, which is neither in my power to avert nor control, you come forward to say that, as children of one family, you will hold to me through life. What must be my emotions I leave to the feelings which dictated your address to decide, for, in truth, I cannot express my own......."

Within a few days of Raffles' departure, the Dutch Baron, van der Capellan, had arrived at Batavia with 3,500 Dutch troops to resume the government of Java. Raffles' dreams were buried forever and he was heading home, a sick and disillusioned man!~

CHAPTER TEN

For the first day or so aboard ship Raffles was more restless than ever. He could hardly believe that instead of a short trip to Sumatra or south Java, this time, his destination was months away in England. Though he was no more Lieutenant Governor of Java, his mind stubbornly refused to relinquish its grip on the problems and opportunities of the Indies. Once through the Sunda Strait he watched the coast of Java fall away astern like an opportunity slipping through his frustrated fingers. While in sight of land he could still visualize Batavia, 'Without a Care', the palaces of the Susuhunan and the Sultan, the incredible verdant jungles with their mysterious stone remains and the brown skinned farmers in the fields with always a happy smile for him in their black eyes. From a land of brightness and optimism, where the sun always shone, he was returning to a dark land of cold and rain in which the only sure thing was that he must face the wrath of the Directors of the Company.

Out of sight of land, many a night, and even day, Raffles lay in his hammock with his eyes closed conjuring up pictures, not only of what had happened in Java, but of his whole life, at home with his mother, at school in Hammersmith, at the offices of the East India Company in

Leadenhall Street, in Penang and, of his dreams with Lord Minto at Calcutta, of the negotiations and wars with the Indies rulers, and of his revolutionary policies to bring freedom and prosperity to all. Despite the kind words about him from fellow officials in India, the attitude of Leadenhall Street and the hatred of Lord Moira left him with a deep sense of injustice, even of humiliation. Even modestly, he could regard himself as one of the most efficient officers in the service, a man capable of overcoming the most apparently insurmountable obstacles, a man with the unique vision to not only be able to see but to secure for the Company and for Britain a second Indian empire stretching from Thailand through the island world of the Indies and right down to Australia, so recently fully charted by Captain James Cook. But his visions and his achievements had been tossed on the scrap heap! Unwanted! Unappreciated!

And what had he to show for almost killing himself with work running the Penang Government and then taking on responsibility for the whole of the Indies? Did he have money? No! His expenses had been huge and he had had to fight a never ending battle with the Company for reimbursement of even the smallest sum. Many of his claims were still outstanding after half-a-decade! Did he have a wife? No! Did he have children? No! Did he have a job of which he could be proud, that he could view as the crown of his achievements to date? Absolutely not! And if he wasn't appreciated or needed by the Company what really was his future to be? An obscure official occupying the smallest post in the Indies! Perhaps dying there! Was this to be his achievement and his reward?

Raffles had always felt that he was born for greatness and he believed that he had achieved greatness only to be spurned like a discarded lover. Napoleon was under lock and key again at St Helena and, viewing only his civil initiatives, Raffles felt a sneaking sympathy for a boyhood hero who had also had grand dreams and who had also dealt himself a losing hand in the dangerous and tricky game of life. St Helena was on the way home and Raffles kept it in mind to drop in upon the former Emperor to see what he was really like and to see how he was coping with the kind of rejection Raffles himself faced.

Meanwhile, as the weeks ticked by, Raffles found that lack of pressure restored his health significantly. He no longer had such savage headaches that he had to spend his days lying in a dark room. The sea air was generally brisk and exhilarating. He had a telescope with him and often stood with Captain Falconer or his officers upon the poop, identifying ships passing by on the horizon. Captain Falconer was an amiable man and his ship comfortable and well provisioned. In the evenings there was no shortage of good food, wine and conversation. After Olivia's death, the news of his dismissal, and his severe illness, Raffles' mind had ranged over his options, sometimes deciding never again to return to the Indies; at other times feeling that the Indies were his destiny. When all was said and done the people, the sights, the sounds, the smells of the Indies had become a love in his life and, in his heart, he knew only death could force him to abandon them.

Captain Falconer steered for Mauritius and the Cape, both, like Java, recently won by British arms. Were these to be given up too in the general peace? And. if not, why sacrifice the lucrative Indies?

Life must go on and Raffles formulated a battle plan for his arrival in London; not only made a plan but commenced an arduous labour to bring a vital part of it to fruition. Much of his reception by the Directors of the East India Company would depend on his stature in society as a whole. If it was great there could be less chance of his being callously swept aside. If it was inconsequential his chances of rescuing his career would be correspondingly small. With him, he had boxes and boxes of data relating to his 'History of Java', the first work in the English language to describe and explain the Indies. With Ali, Muhammad and Travers he forged ahead with the work, sometimes researching, sometimes translating sometimes composing. If the book could be launched in London on arrival or soon after it could be calculated to cause a sensation.

To be certain that it would he had already decided to dedicate the unique work to Britain's future king, the Prince Regent. Thus he would be noticed by society, by scholars and by royalty, whose patronage could be even more important than any decision of the Company. The Prince had sent his congratulations on the conquest of Java. What might his reaction be now, if he could be convinced of Raffles' key role in bringing about that conquest? Could honours be involved? And, if they were, how would an honour, for example, such as a title, affect his position in the Company? Raffles, of course, knew the answer only too well. If society honoured him and if the Prince made him an Earl, almost overnight, he would be on the same footing with Lord Moira, accept a thousand times more knowledgeable about the Indies. If he could achieve this scenario what might the opportunities be then?

Raffles had by no means finished with the Directors. He was realist enough to know that the abandonment of Java and the Indies was a political decision by the national government and not one taken by the Company alone although, had they wished, they could, of course, have applied influence which it might have been difficult to resist. But his sacking hurt and irritated him because it had been so manifestly unjust. Along with the ongoing preparation of his 'History of Java', Raffles and Travers worked on a profit and loss statement for Java in which Raffles sought to illustrate the viability of his policies. Its most telling paragraphs were those which showed that, unlike his own administration, which had been obliged to start from scratch and pay for everything, the government which succeeded him would begin with a positive balance which could be augmented by strong commodity sales, especially coffee, and by land rents, which, in the pilot areas had nearly doubled. This he would present to the Directors upon arrival in London and with him pressing for an interview in person they could hardly follow their usual practice of consigning it to a file unread!

Raffles reviewed his other commitments immediately after landfall - who should he see first, where should he go first? He would have to send messages to his mother and sisters so that they could be reunited as soon as possible. There was no question that he had to stay in London but in what part of town? He felt sure that with the steamroller advance of industry and trade there must have been many changes in his eleven-year absence. A meticulous man, Raffles eventually drew up a sequential list of his priority visits and discussed arrangements with Travers and Garnham.

Toward the end of May, and in much better health and spirits, Raffles sought and was granted permission to meet the former Emperor Napoleon at his prison on St Helena. In addition to the boyish optimism that seemed always to motivate his eyes Raffles always liked to think good of everyone. How wrong he found himself to be about Napoleon. Whatever his positive achievements Raffles wrote that he found the Emperor "a monster, with none of those feelings of the heart which constitute the real man. I compassioned his situation but from the moment I came into his presence these feelings subsided, and they gave place to those of horror, disgust and alarm; I saw in him a man determined and vindictive, without one spark of soul, but possessing a capacity and talent calculated to enslave mankind. I saw in him that all this capacity, all this talent, was devoted to himself and his own supremacy. I saw that he looked down on all mankind as his inferiors and that he possessed not the smallest particle of philosophy. I looked upon him as a wild animal caught, but not tamed."

Raffles' summing up of Napoleon stands in stark contrast to Travers' description of Raffles, which he entered in his dairy the night Raffles celebrated his thirty fifth birthday, on July 6, 1816.

"Few men have pushed themselves forward with the rapidity that Mr Raffles has done and I have no doubt if his health improves but that he will shine in the world one of these days. A better or wiser stored head will seldom be found on such young shoulders."

St Helena is located just off the coast of West Africa and as the 'Ganges' sailed north Raffles thought about his father and of the many tales he had told about his trips from English ports to Africa and across to the islands of the Caribbean.

As they approached the coast of England, the weather wasn't dark and rainy but cool and fair. Raffles felt fitter and the English summer already seemed to offer a new beginning. They touched land at virtually the first signifi-cant port on the west coast, at Falmouth. As Raffles and his party were rowed ashore, the town's people were surprised to hear a nineteen gun salute thunder from the ships can-nons - the full salute due to a Lieutenant Governor! Raffles' heart lifted at the sight of white English cottages and stone buildings, at brass and flower boxes, at quaint inns bearing names of royalty, prominent leaders or reflecting local trades. Most of all he was pleased to see the ruddy faces of his fellow Englishmen with their cheerful humour. Certainly, things were looking brighter. With the green fields and fresh air of Old England so close, the entire party were frustrated at being delayed by immigration officials who doubted that they were in good health! Raffles looked particularly emaciated and sallow but the whole party seemed to have thin, drawn faces and to have eaten less than they should. Finally, after swearing on oath, the party were allowed to land at last. Raffles was home!

Raffles was so delighted merely to be in England that he took his whole party sightseeing on the way to London. The 'Ganges' had anchored about as far west of London as it was possible to be and, as much as his 'guests' from the Indies, Raffles enjoyed every minute of Cornwall and Devon, which seemed to epitomize the English way of life. In addition to fine country food and ale, they stopped at Truro to see one of the oldest and most famous copper mines in Cornwall and, despite his weakness and the remonstrances of his friends, Raffles insisted on going down. They visited a carpet factory at Axminster, walked round the cathedral at Salisbury, poked and prodded at the ancient stones of Stonehenge and visited the new military college at Bagshot. Abdul and Mahmud, Ali and Mohammad were open mouthed at all they saw and were drawn along by Raffles like men in a trance.

"It's so good to be home", Raffles enthused, the face that had been sad and ill for so long creased again in his famous bright eyed, boyish smile.

From Bagshot he sent his aides ahead to London to secure an appointment with the Directors of the East India Company and also to arrange accommodation. Travers secured a house at 23, Berners Street for Raffles and Sir Thomas Sevestre and another for himself and other members of the party across the road at number 52. Garnham arranged for Raffles the all important appointment with the Directors on the morning of August 17, 1816. Would Raffles be welcome? Or, would his reception be as chilly as that received by all his recent dispatches? Would they be prepared to listen to him? Were they interested in him at all?

His old boss at the Secretariat, William Ramsay, met him in the presence of Company Chairman, Thomas Reid, and neither could have been more friendly. No additional acrimony was heaped on Raffles and, with many pleasantries, his final report on Java was accepted for perusal. The two men had some good news for Raffles about a dispute which had dragged on for five years about some of his cash drawings in Penang but no other news, good or bad. It seemed that what had been written in the dispatches was full and final, with neither additions nor deletions. He was welcome and the door to Bengkulu was open. That was all. It was the least and perhaps the most Raffles could have expected. Now, he had to get on with the rest of his programme and see how one piece of the jigsaw might come to affect or change another. With the Directors behind him his next priority was to see his mother, now living at St Ann's Cottage in the very pleasant, rural suburb of Hamstead.

What a reunion it was. Mrs Raffles was positively dancing in her front garden when Raffles' carriage drew up. There were relatives and friends everywhere. His mother called him "my boy" and "Tom" and pushed him into the house for tea.

"Look at you. What's happened to you. You need feeding up", she said, her face alight with a happiness she had not felt since the day her only son had left for the Indies.

Mrs Raffles had still kept the old chair in which Raffles used to sit and after a hubbub of laughter and hugs from his sisters he sat there again, a cup of tea in one hand

and a plate of sandwiches and cake in the other.

"Have some more, Tom, have some more", the good mother pressed as soon as his plate looked even slightly empty. "We'll soon get the colour back into those cheeks."

Mrs Raffles behaved like a concerned mother, Raffles' sisters behaved like doting sisters and Raffles was the same son and brother he had been before. For a few hours the Lieutenant Governor of Java was completely forgotten.

It was the fashion for officers newly returned from the tropics to travel to Cheltenham Spa to imbibe the health restoring waters of the natural springs.

"It will do you good Tom. Don't worry about me. You go. Your health is all that matters," said Mrs Raffles.

Raffles decided to go. After all, without his health what was the point of thinking and strategizing for the future! Travers agreed to accompany him and also his favourite sister, Mary Anne. He decided to invite Bill Ramsay, who had tipped him off about his impending dismissal and with whom he had kept up a constant correspondence from the Indies. Ramsay senior was a kind man but Ramsay junior was more Raffles' age and Raffles felt he could be more open and relaxed with him than with his father. Anyway, ever since their first meeting at the Ramsay home they had liked each other and Bill Ramsay had kept Raffles faithfully, but informally, abreast of matters affecting him. Abdul went along but Mahmud was left in charge at Berners Street together with the Javanese clerks.

The little party went by carriage to Cheltenham but Raffles insisted on making a picturesque detour through Windsor, where the King and the Prince Regent often stayed and then on to the "dreaming spires" of the university city of Oxford where they walked among the ancient quads and visited the library. Cheltenham, with its sweeping terraces of gracious Georgian homes, was a bustle of activity following the end of the long war with France. Upon arrival they were lucky enough to be able to secure rooms at 3, The Royal Crescent overlooking a peaceful woods surrounded meadow around which couples loved to promenade in the late afternoon.

Raffles did not find Cheltenham particularly exciting. He drank the spring water out of hopes that it might improve him. So many doctors had told him that the cause of all his problems was his stomach and the waters of Cheltenham were supposed to be a potent cure for such ails.

"It doesn't seem to do anything at all for me", Raffles observed one day to a young lady also waiting in the pump room her turn for a supply."

"Nor me", she said with a pleasant smile, adding at once, "because I'm not taking it. The water is for my father."

"He has a very kind daughter", Raffles smiled again.

"My father served with the East India Company in Bombay and from time to time he feels the water here to be beneficial", the young lady explained.

"Good heavens", exclaimed Raffles. "I am also with the East India Company."

Raffles introduced himself and the young lady explained that she lived in the town with her parents.

"Really", said Raffles. "Perhaps, Miss, er...."

"Miss Hull".

"Perhaps, Miss Hull, I may have the honour of inviting you with your parents to tea - tomorrow, maybe?

"I will have to see if my parents are free, but my father is retired so I'm sure they'll be delighted to meet you."

Raffles wrote down his address at the Crescent.

"Until tomorrow, then. I look forward to it. Shall we say, four o'clock".

Tea with this young lady promised a more curative impact on his health than all the water in Cheltenham and Raffles was impatient for the appointed time to arrive.

Sophia's father was a spare man, with a military bearing and a mustache. His wife was small and slender with no sign of middle age spread. At first all the conversation was about what they had in common and who they knew.

Like Raffles, Sophia's father had started as a clerk in the East India Company before finishing his career as a wealthy factor and returning, first, to Ireland, and, latterly to Cheltenham. Her mother and father had married in Bombay, just as Olivia's parents had married in Madras. The only difference between them was that Sophia had never lived in India.

"But I do so want to go," she said at tea.

Raffles smiled at her. "I'm sure you will, one of these days."

"You know Peter Auber, of course," James Hull asked Raffles.

"The Company's Assistant Secretary. I know of him but I don't yet know him," said Raffles.

He's a very nice chap, very clever. Ask Ramsay to introduce you. More to the point, he married one of Sophia's younger sisters just last year".

What a small world it was, thought Raffles. Here he was in Cheltenham, and ostensibly far removed from the East India Company, when, by a chance meeting with a young lady, he was back in the thick of it again.

Captain Travers had returned to Ireland on family business and also to be married so, at Cheltenham, Raffles had no work to take up his time. And without work he found life rather tedious. A man should always have some project before him, was his opinion.

After the Hulls had left The Crescent, Raffles told Mary Anne how much he liked Sophia.

"She's very natural, sweet and kind", he said.

"Are you falling in love again Thomas," she said, with typical female intuition and candour.

"If you will be chaperone, I think we should invite the young lady again," Raffles replied.

Raffles had no wish to stay long in Cheltenham but the next few days were occupied wonderfully with a visit to her parents house at 349, The High Street, a return visit to The Royal Crescent and several outings around the town with Mary Anne.

Weddings were in the air. Travers had gone off to be married. Sophia's sister had recently married and Raffles returned to London within a couple of weeks of meeting the Hulls to attend the wedding of his sister Harriet who was marrying Thomas Browne of Somerset House.

Raffles' free wheeling life was brought to a sudden halt. The waters at Cheltenham had done him no good and, back in London, he was struck down by a vicious headache. The doctors gave him mercury which so poisoned him that he was in bed for a month. Travers was so worried about him that he postponed his wedding and hurried to London to be near his old chief. With as little rhyme or reason as it had arrived, Raffles headache disappeared, perhaps banished on its way by letters from the Indies.

Within a few weeks he had received letters, in

distinctive silk envelopes, from all the rulers of Java. In various words and phrases, the rulers expressed their regret at Raffles' abrupt departure and conveyed to him their respect and admiration for all that he had been able to achieve during his short years in office. Buoyed by such protestations, Raffles worked in earnest on his "History of Java', sending the daily product of his pen out to the printer every afternoon.

By Christmas, he was once again on the road to recovering his health, and hosted a magnificent gathering of fully thirty members of his family, including his cousin and namesake, Dr Thomas Raffles, a Liverpool preacher.

Upon arrival in London, Raffles had arranged to meet William Marsden, the Orientalist, whom he had helped from Penang with information about the Malays. The two discussed his forthcoming book, and Marsden put him in touch with Sir Joseph Banks, President of the Royal Society, and a man who had accompanied the explorer Captain James Cook, on his voyages of discovery to Australia and New Zealand. Banks was a man after Raffles own heart, intensely interested in the evidence and explanation of every natural phenomenon and, particularly, how such things could benefit man.

Raffles was elected a Fellow of the Royal Society and, through these channels, he entered London's scholastic society and thereby implemented another stage of the plan he had pencilled together during the months aboard the 'Ganges'. He was invited to give learned talks about the Indies, appeared frequently at social gatherings, attended by leading men of letters, and kept up a heavy schedule of breakfasts, lunches and dinners at Berners Street, much as he and Olivia had in Penang and Java.

At the Royal Society he became close friends with the Duke and Duchess of Somerset and with the Duke of Hamilton. His name became known to royalty. High ranking people were of the utmost importance because they could use their influence to achieve objectives hopeless for others. Raffles was invited to a levee given by the Prince Regent and to a drawing room hosted by Her Majesty the Queen.

Raffles was moving and mixing at the very pinnacle of society in a way that the Directors of the East India Company could not afford to ignore. He was a Company man but he was also famous. It would not be worth their while to detract from that fame.

Very soon it was reconfirmed to him in writing, by the Directors of the East India Company, that his character was unblemished in the wake of the charges by Gillespie, Blagrave and Robison and his appointment as Lieutenant Governor of Bengkulu was also reconfirmed. In conversations with the Directors, Raffles felt that there was "an inclination to see my political authority extended there," in Sumatra. This was just the kind of new opening he had begun to hope for. If, indeed, he was to go back to the Indies it would be better if there was some prize bigger than tiny Bengkulu. Java was now irredeemably lost but, if the Directors were suggesting the whole of the island of Sumatra as a substitute, that might be a sufficient prize for him to return. Sumatra was about three times larger than Java, largely unexplored and, said Raffles, "for all anybody knows maybe three times richer than Java as well."

Sophia and Mary Anne had become good friends and, as women will, had continued corresponding. Sophia had lived in London before removing to Cheltenham and Raffles knew that she missed city life. He suggested to Mary Anne that she might like to come up to town for a visit. Sophia attended many of the gatherings at his house and the two went often to the theatre and the opera - both of them, for different reasons, having been starved of this entertainment during the past few years. As Raffles' mind moved towards acceptance of Bengkulu so it moved closer to the idea that it would be preferable to return with a European wife and, therefore, closer to the idea of Sophia as that wife. He discussed the possibility with Bill Ramsay.

"I loved Olivia very much. If I marry again now maybe unkind people will say it is too soon."

"You have to think of yourself my friend. You loved Olivia and would love her still if she were alive. But God, in his wisdom, snatched her from you, leaving you alone and sick. You need a wife, especially if you go back to the Indies."

Raffles promised to think more about it and asked Ramsay to keep their talk in the strictest confidence.

"It will be better if people don't know I'm thinking of remarrying," he concluded.

The English Spring had transformed the stark winter landscape with buds and shoots when those in Raffles immediate world finally came to know that he intended to marry Sophia. It was a shock even to his closest family. One morning, after breakfast, he simply said, "I'm going to St Marylebone to be married' and in the evening he returned with Sophia with a ring on her hand and a happy smile on her face!

Physiognomically, Sophia and Olivia couldn't have been more different. Olivia had sultry, Latin looks whereas Sophia had the sharp features and fair complexion of an Irish colleen. Olivia's eyes had been brown. Sophia's were green. Olivia had been ten years older than Raffles; Sophia was five years his junior. But like Olivia, Sophia was a sensible, good natured woman, at home in any society. Raffles was deliriously happy. He swept her off for a private two day honeymoon at a hotel in Henley-on-Thames and then to Hampstead for a week at his mother's cottage.

Alone in their hotel room at Henley the couple realized that they hardly knew each other. They had never been alone together, never kissed, never held hands. From the moment they had met they were attracted to each other; to some extent they had a common background from which Sophia understood both the opportunities and exigencies of life in the East. Although Raffles would never have admitted it and, perhaps was genuinely not thinking about it, each met the other when they were searching for something, she for a husband and he for a wife. From Raffles' point of view Sophia was presentable, amiable, well brought up and capable, all that he felt he needed at this time in his life in a companion whom he saw more as a consort and mother to his children than as the career partner Olivia had been. For Sophia, while Raffles was not young and vigorous, he had already attained the rank of Lieutenant Governor of the East India Company and for all she knew might one day become Governor General of one of the Presidencies in India or perhaps of all of them. Just as her father had been a high official in Bombay her grandfather had been Superintendent of the Bombay Marine so it fitted the family tradition perfectly for her to marry a man with Raffles' apparent prospects. Her family were as pleased with the match as was Raffles'.

"You have always dreamed of going to India," Raffles had told her, " and now you shall." In an exact reversal of his role with Olivia, who had shown India to him, Raffles promised Sophia that he would be her mentor and guide, making her dream come true.

At the hotel in Henley, suddenly they were both nervous, she more than he because Raffles was Sophia's first lover. Alone in their room before bed, Raffles drew her to him at the foot of the bed and kissed her lightly on the lips.

"Let's go to bed", he said softly.

Raffles undressed on his side of the bed, flinging his clothes over a chair and struggling into his long night shirt. Sophia concealed herself shyly behind the door of a huge wardrobe that all but filled one side of the room, emerging in a white night dress with lace frills around the neck and sleeves. She walked directly to her side of the bed and they both lay down quietly together, side by side. Raffles blew out the candle flickering by his side and reached across for her. The curtains were heavy, the room pitch. Neither could see anything. Raffles slipped his arm around her shoulders and kissed her again and Sophia felt his right hand caressing her knee and thigh under her nightdress. She held his hand for a moment.

"You have been married before," she whispered. "You must help me."

"Of course", my dear, "of course. There's nothing to worry about," he said softly raising his hand gently higher.

Sophia was surprised by how thin Raffles was beneath his heavy clerical clothes and knowing the frailty of his health she was relieved and excited that he had lost none of his sexual vigour. Next day, they walked by the River Thames and, when they went to bed the second night, Sophia felt more confident and entered more enthusiastically into their love making.

"I shall love you for ever," she whispered into Raffles' ear.

"And I you, my princess."

Sophia laughed.

"If I am your princess you must be my sweet prince, like Hamlet."

On the third day the couple moved to

Hamstead where Raffles' mother fussed over them both, laughing conspiratorially when it came to bedtime. It was February and very cold, but bundled up in warm coats and scarves the still young couple walked hand in hand through the woods and byways of Hamstead, skating on the pond and eating hot chestnuts in their gloved hands. Raffles' pallid face was red with cold and his eyes bright with happiness. Sophia's porcelain complexion was rosy with the chill.

At the end of a week, the newlyweds returned to Berners Street where Raffles hosted a celebration for Sophia's parents and immediate family, his mother and family, Travers, Sir Thomas Sevestre and Ramsay junior.

At Berners Street, Raffles' love making was passionate. Sophia could give him something he had now decided he wanted badly - children, lots of children and he wanted to have them before he was too sick to try. His frequent and extended bouts of inexplicable illness had left him with a residual pessimism about his long term future - not that he told Sophia that. Within a few months Sophia was able to tell him:

"I'm pregnant."

"Pregnant, my little princess," cried Raffles, beyond control with joy, "pregnant. I can hardly believe it. That's wonderful. We must drink champagne to celebrate."

Six weeks later his other 'baby', the 'History of Java' was born and, upon publication, took London's erudite society by storm. With royal assent it was dedicated to the Prince Regent. Within a few days Raffles was invited to dinner with the Prince's daughter, Princess Charlotte and her husband, Prince Leopold of Saxe-Coburg. From Java, Raffles had sent the Princess some valuable presents, including six Javanese ponies, which she still used to pull her carriages phaeton. In the 'Ganges' he had brought presents of ornate Javanese furniture. Before the month of May was out Raffles was again invited to a levee given by the Prince Regent.

Raffles had outfitted himself with new shirts, cravats, coats, trousers, stockings and shoes, soon after arriving in England, and cut a dashing figure that day with his sun tanned face set off by a high white cravat and stiff white collar framed by his black tail coat. There were many other men from government and business in expensive suits and officers in uniforms emblazoned with medals and ribbons with swords at their sides. All gathered in a huge rectangular reception room with deep pile carpets, maroon velvet curtains and glittering transparent chandeliers. Among them, from some interior apartment, soon came the Prince of Wales followed by a train of courtiers and moving slowly through the throng so as to meet as many gentlemen as possible. Only men were invited to levees.

But this time, Raffles was destined to be no mere spectator nor just another face in the crowd of those being presented to the future king. When his turn came, the Prince Regent, who had been uttering mere pleasantries to everyone else, interrupted his programme for twenty minutes to thank Raffles for his work in the Indies and, in particular' for the inestimable contribution to science of the 'History of Java.' Asking Raffles to kneel before him he tapped him lightly on each shoulder with a ceremonial sword before saying:

"Arise Sir Stamford."

Raffles had been made a knight!

Back at Berners Street there was jubilation.

"No-one on this earth deserves it more than you," Travers told him, pumping his hand and echoing the thoughts of all those present.

Sophia ignored his staff and family and ran impulsively into his arms. Raffles swung her round to face the little audience of aides and family.

"I have the honour to present to you Lady Sophia Raffles", he said with a broad smile.

London society feted Raffles more than ever, enabling him to consolidate his position as the most knowledgeable and respected authority on the East Indies in Britain. Out of the disaster of Java had been born the victory of his knighthood. Raffles basked in a degree of confidence that he had not felt since the invasion of Java with Lord Minto. Raffles had made his peace with the Directors, published his 'History', won the admiration of society and been given a knighthood. He decided that the time was now right to treat his 'Lady' to a grand tour of Europe. Sophia fairly danced with joy at the news. "To Europe," she cried with laughter and happiness. "When, where."

"Wait, wait", said Raffles also laughing. "We have to plan and make arrangements. But we'll go very soon."

"Oh, I'm so thrilled my prince, so thrilled."

Within a few months Raffles' impetuous marriage had worked out extremely well for both of them. Raffles knew he could get on with Sophia who was already pregnant. Sophia had not only married a high official of the Company but was now already mixing in Royal circles, something her father and grandfather had not yet managed.

By June, they were ready to depart. Raffles invited Travers but the young man was anxious to return for his own wedding to Ireland. Besides Raffles and Sophia, there was Dr. Thomas Sevestre, Raffles' cousin, Dr. Thomas Raffles and his sister Mary Anne. Sophia's brother, Lieutenant William Hull also went along. Raffles took the lucky young Abdul with him and Sophia took her maid. The sky was blue and the sun was shining as they left Brighton by sea for Dieppe in France. None of them had been to France before and much though they looked forward to it, all were not a little apprehensive at what welcome they would receive from a people their forces had recently defeated in the long war. Raffles and Sophia spoke French and, as always when one can speak the language of foreigners, the French they met were delighted to be able to converse with them in their own language. And, as usual, Raffles was as cordial and respectful as if he was meeting highly sensitive Javanese princes.

Napoleonic Paris, with its great imperial buildings and quaint back streets, seemed the very centre of sophistication. From Paris they made their way slowly by carriage to the towering, snow covered peaks of the Swiss Alps where Sophia insisted on getting down and playfully throwing snowballs at her knight. En route they stayed beside the breathtakingly beautiful Lake Geneva in a charming and romantic Swiss inn. They traversed the perimeter of the Alps for many delightful days, stopping here and there for picnics before entering the great, dark, forests of Germany with their steep mountain gorges and rushing rivers to reach their ultimate destination, The Netherlands.

Raffles had been increasingly concerned by reports that had reached him in London that the new Dutch masters of Java were ostracizing all those Dutch men who had worked with him. Able men and good friends like Muntinghe and Crassens, both loyal Dutch patriots, were being treated as collaborators and traitors and denied posts in the new government. Raffles was determined to help them and in Brussels he succeeded in meeting with the Dutch Colonial Minister, Anton Falck. Raffles pleaded that his old friends be spared from slight or injury. Four days later, at the Hague in Holland, Raffles dined with the Dutch King, the Prince of Orange, upon whom he felt his pleading had also made an impression.

"I cannot let my friends be driven from the Indies broken hearted and in poverty," Raffles told Sophia. "There is nothing I wouldn't do to help these men who supported me with such loyalty."

Eventually, the happy group arrived at Ramsgate in southern England and, within the day, returned to Berners Street. Travers had also returned to London after an engagement to a young lady in Ireland and his old colleague, Thomas McQuoid, was visiting him from Java, with all the latest news.

McQuoid told Raffles of renewed oppression and cruelty by the Dutch colonialists, of the banning from office of all who had befriended the British Government of Java and of the irritation of British merchants, soldiers and bureaucrats alike at having to hand over to the Dutch what they had fought so hard to gain. The Dutch felt that the British were dragging their feet in leaving Java and were pressing to get them out.

After almost a year-and-a-half in England Raffles knew that he had to make up his mind about his future. From the Company he had received a letter confirming his title not as resident but at Lieutenant Governor of Bengkulu, "as a peculiar mark of the favourable sentiments which the Court of Director's entertains of your merits and services." Raffles had attended debates in the Houses of Lords and Commons and found himself so drawn to parliamentary life that he wondered if a career in politics might now be preferable to a return to the Indies. Sir Hugh Inglis even combined his duties for the Company with those of the MP. But there were still so many loose ends in the Indies, so many things to be done.

"The Indies is now my whole life", he told Sophia. "What else do I have to recommend me that is stronger!"

Still only thirty six, Raffles felt that maybe it would be best to return to the Indies now, make some money at last, and, only after that, return to England, hopefully, to be awarded more honours and, perhaps, to enter Parliament. London was more bustling then ever but the home economy was depressed in the wake of the end of the war with Napoleon and all the interest was in selling the output of Britain's new industries abroad. People involved in the domestic market argued for protection and relief from inflation but those in the export sector continued to press for free trade.

"There's no choice, my sweet," he told Sophia. "It's trade and the Indies for us."

To Travers and McQuoid he commented: "The people of the Indies prefer the British to the Dutch. Now that London has been seen to befriend Holland by handing back Java, maybe there is still something to be done to save Sumatra. The Dutch have almost nothing there so we can't be accused of taking that is theirs!"

Raffles finally decided that he would accept the position at Bengkulu and, once his mind was made up, preparations for departure were swiftly put in hand. His last days in Britain were hectic. Goodbyes had to be said to his extensive family and to Sophia's in England, and in Ireland. Raffles paid visits to many of the influential people he had met through his membership of the Royal Society, particularly, the Duke of Hamilton in Scotland and the Duke and Duchess of Somerset. Almost at the last minute, the Queen summoned him to meet her, to express interest in the unusual treasures he had brought back from his part of the Indies, some of which he had presented to her granddaughter, Princess Charlotte. The Queen was especially interested in the regal, carved, Javanese furniture he had given, and Raffles immediately sent some fine Javanese tables to grace Her Majesty's home.

Raffles wanted to be much more clear about his brief in Sumatra than events proved him to have been in Java and he was fortunate to be able to spend two weeks as a guest of the Deputy Chairman of the British East India Company, Sir Hugh Inglis. Sir Hugh introduced him to Charles Grant, three times Chairman of the Company. These men knew the Company's policies inside out and could provide Raffles with certain advice.

The Company arranged for Raffles to return to the Indies in a new ship, flatteringly called 'The Lady Raffles", now awaiting them at the southern port of Portsmouth. With Raffles and Sophia were to go Sophia's brother, William Hull; Otho Travers and his new bride, Mary Lesley; Sir Thomas Sevestre, Abdul, Mahmud, Ali and Mohammad. Sir Joseph Banks had also arranged for Raffles to take with him Dr Thomas Arnold, the botanist.

Sophia was five months pregnant with her very first child and not a little afraid of the near certain prospect of giving birth at sea. She knew from her family how cruel the sea could be and that it was not uncommon for healthy people to be dead from sickness and disease before they reached their destination. Accordingly and indispensibly, Raffles engaged a nurse, Mrs Mary Grimes, to assist Sophia when her time came.

The couple's last major social event was a banquet at the Albion to celebrate the British conquest of Java. Raffles looked statesmanlike as he spoke about what had been achieved and lost and called for toasts to those, like Lord Minto, who had made possible so much. Beside him, Sophia looked ravishing in a low necked turquoise gown with high puffed sleeves. Her chestnut hair peeped out in curls from beneath a diamond and ruby tiara, the stones set in white gold. A string of pearls adorned her throat with more rubies and diamonds suspended as a pendant. Raffles and Sophia made a radiant young couple, deeply in love, committed to their lives and honoured by the very highest in society. Raffles had left Java, it seemed to him, in disgrace and with his most cherished hopes dashed. Now, like a man risen from the grave, once again the world was at his feet! After the last toast at the Albion the new Lieutenant Governor of Bengkulu was given a standing ovation by a gathering of some of the most powerful businessmen in the City of London.

The news that Raffles' friend, Princess Charlotte, daughter of the Crown Prince, had died in childbirth, toward the end of November 1817, scarcely filled poor Sophia with confidence as she thought ahead to her own birth - at sea. The furthest she had sailed was across the English Channel to Europe- and in fine weather. Sophia's worst fears were realized along the south coast as violent gales tossed the little vessel so pugnaciously that she and Mary Travers were so sick and weak that they could hardly stand up. Sophia was transformed from a healthy woman with rosy cheeks to a pale skeleton, unable to keep down food or even water. The further away from the shores of England they sailed the better the weather became. The "Lady Raffles" had just rounded the Cape of Good Hope when Sophia gave birth, without the slightest difficulty, to a daughter, Charlotte Sophia. Like Raffles himself, his first child had been born at sea! There couldn't have been a merrier or more optimistic party on a ship anywhere in the Indian Ocean than those aboard the "Lady Raffles", as she made way, under full sail, through sunny seas, toward Sumatra.

CHAPTER ELEVEN

As the 'Lady Raffles' approached the low, tree covered coast of south Sumatra, the last images in the mind's of all the members of the party were of the bustle and glitter of London, a city fast on its way to becoming the economic capital of Europe. On the March day of their arrival at Bengkulu, after four long months under sail, the ocean was calm, the flatness of sea and land made the grey sky seem huge and it, too, was lifeless. Wide, empty beaches stretched to left and right. In this dismal quiet the "Lady Raffles"' long boats headed for a tiny cluster of buildings on the sun seared shore.

"It's a very small place," remarked Sophia as they neared the stone jetty where they could see troops drawn up, wilting in the heat.

"We will make it bigger", replied Raffles with unquenchable optimism. "We will turn it into the capital city of Sumatra."

Sophia smiled hollowly, without reply.

Raffles knew that he was being sent to take charge of a tiny, five hundred kilometre, strip of coastal land governed from Fort Marlborough, Bengkulu. Personally, he had not expected anything comparable to Calcutta, Batavia or even Penang. Sorry though he felt for any disappointment Sophia might feel, he had tried to prepare her in London. While describing the Indies in rosy colours, he had told her honestly that Bengkulu was a station far from the centre of events and that, whatever happened, they would only be there for five years at the most.

The little garrison's troops had turned out to welcome the new Lieutenant Governor and Raffles noticed that they seemed to share the neglect of the panorama behind them. No amount of optimism could disguise the fact that at that moment Bengkulu was almost in ruins. An earthquake had devastated the town only the day before their arrival. The heavy and solid looking stone bastions of Fort Marlborough stood upon a little hill to the left and, on flat land to the left of that, there seemed to be a tent city of people living outdoors for fear of a further earthquake or of after shocks.

Raffles said nothing to depress the already low spirits of his party but later he wrote to friends in Britain: "This is without exception the most wretched place that I have ever beheld."

They were escorted ashore from the 'Lady Raffles' by the Master Attendant, Captain Francis Salmond. At the jetty, the British Resident, William Jennings, was waiting.

"Sorry everything's such a mess, sir. The whole post's like a battlefield. We're trying to get things sorted out."

Quite alright, Mr Jennings," replied Raffles understandingly. "We can't overrule nature. But, tell me, is there anywhere left standing for us to stay?"

"If you'll kindly walk this way, sir I'll show you Government House."

When Raffles quit the Indies, he drove in style in a carriage, escorted by cavalry and infantry, bands playing, flags flying and with the roar of cannon in his ears. Now, he and his group picked their way, on foot, through piles of fallen masonry and rubble!

They stopped about five hundred metres away from a low, single storey, building standing at the top of a slight and completely barren incline, with the usual high roof, deep eaves and with a colonnade of pillars on all four sides made from whole tree trunks.. Some of the walls were cracked, chunks had fallen down and every door and window had been unhinged by the tremors. Mangy dogs and polecats ranged the grounds and could even be seen even the lower rooms.

"I'm afraid this is Government House, sir," said Jennings with an apologetic grin.

There was no answering smile from Raffles or on the faces of any of his party. Before them was a truly depressing vista of devastation. And not merely because of the recent earthquake. On questioning, Jennings explained that fear of attack by the natives had been so great that the former governor had ordered all trees and shrubs around Government House razed and uprooted so that the baked red earth could afford no cover for an enemy and not only an unimpeded field of fire to the defenders but for cross fire from the stone bastions of the nearby fort..

Shooing away the quadrupeds as they walked, the whole party, escorted by Jennings and Captain Salmond, entered the house via the rectangular front door and stood together in the cavernous entrance hall, looking apprehensively around them. Sophia cried quietly and held her baby close. Mrs Grimes and Mrs Travers put comforting arms round her shoulders. Abdul and Mahmud rolled their eyes, Ali and Muhammad looked terrified. Without exception, the Europeans were grim faced. Many of them were thinking: "If there's a hell on earth, this is it!"

Raffles and his party could not stay here and, as the new Lieutenant Governor, he could hardly camp out in a field.

"If you don't mind, sir, perhaps you and Lady Raffles might like to stay with me for a day or two at the Residence while the rest of your party stay at other less damaged homes or even at the fort."

Raffles felt intuitively that this arrangement would not be the best way for the new Lieutenant Governor to arrive. They could simply have gone back aboard the 'Lady Raffles' but after four months tossed about on the ocean no-one would have welcomed that except in a life threatening emergency.

"Thank you Mr Jennings but I think we shall move in here."

Jennings was incredulous. "But there's such a mess, sir and it might be unsafe."

"We'll clean it up and make it safe", Raffles said firmly. "Please get some work gangs here right away and get things ship shape enough for us to be able to at least have a place to lay our heads. And get those wretched animals out of here."

Raffles directed that the luggage be held aboard the 'Lady Raffles' for a day or two more until they could see whether the quake would return. He allocated everyone temporary rooms on the ground floor of the crumbling edifice which was now to be the newlyweds home - just in case they had to make a hasty exit. While his party were getting settled, Raffles went with Captain Salmond to check what they might do if a strong quake returned. Fort Marlborough was only a short distance away and the huge stone walls showed few signs of damage.

"I should think that the Fort's the best place for us if the tremors return", he told Salmond.

"I should think so, sir. But the accommodation is not very comfortable I'm afraid."

"Can't be worse than Government House!"

No, sir."

When he returned to Government House there was a hubbub of banging hammers and streams of workers with baskets of rubble going in and out. In the middle of it all, Sophia was sitting on a pile of luggage crying quietly, rocking little Charlotte in her arms. Raffles rushed to her.

"Don't worry, don't worry," he said urgently, creating a bustle of activity around her with orders for men to bring this, take that or clear away. "We'll soon get things straightened out. Come, Captain Salmond has a nice lunch for us at Fort Marlborough."

The Fort was a low, squat, building, rather like Fort William in Calcutta, and although on a smaller scale it was known to be the largest outside British India. The stone walls were fully fifteen metres thick with embrasures at each corner and a single arched entrance, approached through a double line of redoubts and deep ditches. It was a soldiers' fort with not a flourish added in the interest of aesthetics. Each embrasure had its cannon and mainly Bengali troops patrolled the walls. Raffles and his party were led across the quadrangle, which formed the centre of the Fort, to a large, stone paved, mess on the right hand side. All the garrison's mostly British officers were assembled here and a wonderful meal of Indian curries and wine was laid out for them. After an hour or so of good food, wine and conversation everyone felt a lot more cheerful.

Even at dusk, Government House was still barely habitable but Raffles' party returned there to spend the night. Although he was not afraid, Raffles had agreed with Salmond that military guards should henceforth be posted outside Government House and that the Company standard should be flown above the roof.

The Governor's party needed every ounce of their courage. During the night, the walls shook and the ground trembled as aftershocks rumbled through Bengkulu.

Lady Raffles and Mrs Travers screamed involuntarily at the first tremor. Nurse Grimes came running with Charlotte, by now crying uncontrollably. In seconds the whole party met each other in their night attire in the reception hall fearing that the house was about to collapse on top of them.

Despite its damage, Government House was a stout building. The doorways in particular were very strong with large stone lintels across the tops.

"Stand in the doorways", commanded Raffles. "We'll be safe there."

From the street outside, they could hear screams and shouts and the sound of people running in panic. Although it seemed like ages, the tremors lasted only a few seconds, and, after waiting a reasonable time, the gently sobbing ladies were led back to bed and the men lay down wakefully to try to get through the rest of the night.

"By sending me here the Company certainly haven't done me any favours", thought Raffles.

The following day, to everyone's immense relief, the sky was blue with puffy white clouds skudding across it. Everyone felt better and Raffles decided to go immediately on a tour of the town with Captains Travers and Salmond. Unfortunately, his impressions were not much better than those of the previous day and were so bad that, later on, he wrote to Bill Ramsay, in London:

"I cannot convey to you an adequate idea of the state of ruin and dilapidation which surrounds me. With the natural impediments, bad government, and the awful visitations of providence which we have recently experienced, in repeated earthquakes, we have scarcely a dwelling in which to lay our heads, or wherewithal to satisfy the cravings of nature.

"The roads are impassable, the highways in the town overrun with rank grass, the Government House was a den of ravenous dogs and polecats.

"The natives say that Bengkulu is now tanah mati or dead land. In truth I could never have conceived anything half so bad."

Sophia later wrote that they had, "risked their lives" at Government House, "with split walls and tumbling down cornices." She added that she had found Bengkulu in "a miserable state of ruin and desolation" with its poor inhabitants appearing "depressed and wretched."

With gradually decreasing violence, the tremors continued for almost a week and then the town was left to pull itself together.

Raffles was not the kind of man to let a few tremors deter him and, in addition to doing what he could to tour the town, he characteristically gave priority to pulling together a total assessment of his new domain. His temporary headquarters was Fort Marlborough and here he sat, day after day, in a dark, high vaulted room, in near continuous briefing and brainstorming sessions with Salmond, Jennings and Travers. As they spoke he made notes.

Salmond reported that the garrison consisted of slaves from Mozambique and Madagascar, military convicts and Sepoys from Calcutta and local troops from Macassar. Raffles raised his eyebrows but said nothing. Beyond the walls was the town with its Chinese section beginning almost behind his own residence, the Malay village along the coast and the houses of the local farming community inland. Jennings informed Raffles that the population of the town was about ten thousand, including the garrison and Europeans, with around fifty thousand more in the environs.

He learned that the Company's interest in the area was more or less only pepper which, to Raffles' absolute horror, he found to be grown under conditions of monopoly which exactly counterparted those of the Dutch which he had been campaigning against virtually since his first days in Penang. Local farmers were forced to grow pepper and sell it either to the Company or the local administration at fixed prices. The pepper was then exported to Britain where it was sold at a profit.

"This is an outrage", stormed Raffles, as the facts unfolded. "All these years the Directors have been receiving from me correspondence against monopoly and forced labour yet they are practicing both right here. I can't believe it. I just can't believe it."

Raffles found that conditions had been so bad that the British Resident, Thomas Parr, had been killed. Because the Europeans were frightened for their lives it was at this time that even the tiniest shrub had been cleared from around the fort and Government House and never allowed to grow back.

With an ending to the tremors, Raffles rode on horseback a short distance into the hinterland. He could see that Bengkulu was almost surrounded by mountains and that the land in between was well watered.

"Not very healthy though, sir", observed Salmond. "Very damp and too many mosquitoes; drive you crazy."

Raffles, Salmond, Travers and Jennings sat their mounts on a little hill overlooking the town.

"Bit of a derelict backwater I'm afraid, sir," said Salmond.

Raffles turned on him fiercely.

"We will try to make it better, Mr Salmond. Even a derelict backwater can be turned to good account."

Salmond said no more but exchanged a glance with Jennings which seemed to say: "He'll soon find out."

It was not that anyone bore Raffles any ill will but Bengkulu had never been a success since the British established it in 1685 and there were precious few indications that it ever would be.

As usual, Raffles was not only concerned or interested in Bengkulu. Bearing in mind that he felt that the Company had once again given him political responsibility for the Indies, albeit, within the terms of the new treaties signed in Europe Raffles looked at his maps.

"It's the same story as at Malacca," he told Travers. "Just as the Dutch can cut off Penang by holding Malacca, here they can cut off Bengkulu by holding Padang."

"But Padang is still British," Travers interjected.

"For the moment", said Raffles. But, just like Malacca, it's due to be handed back. Our new treaty stipulates that the Dutch must regain Java and all its dependencies - and both Padang and Malacca are held to be dependencies. If we're to make anything of Sumatra we must hang on to Padang."

"What about Palembang?"

"Not so strategic. I prefer Bangka island."

"Which we still have."

"Hopefully, under the terms of the treaty Colonel Gillespie agreed with Sultan Ahmad Najimu'd-din. A crucial aspect of the 1814 agreement, handing Java and its dependencies back to The Netherlands, is whether or not the Dutch keep their promise to honour the treaties I made with the separate rulers. If they do, Britain can still have good access to the Indies. If they are determined to drive us out of the Indies, we're right back where we were before we invaded Java, with no certain route through the islands and no foothold in them other than Bengkulu - and Bengkulu is useless! Nobody uses the Sunda Strait any more to get to China. If both Padang and Malacca are returned, it will leave the Dutch in command throughout the Indies and they will easily be able to cut us off at Penang."

So, we'll have nothing!'

"That's my fear. I believe that Sumatra is rich and it will be nice if the whole island can be kept by the Company. If not, it is essential that we keep Padang.

"Otherwise, we may as well give up Sumatra altogether."

"Precisely. If that happens, we have to fight to keep Malacca British and establish another base to the south, close to Riau, to make sure our ships have open access to the South China Sea through the Strait of Malacca."

Raffles called for detailed data about the garrison and its functions, about the Company's human establishment and their functions, about the Bengkulu economy and about the nature of the local people and hinterland.

"Not much is known about the hinterland, sir," Jennings explained. The middle of the island is all mountainous and no European has ever been up there."

Raffles looked at him keenly.

"Maybe I should go!"

Jennings laughed.

"Much too dangerous, sir. The terrain's difficult and the mountain people fear and hate us. If you went, the chances are very high that you'd never come back!"

With the first week behind him, their luggage ashore, and life at Government House taking on a semblance of normality Raffles got down to the business of government.

As at Batavia, his first act was to grant freedom to the black slaves serving in the Company's forces and to abolish slavery and forced labour throughout his jurisdictiction. And a school was immediately established for the children of former company slaves, under the supervision of the Reverend Charles Winter. Indian convicts who had been drafted to Bengkulu were encouraged to marry and to take land or gainful employment, turning them, at a stroke, from a resentful liability into a useful body of settled and willing labour. Emulating the high moral tone Lord Minto had set at Batavia, tax farms in gaming and cockfighting were cancelled forthwith. To encourage trade ,Bengkulu was declared a free port.

His early days at Bengkulu seemed even to Raffles to be very much a re-enactment of all that had happened at Batavia and throughout Java. With the slave and convict element of the garrison retained on a new basis, and his base thereby secure, Raffles next turned to mending relations with the native leaders, just as in Java he had given priority to his relations with the Susuhunan of Solo and the Sultan of Yogjakarta. Since the murder of Thomas Parr, the local community was fearful of retribution. On their side, the Europeans were fearful of more murders.

Raffles struck a relaxed pose. As an indication of his confidence, he ordered the dismissal of military guards around Government House and trees and shrubs to be planted all around the denuded areas close to his residence and to the fort. In the second week, he hosted at Levee at Fort Marlborough to which were invited Bengkulu's leading citizens. The very next day he sent messengers inland to contact local chiefs and invite them to meet with him and to share his hospitality.

Sophia now found herself managing a large

household, and hostess at Raffles' usual hectic round of social functions. Though delicate looking, Sophia was no mamby panby. Her first hours in Bengkulu would have been shocking to anybody but, with the nightmare of the earthquake behind her, she had soon imposed a firm hand on her staff. In addition to Mahmud, she had inherited a small army of domestic helpers who trickled back once the earthquake was finally passed. Just as Raffles had done during his very first voyage to the Indies, on the way out from England, Sophia had learnt Malay. Thus, she could communicate directly with her staff and, more importantly, win their friendship. Sophia was, in any case, a naturally good natured person, and she certainly wanted to support the image being built by her husband that the new Lieutenant Governor was a friend of the peoples of the Indies. Mahmud now acted like a butler while Abdul was very much Raffles' 'man', looking after his personal needs. Gradually, the Raffles' guests at Government House declined in number as the Travers found accommodation of their own. Ultimately only Dr Sevestra and Dr Arnold remained, Arnold being a physician as well as a botanist and, therefore, able to help safeguard Raffles' delicate health. Raffles had established his secretariat inside Fort Marlborough and Ali and Mohammad worked and stayed there.

Inside the fort, Raffles now oriented his daily activities firmly toward Sumatra and the Dutch. Raffles was now well know throughout the Indies and, even without the need to send spies, 'friends' came to him or wrote to him with information about the progress of Dutch policy. Assessing everything he had been told, Raffles eventually concluded to Travers:

"I'm certain that the Dutch want to drive us out of the Indies. Let's look at what they've been up to:-

"They're trying to denigrate the British in the

eyes of the natives:

"They're trying to annihilate our commerce with the native rulers:

They have sent commissioners to every port in the archipelago, where it is likely that we might attempt to found settlements or establish new relationships, warning the rulers not to co-operate with us:

The Dutch flag has not only been hoisted in Java but has been rushed to Pontianak, Bali and even to Lampung and Palembang, close to us here in Bengkulu."

Raffles wrote to his young friend, Ramsay, in London:

"The Dutch possess the only passes through which ships must sail into the archipelago, the Straits of Sunda and Malacca, and, apart from Penang, the British have not an inch of ground to stand upon between the Cape of Good Hope and China, nor a single friendly port at which they can water and obtain refreshments.

"The Dutch would willingly confine the authority of Bengkulu to the almost inaccessible shores of the west coast of Sumatra."

If Raffles was alarmed by the activities of the Dutch, van der Capellan was even more frightened by Raffles' re-appearance in the Indies. His comments to his staff at Rijswij sounded like a strident repetition of Raffles' own.

"If the British control the Strait of Sunda the risk to our shipping will be very great. They could close the Strait at any time. The alternative would be the Malacca Strait but, while they hold Penang, we cannot safely rely on this either. Our best chance is to drive them out of Sumatra!

"I don't care how thinly our resources are stretched," he roared. "Every post we ever occupied must be re-occupied immediately. Wherever the Dutch flag doesn't fly this restless Englishman may try to make claims."

303

Van der Capellan was right. In several conversations Raffles had in London with the Directors of the British East India Company, he felt that it had been made clear to him that an important part of his brief at Bengkulu was to represent, defend and extend British interests in the Indies. Indeed, he had refused to accept the post at Bengkulu unless he was to be regarded as the Company's Indies agent. The Court of Directors had confirmed his appointment!

Now that he was once again in the field, from Raffles viewpoint, as in the case of Java, neither Leadenhall Street nor Parliament seemed to be able to grasp the strategic danger to Britain's trading interests in the Far East represented by Dutch domination of the Indies.

"It's not only the Dutch we have to worry about and the English are not the only people for the Dutch to be anxious about," Raffles told one of his brainstorming sessions. With peace in Europe the French may try to come back, the Russians are expanding into the Pacific and American ships are already doing good business here. What if any of them decide to set up posts?"

Raffles felt more strongly than ever that it was up to him to devise a plan which would maintain the freedom of the seas for British or, for that matter, international shipping. In fact, he devised two plans. The first was to try to secure the island of Sumatra for Britain. His fallback plan was to seek to establish a British post and entrepot at the southern extremity of the Malay peninsula, perhaps among the Riau islands.

Travers was sent to Batavia as an envoy. He was briefed to argue that since Lampung was not occupied by the Dutch at the time of the signing of the 1814 settlement and since the British had been there since 1811, it should continue under the British flag. Lampung directly faced the Strait of Sunda on the Sumatran side. Furthermore, in case the Dutch were considering re-occupying Padang, Raffles insisted that this could not be permitted until Holland had paid Britain for the cost of administering the settlement during the war with France. While Travers was away, Raffles decided to make use of the time by finding out more about the island which he might yet be able to hold for the Company.

The first short trip, for personal reasons, was about fifty kilometres to the north, where he ordered ground cleared and a Calcutta style bungalow built which the family could use as a hilltop retreat. There, he also planned to establish an aviary and to continue his collections of flora and fauna. The house would have a verandah running all around and was to be erected on a hill named, romantically, the "Hill of Mists" at Pematang Balam. Raffles remembered too well the many deaths at Batavia at locations low down and close to the sea and at the 'Hill of Mists" he hoped that he and Sophia could create a home environment similar to 'Without a Care", at Bogor.

Raffles questioned closely his colleagues at Bengkulu about the nature of the land away from the shore. He learned that there were no roads inland and that Europeans mostly confined themselves to travel between river mouths along the west coast's wide beaches. Sand bars blocked the rivers to navigation but, like canals in Britain, Sumatra's rivers were highways along which commodities and goods were carried up and down. South of Bengkulu there were several British forts and a post at Manna which Raffles felt it his duty to see. This part of Sumatra was thinly populated but there were substantial upland communities of Pasemah people inland from Manna, he was told. Raffles decided to see both the forts and the people. However far the ride along the beach turned out to be, the going should be easy. Only the journey inland might be difficult.

305

"I'm sure it will be very difficult", Jennings assured him. "And the people are not at all friendly. Why not just go to our own posts, sir?"

But Raffles had no choice. If the Company was to establish more posts in Sumatra, it was essential that he know its people. He invited Dr Arnold to join him and broke the news of his trip to Sophia as they prepared for bed. He was shocked to hear her say:

"I'm coming with you."

"It's impossible, my dear", he smiled caringly. "No European has ever made the journey inland. We have no idea what dangers we shall face. At the very least there will be lions and tigers and the people are said to be hostile."

Sophia's slight frame suggested weakness but, as any well toned woman can be, in fact she was very strong. And, she had been brought up in the countryside where she loved to take long walks and ride.

"I want to see Sumatra too," she pleaded.

"No, no, no. A thousand times, no," said Raffles kindly. "What will happen to little Charlotte if something happens to you.

Actually, Sophia's marriage to Raffles had uncaged her from the family home where she lad lived for thirty years. She was not only free and her own mistress but in the fabulous Indies with a man she worshipped.

"If it is safe for you then it is safe for me", she said putting both arms round his neck and kissing him gently on the lips "I will follow you to the very ends of the earth, my prince", she whispered.

And so it was settled. Sophia, with her cute smile and doll like features, would accompany him to the wilds of the Sumatra hinterland.

Raffles, Dr Arnold, Sophia, the invaluable

Abdul, about sixty porters and an armed escort of six Bugis officers galloped south along the sandy shore to Manna. All wore hats against the sun and Sophia, as befits a lady, rode side saddle. She was a confident rider, easily comparable to any man. The journey took two nights and each night they stayed at one of the tiny British forts along the way. The first night was one that Sophia would remember for ever.

The fort was austere and cheerless but, with a great orange moon in the sky and with only two Bugis guards and Abdul to keep them company, Raffles and his lady walked side by side along the shore, he in full dress, she in a wide skirted riding habit and a small hat with a long scarf used to keep it on but now trailing down her back. The night was warm but there was a refreshing breeze blowing off the sea, whipping up the sand. The voices of men at the fort echoed strangely in the silence."

"We could be Adam and Eve, couldn't we," Sophia asked mischievously. "It's so perfect here."

"Only because we are together. Without you I should not be walking here alone."

"What would you be doing?"

"Drinking claret back at the fort, I expect."

"Tonight, I shall be your wine. You can drink me."

About two hundred metres from the little brick fort she stopped with an impish look in her eyes.

"Do you remember the dance we had at the Prince Regent's ball", she asked, starting to hum and taking hold of his hands.

"Sophia, no, the men are watching."

Let them watch. It doesn't matter. We are only dancing."

The orange moon rose higher bathing them in

its light. Sophia hummed and danced and twirled Raffles round and round on the sand, while small waves hissed ashore in the darkness. As she danced she leaned away from him, her eyes lightly closed, like a satisfied kitten. She smiled gently, like a person in a trance, he laughed, and round and round they danced until Raffles could dance no more.

"Enough, enough princess," he said holding her to him in the darkness. Abdul and the Bugis guards smiled to themselves at the antics of the crazy white people.

The second night they were not so lucky because it poured with rain, peels of thunder seemed to shake the very sand on which they stood and bolts of lightening lit up the sky in an electric storm of immense power and turbulence.

On the third day they arrived at the small settlement of Manna where they were met by the British Resident, Edward Presgrave.

Presgrave told Raffles with alarm that the Pasemahs were savage and ungovernable.

"I beg you not to go there, sir."

Raffles laughed. "We are Englishmen, Mr Presgrave. I am not afraid to go anywhere. Not only am I going, but you are going too!"

"There's smallpox everywhere, sir, it's a risk."

"Make the arrangements, Mr Presgrave." Raffles ordered. "We'll depart at sunrise."

The mounted party, augmented by guides, made good time in the cool of the dawn, easily reaching and crossing the Manna River before lunch. In the late afternoon they rode on to reach the foothills of a range of mountains which Raffles decided they would climb next day. While it was true that there were no roads over the two thousand metre tall ridges, there were paths, although extremely precipitous and barely wide enough to walk, single file. The horses were sent back to Manna and, in the cool of another dawn, on foot, the party began the ascent.

The lowlands were soggy with water draining off the peaks and, from the outset, men cried out now and again as they discovered hideous looking leaches sucking out their blood. Some of the slopes were very steep but, so long as giant upward strides were taken from one exposed root to another, they were relatively easy to negotiate. Sophia sometimes pulled herself up by hanging onto vines and creepers. Often, to speed their journey, she had the assistance of one man walking in front and another behind, each holding her hand in case she lost her balance. Between the steep upward slopes, the path often continued more or less levelly around the perimeter of the mountain, but, in these places it was usually soggy with mud, into which the trekkers sank virtually up to the knees. Sophia was wearing stout walking boots but the lower half of her long dress was quickly drenched with mud and water and her boots felt cold and damp. Sometimes they lost sight of the track completely and then their guides and guards had to hack a path through the dark virgin rain forest. The paths went up the side of a mountain and down the other, across turbulent streams, with boiling rapids in the gorge below and then up and down again, peak after peak.

Occasionally they came across villages of tumble-down bamboo and rattan huts, abandoned because of the smallpox epidemic, and, with the journey taking three nights, Raffles always insisted that they made their own shelters from the forest around them rather than run the risk of contracting the virus. Once they slept on the open ground with roots for pillows and, as bad luck would have it, this was their worst night because all around them, all night, wild elephants crashed around them in the dense foliage, kept at bay by the flaming torches of the guards. The paths and precipices were so bad and the crashes and bangs of the night so frightening that a number of porters, terrified of evil spirits, threw down their loads and ran home after the third night.

On the fourth morning, as if to mark a turn in their fortunes, scouts came running back to Raffles and Dr Arnold to report finding a huge, red, flower. Raffles and Arnold went forward and were amazed to see a bloom about five centimetres thick and fully a metre wide.

"The world has never seen such a flower," said Raffles.

"But they deserve to. Let's take a sample back," suggested Dr Arnold.

While porters carefully uprooted and stowed the giant flower, Raffles and Arnold supervised anxiously.

"I hope it will stay fresh until we can get it to Bengkulu", said Arnold.

"We'll have to name it you know. We discovered it so I suggest that we call it the Rafflesia Arnoldi after Mr Raffles and Dr Arnold."

"Rafflesia will be enough," said Dr Arnold modestly.

"Enough but not quite fair," countered Raffles. "No. Let it be Rafflesia Arnoldi because it was not my discovery but ours."

As if to emphasize the change in their luck, a Pasemah chief appeared and offered to guide them further. As they walked, hour by hour, they were joined first, by porters, and then by more chiefs until, at the very highest summit of the chain they had spent nearly four days crossing, they emerged on a great and fertile plateau, surrounded by a ring of three thousand metre peaks and dotted with prosperous villages.

If Raffles had expected to be the centre of attention he was mistaken. Gangs of children, little knots of women, and crowds of men, ran to watch their entry into the paramount village. But, although the chiefs paid Raffles full courtesey and were not even slightly "savage", as Raffles had been told they would be, it was Lady Raffles who stole the show.

"They've never seen a white woman before", she said incredulously as they pressed close to her, touching her clothes, then her hair and eventually even her face.

While Raffles went off to talk with the chiefs, somehow or other Sophia managed to take a bath in natural hot springs, and even wash her stinking clothes, waiting for them to dry, spread out on branches in the hot sun, while she dressed in a borrowed sarong. She retired to the hut to rest, with guards posted outside, but slowly the guards were good humouredly circumvented until, on Raffles return, he found the whole hut full of adults and children, squatting down and watching every move his lady made.

Raffles' talks with the chiefs were amicable and successful and they agreed to accept the protection of the British East India Company. But not until after Raffles had given many examples of his goodwill. He freed the cultivation of pepper from the Company's monopoly, scrapped all transit duties on commodities and goods moving along rivers subject to the British resident's control and ended all forced services, including labour. Raffles had found the chiefs and their people living in poverty and wretchedness, their economy paralyzed. In an instant he freed them and left them smiling with hope.

He told Jennings later at Fort Marlborough: "The presence of the Lieutenant Governor in the outer Residencies was something that had never occurred before and of course the people were excited. They looked up to me and hope seemed to give them the courage to state their grievances."

Raffles had already accomplished more than any other Englishman in Sumatra, since the first arrival there of British ships in the Sixteenth Century. When they left the land of the Pasemah, at first, they seemed to be escorted by every living soul on the plateau. As they descended, the crowds thinned, until, at the last they were waved farewell by the chief who had first met them and a group of laughing boys.

On the descent, Raffles went ahead with Dr Arnold and Abdul, leaving Sophia to catch up with Resident Presgrave. The porters were somewhere in the rear. For some minutes, Sophia and Presgrave could hear voices in front and behind them and the sound of snapping twigs, as parties forced their way through. Gradually the voices of Raffles and Arnold died away and, after a while, each realized, more or less simultaneously, that there were no sounds coming from the rear. From time to time, their path was joined by others, or seemed to branch off, but Presgrave was certain they were following Raffles trail. Sophia was not quite so certain.

"I hope we haven't missed the path," she said anxiously.

" I don't think so," said Presgrave, now beginning to take a keener interest in the blanket of greenery around him. "But let's speed up so that we can rejoin them."

Out of deference for Sophia, the two had been walking slowly but now, with dusk falling, they strode briskly forward. Not only had it gradually become dark but it was now very wet, with a rain that had begun as a fine mist but quickly became a tropical torrent, soaking them to the skin. The path was narrow and dark, and Sophia and

Presgrave screamed together as she saw him disappear without warning into a deep pit. Sophia fell to her knees and peered down into the muddy hole.

"Are you all right."

For a second or so there was silence. Sophia had a flashing vision of Presgrave dead and herself lost in a forest roamed by wild elephants and tigers!

"Mr Presgrave, answer me. Are you alright."

To her relief she heard groans and could dimly make out his form far below.

"Alright", Presgrave moaned. "Nothing broken. Just shaken up that's all. It was quite a fall."

"Can you get out?"

There was silence again, presumably while Presgrave explored.

"I don't know, the sides are very steep and muddy. If you could find a creeper or something, maybe I could hang on to that."

"Yes, yes, or course. Wait, I'll look."

Sophia scrambled to her feet and began tugging at anything that looked like a strong vine or creeper. She found something and lowered it over the edge.

He called up.

"Lady Raffles. Can you tie it to something?"

There were plenty of trees. The problem was in tying the stiff and inflexible vine. Eventually, as much by twisting and wedging as tying, she somehow managed to secure the vine.

"OK. I'll try it."

She watched, wide eyed, as he tensioned the vine, and then, with a frantic scramble, and many sounds of grating and grazing, his head rose above the top of the pit and he was on his knees before her."

"Thought I'd better try to do it in one go", he

313

smiled.

Sophia fell back sitting on the ground, her dress a dirty soggy mess around her.

"Thank God you're safe", she smiled in return.

Raffles planned to exit the mountains by river on the sensible grounds that this would be faster, less arduous and less repetitive. He had seen what he came to see so he didn't want to waste time. He had rushed ahead not only to find the river and, hopefully, men, to take them down river, but also to establish a shelter and light a fire.

"We have to find the river", Presgrave told Sophia in the now total darkness. "Listen carefully and if you hear water let me know.

They walked along in silence through the damp darkness, each with his own nightmare of what the night might turn out to be. After what seemed an age they heard, not water, but voices.

"I hope they're friendly", said Sophia.

As they neared the voices the ripple of water could be heard and when eventually they reached its source there was Raffles!

Sophia ran into his arms crying out that they had been lost, that Mr Presgrave fell into a deep pit, and, how glad she was to see him.

"Hush now", said Raffles. "You're safe. But come near the fire so that you can dry those wet clothes. You too Presgrave."

He produced a bottle of claret from a small bag he was carrying.

'Emergency rations", he joked, offering it to Sophia first and then to Presgrave.

It was the worst and wettest night Sophia had spent, not under romantic stars, but under angry rain clouds, and she was extremely glad to see even the faintest glimmer of first light.

"Let's be off", Raffles ordered. "The sooner we're down river, the sooner we can be back at Manna."

There was a steersman at each end of a bamboo raft, each with a long pole. Sophia wondered why there were only two men but, even before they pushed off she could see that a strong current would sweep them along. The trip down the narrow, winding, Manna River, was something else Sophia would never forget!

Rapids occurred like watery steps all down the course of the river, as it gushed and roared its way in clouds of white spray down to the sea, sometimes through the overhanging jungle, sometimes between jagged, rocky, walls, against which the two steersmen jabbed their poles to fend them off. Aboard Sophia's raft was Raffles, Abdul, Dr Arnold and Presgrave. All had to cling on tight for their lives as the raft bounced terrifyingly along, now narrowly avoiding huge rocks in the bed of the river, then ricocheting off overhanging rocky walls on either side. A short, thick, bamboo pole had been lashed upright in the centre of the raft and Sophia was told to hang on to this at all times, in case she was swept over the side. Spray from the ceaseless rapids drenched them even more totally than the rain the previous night. Nobody spoke because it was all too obvious that one mistake in shooting the near continuous rapids could mean a very nasty accident, perhaps even death. Ducking, diving, rolling, smashing, the voyage took seven gruelling hours during which time it was impossible to eat, drink or do anything other than hold on tight and hope for the best. But it was better than the three days it had taken to ascend and, before nightfall, they were back at Manna. Arriving late at the outskirts, none of the villagers would come out of their homes to help them locate their horses, in case of evil spirits or wild animals. Abdul had to be sent all the way to the British Residence before the horses could be brought up and the tired group could reach the comfort of the post.

Although, next night, they were home at Bengkulu, the trip was far from uneventful. They were obliged to ride in the noon heat, which made it extremely hot, and, at one point, the high tide almost drowned the whole party at a spot on the shore known locally as "the place of death". Sophia had to abandon riding side saddle and sit fully astride under her long dress as, with the horses virtually swimming, they fought to turn them so as to be able to regain dry land before being completely cut off. They were all expert horsemen and the horses, fortunately, also kept their heads. The beach route was quickly abandoned and the party rode through shoreline forest until the dangerous cliffs could be passed.

The Company's officers at Fort Marlborough were astounded when they appeared at Bengkulu.

"We thought we'd never see you again," said Jennings with obvious relief.

The little party was vigorously applauded as they rode through the arched gates of the fort and into the great central parade ground.

That evening, which happened to coincide with a dinner in the officer's mess to mark the birthday of King George, an exception was made to the men only rule. Bathed and refreshed, Lady Sophia Raffles entered the hall to be greeted by a standing ovation from the tough soldiers of the garrison. Once she was seated, Raffles rose to propose the first toast of the evening:

"My wife, my heroine."

Not only a toast but three cheers were raised for the First Lady, who had scaled mountains, braved wild animals, shot countless rapids and travelled where no white woman had ever been before.

The cheerfulness of that evening found no counterpart next day when, bright and early, Jennings reported to Raffles that, in his absence, the Sub-Treasurer had absconded with most of the Fort's financial reserves, over 160,000 Spanish dollars!

Raffles was aghast.

"So, we're broke!"

"'Fraid so, Sir."

"Didn't anyone see what he was doing?"

"Not a sign, Sir. In fact, since he applied for sick leave, we all felt sorry for him. You know how easy it is to be hale and healthy one day here and dead the next."

While nobody starved, the next few months were miserable for want of hard cash and, worse still, in reporting the matter to London Raffles felt that it not only made him look negligent but might lead the Directors to believe that almost as soon as he had arrived in Sumatra he was already again demanding a financial bale out instead of turning in the profit they hoped for.

"Damn the man," exploded Raffles with exasperation.

Travers returned from Batavia with the news that the Dutch seemed belligerent and intended the fullest resumption of their posts in Sumatra.

"Then, we must act before they do", Raffles responded.

He sent a survey team south to Lampung with Sophia's brother, Lieutenant William Hull, in charge, and the party was instructed to find a suitable place to establish a post and hoist the Company's flag. One of the few Dutch men who had worked with Raffles, Herman Muntinghe now appeared at Palembang to take command of the post on behalf of Holland. Sultan Ahmad Najimu'd-din sent a messenger to Raffles to ask what to do. No European had ever travelled to Palembang from Bengkulu overland before but, with his recent explorations in mind, Raffles dispatched Captain Salmond overland with a small force to "find out the facts". Raffles also now needed to know urgently about the situation in Padang and, no sooner had Captains Hull and Salmond left, than he announced a second trip to the interior. To save time he decided to sail north along the coast in the 'Lady Raffles.'

The American, Dr Horsfield, had joined Raffles from his studies in Java and asked to accompany the expedition along with Dr Arnold. Raffles had in mind several objectives. First, he wanted to assess for himself the importance to the Company of Padang; secondly he wanted to see whether he could sign a treaty of friendship and cooperation with the rulers of the Minangkabau Empire, located among the mountains above the town.

In addition to his scientific studies, Raffles was deeply interested in the Minangs as the custodians of Malay culture. Arriving, as he had, in the Indies at Penang, at first he had assumed that the peoples of the archipelago were all Malays. Only later had he discovered that the Indies were home to many disparate peoples, speaking many languages. Malay tended to be the lingua franca among many of them and it was for this reason alone that he had, for example, been able to communicate with the rulers of Java, who were not Malay but Javanese. Aware that the area north of Padang was known as the cradle of Malay culture Raffles had to go there.

The voyage along the coast was very scenic, with the usual evening thunder storms. The approach to the little town of Padang was also exceptional and quaint. The "Lady Raffles" took in sail and was towed slowly up the Padang river until, on one side, appeared the town and, on the other, a Malay kampong.

The town was made up of European and Chinese houses fronting in a dead straight line along the banks of the dead straight river. When they disembarked, to be greeted at the foot of the gang plank by Resident William Farnaby, Raffles was vexed to discover that, despite messages being sent on in advance, the Resident had made no arrangements for a trip to the interior thinking, as Presgrave had earlier, that once Raffles realized the difficulties he would change his mind. Like Presgrave, Farnaby immediately discovered that he was very wrong.

On this trip, Raffles felt that he was about to enter an ancient kingdom, and he ordered the provision of an escort of fifty Sepoys. This was easy enough but he also needed two hundred porters and this took a few days to arrange. Raffles put the time to excellent use, discovering that Dutch rights in Padang were purely commercial and that sovereignty was still in the hands of the Sultan of Minangkabau! Raffles was jubilant.

"They have no political rights here", he told Farnaby. "If I can negotiate them, Padang can be ours forever."

Eventually, toward the end of July, 1818, to the beat of a drum and with a cannonade from the little fort, Raffles set out in procession from Padang to try to meet the Sultan of Minangkabau. With him went the local ruler of Padang, two Minagkabau princes, Resident Farnaby and the principal traders of the town but not Dr Arnold, who had contracted fever on the ride back from Manna and was now very ill.

No European had ever visited the hinterland and Farnaby wore his doubts on his sleeve. He was less concerned about the terrain than about the fact that the Minangs were thought to be hostile.

"I hope I get back from this with my life", he told his wife, before departure.

Mrs Farnaby was in tears, holding their little son close to her bosom.

The weather was torrentially wet and messages reached Raffles' column that, ahead of his advance, there were more than twenty swollen rivers, some of them impassable. As usual, Raffles decided to press on. In his mind nothing was impassable! They were mounted but very quickly obliged to lead their horses. The forest covered Barisan Mountains, ahead of them, were the same range that they had climbed on their trip inland from Manna and Raffles knew a two thousand metre ascent lay ahead. But, unlike in the country of the Pasemah, swollen rivers aside, for the first two days, the ground remained suitable for horses and, despite incessant rain, good time was made. After the rice fields of the coast they even passed through pastures with herds of cattle and buffalo.

Raffles had heard of the legendary business acumen of the Minangs and now came to experience it first hand and at an early stage of his visit to their homelands. Roughly a day's journey apart, large sheds made of woven rattan, thatched with atap were available to travellers - on payment of a fee. Some of these sheds, in which travellers slept on the ground, accommodated the whole of Raffles three hundred strong party, and Raffles and Sophia could win no privacy over and above that available to everyone else. Raffles was never a man to stand on ceremony or to let a little discomfort stand between him and his objective and he was happy that Sophia accepted the situation good naturedly. Many a lady would have complained loudly and long but adventure as much in Sophia's blood as in Raffles and far from objecting she revelled in the situation.

For three days, they wound up through the

forest covered mountains in drenching rain, staying each night, bar one, at a toll house and paying their fees. The third day and night were the worst. Most of the day they picked their way over slippery rocks beside roaring cataracts. Their clothes and shoes were wet through. Their muscles ached, especially the calves. One porter lost his footing and was swept away. That night they were forced to camp, with a steep cliff behind them and a rocky precipice in front, with not a single tree for shelter. And the rain was even more torrential than during the day.

After a steep and tiring ascent, around noon on the fourth day, the sun came out and they found themselves, not among the kind of tumble-down huts they had encountered near Manna, but in a gentle, verdant, valley amid hectares of well cultivated rice fields, rising one above the other up the slopes of the mountains and among orchards and plantations dotted with sturdy and distinctive Minang houses with pointed roofs like church spires, each having numerous spires at the top of equally numerous gables. Raffles' eyes were wide with excitement.

The plains had been sparsely populated but now, with every step they took, people appeared on either side of the track, mainly men and all armed with dangerous looking spears. As the approached a village, a wooden drum at least six metres long and hanging from the branch of a tree was beaten to give warning of their arrival. The more the drum was beaten the more people appeared, until Raffles' party found itself with an escort of thousands of villagers, all shouting lustily and brandishing their weapons - mot in hostility but in welcome!

After yet another example of Minang business acumen, tolls were agreed and paid and Raffles' column moved on with the self same scene repeated at village after village almost every hour of the day. Villagers not only crowded the track to see them but groups could be seen standing on the very hilltops, straining to catch a glimpse of the unusual cavalcade. At every village, Raffles was entertained in the home of the local headman or chief and none would let him leave without pressing upon him copious quantities of food and drink.

As in the country of the Pasemah, Sophia was the focus of all attention. Once again, no white woman had ever been seen here and, with her fair complexion, Sophia looked to them more like an angel than a woman. As before, women and children pressed around her pushing and pulling to such an extent that she was afraid of falling down. Babies were brought to her to be blessed, the people supposing that she had divine powers.

Soon, there stretched before them a great lake and, around the lake, numerous villages and towns were plainly visible, with the 'horns' at either end of the distinctive saddle back roofs of the houses pointing skywards among the tree tops. The land was as rich as it could be with the fields crowded with cows, oxen, horses and buffaloes and the hillsides green with coffee plants, olive trees, sugar cane, indigo and maize. Many a house or village was sheltered by coconut groves.

"I wish Bengkulu was like this," Raffles observed to Farnaby.

Farnaby, who had been so opposed to the trip looked blank and glazed.

In the distance they could see the smoking volcano of Mount Merapi, rearing up into the clouds to a height of well over three thousand metres. Many large canoes plied the lake, each one capable of carrying a hundred men or up to six tons weight. The leaders of Raffles' party boarded a canoe for the beautiful journey across the dark waters, while the remainder proceeded by land. They crossed the lake in a single day but had to wait another for the main party to catch up. Raffles' final objective was the home of the Sultan of Menangkabau, high in the Barisan Mountains. As they wound higher, Raffles discovered that many minerals were mined and he learned that gold was plentiful about ten days march away.

"It's fantastic, Farnaby, said Raffles with disbelief. "They have everything here. Java is supposed to be rich but I think Sumatra is richer."

On the seventh day, they approached the capital city of the Menangkabau. As before, the great warning drums were beaten and, as before, men in turbans and women with their heads, and most of their faces, covered, mobbed them into the town. Here, the Minangkabau were almost exclusively an agricultural people and the capital had no focus similar to the palaces at Yogja and Solo. A great palace there undeniably was, many times larger than even the wealthiest farmers house but all the houses were dispersed among the coconut groves and fields and hardly looked like a town in the European sense at all.

Raffles had brought pipes and drums all the way from Padang and now these led his party up to the great palace. There was a guard of Sepoys in front of him and another behind and the Europeans and local leaders all rode with him. The porters brought up the rear. Minangkabau spearmen lined the path leading to the palace and musicians played at the foot of the steep, narrow entrance steps. Inside and out, the palace reminded Raffles of a great sailing ship. Once inside, to left and right, the floor of a single, cavernous, room rose upwards in tiers as if to the high poop deck of a ship. Two columns of wooden pillars supported the many roofs, very much like the masts of a ship. The roofs rose in three spired gables to the left and three to the right with a saddle formed in the centre above the main entrance. Above the saddle something like a small house had been added, with gable roofs on all four sides and providing a small first storey and a diminutive second storey, amounting to not much more than an attic. The floors were of polished planks, the walls of carved and decorated timber and the roof of palm thatch.

Raffles, Sophia, Farnaby, Dr Horsfield, the Menangkabau princes, the ruler of Padang and the leading merchants, were all invited to join the Sultan in a large circle seated on the floor. The guests were requested to leave their shoes outside. Raffles had brought several pack horses with him and now their burdens were carried in and fine and unusual gifts presented to the Sultan. Raffles explained the purpose and hope of the British East India Company and the Sultan described the sufferings of his people at the hands of the Dutch, when they were able to operate from their base at Padang. Raffles was delighted to hear several chiefs express the hope that, after their absence of twenty three years, the British would continue to keep the Dutch out of this part of Sumatra. Before nightfall a treaty of friendship and cooperation was signed.

The leaders of Raffles' party were invited to spend the night at the huge palace, which could accommodate fully one hundred and fifty other guests. The Sultan and his family stayed in small rooms along the rear wall of the great hall. It was thought that Raffles and his lady might like the privacy of the large room on the first floor and their personal effects were taken there in readiness. After the treaty signing, food and drink were brought and, in the cool darkness of evening, illuminated by burning torches, the young men and maidens of the town entertained the foreigners with lively traditional dances. By about nine o'clock the dancing was over and, tired but satisfied, Raffles and Sophia were free to rest.

For the first time in more than a week they were alone. Rattan screens had been hung across the bottom of the wooden stairway to prevent unauthorized access. There was no bed, but, the floor's covering of reed mats was curiously soft and there were large, gaily woven, pillows for their heads. They lay down together, their heads against a large window with open wooden shutters, Sophia cradled in Raffles' left arm. Raffles propped himself up on one elbow.

"Who could have imagined in the Pump Room at Cheltenham that within a few months you would tread where no white woman has ever trodden and that together we should discover this great empire of the Minangkabau."

"It's like a fairy story," whispered Sophia. "I'm so happy."

Raffles bent and kissed her on the lips.

For the first time in more than a week they were at least able to step out of their grubby and smelly clothes and into clean night attire. Sophia looked curiously angelic as she lay in the moonlight in her white nightdress, her long hair framing a pale face.

"I love you so much", whispered Raffles moving on top of her and feeling her legs open beneath him.

"I love you too, my darling", said Sophia softly as they made love gently and lovingly, each hoping that a creaking floor board would not embarrass them.

Afterwards, they lay together peacefully, eyes closed, needing no further words to reflect the happiness and love they felt.

Sophia suddenly opened her eyes wide.

"Won't it be funny if I get pregnant," she laughed. "One child born aboard ship, another conceived in the roof of a palace in the Indies."

Raffles gave her a final hug and they fell asleep,

arms wrapped tenderly around each other.

Raffles decided to return to Padang by a more direct but not necessarily easier route. As usual, now that he had achieved his objective in surveying the land of the Minangkabau, he was anxious to return to base. The Sultan advised him which route was best and gave him guides. Despite its relative shortness the terrain on the return trip was little different to what it had been during the advance. Instead of climbing perpetually through rocks, mud and swollen streams now they were descending perpetually and, if anything, finding the going even more difficult and tiring.

It took five days to regain Padang, having covered over three hundred and fifty kilometres, on horseback and on foot, in fourteen days, across some of the most challenging travelling country in the Indies. At Padang, before doing anything else, the one things most yearned for by the Europeans was put in hand - a wash.

Raffles' exhilaration at his achievements was only marred by the very sad news that in his absence Dr Arnold had died.

After a gorgeous sail back to Bengkulu, in what now seemed like the unbelievable luxury of the 'Lady Raffles', Raffles arrived back at Fort Marlborough. Without pausing for food or rest he called a briefing.

The news was bad. Captain Salmond had ill advisedly gone ahead of his troops into Palembang to try to see the Sultan. Captured by the Dutch he had been sent as a prisoner to Batavia. In retaliation, Raffles sent more troops up the Musli River toward Palembang but with instructions only to intimidate not to attack.

"We urgently need to know where we stand," Raffles told his staff. "Is Sumatra to be British or not? Shall we resist the Dutch or not?"

Raffles had signed new treaties with the Pasemah and the Minangs. Padang was still British, Palembang might still be, if his earlier treaty was respected, Bengkulu was British, Aceh might be and there were a host of smaller posts.

"Now is the time to strike, while we are strong and the Dutch are weak," He said.

Raffles needed little time to reach a decision. Rushing to Government House, even before Sophia had time for a night's sleep, Raffles broke the news:

"I must go to Calcutta immediately to meet Lord Moira."

Sumatra was a land of immense potential, perhaps more so than Java. The British had been in Bengkulu for a century or more, in Padang for a quarter of a century, they had a treaty with Palembang and the Dutch had been forced to give up Aceh.

"Sophia", said Raffles. "I must go. If I can convince Lord Moira, Sumatra can be ours."

"I understand, my prince," said Sophia putting her hands around his neck with her smiling face with its mischievous eyes close to his.

"I'll come too."

CHAPTER TWELVE

It was a joyous day indeed when ships of any size stopped at Bengkulu and the arrival of the tiny brig 'Udney' seemed to offer Raffles the best chance of getting to Calcutta quickly. The 'Lady Raffles' had sailed on, and time was critical. If he delayed, the British East India Company might lose Sumatra to the Dutch. If he offered armed resistance, he lacked sufficient troops and guns and still might lose. And if he challenged the Dutch without proper authorization he risked the same kind of censure from Leadenhall Street that he had received over his handling of Java. Action and resources were bound inextricably to policy and only a visit to Calcutta could sort out what the Company's policy was toward Sumatra - in time.

The 'Udney' was very small and not equipped to carry passengers. A tiny cabin was made available, alive with scorpions and centipedes, and with only one porthole admitting air or light. If the porthole had to be closed, the cabin was plunged into total darkness. Sophia said nothing. After all it was she who had insisted on coming. And Raffles also said nothing. What he was doing had to be done. The voyage along the south coast of Sumatra was pleasant enough and long hours were spend in a quiet corner of the deck. But as they sailed up the Bay of Bengal the forces of hell were unleashed against them. Every night, rain fell in torrents, forks of lightening tore across the dark sky and thunder clapped loudly enough to stop the heart! Even with minimal canvas, the 'Udney's masts were bent double before the wind and the little ship was tossed in waves several times its height. Sophia found it impossible either to eat or sleep and, as when she first boarded the "Lady Raffles' off the English coast, she once again became a skeleton hardly able to speak or move. All day long the seas were heavy, the wind blew and each night rain sheeted down from angry clouds, thunder roared like massed cannon and bolts of electricity formed fiery tracers on every side. The ship had taken a terrible pounding and Raffles and Olivia held each other tight one night as they heard a fearful bang from the deck accompanied by frenzied shouts and commands.

"Mizzen's gone," screamed a voice.

"Cut away the rigging," came the shouted command. "Hold her into the wind helmsman."

The ship bucked and tossed like an angry stallion wrenching away from its halter. Sophia was tearful.

"What is it? What is it?" she asked burying her face in Raffles' chest.

"I think we've lost a mast", said Raffles, gravely. "Will you be alright here while I go and look?"

It was impossible to gain the deck without risk of being swept overboard. Raffles put his head up above the companionway, rain instantly pouring down his face. At the bow, he could see men frantically hacking away at tangled rigging with hatchets, the captain standing high up hollering commands. The mainmast was still intact and Raffles knew enough about sailing to know that in a wind like this the last thing wanted was a lot of sail. The 'Udney' just needed enough to keep into the wind. He closed the hatch on the screaming wind and teeming rain and returned to Sophia. The cabin was pitch black because it was impossible to have a lighted candle. He felt for her on her bunk and lay down beside her in the pitching vessel, cradling her in his arms.

"We are in God's hands, my dear," he said.

Sophia snuggled closer.

At the mouth of the Hoogly, they were boarded by a pilot from Calcutta but it was plain to everyone that the man was much the worse for drink. He could work but not without slurring his words and stumbling about the deck. Within a hour of his arrival the poor 'Udney' was broadside on to a sandbar with giant waves crashing into her and over her.

"Get us off this bar you drunken bastard", roared the captain with a hand on the pilot's neck. "If you sink my ship it's the bottom of the Bay for you."

Somehow or other, the 'Udney' made it into calmer waters across the bar, but her damage was great and the pumps could hardly keep pace with the inflow of water below. Once within the relative safety of the Hoogly, another ship was sent for from Fort William and, despite their brush with death and their unkept appearance, Sir Stamford and Lady Raffles were eventually welcomed at Calcutta with a nineteen gun salute.

Never had human beings been more glad to set foot again on terra firma!

Lord Moira knew that Raffles was in the Hoogly, bound for Fort William, because of the SOS that had been sent for a new ship. When Raffles and Sophia stepped ashore, his personal carriage was waiting at the dock with a liveried driver and footmen. Raffles and Sophia were inexpressibly relieved.

"Last time I was here I had to find my own

way", Raffles told Sophia, squeezing her hand in the privacy of the luxurious coach. Once again he drove under one of the great entrance archways to Government House with a stone lion pacing threateningly above. This time the couple were met by one of Lord Moira's European adjutants on the very steps of Government House.

"Welcome, Sir Stamford. Welcome Lady Raffles," the aide beamed, assisting each from the coach. Indian bearers rushed forward to pick up their few bags.

"I am Major Forbes-Miller and His Lordship has asked me to escort you to the guest apartment here at Government House."

Raffles and Sophia smiled gratefully.

"His Lordship bids you a good rest and expresses the hope that he will have the honour of meeting you at dinner tonight."

Raffles could hardly believe what was happening. He and Moira had never met and they had been at daggers drawn ever since the Governor General had chosen to take the part of Colonel Gillespie. On the other hand Moira had written to him in Bengkulu to say that he was welcome to come to Calcutta to discuss the crisis in Sumatra.

"Perhaps, now, he's come round to my way of thinking," Raffles told Sophia. Dinner was a purely social occasion and Raffles had no opportunity to find out. However, he noted that Lord Moira was far more respectful and solicitous than he had been in many of his dispatches. Next morning, after and early breakfast, he sat with Lord Moira in the self same reception room where he had met Lord Minto for the first time, now, so long ago.

Moira was a very different man from his predecessor. He was tall, with the ramrod back of a soldier. His face was thin and pale with no hint of even the smallest enjoyment of life. His eye seemed to have a perpetual cynical glint as if doubting every word he was told. And yet, facts were facts and cynical or not, like it or not, the noble Lord now found himself with more in common with the 'troublesome' Raffles than ever before. Moira was a man under fire. The merchants of London were shouting, the British merchants of India were shouting, the British merchants of Penang were shouting, the China traders were shouting; even the Penang Government had joined in the shouting. Everybody touching the Dutch controlled ports of the Indies was shouting because of the imposition of swinging new fees!

Because it took months for news to be disseminated, Lord Moira's opening statement, while not surprising, was unknown to Raffles.

"Malacca has been handed back to the Dutch," Moira told Raffles. "The new governor, Timmerman Thyssen, is already there. Now, the whole British trading establishment is up in arms in case we lose the Strait of Malacca."

Raffles smiled a tight smile.

"Quite so," my Lord he said but with professional detachment and with none of the bitterness which might have been expected from a less generous man.

"And we have received a protest about your activities in Sumatra from the Dutch Governor of Batavia, Van der Capellan. He says that you are a restless spirit and that so long as we let you loose in the Indies there can be no peace."

Raffles mentally prepared himself for the usual criticism and censure he had come to expect from the Company but Lord Moira softened the blow by adding with a smile:

"Our merchants are calling you their restless warrior."

Raffles looked modestly down at his shoes. To the Dutch he was a restless spectre they would dearly like to be rid off. To the British he was a restless warrior. Between the two lie the trading interests of each nation and the policy decisions flowing from them which could only be taken in Britain and Holland. For thirteen years Raffles had been fighting a lonely and thankless war in the Indies to safeguard British trading interests. Often it had seemed to him that he was the only Englishman who could see the terrible catastrophe waiting to ambush British trade in the East. Perhaps, at last, he was about to get some support from where it counted - London.

"Tell me what's happening in Sumatra," asked Moira.

Raffles spoke candidly of Dutch efforts to banish the British East India Company from Sumatra, Java and everywhere else in the Indies and of his old fears for the Company's sea routes from Britain to the Far East - fears Moira now knew only too well were shared by the entire merchant community. On the other hand he was not Lord Minto and orders were orders.

"My orders from London are that we should do nothing to antagonize the Dutch. That's the problem. But there may be another way."

Raffles looked at him keenly.

"Another way, My Lord?"

"Van der Capellan is suggesting an exchange of posts so that The Netherlands will basically end up with the Indies south of Riau and the British will be free to operate in the Indies north of Riau and as far to the north as we wish - into Thailand, if we want."

Raffles was by no means unfamiliar with the ideas about swapping posts, that had for some time been circulating among the Company's officers. He would have

preferred Sumatra and, until the last, continued to entertain hopes that it could be retained for Britain, but if Sumatra
was not to be British maybe the least they could settle for
should be free access to the Strait of Malacca.

"Their suggestion is," Lord Moira went on,
"that they will give us Malacca if we give them Bengkulu."

Raffles was often accused by jealous colleagues
and subordinates of being an entirely self serving and ambitious man. For all its insignificance Bengkulu was the only
post he now held or could expect to hold in the Indies and,
had he been selfish, he could easily have fought for its retention. Without it he was nothing. But, objectively, Raffles
felt that, accept in the context of the whole of Sumatra,
Bengkulu would be no loss to the Company and told Moira
so.

"But, if we are to be left only with Malacca we
must have a base to the south, otherwise the Dutch will
always be able to cut us off from China and Japan."

Raffles was not surprised that Lord Moira
agreed with this but he was very surprised that His Lordship was prepared to authorize, without so much as a refer-
ence to Leadenhall Street, that Raffles should explore to the
south of Malacca in more detail to see where a new base
might feasibly be established.

"But don't, for Heaven's sake upset the
Dutch," he emphasized. "Try to find a place where the
Dutch have no claims and negotiate a treaty. And on no
account raise a flag where there wasn't one before."

"May I take the liberty of asking why, My
Lord. Surely an uninhabited isle or a place where no foreign flag has ever been planted will be ideal."

Moira looked at Raffles as if he was about to
impart the most secret secrets of state.'

"This is for your ears only, Raffles, but I have

been given to believe that talks will, in fact, begin soon in London to try to arrive at an agreement to partition the Indies between us and the Dutch. We don't want the founding of any new posts to disrupt these discussions."

"How do you assess the probabilities, My Lord."

"My guess is that those parts of Sumatra where the Dutch have already established posts will go to them and that they will therefore control the Strait of Sunda."

"Then, our only option is the Strait of Malacca."

"Exactly."

Raffles sounded him out about the possibility of a treaty with the ruler of Aceh, for centuries a strategic, independent trading port on the northern tip of Sumatra. Moira agreed that it might be a possibility, along with the Riau islands or Johore - so long as the Dutch had never had a post there.

"In this case, we must give unto Caesar what is Caesar's", he said.

"I am quite clear, My Lord.

"I hope so, Sir Stamford," said Lord Moira, " because we don't want to give the Dutch further grounds for attacking us. You may depend on me with regard approval for the establishment of a base south of Malacca but, concerning Sumatra, it may be distasteful to you to learn that I have been obliged to already write to Governor General Van der Capellan disavowing your activities there. You must withdraw your troops and Padang must be handed back without delay."

"As your Lordship wishes," was all Raffles felt he could say.

"It may not be as I wish but those are the political realities and we must respect them."

Politics was politics and for the whole of his career in the Indies Raffles had been emeshed in the web of European politics, struggling vainly to pull London round to a point of view he felt most favoured the British East India Company and British trade in the Far East. He could try his best to influence events but, ultimately, politics was in command.

Moira told Raffles that he should return to the Indies as soon as possible and begin the search for a base south of Malacca, capable of providing free access to the South China Sea, adding the warning that negotiations between the Dutch and British in London could change the scenario at any time.

Captain John Coombs of Penang was deputed to assist Raffles in any negotiations south of Malacca, together with the Former British Resident of Malacca, Major William Farquhar, who would be put in command of the new post.

Moira's apparent regard for Raffles, a man he could hardly snub now that he had been knighted by the Prince Regent, even went so far as to extend to confirmation that any new post east of Malacca would fall within Raffles' jurisdiction as Lieutenant Governor of Bengkulu, rather than under the command of Prince of Wales Island.

Moira now put two ships at Raffles' disposal for his mission, the 'Nearchus' commanded by Captain William Maxfield and the 'Minto' commanded by Lieutenant J. S. Criddle. With him were to sail Dr Arnold's replacement, Dr William Jack, also a botanist, two young French naturalists and the missionary, Dr Nathaniel Wallich.

There was no point dallying longer in Calcutta. Raffles had been told what he had come to find out. The loss of Sumatra was more or less confirmed. Now the race was on to establish a base south of Malacca which could guarantee freedom of access to the Malacca Strait.

Raffles and Sophia sailed in the 'Nearchus' and the others in the 'Minto'. In addition, two company cruisers were assigned to Penang to survey the Malacca Strait, the Investigator' captained by J.G.F. Crawford and the ' Discovery' captained by Captain Daniel Ross, the famous hydrographer. Moira and London wanted to be absolutely certain that the Malacca Strait really was a viable alternative to the Sunda Strait.

Up 'till the day they sailed for 'home', Raffles and Sophia had remained in Calcutta fully three months. Soon after their arrival, they had moved out of Government House to rented accommodation of their own. Sophia found the heat extremely trying, especially since, true to the thought she had voiced in the palace of the Sultan of Minangkabau, she was pregnant with her second child! Pregnant or not, she had managed to go on a number of elephant rides with Lord Moira, seated comfortably in a howdah. They had even gone on a tiger hunt together. And, as was ever the case, their temporary home in Calcutta was full, morning, noon and night, with scholars, missionaries and, most of all, merchants pressing Raffles to look after their interests in the Indies.

"You are our only champion", Sir Stamford. "If we rely on Government, our business in the Far East will be wiped out by the Dutch."

Feeling more than ever the only man likely to be able to save British trade interests in the Indies, Raffles and Sophia set out for Penang. Sophia was extremely apprehensive about bad weather and Raffles' sense of responsibility weighed on him to such an extent that, while Sophia often enjoyed the warm sunshine above deck, he was confined below in darkness with a pounding headache. Aside from his responsibilities, Raffles was besieged by fears which he kept from Sophia. If Bengkulu was lost his lieutenant governorship was lost with it. Given the Company's apparent hostility to him, at best probably he could expect a residency, perhaps not in the Indies but in India proper. Where would his interest in the Indies be then? What would his prospects for advancement be then? What could he expect to earn as a mere commercial official? With a second child on the way could they afford to live to the standard they wished? During the invasion of Java, at least he had had the comfort of knowing that he would govern Java so long as it was in British hands - even the hope that it could remain British. On this trip not a single prospect was certain and the ground beneath his feet at Bengkulu might soon be swept away. It was enough to give even the strongest man a headache. More than any other of his ventures, Raffles had a sense that the latest was make or break, do or die and he arrived at Prince of Wales Island in this frame of mind.

The Council and company bureaucracy at Penang had never forgiven him for stepping outside the Company's career structure and taking his destiny into his own hands by fighting for the interests of British traders in a more visionary and aggressive manner than his superiors or even his Government in Whitehall. Just as he had not expected much from Lord Moira, he did not arrive in Penang with high hopes of support and assistance. The new Governor, Colonel John Bannerman, was an old soldier whose impression of Raffles was as an ambitious adventurer to whose grandiose schemes the military should be subservient. He stood firmly on what he thought was the side of Lord Moira and the late Colonel Gillespie.

But, just as he had been pleasantly surprised by his reception in Calcutta, at Penang, Raffles found Bannerman besieged by the same chorus of alarm from merchants about free access to the Strait of Malacca as Moira was experiencing at Fort William. Timing favoured Raffles for once. If anything, opinion among Penang merchants was much harder than anywhere else because, with Malacca once again in Dutch hands, all could too easily foresee an abrupt end to the fortunes of Penang. Like Moira, Colonel Bannerman had already been forced to bow before the wind and had dispatched Major Farquhar, the former Resident at Malacca, to points south of that city to try to negotiate the same kind of treaties that Raffles now held in his brief.

Farquhar had signed a treaty with the ruler of Siak in Riau and was about to make a second trip, not only to the Riau islands, but to the next island group known as the Linggas, his purpose to sign as many treaties as possible at places where the Dutch had no presence. Though the Riau and Lingga islands penetrated deeply into the Indies archipelago, in fact, they were part of the Sultanate of Johore, on the southern tip of the Malay mainland, and, despite the Anglo-Dutch talks in London, Company officials in Penang were prepared to take the risk that dependencies of sultanates on the Malay peninsula would not be handed to the Dutch but could remain British if the British sphere of influence was deemed to be the peninsula. Raffles' brief from Lord Moira differed from Bannerman's to Farquhar in that his first objective was to be Aceh and, if negotiations there failed, followed by some other suitable place, including some of those on Farquhar's hit list. Raffles foresaw no conflict between himself and Farquhar because, while in Calcutta, he had once again been appointed Agent to the Governor General among the Malay Chiefs. Thus, his position was senior to that of Farquhar.

On arrival in Penang, Raffles learnt that Aceh had already been occupied by the Dutch. His snap judgement was:

"Then, there's no point in going there!"

Colonel Bannerman disagreed because it had also been learned that the Dutch were not welcome in Aceh and that there still existed a possibility that the British could negotiate a deal to exclude them with one or other of two rival pretenders to the throne. Nothing had been heard from the talks in London so, in theory, anything was still possible.

"In any case," Bannerman told Raffles, "I think you should obey Lord Moira's orders which state clearly that your first objective is to be Aceh. Let's at least try and, if we fail, we'll be right to look somewhere else."

Raffles (and others) regarded Bannerman as a singularly unimaginative man and, knowing how the Dutch thought, he was convinced that they intended to occupy every strategic port in Sumatra and that it was a waste of time going to Aceh if their troops had already landed.

In London, the Dutch were lambasting Raffles at the talks with the British Government and the British were so unwilling to offend them that they not only accepted the lambasting but supported its propriety. Leadenhall Street even wrote to Moira sounding him out as to whether Raffles should be dismissed from his post a second time! Its letter would take three months to arrive during which time Raffles was bustling about the Indies as never before - it was make or break, life or death.

Maps had been extremely important in Raffles career and, once again, he poured over a chart of the Strait of Malacca with Farquhar. As a new base, the major favoured the Karimun Islands, close to Riau but Raffles pointed time and again at the island of Singapore.

"This is the spot."

Raffles dispatched Major Farquhar in the 'Ganges' to the Riau islands to link up with the survey ship 'Discovery' and ascertain if any base for a post had been found in the Karimuns or Riau more suitable than Singapore. So certain was he of the strategic correctness of Singapore and fretting with impatience at Penang, Raffles promptly sailed after Farquhar.

"I can't wait. I just can't wait", Raffles told Sophia.

Since the Dutch were already in Aceh, Colonel Bannerman had ruled that Raffles should not go there until there could be time for a dispatch to be sent to Lord Moira, explaining the new position, and a reply received.

"Typical soldier", smiled Raffles quietly to Sophia. "He can't bear to disobey orders, even if circumstances have made them obsolete."

Bannerman hoped that Raffles would remain quietly in Penang until the reply came. But, by this stage in his career, Raffles had become an experienced tactician, and he had written back to Colonel Bannerman, assuring the good soldier that he would not go to Aceh. Knowing that if he suggested proceeding anywhere else to the east Bannerman would use the same rationale to try to stop him, without further consultation with Bannerman, or even his fellow commissioner, Captain Coombs, Raffles had ordered his luggage stowed aboard the sleek and fast 'Indiana', a ship, the presence of which in Penang, he had arranged clandestinely.

With him went the 'Minto', which had accompanied him from India, and also the schooner 'Enterprise. Including the two survey ships he now commanded a little fleet of eight vessels off the Malay coast with nothing to do other than establish a new post for the British East India Company. As the fleet sailed past Malacca Governor Timmerman was more than a little suspicious and could Governor van der Capellan have seen them from Batavia he would have been livid. Just as he believed that The Netherlands was about to drive Britain out of the Indies the bette noir of the Dutch, Sir Thomas Stamford Raffles, was re-entering waters that they felt to be theirs with a battle fleet!

"Anyway, what can Bannerman do," Sophia had asked, largely rhetorically, as she had helped him pack his bags.

Bringing up with Farquhar and without even asking for the results of the survey, Raffles ordered him immediately to Singapore and also to nearby Johore to spy out the situation there. Farquar was accompanied by the 'Nearchus' and the 'Mercury', each containing military contingents sent from Penang. At the same time, Raffles sent a note to Resident Jennings at Bengkulu ordering that a battalion of troops about to be relieved there should be diverted urgently to the Riau islands.

Though he had no definite idea where it would be, Raffles had not the slightest doubt that he would establish a new post south of Malacca nor that Singapore was the hot favourite. He wrote to John Adam, now the Company's Chief Secretary at Calcutta and a man who had sat in on most of his talks with Lord Moira:

" The island of Singapore seems in every respect most peculiarly adapted for our object. Its position in the Straits of Singapore is far more convenient and commanding than even Riau, for our China trade passing down the Straits of Malacca, and every native vessel that sails through the Straits of Riau must pass in sight of it."

He added:

"The larger harbour of Johore is capacious and easily defensible and the British flag, once hoisted, there would be no want of supplies."

On the fateful morning of January 28, 1819 the squadron anchored off Singapore!

Raffles called a council of his captains and Major Farquhar and no landing was made that day. Meanwhile, a deputation arrived from shore to enquire the mission of the British ships. Raffles told them and learned from them that no Dutch post had ever been established at Singapore.

"This is absolutely perfect", Raffles told the Council triumphantly. "And exactly what Lord Moira stipulated."

The British learned that Johore itself was deserted but that a senior official of the Sultan of Johore still lived at Singapore.

Next morning Raffles went ashore with Farquhar and one Sepoy guard to meet the Sultan's representative, Maharaja Abdu'l-Rahman, who bore the official title of Temenggong or governor.

"We don't want to frighten them", Raffles had told his captains. "I will go ashore with a small party."

Of course, Raffles was in his element because he spoke fluent Malay, knew the Malays and their ways and knew exactly how to relate to them. He was certainly not afraid. Abdu'l-Rahman greeted him in a very friendly manner at his house, close to the Singapore River, and told Raffles that if he wanted to set up a post at Singapore he would have to ask the Sultan. Though Raffles fleet was relatively small, Abdu'l-Rahman was among those who had seen the great battle fleet sail past Singapore to Java in 1811 and he knew the power of the British.

Abdu'l-Rahman told Raffles that his namesake Abdu'l-Rahman was now Sultan but that since he was the son of the deceased Sultan Mahmud's second wife, his position was disputed by the eldest son of his first wife. The name of the disputant was Husain Muhammad, also known as Tunku Long. Abdu'l-Rahman had only been made Sultan because Tunku Long had been away visiting a sultan in the north. Before he died, the old Sultan had declared Tunku Long his successor but Abdu'l-Rahman refused to recognize the legitimacy of his claim.

Temenggong Abdu'l-Rahman assured Raffles that he personally had no objection to the British establishing a post at Singapore, a large sparsely populated island with more than enough room for everybody. Accordingly, Raffles signed a provisional treaty guaranteeing Singapore protection from its enemies and its ruler an annual payment of $3,000. No other nation was to be allowed to establish a similar post. Since Temenggong Abdu'l-Rahman saw no reason why final agreement would be withheld by the Sultan, Raffles also secured permission to begin landing men and supplies and to hoist the standard of the British East India Company.

Instead of going directly to Sultan Abdu'l-Rahman, then living in Lingga, Raffles decided to send Major Farquhar to Riau to bring back Tunku Long.

"Abdu'l-Rahman already has a treaty with the Dutch", Raffles explained to Farquhar but Tunku Long doesn't - and he's the legitimate ruler."

Farquhar already knew Tunku Long, and his own wife was Malay, so he was therefore the ideal choice to win the pretender's confidence and escort him to Singapore. While British Resident of Malacca, he had received a complaint from Tunku Long about the loss of his throne and now he could honestly say that he had come to help him.

"Treat him with all the honour due a member of Malay royalty", Raffles had told Farquhar before he sailed in the 'Ganges'. The 'Nearchus' also went along to endow the mission with suitable prestige. Among Malays, form and spectacle was everything. If Tunku Long was impressed he would come the more easily.

Tunku Long was delighted at Farquar's news and needed little encouragement to accompany the Major to Singapore where he perceived a unique opportunity in the offing to recover at least something of his usurped throne. Soon after his arrival, an extraordinary gathering formed beneath the trees beside the Singapore River. The Malays living in the area were all invited to meet Tunku Long.

"Is this man your Sultan", Raffles asked them in Malay, "or is your sultan Abdu'l-Rahman?"

Sitting in a circle, the Malay headmen replied unhesitatingly and unanimously that Tunku Long was their rightful Sultan.

Raffles, Farquhar and Tunku Long and the Temenggong were seated on chairs to one side of the gathering, parasols held over their heads to keep off the sun. Behind them sat their respective secretaries.

Raffles had never met Tunku Long but he knew the Malay character so well that he could speak to him in a way calculated to put him at ease and win his friendship. Raffles smiled continuously and addressed him deferentially as "Your Highness". He quickly saw visible signs that his flattery was appreciated. He spoke softly and by suggestion and used no words of command. He told Tunku Long how much he sympathized with him for the loss of his throne, how much he would like to help him regain his birth right, how much he needed the Sultan's help in establishing a post in Singapore to keep out the greedy and cruel Dutch, how appreciative His Britannic Majesty, King George, would be, how the British would protect him and how much he stood to gain from the relationship.

"Sir Stamford's words could have melted a stone," Farquhar later told his fellow ship's captains as they toasted Raffles' success.

Tunku Long also agreed to the establishment of a Company post at Singapore and Raffles acknowledged him as the rightful Sultan of Johore with the title Sultan Husain Muhammad Shah. In Malay terms it was a good deal. Each had secured mutual benefit.

On February 6, 1819 the captains and all available officers from Raffles' fleet mustered on shore for the formal signing of the treaty granting permission to establish a post. His Majesty, Sultan Husain Muhammad Shah, was provided with a seat of honour in a large marquee specially prepared for the occasion. The chair was draped in scarlet broadcloth which extended like a red carpet outside the tent. Raffles and Farquhar took their places early on either side. Offshore, the ships of the fleet were moored in line, dressed overall with gay flags fluttering in the tropical breeze. When the Sultan, his son, the Temenggong, and their staff, arrived at the tent with an escort of pikemen, an artillery battery commenced firing a royal salute which was taken up by all the guns of the assembled fleet. An honour guard of Sepoys lining the route presented arms.

The Sultan and the Temenggong sat expressionless while Raffles read and presented the Sultan with a Malay language copy of his commission from Lord Moira, Governor General of India. Lieutenant Crossley then read the treaty Raffles intended to sign with the Sultan, including a payment to him of $5,000 per year. Raffles and the Sultan each signed three copies and affixed their respective seals, one for Moira, one for the Sultan and one for the new Resident of Singapore, Major Farquhar. Sepoy guards fired a salute of three volleys. Next, Raffles presented expensive and rare gifts that he had once again brought with him from India. The Sultan was then escorted to some chairs that had been arranged outside and Raffles invited him to formally witness the hoisting of the Company's flag, which had been hauled down for the purpose. As the flag fluttered bravely at the top of the mast, the artillery again fired a royal salute and the salute was again taken up by all the ships of the fleet.

Perhaps as a portent for the future, the cosmopolitan audience in the field that day included not only Malays but Chinese, Indians, English merchants, French, Dutch and even Danes. With the principal ceremony over, Raffles and the Sultan led the guests into a large banquetting tent, where food and drink was plentifully available. That night, Raffles hosted a dinner for all British officers aboard the 'Indiana'.

When the officers dispersed for the night and he went alone to his cabin, Raffles wished Sophia could have been with him. Unfortunately, in view of her pregnancy, she had stayed behind at a rented house in Penang with Dr Jack. As he lay on his back on his bunk, hands clasped behind his head, he could see the Sultan and his party arrive for the ceremony, see the ships' flags flying bravely and their guns firing, see again the Sepoys snap to attention, hear their rifle fire. The great, red, seals of the treaty danced before his eyes together with his own signature above the title: Honourable T.S. Raffles, Lieutenant Governor of Bengkulu and its Dependencies and Agent to the Governor General of India. A few weeks ago he seemed on the brink of losing Bengkulu, his job and his life's work. Today, at Singapore, he was complete master of a post he was convinced no power on earth could force Britain to abandon.

More to please the Dutch than anything else, at this very moment the Court of Directors at Leadenhall Street was writing to Lord Moira in Calcutta:

" Although sensible of his zeal and talents, we cannot but entertain strong doubts whether Sir Thomas Raffles ought to continue to hold the situation in which he so widely and inconveniently overstepped the limits of his authority."

When news of this and other criticisms of Raffles reached Batavia van der Capellan threw a party!

Raffles was acutely aware of how much hatred his establishment of a post at Singapore would attract from the Dutch, and he specifically cautioned Farquhar to do nothing to excite it further. On the other hand, he knew that the Malays preferred trading and dealing with the British and the encouragement of exemplary relations with Malay rulers everywhere might yet lead to substantial advantages for the British East India Company.

"We must encourage them to think of Singapore as a Malay port", Raffles told Farquhar.

After the signing of the treaty, troops, tents and baggage streamed ashore and work gangs swiftly ran up temporary houses made, as usual, from bamboo and rattan with thatch roofs. Singapore island was low and tree covered, with most its tiny native population clustered at the mouth of the Singapore River. Fisher people lived in houses on stilts along its banks and Malay huts had been built to left and right. Overlooking the river was a modest hill. Inland, a handful of Chinese farmers tended gambier plantations.

Raffles instructed that a fort, mounting up to ten twelve pound cannon, and a barracks for troops, be constructed on the crest of the hill, dominating the river and its anchorage. Smaller batteries should be sited along the coast in the immediate vicinity and a cantonment for the troops laid out with adequate defenses. Raffles knew he was not establishing a mere factory at Singapore. He dreamed of a town, maybe even a city which would become the dominant entrepot of the whole Far East, one day perhaps, with great buildings reflecting its success and wealth, equal to

Calcutta or even London. Using a map hastily drawn for the occasion, he indicated to Farquhar how the new town should be laid out. He marked the site of European, Malay, Chinese and Indian quarters and pencilled in roads. Several plots of prime land he reserved for his family and friends.

Nine days later, he returned in the 'Indiana' to Penang, leaving Farquhar to build up the post and allowing time for word to spread throughout the region that the Company's flag had been hoisted irrevocably at Singapore.

As he sailed northwards along the Malay coast, the news of the settlement travelled in parallel overland to the Dutch governor of Malacca.

"We must wipe them out", he fumed to his Council. "I will have Raffles in chains for this."

In Penang, meanwhile, Raffles was writing calmly and dispassionately to John Adam:

" The occupation of Singapore destroys the political importance of Malacca, it paralyses all plans for the exclusion of our commerce and influence with the Malay states, one independent post under our flag may be sufficient to prevent the reappearance of the system of exclusive monopoly which the Dutch once exercised in these seas and would willingly re-establish."

But Raffles' victory was only in his own mind. Colonel Bannerman was furious. The years of jealousy among former colleagues in Penang now welled uncontrollably to the surface. Instead of being welcomed to Penang as a conquering hero, Raffles found himself condemned for "ambition and self aggrandizement." Moreover, the establishment in Penang was mortally afraid that the founding of Singapore was sounding their death knell! Bannerman was also terrified that Timmerman would carry out his threat to send troops to drive the British from Singapore.

He instructed Raffles, in writing, to order Farquhar to evacuate the post rather than "allow a single drop of human blood to be shed in maintaining it."

Raffles' authority was directly from Moira so he ignored the irate Governor. Bannerman even wrote to Timmerman disowning Raffles and voicing the hope that nothing premature would be done until he could obtain fresh orders from Moira. Meanwhile, he refused all Raffles' requests for money, supplies and troops.

At Batavia, Van der Capellan played into Raffles hands. Instead of ordering an immediate Dutch invasion he tried to cash in on what he thought was Raffles unpopularity in London by restricting himself to a written protest. Poor Colonel Bannerman had humiliated himself in front of the Dutch about a possible invasion that was already ruled out!

"Sticks and stones may break my bones but names can never hurt me," thought Raffles, when he heard.

In India, the influential Calcutta Journal wrote:

" We believe and earnestly hope that the establishment of a settlement under such favourable circumstances, and at a moment when we had every reason to fear that the efforts of the Dutch had been successful in excluding us altogether from the Eastern Archipelago, will receive all the support which is necessary to its progress, and that by its rapid advance in wealth, industry and population, it would attest hereafter the wisdom and foresight of the present administration and its attention to the commercial and political interests of our country."

Raffles couldn't have put it better himself!

Under pressure from the British Government not to upset the Dutch and from the merchant lobby to support Raffles, at first, Moira tried to mollify the Dutch by appearing critical of Raffles. This criticism was reflected in his correspondence with Raffles, yet he could not afford to ignore reality. The difficulty of his position is reflected in the letter circumstances eventually obliged him to write to Raffles:

" The selection of Singapore for a post is considered, as to locality, to have been highly judicious, and your proceedings in establishing a factory at that place do honour to your approved skill and ability though the measure itself, as willingly incurring a collision with the Dutch authorities is to be regretted. Your engagements with the presumed legitimate Chief of Johore and the local Government of Singapore are provisionally confirmed. It is intended to maintain the post of Singapore for the present."

Colonel Bannerman was roundly castigated and commanded to extend to Raffles every support. Men, money and supplies were rushed to Singapore! Bannerman responded to Moira that he had learned a lesson in realpolitik he would never forget as long as he lived! As his letter winged its way to Calcutta, another was on its way to him from London, forthrightly condemning his actions as "totally irreconcilable with every principle of public duty."

When he had first landed at Singapore, Raffles had inherited nothing but a near empty island and a cluster of huts. As he wrote to friends, Singapore was like a child of his own that he had "made what it is." When he arrived back in Penang Raffles had found that Sophia had given birth to a real child, a son, Leopold Stamford, named after Prince Leopold, the husband of the daughter of the Prince Regent. Within three short months Farquhar reported that five thousand people had crowded into Singapore, about half the population of Penang when Raffles first arrived and which had taken years to build up with painful slowness - living testimony to the popularity of the British in the Indies. Raffles now dreamed of the restoration of

Malacca to the Company and the consolidation and extension of its power anywhere in the Indies where the Dutch had not established posts.

But while he dreamed, Leadenhall Street and the British Government at Whitehall were again furious with him. As Moira had revealed in Calcutta, Raffles' treaties in Sumatra had been repudiated and orders issued for the return of all Dutch possessions. Just as it looked as if London could reach agreement with Holland to partition the Indies between them, news arrived that Raffles had founded Singapore! There was pandemonium in the corridors of power and The Hague was naturally furious. Knowing Britain's fear of renewed war in Europe over Dutch possessions in the Indies, Holland mercilessly pressed its attack. Whitehall turned on Leadenhall Street and Leadenhall Street fired off a string of viciously critical and unappreciative letters to Raffles.

Outside the corridors of power in London, one of Raffles' loyal assistants in Java, Charles Assey, hardened merchant opinion against the Dutch by publishing a paper highlighting the threat from Holland to Britain's entire Far East trade. Like Moira before them, Leadenhall Street and Whitehall now found themselves trying to please the Dutch by again disowning Raffles while at the same time trying to please the merchants, whose applause for the establishment of the new post at Singapore was deafening. Slowly the Government line changed from initial annoyance at Raffles to grudging acceptance of both the gravity of the threat from Holland and the immense value of Singapore. At the same time the reality sank in that Raffles had acted by no means alone but with the full knowledge and authorization of Lord Moira. Like it or not with the founding of Singapore a new game was afoot!

From Penang, Raffles, far from feeling chastised, launched an intervention in the Anglo-Dutch talks in London, urging, through correspondence, that the Dutch had no claim on Sumatra, Borneo and the thousands of other islands of the archipelago, except Java.

"Let them not involve our allies (the sultans) and the British Government in the general vortex of the ruin they are working for themselves", he thundered.

Bowing, as others had done, before the remorseless pressures of the commercial lobby, British Foreign Secretary, Viscount Castlereagh, now firmly laid down the policy that no power could be allowed to threaten British shipping routes through the Indies to China and Japan. The talks with Dutch representatives in London now assumed a new character. The British stressed how, after the Napoleonic Wars, how scrupulous they had been in restoring posts that were rightfully Dutch and how they had several times disciplined Raffles for challenging this friendly policy. But, now, it was stressed equally, in all fairness, the British and everyone else must be left with at least one open and free sea route to the Far East and Singapore appeared to guarantee this.

While the Dutch fumed, could he have seen them, Raffles would have been proud of the British negotiators for their emphasis on the need for co-operation, mutual benefit and fair play. "You have Sunda and we'll keep Malacca" was what it came down to. And, anyway, the Indies was vast and no one power could hope to dominate them. Unexpectedly, the King of the Netherlands agreed with the British and expressed incredulity that anyone in his government should ever have thought of possessing both Sunda and Malacca. He had met Raffles during his honeymoon tour of Europe with Sophia. He liked Raffles and respected him for his talents, sincerity and fairness. The king was not in the money grubbing business of trade and he wanted his country to be thought of well in the community of nations. From this moment on, whoever played a role or thought they played a role in the process, the fate of Singapore was in the hands of four men, Viscount Castlereagh, King William of The Netherlands, Lord Moira and Thomas Stamford Raffles. The British and the Dutch 'sides' reached agreement in the person of the Dutch King and from that moment on the future of Singapore was hardly in doubt.

But the talks between delegations dragged on and on, bedevilled by painfully slow communications with officials in Europe, India and the Indies. Despite the furore his founding of Singapore had caused in political circles, Raffles was confident that he had executed Lord Moira's wishes to the letter. And he was well pleased. If he had achieved nothing else during his turbulent career in the Indies and, virtually against all odds, he felt that, with the founding of Singapore, British access to the great markets of the Far East was assured.

"I only wish we could have done more to help the Malays," Raffles said sadly to Sophia. "We had the opportunity to bring freedom and prosperity throughout the Indies and we have handed it back to the Dutch to monopolize and brutalize. I shall always feel very sad that I allowed this to happen."

"There was nothing more you could do, my sweet", said Sophia, standing behind him at his writing desk and stroking the back of his head. "You spoke, but London refused to listen. You've ruined your health and almost lost your job trying to keep the Dutch out of the Indies. What more could any man do?"

"What more?" whispered Raffles, gazing reflectively out of a window looking across the strait to the mountains of Malay mainland. "What more?"

While London and The Hague argued and dispatches were carried hither and thither, Raffles decided that the time had come to check on progress at Bengkulu. He had already sent dispatches ordering the return of his troops from Palembang and complete withdrawal from Padang but he still had responsibility for Fort Marlborough and Bengkulu. Raffles' consumate political intuition told him that time must now be allowed to elapse to see how events would develop and how the London talks would conclude. While hoping to keep his finger as close to the pulse as distance and lack of rapid communications would allow, he decided to leave Penang and return to Bengkulu in the 'Indiana' with Sophia and baby Leopold. Governor Bannerman did not even wish him Bon Voyage!

CHAPTER THIRTEEN

The islands of the Riau archipelago dot the sea so numerously that there seems hardly a space between them large enough for a substantial ship. Sophia sat in the shade on the deck nursing little Leopold as the three masted 'Indiana' made its way through the enchanting island world. Around every point was a new vista. Here a cliff, there a mountain, over there enormous rocks, everywhere, white, sandy, beaches. Carpets of mangroves extended far into the sea, flying fish and dolphins leapt and arched above the sun-glittered waves. Here giant trees stood far into the sea because of the erosion of the land in which they grew, there they teetered on the crest of crumbling cliffs. Mostly the islands were deserted but occasionally they saw the quaint sight of a cluster of fishermen's huts, on stilts, over the water and in many places they saw nets set to entrap unwary residents of the deep. From time to time Raffles stood beside her, the light breeze blowing his hair.

"Surely, there could be no place more perfect", said Sophia.

"Quite wonderful", said Raffles smiling, throwing out his chest and drawing in deep breaths of fresh air. "Utterly magnificent."

That night, in the dark, the narrow, rock infested spaces between the islands being imperfectly known, the ship ran aground! Even at high tide it could not be floated off.

"I'm more worried about pirates than I am about the rocks", said Captain Pearl. "If they catch us here we'll be in a very difficult position."

The Captain offered to provide Raffles with a small boat so that his family could return to Singapore but, as a last resort, he suggested jettisoning their water, to lighten the ship. It worked! Next high tide the 'Indiana' was free. But now they had no water for the long trip through the islands, through the Sunda Strait and home to Bengkulu.

"We'll have to apply to the Dutch Controller at Riau", suggested Raffles. "I'm sure he will not refuse humanitarian aid."

But the Controller did refuse, and the 'Indiana' sailed on with its passengers and crew feeling deepening thirst, perhaps intensified by the knowledge that there was no water with which to slake it. On the fourth day, in heavy seas, they signalled a passing American trading vessel and Captain O'Hara even risked life and limb to come across himself in a bosun's chair to see what was wrong. The American captain was introduced to Raffles and Lady Sophia and couldn't have been more solicitous. Casks of water were hauled from ship to ship by ropes and O'hara refused to leave until he was quite satisfied that the 'Indiana' was safe and had all supplies needed to make port at Bengkulu.

"The Americans are so generous", observed Raffles to Sophia. "What a contrast with the Dutch!"

The eventual sight of the tiny Fort Marlborough at Bengkulu depressed Raffles. It may not now be the most wretched place he had ever seen but the domain over which he was Lieutenant Governor was less than a dot on the map.

"Don't be sad," said Sophia fondly as they anchored off Rat Island. "Perhaps, with the founding of Singapore, we won't have to stay here five years."

"Perhaps", said Raffles, "perhaps not. Unfortunately, even some of our own people in London want me to be shut up in this place like Napoleon on Elba.

"It's so unjust."

"Sometimes, I feel that they see in me more of an enemy than the Dutch. I've sent them enough reports to furnish a library and still London treats the Dutch as bosom friends and me as a trouble maker."

"Yet, you are the only person in the world to defend Britain's trade routes to the East."

"Not the only person, perhaps," said Raffles modestly. "But, I've tried my very best to do a duty that has to be done."

"Maybe, some day, London will realize the value of what you've achieved."

"I hope so. I really hope so."

"Coming back to Bengkulu is depressing you," said Sophia. "Come, let's get ashore, see Charlotte and see how our menagerie is faring on the 'Hill of Mists."

As their longboat approached the little dock, Raffles and Sophia could see Nurse Grimes, Otho and Mary Travers with little Charlotte jumping up and down with excitement beside them. Sophia could hardly wait to land and, while a Malay nanny held Leopold, she positively danced on the dock with Charlotte held high in her arms. The shy little child clung to her mother like a limpet.

"And who is this?" said Sophia plucking Leopold from his nanny's arms. "It's your new brother, Leopold." She bent down so that Charlotte could see her brother and hold his little fingers. Leopold smiled with hap-

358

piness at all the attention.

"Come, let's go to the house", said Sophia, leading her little daughter with one hand and continuing to hold Leopold.

Mahmud, Abdul and a party of house staff were also at the dock and quickly scooped up the couple's luggage.

Raffles had his official duties, of course. Upon arrival the usual salute had been fired from the fort and an honour guard was drawn up. Captain Salmond had been released by the Dutch and was there to welcome him, and Resident Jennings stepped forward with a broad smile.

"If I may say so, you're looking very well, sir."

"I feel well, Mr Jennings. I feel very well, replied Raffles with a smile, broadened by the knowledge that over his shoulder his dream emporium of the East was daily taking shape.

Returning to Government House cheered him up. It was transformed. No more a barren landscape but green with the trees and shrubs he had ordered planted - casuarinas, coco, nutmeg and cassia.

"It's good to be home", said Raffles as they entered Government House, dreams of further journeys into the unknown interior of Sumatra already beginning to simmer in his mind.

Back in a working environment, he was eager to get to see what had been achieved during his absence and walked directly to Fort Marlborough with Salmond and Jennings for an outline progress report - how many vessels were using the port now that it had been declared free, how the freed slaves were progressing, how many children were attending the school for the children of former slaves, how much of the data he had called for had actually been collected, what were the reactions of the local people and the native rulers and finally, what news of the latest activities of the Dutch.

Unlike the situation in Java, ironically, Raffles was not short of staff in Bengkulu. He had more than twenty civil servants with too little to employ them and others had been posted from Java when the British withdrew. Thus, he was ideally placed to form committees, commission enquiries and frame policies for the benefit of the townspeople and those inland territories influenced by the Company.

Raffles was concerned that without any form of education local people would lack the basis to improve themselves. He had already established a school for the children of ex-slaves but, ideally, he wanted to see every child have an opportunity to at least learn some basic skills. Within a short time of his return to Bengkulu, he declared that education should be available to all who wished it and, although teachers were in short supply, he proposed to overcome the deficiency by an approach adopted in England under which senior pupils stood in for teachers.

"A better educated people will make a more industrious and a wealthier people," he said, "and productive and wealthy people mean more trade."

Raffles' visit to England, where he had seen at first hand the striking and dramatic contribution to wealth creation of extending property ownership, had also fanned his enthusiasm for replicating his Java land ownership plan in Sumatra. Regulations were framed and promulgated which acknowledged the traditional chiefs as owners of the land but recognized the right of all who dwelt on it to lease that land and work it themselves or to be paid wages for working other people's land. Forced labour and forced deliveries had already been halted.

With new life breathed into public policies at Bengkulu, Raffles spent more time at the 'Hill of Mists'. After his visit to India, it was clear that, from the point of view of public policies, there was nothing more he could do in Sumatra as a whole. Time must be allowed to pass and attitudes and ideas to ebb and flow, pending the final outcome on the new round of Anglo-Dutch talks in London about partitioning the Indies and his new 'baby' at Singapore had to be given time to grow.

But, Raffles could never bare to be idle. His idea of relaxing at his country retreat was to add to, examine, describe and record his growing collection of flora, forna and even marine life, a task which Dr Horsfield had been continuing both on his own and on Raffles account while the Lieutenant Governor had been in India, Penang and Singapore. As he had seen done in England, as a boy, he was soon experimenting with crops and had a dozen ploughs at work on his land. Whenever he put some new idea into practice, groups of curious local farmers came to squat on their haunches and watch the proceedings. There were many questions, asked not of him, but discreetly of his Malay assistants, and Raffles hoped that they would benefit by copying some of his experiments.

Although Britain's cities were growing apace, the country was still largely rural and the mark of true wealth was to have a large country estate and a townhouse in London for the 'season' or for business. Raffles wrote to his many friends in Britain that, though in Sumatra, he felt just like an English country gentleman. And around him was the happy laughter of his own growing children, who now formed as much of the substance of his unofficial letters as details of his work and travels.

"They are delightful prodigies, curious about everything and forever filled with happy optimism", he wrote.

Raffles' life with Sophia at the bungalow on

the 'Hill of Mists' was the happiest of his whole life.

Sophia wrote: " This is one of the happiest periods in Sir Stamford's life. Politically, he has obtained the object which he felt so necessary for the good of his country. He is beloved by all those under his immediate control, who unite in showing him every mark of respect and attachment and many are bound to him by ties of gratitude for offices of kindness or private acts of benevolence and assistance which he delights to exercise towards them."
Sophia was Raffles' willing companion on even the most dangerous adventure, his beautiful young lover and her humour and enjoyment of life filled his every hour with charm and fun. The tropical night descends early, the heat is intense and there was many a night when they would throw off the bedcovers and discover each other's sexuality anew. Sophia held her too him as if she would never let go. Outside, birds howled in the tree tops while elephants, tigers and rhinos crashed about in the undergrowth below.

"I love you so much," they each whispered to the other.

Out of the blue, a messenger rode hard from Fort Marlborough to the 'Hill of Mists' with the news that old Governor Bannerman had died of cholera in Penang! Raffles sat down heavily, one arm draped over the arm of his chair, the paper held loosely in his hand. Instantly he was transformed from farmer to careerist.

"What is it", Sophia asked seriously. "Bad news?"

"Not bad but interesting", replied Raffles. "Colonel Bannerman is dead."

"Poor man but at least you won't have to worry about him any more."

No. But his death opens up a major new possibility."

"You don't want to go back to Penang!"

"Not really. Penang is another life and it's over now. But I don't want to stay at Bengkulu for ever either."

Raffles had already hinted to Lord Moira how desirable it would be if the governance of the Company's posts east of India could be placed in one hand.

"It would be so much cheaper than maintaining governors and civil establishments in so many posts. Such establishments overweigh the local economies and turn profit into loss," Raffles had commented.

Lord Moira seemed interested but, since the management of posts in the Indies had not then been the subject of their talks, it passed by quickly in the general conversation.

"Now that Colonel Bannerman is dead there may be an opportunity to bring Penang, Singapore, Bengkulu and our smaller posts in the Indies under one head."

"Shall you write to Lord Moira?"

Raffles thoughtfully stroked his chin without replying. Then he got up and walked to the edge of the wide verandah surrounding the house. Charlotte was playing with some sea shells. Little Leopold gurgled happily in a rattan crib. He looked out over his green fields, at the villagers dotting them here and there and at the fantastic shapes of the mountains beyond.

"So perfect," he murmured so that no other could really hear.

"Sorry?"

Raffles turned decisively and held both Sophia's hands in his.

"Writing will probably not be effective, my sweet. I must go again to India."

Oh, Thomas, no. You've only been back four

months and the sea voyages are so awful."

"There is too much at stake. I must go. If I can convince Lord Moira to make me Governor of the Indies, in a few years, the next step might be Governor General of India. I can never be made governor general from a small post like Bengkulu. I need a larger power base and the Indies could be it."

"Of course, you're right. You must go. When will you leave?"

"The brig 'Favourite' is in port and bound for India tomorrow. It is like the 'Udney' but I will go alone with Abdul."

Raffles wrote a short message for Resident Jennings and sent the horseman back to Fort Marlborough at top speed.

"Abdul", he called, bustling about in a frenzy of preparations."

"Yes, Tuan."

"Get ready Abdul, you and are leaving for India tomorrow morning!"

Raffles took with him a secretary, Captain Watson and, in case of sickness, Dr Jack. The weather en route to Calcutta across the Bay of Bengal was as rough as ever with screaming gales and teeming rain battering the little ship. But this time, there were no accidents and the 'Favourite' reached port safely.

Raffles used as much of the time aboard ship as he could to compose a detailed memorandum for Lord Moira setting out the rationale for consolidating the government of whatever there might eventually be of the British East Indies in a single hand and, despite, the pitching decks, the memo was ready upon arrival. Reflecting the thinking in Britain at the time, his basic argument was to reduce government in the Indies to the bone and concentrate only upon the creation, nurturing and management of commercial posts. Raffles knew from his bitter experience in Java how steadfastly the Company's back was turned to acquiring territory, so he studiously avoided any such suggestion.

"It is not territory we want but trade," he wrote.

To the territory versus trade debate, which had raged for years in Britain's corridors of power, Raffles felt more than a little ambivalent. Much as he admired the approach taken by Warren Hastings in building trade upon treaties with local rulers, on the other hand, the British Government had felt it to be quite alright for Captain James Cook to sail to the antipodes, raising the British flag wherever he could! For Raffles in the Indies, any suggestion of hoisting the British flag or even the Company flag had been met with barrage after barrage of condemnation so severe that twice it had almost cost him his career.

"Poor Thomas, there is no justice in the world, Sophia always remarked philosophically.

Despite the traditional reluctance in Leadenhall Street, the British East India Company now ruled virtually the whole of India, and Raffles knew very well that for this reason alone his argument for policy in the islands of the East Indies could take no form other than in his memo.

"By this means", he wrote, " we will open new channels of trade, encourage industry, diffuse wealth and excite enterprise, thereby tending to promote the best interests of mankind."

Like many of those he mixed with at the Royal Society, a man like Raffles felt himself to be alive at an historic moment - when men were finding out more about their world than ever before, when miraculous new technologies were transforming the means of production and when human being seemed on the brink of being able to achieve standards of health, education and wealth which could create a utopia on earth. Money and markets were undeniably what made the world go round, but, the motive was not unadulterated greed so much as the desire of good men to do good among their fellows. Raffles' memo touched all the right nerves by emphasizing limited government involvement and, therefore, expense, and maximum markets for the products of the Indies and, more importantly, for the products of India and Great Britain. He was shrewd and he was right.

Lord Moira read his memo carefully and replied promptly that: " The consolidation of our eastern possessions into one government would unquestionably be a desirable arrangement."

"Your qualifications and experience make you the ideal candidate for the job," he later told Raffles personally, in a most friendly manner.

The problem, Moira explained to Raffles, was that no decision could be made until such times as agreement could be reached between London and The Hague about a possible partition of the Indies between the two countries.

"Meanwhile, would you wish to consider Penang?"

Raffles had been happy and unhappy in Penang. He had been happy there with Olivia and for that reason would prefer not to return to the scenes of his former happiness. But, he had been unhappy with his excessive workload, the incessant jealousy of council members and colleagues and the perpetual opposition to everything he tried to achieve to the east.

"I think not, My Lord," he told Moira. "I'm

prepared to wait."

Lord Moira smiled knowingly, guessing at the ambition which drives many a self made man.

"Let's wait then", he said. "And let's also hope it won't be too long."

Privately, Moira had already decided that if Raffles declined Penang he himself would govern it directly from Calcutta.

Raffles' visit was the first opportunity Moira had of being briefed about progress in Singapore, and Raffles now found no wavering in His Lordship's support.

"I think the winds are blowing from another quarter in London," he said. "The Dutch are still complaining loudly and, whatever the Court of Directors at Leadenhall Street may say, the fact is, that the British Government now sees the unique value of a post at Singapore to keep free the sea lanes to China. Frankly, I believe there is very little chance of us giving it up."

Relying to the end on what he assumed to be the sympathy for the Dutch case of the British Government, van der Capellan was driven to write to Whitehall from Batavia:

" Raffles has to be removed from the Indies or there can be no peace for the Dutch Government out here!"

Had Moira, Raffles or van der Capellan known it, virtually as they spoke and wrote, the Anglo-Dutch talks were being broken off in London! The British, who had bent over backwards to accommodate the Dutch before, were now not prepared to give an inch of ground concerning Singapore!

Not that this helped Raffles very much because, now, he was once again in the same position of paralyzing uncertainty that had dogged his days in Java. Was it really true that Singapore would be retained by the

British? Would Bengkulu be swapped for Malacca? Would the British hang on to any posts at all south of the equator?

"Until these issues are clarified in London there is nothing we can do," Lord Moira told him.

When his sister, Mary Anne arrived in Calcutta with her husband William and baby son Charles, Raffles was almost ready to return to Bengkulu. For a decisive and restless man, the indecisiveness of his situation depressed him and he was glad to have at least some of his family on hand to boost his flagging spirits. As usual, low spirits and constant anxiety produced ferocious headaches which knocked him out for a month. Plunged into sadness Raffles wrote to his good friend the Duchess of Somerset:

" I do all I can to raise myself above these feelings in the hope that there is even in this world more happiness than we weak mortals can comprehend. I have had enough of sorrow in my short career and it still comes too ready a guest without my bidding. But I drive it from my door and do my best to preserve my health and spirits that I may last out a few years longer and contribute as far as I can to the happiness of others."

Mary Anne sometimes held his head in her arms and cradled him to her bosom, her fingers soothing his aching brow.

"I wish so much that this pain would go away," Raffles whispered. "What have I done so evil that I should be cursed with this?"

Dr Jack bled him and kept a strict watch on his diet, which, like so many doctors before him, he blamed for Raffles' sickness.

"You must be extremely careful with your diet and also with your digestion", he advised. "When you eat don't eat too much or too fast."

Raffles spent Christmas and New Year in Calcutta with the Flints, until he felt well enough to face the sea voyage to Bengkulu. He wrote long and apologetic letters to Sophia, expressing has sadness at her and the children spending the holidays alone and promising to be with them again soon. Sophia was pregnant with her third child and Raffles wanted so much to be close to her. He sailed from Calcutta in the 'Indiana' in February 1820.

Looking out from the ship, over the empty expanse of ocean, gave him an empty feeling inside.

"Was I too optimistic after the death of Colonel Bannerman?" he asked himself. "Was I too impetuous in rushing to Calcutta?"

As the 'Indiana' forged its way back to Sumatra, Raffles was dogged by the feeling that he was coming home empty handed!

Off the coast of Sumatra, north of Nias, the 'Indiana' sailed into the Mentawi Strait, a stretch of water dividing the mainland from a chain of offshore islands. At the entrance to the strait, far north of Padang, at Poncan Island the Company had a small post and Raffles decided to pause there to recover from crossing the choppy Bay of Bengal and also to try to see something of the Batak country inland. Travellers had stopped here from time immemorial and the coast was littered with the remains of the first European explorers, the Portuguese. William Marsden had sparked his interest in the people who lived in the part of Sumatra by his descriptions of them as cannibals.

Landing first at Poncan Island, Raffles met the British Resident, John Prince, and explained his purpose. Prince agreed to provide guides and porters for Raffles to make the journey inland to the mountain home of the Batak people. Beaching their boats at the village of Sibolga, Prince negotiated for porters and horses from the local people. While Mary Anne and little Charles stayed at Prince's house, the Resident, Raffles, Dr William Jack and Captain Flint set out into the interior, the Europeans and guides riding, and the porters walking. Prince said that the journey was about two hundred kilometres, once again, up and down the beautiful but rugged Barisan Mountains.

In addition to cannibalism, the Bataks had a warlike reputation, but their chiefs received Raffles warmly and he discovered that cannibalism was only used as a punishment for crime. Still, it <u>was</u> used and he wrote letters, filled with suitable horror, home to friends in England. As he had experienced upon arrival at the homeland plateau of the Minangkabau, here, too, Raffles found the soil rich and many gardens of carefully tended fruit and vegetables. He found the Bataks very dark skinned and, from what he was told of their history and the stone remains he saw, he felt sure that they originated either in India proper or in the northern region around Burma or Thailand. Their houses were most spectacular, built on stilts, with each end of the roof rising up from a saddle in the middle and decorated plentifully with buffalo horns. Anthropology aside, he found Lake Toba, a huge mountain-locked expanse of water at the heart of the Batak homelands, one of the most beautiful lakes he had ever seen.

"It was worth coming here just to see this," he sighed looking out over the island dotted lake. "Utterly magnificent."

Back at Poncan Island, Prince persuaded him that Nias was even richer in agrarian produce than the Batak lands, and its people not only industrious but keenly desirous of British protection from pirates. While Raffles returned to Bengkulu, he sent John Prince and Dr Jack to meet with the Nias chiefs. Upon their reporting to him in Bengkulu he decided to establish a British post on the island and to extend to them the protection they wanted.

"Why not?" he asked his senior staff rhetorically. "Nothing has been settled yet in London. Who knows. Maybe we shall be able to keep these posts in Sumatra. Everything depends on where the line of partition is drawn. Would that it could still be Sunda!"

Although, on Raffles return to Bengkulu from Calcutta, Dr Horsfield at long last departed, Raffles' family was now larger than it had been for several years. Regrettably, the Flints could not stay long before Raffles sent them to Singapore where he had found a post for William. When Singapore was founded Major Farquhar was about to return to Europe on leave but had postponed sailing to fulfill Lord Moira's instruction to take charge of the new post. Knowing what it was like not having been home for many years, Raffles dispatched Otho Travers to Singapore to take over from Farquhar as Resident.

"I shall miss you Otho," Raffles told him. But, you mustn't remain a mere aide all your life. I cannot be selfish. I must help you get on."

Travers had been together with Raffles now for many years and almost nothing could sadden him more deeply than parting from his chief. But it was only to Singapore and, later on, Raffles might turn up there. And it was a promotion! The Travers and Flints sailed together.

Raffles rejoined his family at the 'Hill of Mists' and life continued in much the same way as it had with Olivia at 'Without a Care'.

Having waited so long for them, Raffles children were his pride and joy. Not that he blamed Olivia for anything. At the commencement of his career the time was not right; now it was. To William Marsden he wrote:

"My children are certainly the finest children that were ever seen."

In April 1820, he wrote to his mother in

Hamstead:

"Charlotte, I can assure you, is not a little proud of her grandmother's finery. She has just come in to show me the dress you worked for her. She is the sweetest and best tempered little darling ever beheld. Leopold is as quick and bold as a lion."

To the Duchess of Somerset he wrote:

"We have a delightful garden and so many living pets, children, tame and wild, monkeys, dogs, birds etc., that we have a perfect menagerie within our walls. On one side are the animals, on another perfect flora, here a pile of stones, there a collection of seaweed, shells etc."

Around the house roamed two young tigers and a bear and the youngsters loved to play with their live, furry, 'toys', watched by cuddly cats and a blue, mountain parrot.

To add to Raffles' happiness, in May, 1820, Sophia gave birth to little Stamford Marsden. The birth was at the 'Hill of Mists', but with Nurse Grimes on hand there was no risk and mother and baby were soon fine.

The house was full of local cooks, cleaners and maids, padding about in bare feet and ever ready to do this or prepare that. Every morning, before breakfast, Raffles rode around neighbouring villages, stopping frequently to talk to the farmers and their families. They listened to his advice as they did to that of their own elders. The population of the area was falling and Raffles made it his business to try to find out why by probing minutely into what type of crops were grown on what kind of soil and under what conditions. Once having identified a problem he rarely failed to recommend a solution. After a breakfast of fresh fruit he worked at natural history, chemistry or geology and supervised a team of six local draughtsmen who made complete drawings of all the specimens in his now vast collection.

Many animals, even the giant rhinoceros, were either stuffed, preserved in spirits or kept as skeletons. The flora and fauna he collected were largely unknown in Europe and therefore of great interest in scientific circles.

As at Malacca, a constant procession of people came to the house to bring plants and animals from the land or sea which they thought might interest him. From lunch time onwards, he made time to be with his children, where practical, involving them in his love of nature. In fact, wherever he went they followed, until it was difficult to get a moment away from them for quiet of studious concentration! In the evenings, he and Sophia liked nothing better than to stroll in their garden beneath the tropical moon, a cool breeze on their cheeks.

Occasionally, people came up from Fort Marlborough to dine and, of course, once a week Raffles and Sophia stayed at Government House, often for several days. Then, the house would be full of guests at every meal, Raffles treating the leading members of the community very much as his 'family', like an latter day Lord of the English Manor. Not that he lorded it over anybody. Such behaviour was not in his make up. Raffles also acted as a magistrate and every week there were cases requiring his attention, usually domestic arguments or disputes about property.

Raffles had formed the habit of sending parts of his unique and valuable scientific collection home to Britain at convenient intervals. Throughout 1820 he sent large shipments of zoological specimens to Sir Joseph Banks and to William Marsden. Leadenhall Street criticized him for the expense.

While engaged in his farming, scientific, magisterial and administrative life in Bengkulu, news trickled through to him from the 'outside world', particularly Calcutta and London. As Lord Moira had told him in Calcutta, the winds of opinion in London were changing and he could virtually track the course from the dispatches. First, he read the violent Dutch criticisms of his activities, then the Company's and the British Government's agreement and condemnations until, finally, the correspondence began to move slowly more and more in his favour. The Dutch still complained, but the Company and Whitehall could be seen to at last be arriving at an understanding of the importance of Singapore to Britain.

He wrote to friends:

"With the founding of Singapore the great blow has been struck, and though I may personally suffer in the struggle, the nation must be benefited. If matters are only allowed to remain as they are, all will go well."

Van der Capellan, meanwhile, was still writing of Raffles efforts:

"God grant that he won't succeed."

Raffles' reply to all his enemies was:

" The more I am opposed, the more my views are thwarted, destroyed and counteracted, the firmer do I stand. I am confident that I am right and that when I appear at home even those who are opposed to me will be the first to acknowledge this."

One day, at the end of a long succession of dispatches written over many months Raffles silently handed Sophia a letter from Charles Grant, the Chairman of the British East India Company, which had for so long criticized him and even taken the sides of his enemies and his country's enemies!

"I consider the possession of Singapore, and the occupancy of that place, to be very important to the British interests; and I heartily wish it may be found consistent with the rights of the two nations that Great Britain may keep possession of it. I think it is remarkably well situated to become a commercial emporium of those seas. I have no doubt that it will very soon rise to great magnitude and importance; and if I may be permitted to allude to the conduct of any individual on this subject, I must say that I think the whole of the proceedings of Sir T.S. Raffles have been marked with great intelligence and great zeal for the interests of his country."

"My dear," said Sophia sympathetically holding her husband in her arms. Only she, and perhaps Olivia, really knew how hard Raffles had fought for this moment.

From Singapore came news from Major Farquhar that trade already exceeded that of Malacca during its most flourishing years and that Malay, Bugis, Chinese, Arab, Indian and even Portuguese settlers were flooding in. Farquhar said that the harbour was crowded with prows, junks and European trading ships.

"Singapore is so admirably situated in every respect for becoming a grand commercial depot and port of transfer trade, that too great a value can scarcely be placed in the possession of it by the British Government."

With no resumption of the Anglo-Dutch talks in London, Tunku Long and his chiefs were beginning to feel nervous that Britain might yet hand Singapore to the Dutch and, just as British merchants were daily filing petitions in London and lobbying Lord Moira in Calcutta, so Chinese, Bugis, Arab and Indian traders were daily pestering the Sultan about their fate. Tunku Long wrote to Farquhar on their behalf expressing "dread and dismay" lest Singapore be given to Holland. Meanwhile, finding government from Calcutta impracticable Lord Moira appointed a new Governor of Penang Island, William Phillips.

"Good luck to him", said Raffles, when he read the news. "He has acted seven times so he surely deserves it. I am happy to wait here until we see what happens in

London, however long that may take.

"I am content with things to remain as they are for two or three years to come; I should then be better prepared for the contest, for contest it must come to, sooner or later, and the longer the adjustment of our differences with the Dutch, on a broad and just footing, is delayed, the better it must be for our interests."

While the Raffles waited a fourth child was born, Ella Sophia.

"We are truly blessed," Raffles told Sophia as she weakly presented him with the latest addition to the family. As the slings and arrows of outrageous fortune crashed around them, their life of idyllic happiness went on as before.

CHAPTER FOURTEEN

It was during Raffles' weekly visit to Bengkulu that Sophia's brother, Captain William Hull, fell ill.

"He has a terrible fever, diarrhoea and vomiting," Sophia told Raffles, looking very concerned.

"Poor fellow," said Raffles at once. 'Let's bring him here. He will be more comfortable at Government House.

Sophia took the carriage and went herself with Dr Jack to collect her brother. The Captain could barely walk and, even in the tropical heat, shivered uncontrollably.

William was put immediately to bed, swathed in blankets and given lots of water in an effort to bring down his fever.

"I think it's dysentry", Dr Jack told them. Tonight will be crucial. Tomorrow is the third day and if the fever doesn't abate we may not be able to save him. He's losing too much fluid."

"The tropical climate is cruel beyond words," said Raffles. "I have been ill on and off practically since I came out here. And so many of my friends have been carried off. After all these years it's a wonder that I'm still alive."

William was in terrible pain from stomach cramps and Sophia remained by his bedside to comfort him.

William's younger brother, Nilson had been staying with him and he too was now at Government House.

The Malay staff, who padded in and out with clean bed linen, water for bathing and drinking and fresh towels and flannels, walked with downcast eyes and grave faces.

On the third day, the fever hadn't broken and, if anything, the symptoms of diarrhoea and vomiting were worse.

"Isn't there anything we can do", said Sophia tearfully to Dr Jack.

"We can pray to God for his recovery", the doctor replied stoically.

On the fifth day, William died and was buried in the European cemetary behind the settlement.

Meanwhile, Raffles had received puzzling news from Singapore. A dispatch from Travers informed him that Farquhar, now promoted to Colonel, refused to proceed on leave and that, for the time being, he was staying at the Colonel's house, awaiting the outcome of events. Farquhar enclosed a dispatch of his own saying that while it was true that he had wanted to go on leave to Britain when appointed to Singapore, now, he was very happy there and he had thought that his appointment as Resident rendered obsolete his previous plans to go home. Raffles clicked his tongue with frustration.

"What a nuisance", Raffles muttered to himself on reading the news "I have sent Travers there but he can do nothing. Just wasting his time. Why do I always have such difficulties with military men?"

He dispatched a letter to the Colonel asking him for the most complete clarification of his position and when, if at all, he now expected to quit the new colony.

Government House now begun to be aware

that others were dying in the enclave from the same symptoms that had reduced Captain Hull from a strong and healthy soldier to a corpse in only five days.

"What is it? What can we do", Raffles asked Dr Jack.

Local people who knew tropical illnesses and herbal remedies were summoned urgently to Government House. They reported that illnesses of the kind which had killed William appeared from time to time but that they knew neither cause nor cure.

"With such a disease it is in the hands of God," they said.

Everyone was deeply worried.

"Let's hope that it doesn't become an epidemic," said Raffles.

But it did. Soon, funerals were an almost daily occurence on the streets, as they had used to be in the unwholesome streets of early Batavia.

Despite the gloom and doom which hung over Bengkulu, Raffles held a banquet to celebrate the King's birthday in June. Three weeks later his eldest son, Leopold, displayed symptoms identical to Captain Hull's. The little child was in great pain and distress and died during the night a few hours after the dreaded symptoms appeared.

Sophia's screams of anguish rang through the cavernous, high ceilinged rooms, bringing every occupant running from their beds. Not only Nurse Grimes, but two Malay maids as well, had to help prise the loving mother's arms from the little body of her dead son.

"No, no," she screamed as they took the child away to prepare for burial. "Not my baby, please, no."

Sophia's eyes were red with sobbing - first her brother and next her eldest son were dead.

"We were too happy," she wept, "too happy."

Nurse Grimes did her best to comfort her. For the second time in eight months a funeral procession wound its way the short distance inland to the cemetary. But this time it was one of the governor's children and leaders of the community joined the procession to pay their respects and express their sorrow.

Raffles wrote to England:

" My heart has been nigh broken and my spirit is gone. I have lost almost all that I prided myself on in this world and the afflication came upon us when we least expected such a clamity. Had you but seen him and known him you must have doted - his beauty and intelligence were so far above those of other children of the same age that he shone among them as a sun enlivening and enlightening everything around him."

A few days later, Sophia's brother in law, Harry Auber, Captain of the 'Lady Raffles', died of similar symptons to those which had snatched away William and Leopold.

Sophia was hysterical. She locked herself in her room, refusing even to see her other children, not eating and crying all day long.

"Better to take me than my young babies," she sobbed uncontrolably.

For days no-one could stop her tears. She was snapped out of her misery not by Raffles, not by Nurse Grimes but by an older Malay maid who told her quietly and kindly that she should be ashamed to grieve so much when she still had a family of fine children who loved and needed her. She knelt on the floor close to her head as Sophia lay on her bed.

"God will take far better care of all those who came to him than has ever been taken on earth," she said.

Three months later, all Sophia's children fell

ill and while Marsden and Ella recovered, her eldest daughter, Charlotte remained gravely ill.

"How much suffering can there be for us," wailed Sophia. "Death heaped upon death until we have nothing left."

Raffles' head pounded with the stress of the epidemic and the remorseless losses to his family. Sophia was distraught beyond description. Luckily, Charlotte recovered but within a few weeks Marsden, the second youngest, had been carried off by dysentry. When he died, Raffles was in his study and Sophia came to him carrying the limp body of baby Marsden in her arms. His little feet dangled lifelessly on one side and the brown hair of his head hung down loosely on the other. Raffles leapt up and husband and wife stood together weeping silently amid a circle of Malay house staff.

No sooner had the new year of 1822 dawned than Charlotte was stricken for a second time and, despite all their efforts, joined her brothers in the grave.

"We must leave here or we won't have even a single child left", Sophia told Raffles.

"To leave the people here to their fate will be so unkind," said Raffles.

"Darling! For once you must think of yourself. You can't help them if you are dead. We must get away!"

"Yes, yes, you're right. We must try to get out by the first ship. We can go to Singapore and see the situation there."

Raffles was mentally a strong man but the deaths had scared both him and Sophia, not to mention the entire European community. He was so ill and depressed that he wrote to the Directors of the Company informing them that his terrible sufferings at Bengkulu had led him to the conclusion that he must quit the Indies. He wrote:

"For the last three weeks I have been confined to my room by a severe fever which fell on the brain and drove me almost to madness.

" During the last year my constitution has suffered so severely from repeated attacks of illness that I can no longer look forward with confidence to protracted residence in an Indian climate."

However distressed he felt, Raffles never lost sight of the possibility of influencing London to keep even a part of Sumatra out of Dutch hands. In the same letter he wrote:

"I am particularly anxious that the lamp we have lighted should not be allowed to shine with a dim or imperfect lustra; the spark has been struck with enthusiasm, and while I remain in this country, the flame shall be fanned with ardour and perseverance. But we must look to a higher power for the oil which is to feed and support it, and, above all, to the protecting and encouraging influence or true principles and British philanthropy."

By mid-summer, while awaiting the infrequent arrival of a ship at Bengkulu, even the Raffles' physician, Dr Jack, was dead.

His only surviving child, baby Ella, was sent home directly to England with Nurse Grimes in a small vessel named the 'Borneo', commanded by Captain John Ross.

It was a legitimate part of his duties for Raffles to visit Singapore and, although concerned about Ella and for her own life, faithful to the promise that she made when she first married that she would follow him to the ends of the earth, Sophia said that she would remain by his side.

"I beg you to save yourself," Raffles told her.

"What is the point saving myself if I lose my

husband," Sophia replied. "I will never leave you until death do us part."

Within days of burying Dr Jack, Raffles and Sophia together with her youngest brother and Captain Salmond made their escape by sea to Singapore. Abdul went along but Mahmud was left in charge at Government House, Bengkulu. Sophia and Raffles went for a last time to the European graveyard and gently placed flowers on each of the graves of their loved ones.

At the couple's romantic hideaway on the 'Hill of Mists' the tigers, monkeys, bears and parrots still romped around the house where children's laughter had also once filled the air. The house staff said that, often, they seemed to be searching for the children, their little playmates. Local people still came with specimens for the tuan, sitting patiently for hours on the verandah waiting for the return of one who was already at sea. Sophia's herb garden was tended with loving care. Villagers still watched the ploughs in the fields. In the evenings, after the rain, a great orange moon hung over the bungalow.

Deep gloom cloaked Bengkulu and there was little ceremony as the Lieutenant Governor and his party departed.

"God bless, keep safe" Raffles told Jennings. God willing, we'll be back soon."

Raffles and Sophia felt intensely lonely on the voyage to Singapore. Only a few weeks before they had had a boisterous, laughing family of four. This one noisy, that one shy, this one asking endless questions, that one always wanting to play. To Raffles it was as if a whole part of his life had disappeared with cruel abruptness - and not temporarily but never to return! Never again would he see the bright eyes of three of them, hear their happy laughter, watch them grow from helpless babies to personalities for which he had already begun to plan. Soon, he had thought, they would be sent to school in England, within two or three years more maybe they would all be living together again in London. At the end of it all the boys would rise to high office in society and the girls would marry well.

"Did ever children have such prospects as ours", he reminisced to Sophia.

Tears merely rolled down Sophia's cheeks.

Whatever either of them did, whatever they said, wherever they looked, in the back of their minds were the images of their dead children, their faces, their clothes, their little bodies, their happiness.

"We shall never forget them", sighed Raffles. "We must thank God for the privilege of being able to have them even for so short a time".

Death upon death had strengthened Sophia. "Hush, my dear," she said, "we must try not to think about it too much."

Raffles and his party had no idea as to whether Singapore was affected by the epidemic or not. Colonel Bannerman had died of cholera, an ever present risk throughout India and the Indies, but there had been no reports of disease or fatalities in Singapore.

"I will inspect the settlement and we will rest here awhile" Raffles told Sophia as they approached the fifth 'baby' in his life after his children.

How different was the approach to Singapore from the approach to Bengkulu. The port was bustling to bursting with shipping from seemingly the four corners of the globe. Every vista was a new scene of industry and achievement. Flags were flying bravely in the wind and the guns of the battery boomed out the salute befitting a Lieutenant Governor. Raffles already felt better! On the dock was Mary Anne with her husband, William Flint and their son Charles, all well and all smiling. In front of them stood Resident Farquhar.

"It's like another world", Raffles whispered to Sophia with a smile as they prepared to disembark at the dock.

An honour guard of Sepoys was drawn up for Raffles' inspection and after the formalities Farquhar said that he quite understood that Raffles' priority was to spend time with his family. The Flints took the Raffles and Nilson Hull home.

To be with the Flints again was, in a sense, like old times. The air in Singapore seemed unaccountably beneficial after Bengkulu and after a few days Raffles felt more like his old self and began reviewing the steps taken by Farquhar's government. Travers, he learned, not being able to take up his post, had proceeded to Britain on leave of his own.

Colonel Farquhar was a kindly man, married to a Malay woman, and much loved by local people in Malacca and Singapore. He had been a Resident at Malacca for many years and continued primarily in this commercial role in Singapore. By and large his decisions went with the flow of reality in which he happened to find himself. On the other hand, Raffles envisioned Singapore as a great city rather than as a humble trading post and the man needed to build it was a city builder. This Farquhar was not. As a result, from the moment Raffles landed, he could see projects that had not been executed properly. The population of the busy town had now swollen to an incredible ten thousand in three years but in place of the order he planned to bring to the settlement there was a strong element of higgaldy piggaldy.

"If we go on like this the whole settlement will be chaotic," he reproved Farquhar, who always had plausible sounding reasons as to why something had not been done. Any reasonable person would have agreed that, on the surface, the Colonel was right, but Raffles was not in the business of merely coping with circumstances as he found them; he was in the business of changing them and moulding them to his will and vision. In this, he and Farquhar parted company. Worse still, Farquhar took Raffles' instructions for corrections and improvements as a personal attack.

Raffles had told Farquhar that all government buildings should be grouped together on the north bank of the Singapore River with godowns, shops and merchant's houses to the south. Farquhar had ignored this because, he said, the land to the south was too swampy. Raffles had a simple solution - drain the land. Orders were issued forthwith and all town planning reverted to his original concept. Farquhar was not pleased. Those people who had settled in the wrong area were forced to move and compensation offered. Henceforth, he decreed that such decisions should be taken by the revolutionary means of a newly established town planning committee. Moreover, the committee would also be concerned with the appearance of buildings, with the regularity of their siting, and with hygeine and cleanliness.

"Cleanliness is next to Godliness", Raffles liked to say, and he had long suspected that lack of it was the basis of so many of the diseases that plagued the East. After the recent loss of almost his entire family, no one could have been more sensitive than Raffles to the desireability of keeping deadly diseases at bay by being clean!

"We don't even have such committees in England", fumed Farquhar, at the same time seeing the sense of it and keeping quiet about his frustrations.

Next, Raffles turned his attention to the terms and conditions on which land had been occupied. Raffles favoured acquisition through competitive bidding rather than through favouritism and partiality. He found many of Farquhar's explanations partisan and as vague as the contracts they described. Neither man was pleased.

The Town Planning Commitee repeated and elaborated Raffles' initial concept that each race resident in Singapore should live in its own area - Europeans, Chinese, Malay, Indian, Bugis, Arab and land was either re-confirmed or duly set aside.

While Raffles and Farquhar quarrelled over land use and allocation Raffles discovered that Farquhar was permitting slaves to be landed at Singapore! He was even sent a slave as a present! Raffles was apoplectic.

"This is absolutely outrageous", he fumed.

Farquhar responded to Raffles' annoyance by saying that he felt that one had to be flexible at a new post, as usual much in need of revenue because of Leadenhall Street's emphasis on strict economy.

"One cannot be flexible with morals", was Raffles' uncompromising retort.

Knowing full well that Raffles at all times favoured free trade, Farquhar next proposed that merchants should be forbidden to negotiate directly with local native rulers, presumably to create semi-monopolistic conditions for those who could.

"There will never be any avoidable monopolies in even the smallest territory administered by me," the Lieutenant Governor wrote Farquhar firmly.

All of these vexations built up to such a pitch of tension, anxiety and irritation that the headaches Raffles had managed to banish upon arrival in Singapore now returned. Before, Raffles had been exasperated with Farquhar. Now he was exasperated and in pain and the pain sharpened his resolve and diminished his patience.

He wrote irritably to Farquhar:

" The objects contemplated by government have been in great measure defeated by the arrangements you have adopted and on this as well as on other occasions which have recently occured you have been more inclined to argue in support of your own measures which have been disapproved than to afford due assistance to government."

Raffles warned Farquhar that his term as Resident must now be brought to a close, the last thing Farquhar wanted now that he could see how successful Singapore was becoming. Feeling increasingly threatened, Farquhar now sent complaints against Raffles to Lord Moira in Calcutta and to the Board of Directors in London.

Raffles had by now had time to see what was wrong in Singapore and to work out how to correct them. He issued a lengthy proclamation designed to make everything clear to new Singaporeans.

He announced work on a constitution and a code of law and the setting up of a magistracy. It was ruled that, in future, to avoid mistakes, misunderstandings and confusion, all decisions of government would be put in writing and accompanied by Malay language translations. Everyone was to be equal before the law and no unnecessary or humiliating punishments were to be permitted for offenders. In framing the constitution and planning the related institutions of the new settlement Raffles laid heavy stress on the need to include a body of people long excluded by the Company from its deliberations and decisions and of whom he had long been the undeclared champion - the merchants. Leavened by wisdom, so much of what he had done and which had brought appalling criticism down on his head, he had done in the interests of merchants and of trade. Raffles seized the chance to underline indelibly Singapore's status as a free port. To halt the muddle surrounding land purchase a government administered land registry was established, and slavery and gaming were outlawed. By these measures, Raffles had stamped a mark on Singapore which would not be easily eradicated.

"It's absolutely incredible to me," Raffles told Nilson Hull, who had now become his secretary, "that after three years none of these steps have been taken by Colonel Farquhar. One has to wonder what he has really been doing here all this time!"

Whatever omissions Farquhar had made on the administrative side there was no doubt about Singapore's success. Figures showed that about one thousand five hundred trading ships were now using the port every year.

"At least Leadenhall Street can't find fault with that," said Raffles.

Raffles felt that it would be more fitting for the chief authority at Singapore to occupy a suitably impressive and commanding house. Soon after arrival, he had ordered the hill behind the Singapore River to be cleared and an Indian style bungalow, about thirty metres long, built there to serve as Government House. The all-wood building, with the traditional thatch roof, designed by a young architect named George Coleman, was now ready, and the Raffles decided to move in. Prestige was by no means the whole reason for the move. Raffles' headaches were unbearable and doctors feared for his very life. Everyone hoped that a move to the cool hill top might improve his health. Temorarily it did.

Insofar as either felt playful, after the death of three children and of so many friends and relatives, Sophia joked that this was their new 'Hill of Mists'. Indeed, once again a botanical garden was begun by Raffles, and people started to bring him animals and plants.

"We cannot allow ourselves to be defeated",

Raffles told Sophia. We must start our family again."

Within a few months Sophia was pregnant with a child they both prayed could be taken back safely to England.

The Raffles did not go out much from Government House. It was hardly necessary. From their front verandah they could see practically the whole of the settlement - the Singapore River with its godowns and busy waterways, Chinatown to the right, the new government buildings to the left, the wide esplanade in front where, in the evenings, Europeans rode in carriages or on horseback. Raffles did not have a carriage of his own in Singapore, another reason for staying close to home. And, since he was inexplicably so ill with headaches for much of the time, the entertaining for which he had been famous at Georgetown, Batavia, 'Without a Care' and Bengkulu was a rare occurrence. Some of the time Raffles felt that if he could get back to his own country he might recover his health - it was notorious that people who lived in the East either never returned home at all or came back with their health much in need of repair. At other times he felt that his time on this earth was very short.

"So much to do, so little time," he sighed frequently.

Raffles and Farquhar continued to irritate each other and Raffles wrote to Calcutta that he was prepared to take over the Resident's post while a replacement for the Colonel was identified and posted.

"I would rather do his job than see him continue to give me these headaches," he told Sophia after she asked if he was really fit enough to handle so much extra work.

Raffles and Sophia had arrived in Singapore looking thinner than ever but the absence of infection and

Singapore's bracing air had soon returned the colour to Sophia's cheeks. Raffles was more stooped than ever and had lost so much weight that his clothes seemed ill fitting. There were deep bags under his eyes and his face was heavily lined from being screwed up against the terrible pain in his head. Only his eyes retained their glint of boyish optimism but increasingly they were more often shut against pain than open to brave new ideas.

"I really don't know what it is in this climate that damages my head so," he almost daily lamented to Sophia. "Even when I'm very careful about my diet I still get a headache".

"Maybe it's not your diet at all. You have too many responsibilities and too much worry, my sweet. That's the real problem. I'm certain."

Raffles was galvanized to activity by the news that a Dutch reconnaissance party had landed temporarily at Johore.

"Disaster," he cried immediately. "They must not be allowed to stay."

Colonel Farquhar was not only Resident but commander of the troops and Raffles instantly ordered a detachment of Sepoys to Johore and the raising of the Company flag. He was past caring about the reaction of Leadenhall Street. They were in London and he was in Singapore and nobody knew better than him of the threat that would be posed to his new 'baby' if an enemy post was to be established inland.

"We could be pushed into the sea", Raffles told Farquhar.

At least on this score the two men agreed, troops were sent and the flag hoisted and left under guard.

Meanwhile, fearful as ever of offending the Dutch and uncertain of the outcome of the still stalled Anglo-

Dutch talks about Indies partition Leadenhall Street wrote to Raffles condemning his signing of a treaty of protection with the rulers of Nias, off the coast of Sumatra.

"I wonder how long it will be before they condemn Johore," Raffles said wearily and rhetorically to Nilson Hull. "Oh, well, I'm used to it now."

Next came news that Farquhar was at last to be relieved - but not by Raffles. The Directors had taken to heart Raffles plea from Bengkulu that he was too ill to continue in the Indies and John Crawford was appointed as Resident of Singapore. To avoid any administrative or other sabotage from Penang, Singapore was to report directly to Calcutta. Captain William Mackenzie would take over from Prince at Bengkulu. Raffles would only retain his position as Agent to the Governor General in India, a post without terratorial responsibilities.

"It will still take a few months for everyone to get into position," Raffles told Sophia, "But we'll be going home soon now."

Ceremony mattered as much to Raffles as it did to many of the peoples of the Indies, especially the Malays and Javans. Raffles now noticed that Colonel Farquhar had begun to dispense with his military uniform, even for official duties. Raffles was incensed and, after repeated and repeatedly ignored warnings, and with his head pounding, he peremptorily relieved Farquhar of his command. A new flood of paper protests instantly flowed from Farquhar's desk to Calcutta and London. Even his private quarrels with Raffles Farquhar felt to be unjust, but a public stripping of his post meant a public humiliation and while this was bad enough in front of Europeans, in front of the many Malays who knew him, the disgrace was extreme. His complaints now took on a new tone of bitterness against Raffles.

With replacements on the way to the Residencies of Singapore and Bengkulu, Raffles felt that there was still one more step in his power to be taken to help the Malays - the people who had first excited his interest when he arrived in Penang and whose culture had lured him deep into the Indies and to the realization that here was a proud people to whom and enlightenment and freedom could bring prosperity and happiness. Raffles wanted to establish a Malay college and he called upon every friend he had ever known to support the scheme. A grand meeting was held at Government House, attended by all the leading Europeans, Tunku Long and Temenggong Abdu'l Rachman. Seventeen thousand dollars was raised and two months later, to a salute of cannon from the batteries atop Government Hill, Raffles laid the foundation stone of the Singapore Institution, a place of learning open to Malays as well as children of all races.

Representatives of every race and segment of society were gathered around him that day as he launched Singapore's first college and, knowing that he must soon depart, Raffles took the opportunity to make a concluding statement which, while meant for a single occasion, also summarized his approach to all that he had tried to achieve in the Indies. He said:

" If commerce brings wealth to our shores, it is the spirit of literature and philanthropy that teaches us how to employ it for the noblest purposes. It is this which has made Britain go forth among nations, strong in her native light, to dispense blessings all around her. If the time shall come when her Empire shall have passed away, these monuments of her virtue will endure, when her triumphs shall have become an empty name. Let it still be the boast of Britain to write her name in characters of light; let her not be remembered as the tempest whose course was desolation, but as the gale of spring, reviving the slumbering seeds of mind, and calling them to life from the winter of ignorance and oppression. Let the sun of Britain arise on these islands, not to whither and scorch them in its fierceness but like that of her own genial skies whose mild and benign influence is hailed and blessed by all who feels its beams."

Raffles determined that June 9, 1823 would be the date fixed for his return to Bengkulu, and onward journey home to England. They would sail in the 'Hero of Malown' commanded by Captain James Neish. Four days before he was due to leave, Raffles received a long memorial from the leaders of Singapore society. It was presented to him by John Crawford. He had lived in Singapore only eight months and for five of those his headaches had kept him in a dark room unable even to think. If people remembered him it was as much for his achievement in founding Singapore as for what he had done this visit. In fact, while his measures were generally appreciated, some, like land use zoning had meant removals, compensation and short term hostility. It had taken a strong hand to overcome the consequences of Farquhar's weaker touch.

"I'm surprised anyone has remembered me", Raffles joked as he opened the letter. The memorial was addressed in the most respectful terms and read:

"To your unwearied zeal, your vigilance and your comprehensive views we owe at once the foundation and maintenance of a settlement unparalleled for the liberality of the principles on which it has been established; principles, the operation of which has converted in a period short beyond all example, a haunt of pirates into the abode of enterprise, security and oppulence.

Accept, Sir, we beseech you, without distinction of tribe or nation, the expression of our sincere respect and esteem and be assured of the deep interest we shall ever take in your own prosperity as well as in the happiness of those who are most tenderly related to you."

Raffles sat down at his desk, closed his eyes and nodded his head quietly after he read this tribute.

"Thank you so much," he said simply to Crawford, calling immediately for Nilson to prepare a short reply. Raffles was the envy of most men for his powers of composition and dictation. Leading back in his chair, statesman to the last, among his comments he declared:

" It has happily been consistent with the policy of Great Britain and accordant with the principles of the East India Company that Singapore should be established as a free port; that no sinister, nor sordid view; no considerations either of political importance nor pecuniary advantage should interfere with the broad and liberal principles on which the British interests have been established. Monopoly and exclusive privilege, against which public opinion has long raised its voice, are here unknown and while the free port of Singapore is allowed to continue and prosper as it has hitherto done, the policy and liberality of the East India Company, by whom the settlement was founded and under whose protection and control it is administered can never be disputed. That Singapore will long and always remain a free port and that no taxes on trade and industry will be established to check its future rise in prosperity I can have no doubt."

The day the 'Hero of Malown' was due to carry their hero away, perhaps forever, Singapore people gathered on the shore in their hundreds to watch him depart. Raffles and Sophia also took with them the Flint's son Charles. After shaking hands with men from all races Raffles and his party were rowed out to the ship under a salute of guns from Government Hill.

"I wonder if we will ever come back," he said with quiet sadness, as the faces of the waving crowd became smaller in the distance.

"As long as the Indies needs you and you have strength you will come back", said Sophia squeezing his arm.

"I hope so, " said Raffles, his eyes fixed vacantly on the shore.

Even as the 'Hero of Malown' weighed anchor an armada of small boats bobbed alongside, their occupants waving until Raffles and Sophia went below with young Charles. Until he could see no more Raffles stood by an open window, tears streaming down his face for all those he knew, all that he had done and all that remained to be done still.

The last boat to fall behind contained Abdul, a young man who had become like a son to Raffles. Before sailing, Abdul had come to him very apologetically and said quietly that he hoped to marry and that if the tuan didn't object it would be better for him this time to stay in Singapore. He had served Raffles since his first arrival in Penang, had shared many of the hazzards he had faced at sea, had looked after him for virtually all of his professional life in the East. Parting was hard but Raffles understood and took steps to try to find him not only alternative employment but work which would be a step up. When they parted, instead of the usual limp Malay handshake, Raffles clasped his hand tightly, as if he would never let go, until there were tears in Abdul's great dark eyes.

"I shall never forget you tuan," Abdul whispered. "May God walk with you always."

Raffles and Abdul waved until each was but a tiny speck to the other, Abdul bobbing up and down in his little boat, Raffles standing at his cabin window.

That night, Raffles said reflectively to Sophia:

"It's strange isn't it. From the Company I have had almost nothing but criticism and hurt and yet out here so many have liked me and respected what I have tried to do. How can two groups of people involved in the same objective have such different reactions?

"When I lived at home in London I wanted to achieve something big. In the end what I have achieved is small. We have already lost Java and I suspect we will soon lose Sumatra."

Sophia held his hand affectionately: "Singapore has begun small but, who knows, one day, it may be one of the biggest cities in the world. Look how fast it is already growing."

"I pray it may be so," said Raffles. "I would feel bad about having done so much and suffered so much if it is all to be for nothing."

"So long as Singapore survives, no-one will ever forget Sir Thomas Stamford Raffles of the Indies."

Sophia hugged Raffles to her breast as she nursed him gently on his narrow bunk until he fell asleep.

As Sophia said, if only Singapore was retained by the Company, the usefullness of Malacca was severely undermined to the point at which the Dutch must feel it to be useless. What could there be left to talk about in London? Of course, the Malay mainland must form Britain's sphere of influence but to the south how much must be allowed the Dutch? All of it? Java and its dependencies only? Yes, these were still critical questions, the answers to which could still be influenced in London by a determined man.

The magnitude of Raffles' achievements in Singapore had been gigantic. As he wrote to friends:

"I have had everything to new-mould from first to last; to introduce a system of energy, purity, and encouragement, to remove nearly all the inhabitants, and to resettle them; to line out towns, streets and roads; to level the high and fill up the low lands; to give property in the soil and rights to the people; to lay down principles and sketch institutions for the domestic order and comfort of the place, as well as its future character and importance; to look for a century or two beforehand, and provide for what Singapore may one day become."

Raffles mostly wrote as the 'Hero of Malown' slowly threaded its way through the beautiful island world using sea channels the safety of which only a decade or so ago had still been doubted. He had been the first to lead large European ships south through the Malacca Strait and it saddened him now to think of the voyage to Java with the great war fleet led by Lord Minto, scores of sail, hundreds of guns, thousands of men and horses. At such moments he closed his eyes and fought to control his emotions.

"We could have had so much," he said quietly to Sophia.

Raffles felt much better aboard ship and away from all the pressures and tensions he had faced in Singapore. Now, his head ached only once or twice a week instead of for days at a time. Once or twice Raffles tried his hand at fishing and the catch was given to the cooks in the galley. Even before he boarded the 'Hero of Malown' Raffles had known that Captain Neish must make a stop at Dutch controlled Batavia.

"There won't be a problem because I won't get off," he had told Neish.

But, on arrival in the Batavia Roads, Sophia was ill from the effects of the sea and needed to land to recover her health and energy. Raffles notified the Dutch Governor General that he had arrived and stressed that he had no intention of accompanying Sophia ashore to stay at the home of Thomas McQuoid, still active in business in Java. Van der Capellan was thunderstruck and, as Raffles observed, his shock robbed him of his manners.

"Had Napoleon returned to life and anchored in The Downs, in England, my arrival could not have excited greater agitation in Batavia."

Van der Capellan wrote him an offensive letter, reminding him of the injuries he had inflicted upon Holland and refusing to meet him or to extend to him the smallest hospitality.

"I never expected anything more," Raffles smiled aboard the 'Hero'.

Ironically, while van der Capellan refused permission to land for fear of what he might do ashore, from the very moment it was known in Batavia that he was in the Roads a continuous procession of small boats put out to the 'Hero' with such frequency and bringing so many that Raffles held an almost continuous levee on the ship's deck. Instead of remaining only a day or two, the 'Hero' remained at anchor for a week by which time Raffles had seen "every English gentleman" in the town.

Raffles and Sophia were both extremely fearful lest the epidemic sweeping Bengkulu should strike them again. Raffles intended to stay only long enough to pack his specimens, books, maps, pictures and papers but, as always, they were at the mercy of shipping; no-one could predict accurately when they would finally leave for home. London had told Raffles to look out for a ship named the 'Fame'.

John Prince met them at Bengkulu with gloomy news. The epidemic was still sweeping the area and people were dying daily. Raffles and Sophia entered Government House grim faced.

"Pray God the 'Fame' arrives soon," said Raffles.

As before, much time was spent at the 'Hill of Mists' but, once his specimens were packed Raffles and Sophia now prefered Government House. The 'Hill of Mists' was too full of the ghosts of little Charlotte, Leopold and Marsden. Not a day passed without one or other of them wiping away tears at some reminder. When they left, for the last time, crowds lined up to touch their hands and stood in groups along the road as their carriage moved slowly on its way.

At Government House, in September, Sophia gave birth to a baby girl, Flora.

"Thank God," smiled Raffles. "Our family is growing again."

Within a few days Sophia was attacked by the kind of fever which had struck down so many. Raffles wrung his hands and paced up and down, hollow cheeked and with wide eyed fear for her life. His head pounded with the strain.

"Save her, try everything," Raffles told his new physician, Dr Bell.

Leeches were applied to Sophia's body to bleed her, she was given laudanum and immersed in hot baths to help the pain and keep down inflamation. Pale and weak with the fever and the exertions of birth Sophia clung on.

Raffles again dispaired that conditions in the Indies were killing him and his family. He wrote:

" If I am fortunate enough to reach England alive, I am certain that no inducement shall ever lead me to revisit India."

With death all around him and middle age approaching, Raffles looked increasingly towards retirement rather than grand new enterprises. He went on:

" I have already passed nearly thirty years of my life in the Company's service, and have always been placed in positions of so much responsibility, that my mind has always been on the stretch, and never without some serious anxiety.

"I naturally look forward to retirement, when these anxieties may cease and I can enjoy that serenity which is above all things necessary for the peace and comfort of this life"

He added characteristically:

" I am aware that I cannot be idle and happy at the same time, and therefore I shall be ready to enter with some degree of zeal upon any pursuits that appear to promise eventual satisfaction."

One such project was a book about Singapore. Just as he had written substantial parts of his 'History of Java' on the last voyage home, this time he looked forward to a work on the founding of Singapore and its consequences and prospects.

Sophia was brought back from the brink but, every day, as sickness and death tore at Bengkulu, the Raffles scanned the horison for a sight of the 'Fame'. Every day they looked anxiously at Charles and baby Flora for the tell tale signs of a fever which might prove fatal. As one friend after another was struck down, the day came when the death list included the loyal Captain Francis Salmond who had become one of Raffles' right hand men in his governance of the Company's posts in Sumatra. Raffles was particularly moved not only to find that Salmond had nominated him as the executor of his will but to read that in doing so the loyal Captain described Raffles as his "only friend."

"How is it that all those we love and esteem, all those whose principles we admire and in whom we can place confidence, are thus carried off, while the vile and worthless remain," Raffles wrote to England.

Before Christmas newly born Flora died of the

fever which had threatened Sophia.

"We are severely afflicted," Raffles groaned.

Sickness, death and the need to escape now dominated the Raffles' every waking moment. The situation was desperate. Where was the 'Flame'? For that matter, where was any ship?

"I'd leave in anything likely to get us to England rather than stay here a moment longer," said Raffles. "At the very least, I must get you away, my princess."

"We will go together," Sophia smiled weakly.

Husband and wife were now so sick and depressed that they hardly left their rooms.

Raffles wrote: "Either I must go to England or by remaining in India die!

"Our spirits are completely broken and we are most anxious to get away from such a charnel-house, but here we are detained for want of an opportunity. How often do we wish the 'Fame' had come here direct but we have neither seen nor heard of her and God only knows when they day or our deliverance will arrive."

Christmas 1823 and New Year 1824 were the most miserable the Raffles' had spent anywhere. Their guests at the celebration tables were largely the ghosts of the dead! Raffles and Sophia prayed hard for better fortune in the New Year. As if by magic, a few days into January, the 'Fame' appeared.

Government House was plunged into an uproar of activity as bags, boxes and trunks were loaded aboard and Raffles and Sophia allowed themselves smiles of relief.

"We might make it yet," Raffles told her with a glimmer of his old optimism.

Aside from the collections he had assembled in Sumatra, Raffles had brought from Singapore hundreds of irreplaceable manuscripts, which had been brought to him at Penang, Malacca and Singapore, recording the history, beliefs and practices of the Malay people. There were also dozens of equally irreplaceable Javanese manuscripts. He had kept them either with him or in safe locations because to lose even one of them would be for the Malay people to lose a part of themselves for all time. Raffles personally supervised the packing and loading.

Raffles' departure from Bengkulu was very similar to his arrival. Sepoys were drawn up at the dock, the few Europeans who had survived were there to say "goodbye", including Resident John Prince. And the leaders of the local comunities had all sent delegations which expressed their heartfelt thanks for all that Raffles had achieved.

When he first set foot in Bengkulu Raffles had written to Leadenhall Street:

"Although the insignificance of the place could not have been unknown to me, I was by no means prepared for the wretchedness and poverty which met me on my arrival; the public buildings had been allowed to go to ruin; the streets and highways were covered with high grass and jungle, nuisances met the eye in every direction; robberies and murders were such constant occurrences that scarce any enquiry was made into them."

Shortly after his departure for England an old Dutch adversary wrote:

"A great variety of broad good roads make attractive the neighbourhood and surroundings of the establishment and a very atractive road, twelve miles long, runs from Fort Marlborough to Pemattanbalan, a Government coffee, nutmeg and clove plantation. Lieutenant Governor Raffles has a very good country house where he sometimes stays. Everything that grows here is in perfect order, neither pains nor expense are spared. Coffee thrives here most luxuriantly but what care is not bestowed upon it! I have seen numerous young trees which are protected by atap screen against sun and wind. Every possible encouragement has been given by the British Indian Government to the agricultural development of this establishment and the produce of planters is free of all export duties and is admitted in all harbours of British India without payment of import taxes.

"What could be done for the moral improvement of the people has certainly been tried by the able Mr Raffles. In all places and districts where the English have any say, native schools have been established where the youth have been instructed in reading, writing, arithmatic and useful general knowledge."

The night the 'Fame' sailed was one of celebration. Raffles entertained Captain Griffiths and officers to dinner and a hearty meal with wine and toasts were enjoyed by everyone. Sophia's brother, Nilson Hull, had opted to accompany them home. Dr Bell had been invited to look after Raffles. The final toast before bed was to "A safe voyage", to which there were many "here, heres".

Raffles and Sophia had just undressed and climbed into their bunks when the hoarse cry of "fire" was raised and quickly taken up by many voices. Boots could be heard everywhere, running hither and thither about the decks and companion ways. Voices shouted urgently for "water."

Raffles had only to open the cabin door to discover that the fire was right beneath their very feet. Choking, white smoke was pouring through the deck boards.

"Sophia, Charles, quick, up, up," Raffles shouted.

The doors of other cabins were open and the whole party rushed, as they were, onto the deck in time to hear:

"The fire will ignite the gunpowder. Lower the boats!"

"Into the boats," shouted Raffles. "Quickly, quickly."

Raffles' boat had barely cleared the stern when the whole of the after part of the 'Fame' burst into an inferno of fire with flames licking greedily up the rigging and into the sails.

"Pull away, pull away", Raffles yelled to the men in his boat.

Out of the darkness another boat appeared, loaded to the gunwales with Captain Griffiths and more men.

"Pull away Mr Raffles, quickly now, before the magazine explodes."

The two boats had no sooner put a safe distance between themselves and the burning ship before the "Fame' was engulfed in a ball of fire and light, there was an earsplitting, blinding explosion, fragments of the vessel rained down around them and what was left sank in a hiss of steam to the bottom of the Indian Ocean! For a few moments everyone sat absolutely still. Then the captain shouted to know if everyone was alright and if anyone was missing. Getting a 'yes' and 'no' he said that their only chance was to row the thirty kilometres back to Bengkulu, preferably before the sun came up.

Raffles and Sophia were numb. Their first thought was, would they ever escape from Bengkulu or had some ghastly fate condemned them to die there! Their second thought was that they had lost everything in the fire, even their clothes. But their immediate challenge was to survive, and the men in the overcrowded and leaking boats rowed with a will against wind and tide. Sophia fainted constantly in the intense daytime heat, and Raffles sheltered her as best he could with the tail of his coat. It was afternoon next day before they were sighted from Bengkulu and a boat sent out to rescue them - its first act of mercy the lowering of a bucket of water!

At Bengkulu dock, the crowd of friends, well wishers and onlookers was huge and there was not a dry eye as the bedraggled party, largely in their night clothes, were escorted either to Government House or to Fort Marlborough.

Raffles wrote later:

"No words of mine can do justice to the expressions of feeling, sympathy and kindness with which we were hailed by everyone. If any proof had been wanting that my administration had been satisfactory here, we had it uniquivocably from all."

When all were safe and rested, Raffles had time to take stock and for the full enormity of his loss to sink in. In addition to the priceless Malay and Javanese manuscripts, Raffles had lost all his dictionaries, grammars and glossaries, the material for his proposed book on Singapore, all the papers from his various administratioons, specimens, he thought, of every animal and plant in Sumatra, over two thousand drawings and the botanical notes of doctors Arnold and Jack. A lesser man would have buckled at the knees at this staggering loss. Not Raffles. The very next day, now that he had to await the arrival of another ship, he set to work to try to re-gather from local sources as much information as possible. He even instructed his draughtsmen to make new drawings!

Raffles was able to discover that the fire had originated in a store room beneath his cabin when a naked light was carelessly dropped by a steward sent there for more brandy with which to garnish the evening's lingering celebration of going home at last!

Informing the Directors of the disaster and of his rescue Raffles wote:

" In espressing my deepfelt gratitude to the inhabitants of this settlement, for their sympathy in our sufferings, and genuine hospitality, I can only say, that having been thrown back on their shores most unexpectedly, we were naked, and they clothed us, hungry and athirst and they fed us, weary and exhausted and they comforted and consoled us, and I pray to God that your Honourable Court, as the immediate guardian of their interests, will bless this land of Sumatra in return, even for their sakes."

Even as Raffles' pen scratched over his paper, in London an Anglo-Dutch Treaty had at long last been signed. All of Sumatra except Aceh was given to The Netherlands; Britain retained Malacca and exclusive rights in the Malay mainland. Holland was to enjoy similar rights throughout the Indies, south of Singapore. As Raffles had so intuitively sensed aboard the 'Hero of Malown', everything that he had won for the Company had been thrown away, with the sole important exception of his 'baby' at Singapore.

Meanwhile Raffles was concluding his report, noting the honour he felt at exercising authority for twelve years in the Indies "over the finest, most interesting but perhaps least known countries in creation.

"This lovely and highly interesting portion of the globe had, politically speaking, long sunk into insignificance from the withering effects of that baneful policy with which the Hollanders were permitted to visit these regions, when it fell to my lot to direct the course of the British arms to the island of Java, and there, on the ruins of monopoly, torture and oppression, in all its shapes, to re-establish man in his native rights and prerogatives, and re-open the channel of an extensive commerce. Political events required our secession from that quarter, but the establishment of Singapore, and the reforms introduced on this coast (Sumatra) have no less afforded opportunities for the application and extension of the same principles.

"In the course of those measures, numerous and weighty responsibilities became necessary; the European world - the Indian world - (the continental part of it at least) - were wholly uninformed of the nature of these countries, their character and resources. I did not hesitate to take these responsibilities as the occasion required them, and though from imperfect information many of my measures in Java were at first condemned, I had the satisfaction to find them in the end not only approved but applauded, far beyond my humble pretensions, and even by those who at first had ben most opposed to me.

"During the last six years of my administration, and since I have ceased to have any concern in the affairs of Java, the situations in which I have been placed, and the responsibilities which I have been compelled to take in support of the interests of my country, and of my employers, have been, if possible, still greater than during my former career: I allude to the struggle which I have felt it my duty to make against Dutch rapacity and power, and to the difficulties that I had to contend with in the establishment of Singapore, and the reforms which have been effected on this coast.

"In addition to the opposition of avowed enemies to British power and Christian principles, I had to contend with deep rooted prejudices, and the secret machinations of those who dared not act openly, and, standing alone, the envy of some and the fear of many, distant autorities were unable to form a correct estimate of my proceedings. Without local explanation some appeared objectionable, while party spirit and Dutch intrigue have never been wanting to discolour transactions and misrepresent facts."

While Raffles wanted the Directors to think well of him, he was too honest a man to desire this on any basis other than the truth as he had seen it and, to the last, defended his every action. At the same time Raffles could see with some alarm that it was imperative that the Court of Directors be encouraged to a more positive view of him if he was to secure any financial assistance from them during this time of serious loss. Without his source materials how could he write more books? If he could not write more books, how would he obtain income? Not to mention the value of the lost shipment, which he put at up to £30,000 - an extremely large sum and all uninsured! All of the valuable gifts which had ever been presented to him went down in the 'Fame' including silver, gold and jewels. Given the precarious state of his health, his basic idea, on safe return to England, was to retire but now, with the loss of everything which could generate income, how was this to be achieved?

Raffles felt strongly that his extensive services to the Company should merit, if not compensation, at least a pension and at the end of this long report in which he fully enumerated what he saw as his achievements, he wrote that he felt he now had no choice but to "throw myself on your Honourable Court to enable me to end my days in honourable retirement, trusting to an all-bounteous Providence to restore me and my family to health and peace in my native land."

While Raffles plea was on its way to London via Singapore, Penang and Calcutta, another ship suitable for the long voyage to England, the 'Mariner' arrived at Bengkulu. On April 8, Raffles' party plus the crew of the

'Fame' embarked.

Just days before he left, the great battles he had waged with Lord Moira fresh in his mind due to the writing of his last report from Sumatra, Raffles received a kind note, not from Moira, but from a new Governor General of India, Lord Amherst. In terms reminiscent of his friend and champion Lord Minto Amherst wrote:

"It would have afforded me pleasure to have found myself in correspondence with you and to have received advantages from those services which have already been so beneficially exerted in this part of our Empire."

"How strange is fate," said Raffles with a tight smile.

Lord Amherst had arrived too late! Like Java, Sumatra was now a past life!

CHAPTER FIFTEEN

When Raffles and Sophia stepped off the 'Mariner' in Portsmouth Harbour, Raffles looked skeletal with hollow eye sockets. His stockings hung limp and twisted around his calves. Sophia looked pale and more slender than ever. Rounding the Cape of Good Hope they had sailed through three weeks of storms which even Captain Young said were the worst he's seen during nineteen roundings. The turbulence was so bad that, at one stage, Sophia had to be tied in her bunk and the sea poured into their cabin from the decks above.

"God have mercy on us," Sophia repeated over and over again as the ship was tossed about on the raging seas like a feather weight cork.

"When we get to England, I shall feel like falling to my knees and kissing the ground", Raffles often said jocularly, partly to dispel Sophia's daily terror.

"I just hope we get there," quipped Sophia from her boarded up bunk.

Raffles had set himself his customary ambitious programme of work which he hoped to complete aboard ship, an account of the founding of Singapore, of his various administrations, study and reading. But the voyage was so rough for so long that he could rarely stick to his plans.

When they at last reached Plymouth, the Raffles had been at sea for four long months and both felt permanently dizzy from the motion of the ship. As he stepped ashore Raffles said:

"Thank God for bringing us safely home. May we never leave these gentle shores again."

Dr Thomas Raffles happened to be preaching in Plymouth when they landed and, after a warm welcome, he broke the depressing news to Raffles that his mother had died.

"Just as I have come home to cheer her final days she has been snatched from us", said Raffles sadly. "I wish I could have seen her just once more."

"She is waiting for you," said Sophia. "You'll see her again one day."

Raffles felt that his return to England had saved his life.

"If only my health will improve, life may still be good," he told Sophia.

"You must give it time," she said "and look after yourself. Now that your poor mother has passed away, perhaps we may go first to Cheltenham and see little Ella. We can stay with my parents and you can again take the waters."

Raffles agreed and, together with young Charles, they set off at once. Never having been in Europe Charles was goggle-eyed at all that he saw and Raffles revelled in treating him as one of the sons he had so tragically lost. Even though he had work to do, plans to make and people to see, en route to Cheltenham, he insisted on taking the boy up in a hot air balloon. At Exeter they went to the horse races. At Bath they drove through the magnificent golden Georgian terraces, so similar to Cheltenham, although, of course, much grander. Not only Charles, but Raffles and Sophia were entranced. Bath was perhaps the leading centre of fashion and society outside London. Among the ornate and graceful buildings, in addition to the usual pump rooms, were assembly rooms, ballrooms, parks and walkways. There were theatres, coffee houses and shops of all kinds. And infirmaries for people like Raffles, their health undermined in the tropics.

It took almost a fortnight for them to arrive at Cheltenham. Along the way they were frequently mobbed by friendly crowds who had heard of their providential escape from the 'Fame' and inn keepers and shop keepers several times refused any payment from the couple, so deep was their sympathy. Sophia was impatient. She had not seen her one surviving child, Ella, for many, many months. On the last lap of the journey home she insisted on driving so fast that one of the carriage wheels caught fire!

Ella had been well cared for by Sophia's parents, James and Sophia Watson Hull. When her mother arrived at the house on the busy High Street promenade, at first Ella hid behind her grandmother's skirts and had to be coaxed forward. She was almost four years old and had little recollection of the parents who, to save her life, had sent her away to safety. The next few days were difficult ones for Raffles and Sophia as they took up the reins of a parentage the child had almost forgotten. Within a few days they had rented "a snug house' nearby at 2 Wellington Place and Raffles found himself and Sophia once again in the Pump Room where they had begun their courtship.

"I hope the water does me more good than it did last time," joked Raffles. 'This time I am in more need."

From James Hull, Raffles learned the news of the Anglo-Dutch Treaty, signed earlier in 1824.

"Singapore is safe and the Strait of Malacca as

the gateway to the Far East is safe but all my work in Java and Sumatra is wasted," Raffles explained to Sophia.

The magnitude of what Raffles had tried to accomplish, the short time available and the enormous workload on himself made the sacrifice of Java and Sumatra to Holland a bitter pill.

"As Lord Minto said, you did as much good as you could while you were there," said Sophia. "Nothing can ever eradicate that."

Despite this gloomy news, the family's time at Cheltenham consisted of relaxed and happy days and, after a few weeks, Raffles felt sufficiently recovered to make the trip to London and Leadenhall Street. Unlike his first return to England, this time, Raffles had no fear that the Directors would pounce on him with a torrent of new criticisms. They had told him that they were displeased with many of his acts in Java and Sumatra but delighted about Singapore and the new Anglo-Dutch Treaty reflected this. Had Raffles been fit, one of two objectives he would have had would have been to enquire about future prospects. Had he not felt that he had to resign for health reasons, while at Bengkulu, the Directors might now have been putting him in charge of all its territories in the Indies. But his resignation had forestalled this and, with his career now effectively ended, there was little point in continued acrimony, even if there had been grounds. The Indies' 'restless spirit' would stir the waters there no more! Not having future postings to talk about Raffles only concern was ways in which the Company could help him financially, after the disaster of the 'Fame'. The Directors would hardly have been human had they not only sympathized with Raffles in his great material loss but also for the loss of four of his five children. Plus, the man before them looked shrunken with illness. Raffles left the meeting very pleased, and optimistic that assistance would be forthcoming, at the very least an adequate pension in recognition of his long years of service.

The Raffles had arrived home in the summer and, with the onset of winter, Raffles caught a severe cold. After weeks of good health, unaccountably, influenza was followed by a headache so severe that he felt he must bid the world his final farewell. Toward the end of October he was considerably cheered by a brief visit by his long time and loyal aide, Otho Travers, travelling specially all the way from Ireland to see him at Cheltenham. Raffles pressed him to stay a few days and the very next day after the arrival of his old friend and colleague he felt so much better that he left his bed and spent hour after hour talking and reminiscing about old times in the Indies.

Not that Raffles was inextricably wedded either to the times or the places. He had always believed that, to be happy, a man must have something to occupy him and he used Travers as a sounding board for some of his varied new plans for the future, the pinnacle of which, he thought, might be a seat in Parliament. At the same time he was very drawn to the life of a country gentleman, as he had been at 'Without a Care' and the 'Hill of Mists'.

"If I could become a country gentleman and perhaps a magistrate that might also do me very well."

"What about your scientific work?" asked Travers.

"I certainly intend to go on with that, as far as I am able. The loss of my collections in the 'Fame' was, of course, a severe blow. My first project is still to publish a small book about Singapore."

Travers could only spare a few days and in less than two weeks he was obliged to return to Ireland.

Monetary reasons compelled Raffles to pursue

vigorously his case with the East India Company and it was difficult to do this from Cheltenham. Accordingly, he rented a small furnished house at 104, Picadilly and with Sophia and his little family of two, Ella and Charles Flint, he arrived there at the end of November 1824, just in time for the Christmas holidays.

Unbeknown to Raffles, while his plea for financial rescue was being considered by the Court of Directors, Colonel Farquhar had lodged with the same Court a long condemnation of Raffles' activities during the Lieutenant Governor's last visit to Singapore and particularly of Raffles' criticisms and dismissal of himself. Farquhar had been widely respected and even loved by all those who knew him at Malacca and Singapore and he felt deeply that Raffles had wronged him. From Raffles' point of view, just at the time when he most needed the Director's sympathy was not a good moment for a complainant to appear.

"Just my luck," he said with momentary gloom. "Another Gillespie, another Bannerman!"

After Christmas, Raffles moved to a larger house at 23, Lower Grosvenor Street and Sophia's parents also moved to London so that the family could see each other more often. If truth be known, the grandparents had become attached to little Ella.

Raffles was obliged to devote many hours responding to, now, Lieutenant-Colonel, Farquhar's charges and he was relieved that his version of events was finally accepted by the Court.

"I hope Farquhar's complaint doesn't affect my application for assistance," Raffles said to Sophia.

"Surely the two cases are quite separate."

"In theory, but Farquhar can't have helped to make them feel well disposed towards me. Some of them probably feel that some of what Farquhar says against me holds more than a grain of truth."

"Try not to worry. We'll know soon enough."

But they didn't and, despite frequent enquiries from Raffles, the whole of 1825 passed without his being able to obtain any decision on his pension. Meanwhile, although he was denied permission to regain his post in Singapore, Farquhar was promoted to Major General.

While waiting for news and making regular calls at Leadenhall Street to see how things were progressing, Raffles pursued an idea he had to try to establish a zoological garden in London, harnessing the support of the Royal Society, now led by Sir Humphrey Davey. A committee was set up to promote the scheme and Raffles was elected Chairman. In this capacity he had soon re-immersed himself in society, especially the nobility, who had the power and resources to help bring his idea to reality. A plot of land was applied for in Regent's Park. The pace of social engagement picked up until "scarcely a day passed" without his hosting or being invited to a breakfast, lunch or dinner. Raffles was as happy as a child in a toy shop to be home at last and he wrote to a friend:

" After so long an absence in the woods and wilds of the East, like the bee, I wander from flower to flower and drink in the delicious nutriment from the numerous intellectual and moral sources which surround me."

Miraculously, his health not only stayed good but seemed to improve. Even during Travers' visit to London he had found Sophia looking "better than ever." The Raffles family fortunes seemed on the road to recovery. Also, Raffles had come to be good friends with that outstanding anti-slaver, William Wilberforce, who now suggested that the two men might share ownership of an estate, on the fringe of London, at Hendon.

Raffles and Sophia immediately fell in love

417

with the house on the hill at Hendon. A torrid white, it reminded them both so much of the Indies, especially of 'Without A Care'. While clearly an 18th Century English structure it embodied something of the flavour of the Indies with a plantation house in Virginia.

"An ideal retreat for a country gentlemen newly returned from the East", said Raffles jovially. The Raffles liked the prospect and entered enthusiastically into negotiations.

Unfortunately, after months of uninterrupted good health and happiness, in May 1825, he unaccountably fainted en route home from seeing a friend.

"There were pains in my chest," he told Sophia later.

Within three weeks, he was back to normal, although, for some time, normal had been unaccountable frailty and an inability to hold things without his hands shaking.

Once again, it was the appearance in London of an old friend from the Indies, Thomas McQuoid, which speeded his recovery. As with Travers, Raffles had much to talk about with McQuoid.

"And what about my savings in your bank? Are they still safe?"

"Still safe, my friend. Don't worry. Whenever you want the money, just let me know."

McQuoid's visit was brief and pressing business drew him rapidly back to Java.

In July, they were able to move into the country house at High Wood, Hendon, and Raffles at once set about creating the atmosphere of rustic charm in which they had all been so happy in the Indies. Not only the charm but also the industry. As at the 'Hill of Mists', High Wood was a farm of a hundred and eleven acres which Raffles farmed himself. Sophia's task was to look after the poultry and pigs. They baked their own bread and even brewed beer. On summer evenings they strolled to the 'Rising Sun', a public house which had been sold with the estate, along with half the village which crowned a hill at the centre. Wilberforce owned the other half and yet another pub, the 'Crown'. The only misfortune was that the local vicar made money out of slavery and consequently disliked both Wilberforce and Raffles.

A menagerie of rabbits, dogs, cats and birds was assembled at the house and while Charles seemed to prefer the dogs, Ella spent hours with a pair of white rabbits she had begged Raffles to get for her. Free of his heavy workload, and delighting in fatherhood, Raffles spent many happy and delightful hours with the two children, not only with the animals and on the farm, but, also in reading, drama and music.

Raffles knew from experience that the Company was always tortuously slow in reaching decisions but by now he was becoming very agitated. Money was running out.

"I hope they're not waiting for me to die," he joked bitterly.

Without saying so, of late, Sophia had had the very same thought. Raffles was magnitudes better than he had been in Singapore or Bengkulu but he was not the man she married. His body weight had not returned and his headaches had not been banished. He was still very careful with his diet in case the wrong food or too much food upset his digestion or stomach and he almost never went out after dark for fear of taking a chill. Raffles was still only forty five years old but Sophia could see that he looked much older. She loved him so much that it hurt her inexpressibly to see her Titan so weakened and circumscribed. And, after

419

all his prodigious efforts and enormous achievements, the British East India Company treated him so badly.

"Daddy, isn't there anything you can do?" she asked her father.

"I'm afraid not, my dear. "I've been retired for so long nobody knows me any more. I have no influence at all."

There had barely been time for McQuoid to return to Java and for a dispatch to be sent to England when Raffles received the devastating news that McQuoid's bank in Java had gone bankrupt and every penny of Raffles last £16,000 of savings had been irrecoverably lost!

"Oh, my God," moaned Raffles holding his head. 'First the 'Fame', then I come home to no pension and now my savings are entirely lost. It couldn't be any worse."

Sophia was also worried, but not about the critical financial situation so much as about Raffles' health. The loss of his savings together with the absence of news about a pension started to bring back his vicious and paralyzing headaches, although, thankfully, still nothing like as bad as in the Indies.

"We mustn't give up hope of the Company helping me and of granting a pension," Raffles told Sophia with characteristic optimism. "Never give up hope, my dear."

Raffles and Sophia often went sightseeing by carriage around London. The city was changing rapidly with grand new buildings going up in the centre and the suburbs fingering remorselessly outwards. Occasionally, they visited grimy workshops so that Raffles could see for himself the incredible power of the revolutionary new steam engines. Steam tools, steam machines, steam carriages and even steam ships were promised.

"What a time to be alive", enthused Raffles, "

and what a country. Where else on earth is there so much dynamism, so much invention, so much capital and so much spirit of change and improvement."

Despite his grievous loss, when McQuoid reappeared again in England, Raffles had not it in his heart to criticize or condemn him.

"He is one of my oldest and dearest friends", he told Sophia with typical generosity.

At long last, on April 12, 1826, Raffles received a bulky letter from the Court of Directors of the British East India Company marked 'private and confidential'.

"It must be about the pension," he smiled, tearing opening the letter with shaking fingers. In his excitement he dropped it on the floor and Sophia picked it up and opened it properly before handing it to him to read.

Raffles started reading with a smile on his thin face which quickly turned to grim despair. He sat down and read page after page of the long letter before looking up at Sophia with almost a look of pain and terror in eyes which had once been filled with optimism and good intentions.

"I can't believe it," he said.

"What is it? What do they say?"

"They approve virtually all that I did in the Indies and even the manner of my doing it but there is not only no mention of a pension but they have sent me a bill for £22,000!"

"A bill! For what?"

Raffles hands shook even more violently then normal.

"You read it," he said, passing the last sheet of the letter to her.

While Lieutenant Governor of Java and, later, Lieutenant Governor of Bengkulu, Raffles had paid himself. His Java salary had been eroded by inflation and he had been obliged therefore to seek permission from Calcutta to draw a higher nominal salary than allowed or suffer losses he could not support. After being posted to Bengkulu he had spent nearly two years in England and upon taking up his post he had drawn salary for that period. Also, to cover the cost of what he considered absolutely essential temporary employments, such as of clerks and translators, his extensive entertaining and of gifts for the Malay rulers, he had paid himself a commission on exports from the territories under his control.

At the time, Calcutta had agreed in writing to all of these financial arrangements. Headquarters in London now chose to override Calcutta and adopt its own view of things. They ruled that Raffles should not have adjusted his salary in Java, should not have drawn pay while in England and was not entitled to expenses which he had calculated against previous averages rather than actual costs. The result - a bill for £22,000, including interest over the fully ten years that the matters had been outstanding.

From the Company's point of view, Raffles' schemes, other than Singapore, had done nothing but cost them money in the East. They were especially irritated at his use of company ships to transport his collections home and to send gifts to friends in England. Some of Raffles claims for the cost of this were also disallowed. Because of his incorruptibility in office and the disasters of the 'Fame' and McQuoid, Raffles was living in England as a relatively poor man. But, knowing the extent to which its officers lined their pockets while in the Far East, Leadenhall Street found this difficult to believe. Before they decided anything about a pension for a man whom they felt had caused them so much trouble they were determined to get some of their money back.

"How inexpressibly mean," exploded Sophia.

Raffles was thunderstruck. On the one hand there was a 'nice letter' acknowledging how much he had achieved; on the other this appalling bill! But the Company was the boss and he was but a servant. He had only two choices:- appeal or pay. Informally, it was soon made clear to him that an appeal would fall on deaf ears. He wrote with a politeness he did not feel:

" I hope I may be allowed the indulgence of time to raise the sum necessary." He noted that his only real option was to sell his property, "a provision for my family after my death." Several mistakes had been made in the Company's claim and these Raffles pointed out.

The Company was unmoved and renewed its demand. Raffles' head ached mercilessly.

"My poor, poor darling," Sophia comforted him. "How the world has misused you."

In fact, at Malacca, in Java, at Bengkulu and in Singapore Raffles had never had enough money for all the expenses he had to meet, not only entertainment but the actual operational expenses of the posts under his command. He had been put in positions where certain steps had to be taken but Leadenhall Street had kept its purse strings as tightly closed as possible. Raffles calculated that, in compounded time, he had spent a year or two of his career arguing about money with them in correspondence. As Olivia had said, they never wanted to pay out, only to receive.

"It was always impossible, "said Raffles. "In business if you don't spend you can never receive. Nothing can be gained for nothing."

Raffles' problem was that all the steps that he had taken, sanctioned by Calcutta, had only been agreed subject to approval by the Court of Directors. This they now withheld. If they had genuinely been well disposed towards him the Company could have written off the bill against the long list of his meritorious and visionary services. But, merit and vision mattered little to men whose own vision was limited by the counting house.

Raffles' head ached for days as he agonized over how he could repay this enormous bill. Meanwhile, his heart ached at the thought of the injustice of the claim.

"I never spent a farthing unless it was necessary."

Despite his headache, he decided to compose a long statement, amounting to a booklet, setting out exactly what he had done in Java, Sumatra and Singapore and beginning with his vision of a chain of British posts and free ports throughout the Indies, from Penang to Japan - a dream at all times threatened by the exclusive and monopolistic policies of the Dutch.

"I want them to understand why I did what I did as much as what I did," he told Sophia.

Sophia was worried about him. At night he couldn't sleep because of the terrible pain in his head. Each day he punished himself, setting down events for many of which the documentation had been burnt in the 'Fame'. His pain was so intense Sophia could see him rocking too and fro in his chair behind his writing desk, his thin hands trembling as he tried to keep hold of his pen.

"Even if they never pay me a penny, I would like the satisfaction of them admitting that I'm right and that I committed no errors," said Raffles grimly.

At six o'clock on the morning of July 5, 1826, at High Wood, still labouring behind his desk, Raffles died. It was Sophia who found him and she lifted his head tenderly and held the worn face close to her bosom.

"Sleep well, sweet prince, sleep well," she murmured lovingly.

Raffles death had not been unexpected and, after all their sufferings together, Sophia took it more stoically than she otherwise might.

Raffles was found to have died, not from any ailment of the stomach or digestive system, as the doctors had always maintained, but from the effects of a brain tumour. All the foods he had eschewed and all the treatments he had suffered had been eschewed and suffered pointlessly!

To the bitter end he was obliged to fight - even in death. The vicar of the Parish church at Hendon officiated at his funeral but, being pro-slavery, while Raffles favoured universal freedom and human rights, he refused to allow any memorial tablet to be erected. As a result, Raffles' grave was soon forgotten and lost.

Raffles was carried from High Wood in a black hearse drawn by two black horses, accompanied by top hatted coachmen and footmen. The immediate family, dressed from head to toe in black mourning, walked behind, through the grounds of his estate and up the little hill to Hendon village church. Here, among the grey tombstones, threaded by narrow, grassy, paths, a handful of Raffles' friends had assembled for a final salute. Among those who respected him or loved him there was a profound sense of regret that his life had ended while he was still so young. All those who were close to him winced at the thought of the terrible pain he must have suffered with his poor head. Of the little 'family' at Bogor, the name he had given his Secretariat, only Travers could be present. Sadly, most of those to whom he had meant as much as they had to him were either dead or still in the Indies. None of his beloved Malays could be present. The British East India Company sent a single representative, who hurried away as soon as decency permitted.

At the graveside, silenced by his animosity, the

Reverend William Cheadle of Hendon said as few words as possible, his stout stature, bloated face and piercing eyes making him look more like a ferocious bull than a kindly conductor of souls. Red eyed but tight lipped, Sophia and Ella each threw a single red rose onto the casket, on the lid of which a pair of crossed Malay krises had been carved resting gently on a bed of water lily leaves, symbolizing grace and strength. Outside the family, Otho Travers was the person who knew Raffles most and best. Just before the dark earth was shovelled down onto the coffin, Travers stepped forward.

He said, with red eyes, "There are many great men, besides him, clever, rich and handsome, but in good disposition, amiability and gracefulness, Mr Raffles had not his equal and were I to die and live again such a man I could never meet again, my love of him is so great."

It was a modest farewell to one who had once known adoration in the Indies, who had been feted by thousands, wept over and saluted wherever he went by the roar of cannons and the crackle of musket fire.

Sophia lent on Travers' arm as they walked slowly out of the cemetery where her prince would at last find everlasting peace.

At High Wood, after the funeral, Sophia sat down in the chair where Raffles had last worked. She looked carefully at what he had been writing. Picking up his pen she herself began to write, carrying on where he had left off. Within a few months and with the generous help of Otho Travers, Raffles' intended explanation and vindication of his policies and actions in the Indies was published under the title 'Memoir Of The Life And Public Services Of Sir Thomas Stamford Raffles'. Even from beyond the grave his voice had been heard.

While the British East India Company quickly

closed any of its files with Raffles' name on it, his legacy was destined to live on.

One of the many press obituaries published at the time said:

"The name of Sir Thomas Stamford Raffles will live long in British history. There can be no doubt that the great designs which he formed, and the measures he pursued, will exalt the character of Great Britain far more than her proudest victories have ever done."

Raffles' healthiest 'baby', Singapore, grew to become one of the most admired and well run city states on earth, its hallmark, justice for all in a property owning free port. To this day, in a shady square in Asia's best planned country, a statue of Raffles gazes out proudly across the city he helped to create and countless places are named after him. The British values Raffles cherished so highly came to permeate the whole of the Malay mainland where the British Government ended its stewardship with the creation of a prosperous democracy in 1957. After the restoration of Java to the Dutch, Travers had predicted that should they ever be driven out it would be because of "want of conduct in the colonial government." In 1949 "want of conduct" eventually led to their expulsion. They were driven out by a rag tail army of native fighters whose principal weapon was the burning desire to be free. The free trade among free peoples that Raffles dreamed about in 1820 and before is finally due to be introduced throughout the Indies in the year 2020 - 200 years after he first promoted such a vision. Thomas Stamford Raffles was a man of his time, a man ahead of his time and a man for all time!

Special thanks

I should like to offer my heartfelt thanks to my daughter, Sarina, for her boundless confidence that I could write this story and, having written it, to my son, Ian, for devoting his holidays to designing the cover and computerizing the entire manuscript.

By the same author

A Clown On The Streets Of Jakarta

The Fortune Teller

All sources fully acknowledged.